SKETCHES,

NEW AND OLD

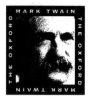

THE OXFORD MARK TWAIN

Shelley Fisher Fishkin, Editor

Personal Recollections of Joan of Arc
  Introduction: Justin Kaplan
  Afterword: Susan K. Harris

The Stolen White Elephant and Other Detective Stories
  Introduction: Walter Mosley
  Afterword: Lillian S. Robinson

How to Tell a Story and Other Essays
  Introduction: David Bradley
  Afterword: Pascal Covici, Jr.

Following the Equator and Anti-imperialist Essays
  Introduction: Gore Vidal
  Afterword: Fred Kaplan

The Man That Corrupted Hadleyburg and Other Stories and Essays
  Introduction: Cynthia Ozick
  Afterword: Jeffrey Rubin-Dorsky

The Diaries of Adam and Eve
  Introduction: Ursula K. Le Guin
  Afterword: Laura E. Skandera-Trombley

What Is Man?
  Introduction: Charles Johnson
  Afterword: Linda Wagner-Martin

The $30,000 Bequest and Other Stories
  Introduction: Frederick Busch
  Afterword: Judith Yaross Lee

Christian Science
  Introduction: Garry Wills
  Afterword: Hamlin Hill

Chapters from My Autobiography
  Introduction: Arthur Miller
  Afterword: Michael J. Kiskis

Sketches,
New and Old

Mark Twain

FOREWORD

SHELLEY FISHER FISHKIN

INTRODUCTION

LEE SMITH

AFTERWORD

SHERWOOD CUMMINGS

New York   Oxford

OXFORD UNIVERSITY PRESS

1996

OXFORD UNIVERSITY PRESS

Oxford   New York

Athens, Auckland, Bangkok, Bogotá, Bombay

Buenos Aires, Calcutta, Cape Town, Dar es Salaam

Delhi, Florence, Hong Kong, Istanbul, Karachi

Kuala Lumpur, Madras, Madrid, Melbourne

Mexico City, Nairobi, Paris, Singapore

Taipei, Tokyo, Toronto

and associated companies in

Berlin, Ibadan

Copyright © 1996 by

Oxford University Press, Inc.

Introduction © 1996 by Lee Smith

Afterword © 1996 by Sherwood Cummings

Illustrators and Illustrations in Mark Twain's

First American Editions © 1996 by Beverly R. David

and Ray Sapirstein

Reading the Illustrations in Sketches, New and Old

© 1996 by Beverly R. David and Ray Sapirstein

Text design by Richard Hendel

Composition: David Thorne

Published by

Oxford University Press, Inc.

198 Madison Avenue, New York,

New York 10016

Oxford is a registered trademark of

Oxford University Press

Library of Congress

Cataloging-in-Publication Data

Twain, Mark, 1835–1910.

Mark Twain's sketches, new and old / by Mark

Twain; with an introduction by Lee Smith ; and an

afterword by Sherwood Cummings.

p. cm. — (The Oxford Mark Twain)

Includes bibliograhical references.

1. Manners and customs—Fiction. 2. Humorous

stories, American. I. Title. II. Series: Twain, Mark,

1835–1910. Works. 1996.

PS1319.A1 1996

813'.4—dc20

96-12321

CIP

ISBN 0-19-510135-9 (trade ed.)

ISBN 0-19-511404-3 (lib. ed.)

ISBN 0-19-509088-8 (trade ed. set)

ISBN 0-19-511345-4 (lib. ed. set)

9 8 7 6 5 4 3 2 1

Printed in the United States of America

on acid-free paper

FRONTISPIECE

In 1874, the year this photograph was taken, Samuel
L. Clemens wrote and published "A True Story,
Repeated Word for Word as I Heard It" and other
pieces that appeared in *Sketches, New and Old*.
(Courtesy, The Mark Twain Project, The Bancroft
Library)

CONTENTS

EDITOR'S NOTE

The Oxford Mark Twain consists of twenty-nine volumes of facsimiles of the first American editions of Mark Twain's works, with an editor's foreword, new introductions, afterwords, notes on the texts, and essays on the illustrations in volumes with artwork. The facsimiles have been reproduced from the originals unaltered, except that blank pages in the front and back of the books have been omitted, and any seriously damaged or missing pages have been replaced by pages from other first editions (as indicated in the notes on the texts).

In the foreword, introduction, afterword, and essays on the illustrations, the titles of Mark Twain's works have been capitalized according to modern conventions, as have the names of characters (except where otherwise indicated). In the case of discrepancies between the title of a short story, essay, or sketch as it appears in the original table of contents and as it appears on its own title page, the title page has been followed. The parenthetical numbers in the introduction, afterwords, and illustration essays are page references to the facsimiles.

FOREWORD

Shelley Fisher Fishkin

amuel Clemens entered the world and left it with Halley's Comet, little dreaming that generations hence Halley's Comet would be less famous than Mark Twain. He has been called the American Cervantes, our Homer, our Tolstoy, our Shakespeare, our Rabelais. Ernest Hemingway maintained that "all modern American literature comes from one book by Mark Twain called *Huckleberry Finn*." President Franklin Delano Roosevelt got the phrase "New Deal" from *A Connecticut Yankee in King Arthur's Court*. *The Gilded Age* gave an entire era its name. "The future historian of America," wrote George Bernard Shaw to Samuel Clemens, "will find your works as indispensable to him as a French historian finds the political tracts of Voltaire."[1]

There is a Mark Twain Bank in St. Louis, a Mark Twain Diner in Jackson Heights, New York, a Mark Twain Smoke Shop in Lakeland, Florida. There are Mark Twain Elementary Schools in Albuquerque, Dayton, Seattle, and Sioux Falls. Mark Twain's image peers at us from advertisements for Bass Ale (his drink of choice was Scotch), for a gas company in Tennessee, a hotel in the nation's capital, a cemetery in California.

Ubiquitous though his name and image may be, Mark Twain is in no danger of becoming a petrified icon. On the contrary: Mark Twain lives. *Huckleberry Finn* is "the most taught novel, most taught long work, and most taught piece of American literature" in American schools from junior high to the graduate level.[2] Hundreds of Twain impersonators appear in theaters, trade shows, and shopping centers in every region of the country.[3] Scholars publish hundreds of articles as well as books about Twain every year, and he is the subject of daily exchanges on the Internet. A journalist somewhere in the world finds a reason to quote Twain just about every day. Television series such as *Bonanza, Star Trek: The Next Generation,* and *Cheers* broadcast episodes that feature Mark Twain as a character. Hollywood screenwriters regularly produce movies inspired by his works, and writers of mysteries and science fiction continue to weave him into their plots.[4]

A century after the American Revolution sent shock waves throughout Europe, it took Mark Twain to explain to Europeans and to his countrymen alike what that revolution had wrought. He probed the significance of this new land and its new citizens, and identified what it was in the Old World that America abolished and rejected. The founding fathers had thought through the political dimensions of making a new society; Mark Twain took on the challenge of interpreting the social and cultural life of the United States for those outside its borders as well as for those who were living the changes he discerned.

Americans may have constructed a new society in the eighteenth century, but they articulated what they had done in voices that were largely inter-changeable with those of Englishmen until well into the nineteenth century. Mark Twain became the voice of the new land, the leading translator of what and who the "American" was — and, to a large extent, is. Frances Trollope's *Domestic Manners of the Americans,* a best-seller in England, Hector St. John de Crèvecoeur's *Letters from an American Farmer,* and Tocqueville's *Democracy in America* all tried to explain America to Europeans. But Twain did more than that: he allowed European readers to *experience* this strange "new world." And he gave his countrymen the tools to do two things they had not quite had the confidence to do before. He helped them stand before the cultural icons of the Old World unembarrassed, unashamed of America's lack of palaces and shrines, proud of its brash practicality and bold inventiveness, unafraid to reject European models of "civilization" as tainted or corrupt. And he also helped them recognize their own insularity, boorishness, arrogance, or ignorance, and laugh at it — the first step toward transcending it and becoming more "civilized," in the best European sense of the word.

Twain often strikes us as more a creature of our time than of his. He appreciated the importance and the complexity of mass tourism and public relations, fields that would come into their own in the twentieth century but were only fledgling enterprises in the nineteenth. He explored the liberating potential of humor and the dynamics of friendship, parenting, and marriage. He narrowed the gap between "popular" and "high" culture, and he meditated on the enigmas of personal and national identity. Indeed, it would be difficult to find an issue on the horizon today that Twain did not touch on somewhere in his work. Heredity versus environment? Animal rights? The boundaries of gender? The place of black voices in the cultural heritage of the United States? Twain was there.

With startling prescience and characteristic grace and wit, he zeroed in on many of the key challenges — political, social, and technological — that would face his country and the world for the next hundred years: the challenge of race relations in a society founded on both chattel slavery and ideals of equality, and the intractable problem of racism in American life; the potential of new technologies to transform our lives in ways that can be both exhilarating and terrifying — as well as unpredictable; the problem of imperialism and the difficulties entailed in getting rid of it. But he never lost sight of the most basic challenge of all: each man or woman's struggle for integrity in the face of the seductions of power, status, and material things.

Mark Twain's unerring sense of the right word and not its second cousin taught people to pay attention when he spoke, in person or in print. He said things that were smart and things that were wise, and he said them incomparably well. He defined the rhythms of our prose and the contours of our moral map. He saw our best and our worst, our extravagant promise and our stunning failures, our comic foibles and our tragic flaws. Throughout the world he is viewed as the most distinctively American of American authors — and as one of the most universal. He is assigned in classrooms in Naples, Riyadh, Belfast, and Beijing, and has been a major influence on twentieth-century writers from Argentina to Nigeria to Japan. The Oxford Mark Twain celebrates the versatility and vitality of this remarkable writer.

The Oxford Mark Twain reproduces the first American editions of Mark Twain's books published during his lifetime.[5] By encountering Twain's works in their original format — typography, layout, order of contents, and illustrations — readers today can come a few steps closer to the literary artifacts that entranced and excited readers when the books first appeared. Twain approved of and to a greater or lesser degree supervised the publication of all of this material.[6] The Mark Twain House in Hartford, Connecticut, generously loaned us its originals.[7] When more than one copy of a first American edition was available, Robert H. Hirst, general editor of the Mark Twain Project, in cooperation with Marianne Curling, curator of the Mark Twain House (and Jeffrey Kaimowitz, head of Rare Books for the Watkinson Library of Trinity College, Hartford, where the Mark Twain House collection is kept), guided our decision about which one to use.[8] As a set, the volumes also contain more than eighty essays commissioned especially for The Oxford Mark Twain, in which distinguished contributors reassess Twain's achievement as a writer and his place in the cultural conversation that he did so much to shape.

Each volume of The Oxford Mark Twain is introduced by a leading American, Canadian, or British writer who responds to Twain — often in a very personal way — as a fellow writer. Novelists, journalists, humorists, columnists, fabulists, poets, playwrights — these writers tell us what Twain taught them and what in his work continues to speak to them. Reading Twain's books, both famous and obscure, they reflect on the genesis of his art and the characteristics of his style, the themes he illuminated, and the aesthetic strategies he pioneered. Individually and collectively their contributions testify to the place Mark Twain holds in the hearts of readers of all kinds and temperaments.

Scholars whose work has shaped our view of Twain in the academy today have written afterwords to each volume, with suggestions for further reading. Their essays give us a sense of what was going on in Twain's life when he wrote the book at hand, and of how that book fits into his career. They explore how each book reflects and refracts contemporary events, and they show Twain responding to literary and social currents of the day, variously accepting, amplifying, modifying, and challenging prevailing paradigms. Sometimes they argue that works previously dismissed as quirky or eccentric departures actually address themes at the heart of Twain's work from the start. And as they bring new perspectives to Twain's composition strategies in familiar texts, several scholars see experiments in form where others saw only form-lessness, method where prior critics saw only madness. In addition to eluci-dating the work's historical and cultural context, the afterwords provide an overview of responses to each book from its first appearance to the present.

Most of Mark Twain's books involved more than Mark Twain's words: unique illustrations. The parodic visual send-ups of "high culture" that Twain himself drew for *A Tramp Abroad*, the sketch of financial manipulator Jay Gould as a greedy and sadistic "Slave Driver" in *A Connecticut Yankee in King Arthur's Court*, and the memorable drawings of Eve in *Eve's Diary* all helped Twain's books to be sold, read, discussed, and preserved. In their es-says for each volume that contains artwork, Beverly R. David and Ray Sapirstein highlight the significance of the sketches, engravings, and pho-tographs in the first American editions of Mark Twain's works, and tell us what is known about the public response to them.

The Oxford Mark Twain invites us to read some relatively neglected works by Twain in the company of some of the most engaging literary figures of our time. Roy Blount Jr., for example, riffs in a deliciously Twain-like manner on "An Item Which the Editor Himself Could Not Understand," which may well rank as one of the least-known pieces Twain ever published. Bobbie Ann Mason celebrates the "mad energy" of Twain's most obscure comic novel, *The American Claimant*, in which the humor "hurtles beyond tall tale into simon-pure absurdity."[9] Garry Wills finds that *Christian Science* "gets us very close to the heart of American culture." Lee Smith reads "Political Economy" as a sharp and funny essay on language. Walter Mosley sees "The Stolen White Elephant," a story "reduced to a series of ridiculous telegrams related by an untrustworthy narrator caught up in an adventure that is as impossible as it is ludicrous," as a stunningly compact and economical satire of a world we still recognize as our own. Anne Bernays returns to "The Private History of a Campaign That Failed" and finds "an antiwar manifesto that is also confession, dramatic monologue, a plea for understanding and absolution, and a romp that gradually turns into atrocity even as we watch." After revisiting Captain Stormfield's heaven, Frederik Pohl finds that there "is no imaginable place more pleasant to spend eternity." Indeed, Pohl writes, "one would almost be willing to die to enter it."

While less familiar works receive fresh attention in The Oxford Mark Twain, new light is cast on the best-known works as well. Judith Martin ("Miss Manners") points out that it is by reading a court etiquette book that Twain's pauper learns how to behave as a proper prince. As important as etiquette may be in the palace, Martin notes, it is even more important in the slums.

> That etiquette is a sorer point with the ruffians in the street than with the proud dignitaries of the prince's court may surprise some readers. As in our own streets, etiquette is always a more volatile subject among those who cannot count on being treated with respect than among those who have the power to command deference.

And taking a fresh look at *Adventures of Huckleberry Finn,* Toni Morrison writes,

> much of the novel's genius lies in its quiescence, the silences that pervade it and give it a porous quality that is by turns brooding and soothing. It lies in ... the subdued images in which the repetition of a simple word, such as "lonesome," tolls like an evening bell; the moments when nothing is said, when scenes and incidents swell the heart unbearably precisely because unarticulated, and force an act of imagination almost against the will.

Engaging Mark Twain as one writer to another, several contributors to The Oxford Mark Twain offer new insights into the processes by which his books came to be. Russell Banks, for example, reads *A Tramp Abroad* as "an important revision of Twain's incomplete first draft of *Huckleberry Finn,* a second draft, if you will, which in turn made possible the third and final draft." Erica Jong suggests that *1601,* a freewheeling parody of Elizabethan manners and mores, written during the same summer Twain began *Huckleberry Finn*, served as "a warm-up for his creative process" and "primed the pump for other sorts of freedom of expression." And Justin Kaplan suggests that "one of the transcendent figures standing behind and shaping" *Joan of Arc* was Ulysses S. Grant, whose memoirs Twain had recently published, and who, like Joan, had risen unpredictably "from humble and obscure origins" to become a "military genius" endowed with "the gift of command, a natural eloquence, and an equally natural reserve."

As a number of contributors note, Twain was a man ahead of his times. *The Gilded Age* was the first "Washington novel," Ward Just tells us, because "Twain was the first to see the possibilities that had eluded so many others." Commenting on *The Tragedy of Pudd'nhead Wilson*, Sherley Anne Williams observes that "Twain's argument about the power of environment in shaping character runs directly counter to prevailing sentiment where the negro was concerned." Twain's fictional technology, wildly fanciful by the standards of his day, predicts developments we take for granted in ours. DNA cloning, fax machines, and photocopiers are all prefigured, Bobbie Ann Mason tells us, in *The American Claimant*. Cynthia Ozick points out that the "telelectrophonoscope" we meet in "From the 'London Times' of 1904" is suspiciously like what we know as "television." And Malcolm Bradbury suggests that in the "phrenophones" of "Mental Telegraphy" "the Internet was born."

Twain turns out to have been remarkably prescient about political affairs as well. Kurt Vonnegut sees in *A Connecticut Yankee* a chilling foreshadowing (or perhaps a projection from the Civil War) of "all the high-tech atrocities which followed, and which follow still." Cynthia Ozick suggests that "The Man That Corrupted Hadleyburg," along with some of the other pieces collected under that title — many of them written when Twain lived in a Vienna ruled by Karl Lueger, a demagogue Adolf Hitler would later idolize — shoot up moral flares that shed an eerie light on the insidious corruption, prejudice, and hatred that reached bitter fruition under the Third Reich. And Twain's portrait in this book of "the dissolving Austria-Hungary of the 1890s," in Ozick's view, presages not only the Sarajevo that would erupt in 1914 but also "the disintegrated components of the former Yugoslavia" and "the *fin-de-siècle* Sarajevo of our own moment."

Despite their admiration for Twain's ambitious reach and scope, contributors to The Oxford Mark Twain also recognize his limitations. Mordecai Richler, for example, thinks that "the early pages of *Innocents Abroad* suffer from being a tad broad, proffering more burlesque than inspired satire," perhaps because Twain was "trying too hard for knee-slappers." Charles Johnson notes that the Young Man in Twain's philosophical dialogue about free will and determinism (*What Is Man?*) "caves in far too soon," failing to challenge what through late-twentieth-century eyes looks like "pseudoscience" and suspect essentialism in the Old Man's arguments.

Some contributors revisit their first encounters with Twain's works, recalling what surprised or intrigued them. When David Bradley came across "Fenimore Cooper's Literary Offences" in his college library, he "did not at first realize that Twain was being his usual ironic self with all this business about the 'nineteen rules governing literary art in the domain of romantic fiction,' but by the time I figured out there was no such list outside Twain's own head, I had decided that the rules made *sense*. . . . It seemed to me they were a pretty good blueprint for writing — Negro writing included." Sherley Anne Williams remembers that part of what attracted her to *Pudd'nhead Wilson* when she first read it thirty years ago was "that Twain, writing at the end of the nineteenth century, could imagine negroes as characters, albeit white ones, who actually thought for and of themselves, whose actions were the product of their thinking rather than the spontaneous ephemera of physical instincts that stereotype assigned to blacks." Frederik Pohl recalls his first reading of *Huckleberry Finn* as "a watershed event" in his life, the first book he read as a child in which "bad people" ceased to exercise a monopoly on doing "bad things." In *Huckleberry Finn* "some seriously bad things — things like the possession and mistreatment of black slaves, like stealing and lying, even like killing other people in duels — were quite often done by people who not only thought of themselves as exemplarily moral but, by any other standards I knew how to apply, actually *were* admirable citizens." The world that

Tom and Huck lived in, Pohl writes, "was filled with complexities and contradictions," and resembled "the world I appeared to be living in myself."

Other contributors explore their more recent encounters with Twain, explaining why they have revised their initial responses to his work. For Toni Morrison, parts of *Huckleberry Finn* that she "once took to be deliberate evasions, stumbles even, or a writer's impatience with his or her material," now strike her "as otherwise: as entrances, crevices, gaps, seductive invitations flashing the possibility of meaning. Unarticulated eddies that encourage diving into the novel's undertow — the real place where writer captures reader." One such "eddy" is the imprisonment of Jim on the Phelps farm. Instead of dismissing this portion of the book as authorial bungling, as she once did, Morrison now reads it as Twain's commentary on the 1880s, a period that "saw the collapse of civil rights for blacks," a time when "the nation, as well as Tom Sawyer, was deferring Jim's freedom in agonizing play." Morrison believes that Americans in the 1880s were attempting "to bury the combustible issues Twain raised in his novel," and that those who try to kick Huck Finn out of school in the 1990s are doing the same: "The cyclical attempts to remove the novel from classrooms extend Jim's captivity on into each generation of readers."

Although imitation-Hemingway and imitation-Faulkner writing contests draw hundreds of entries annually, no one has ever tried to mount a faux-Twain competition. Why? Perhaps because Mark Twain's voice is too much a part of who we are and how we speak even today. Roy Blount Jr. suggests that it is impossible, "at least for an American writer, to parody Mark Twain. It would be like doing an impression of your father or mother: he or she is already there in your voice."

Twain's style is examined and celebrated in The Oxford Mark Twain by fellow writers who themselves have struggled with the nuances of words, the structure of sentences, the subtleties of point of view, and the trickiness of opening lines. Bobbie Ann Mason observes, for example, that "Twain loved the sound of words and he knew how to string them by sound, like different shades of one color: 'The earl's barbaric eye,' 'the Usurping Earl,' 'a double-

dyed humbug.'" Twain "relied on the punch of plain words" to show writers
how to move beyond the "wordy romantic rubbish" so prevalent in nineteenth-century fiction, Mason says; he "was one of the first writers in America
to deflower literary language." Lee Smith believes that "American writers
have benefited as much from the way Mark Twain opened up the possibilities
of first-person narration as we have from his use of vernacular language." (She
feels that "the ghost of Mark Twain was hovering someplace in the background" when she decided to write her novel *Oral History* from the stand-
point of multiple first-person narrators.) Frederick Busch maintains that "A
Dog's Tale" "boasts one of the great opening sentences" of all time: "My father was a St. Bernard, my mother was a collie, but I am a Presbyterian." And
Ursula Le Guin marvels at the ingenuity of the following sentence that she encounters in *Extracts from Adam's Diary*.

> . . . This made her sorry for the creatures which live in there, which she
> calls fish, for she continues to fasten names on to things that don't need
> them and don't come when they are called by them, which is a matter of no
> consequence to her, as she is such a numskull anyway; so she got a lot of
> them out and brought them in last night and put them in my bed to keep
> warm, but I have noticed them now and then all day, and I don't see that
> they are any happier there than they were before, only quieter.[10]

Le Guin responds,

> Now, that is a pure Mark-Twain-tour-de-force sentence, covering an im-
> mense amount of territory in an effortless, aimless ramble that seems to be
> heading nowhere in particular and ends up with breathtaking accuracy at
> the gold mine. Any sensible child would find that funny, perhaps not fol-
> lowing all its divagations but delighted by the swing of it, by the word
> "numskull," by the idea of putting fish in the bed; and as that child grew
> older and reread it, its reward would only grow; and if that grown-up child
> had to write an essay on the piece and therefore earnestly studied and
> pored over this sentence, she would end up in unmitigated admiration of
> its vocabulary, syntax, pacing, sense, and rhythm, above all the beautiful

timing of the last two words; and she would, and she does, still find it funny.

The fish surface again in a passage that Gore Vidal calls to our attention, from *Following the Equator*: "'The Whites always mean well when they take human fish out of the ocean and try to make them dry and warm and happy and comfortable in a chicken coop,' which is how, through civilization, they did away with many of the original inhabitants. Lack of empathy is a principal theme in Twain's meditations on race and empire."

Indeed, empathy — and its lack — is a principal theme in virtually all of Twain's work, as contributors frequently note. Nat Hentoff quotes the following thoughts from Huck in *Tom Sawyer Abroad*:

> I see a bird setting on a dead limb of a high tree, singing with its head tilted back and its mouth open, and before I thought I fired, and his song stopped and he fell straight down from the limb, all limp like a rag, and I run and picked him up and he was dead, and his body was warm in my hand, and his head rolled about this way and that, like his neck was broke, and there was a little white skin over his eyes, and one little drop of blood on the side of his head; and laws! I could n't see nothing more for the tears; and I hain't never murdered no creature since that war n't doing me no harm, and I ain't going to.[11]

"The Humane Society," Hentoff writes, "has yet to say anything as powerful — and lasting."

Readers of The Oxford Mark Twain will have the pleasure of revisiting Twain's Mississippi landmarks alongside Willie Morris, whose own lower Mississippi Valley boyhood gives him a special sense of connection to Twain. Morris knows firsthand the mosquitoes described in *Life on the Mississippi* — so colossal that "two of them could whip a dog" and "four of them could hold a man down"; in Morris's own hometown they were so large during the flood season that "local wags said they wore wristwatches." Morris's Yazoo City and Twain's Hannibal shared a "rough-hewn democracy . . . complicated by all the visible textures of caste and class, . . . harmless boyhood fun and mischief right along with . . . rank hypocrisies, churchgoing sanctimonies, racial hatred, entrenched and unrepentant greed."

For the West of Mark Twain's *Roughing It*, readers will have George Plimpton as their guide. "What a group these newspapermen were!" Plimpton writes about Twain and his friends Dan De Quille and Joe Goodman in Virginia City, Nevada. "Their roisterous carryings-on bring to mind the kind of frat-house enthusiasm one associates with college humor magazines like the *Harvard Lampoon*." Malcolm Bradbury examines Twain as "a living example of what made the American so different from the European." And Hal Holbrook, who has interpreted Mark Twain on stage for some forty years, describes how Twain "played" during the civil rights movement, during the Vietnam War, during the Gulf War, and in Prague on the eve of the demise of Communism.

Why do we continue to read Mark Twain? What draws us to him? His wit? His compassion? His humor? His bravura? His humility? His understanding of who and what we are in those parts of our being that we rarely open to view? Our sense that he knows we can do better than we do? Our sense that he knows we can't? E. L. Doctorow tells us that children are attracted to *Tom Sawyer* because in this book "the young reader confirms his own hope that no matter how troubled his relations with his elders may be, beneath all their disapproval is their underlying love for him, constant and steadfast." Readers in general, Arthur Miller writes, value Twain's "insights into America's always uncertain moral life and its shifting but everlasting hypocrisies"; we appreciate the fact that he "is not using his alienation from the public illusions of his hour in order to reject the country implicitly as though he could live without it, but manifestly in order to correct it." Perhaps we keep reading Mark Twain because, in Miller's words, he "wrote much more like a father than a son. He doesn't seem to be sitting in class taunting the teacher but standing at the head of it challenging his students to acknowledge their own humanity, that is, their immemorial attraction to the untrue."

Mark Twain entered the public eye at a time when many of his countrymen considered "American culture" an oxymoron; he died four years before a world conflagration that would lead many to question whether the contradiction in terms was not "European civilization" instead. In between he worked in journalism, printing, steamboating, mining, lecturing, publishing, and editing, in virtually every region of the country. He tried his hand at humorous sketches, social satire, historical novels, children's books, poetry, drama, science fiction, mysteries, romance, philosophy, travelogue, memoir, polemic, and several genres no one had ever seen before or has ever seen since. He invented a self-pasting scrapbook, a history game, a vest strap, and a gizmo for keeping bed sheets tucked in; he invested in machines and processes designed to revolutionize typesetting and engraving, and in a food supplement called "Plasmon." Along the way he cheerfully impersonated himself and prior versions of himself for doting publics on five continents while playing out a charming rags-to-riches story followed by a devastating riches-to-rags story followed by yet another great American comeback. He had a long-running real-life engagement in a sumptuous comedy of manners, and then in a real-life tragedy not of his own design: during the last fourteen years of his life almost everyone he ever loved was taken from him by disease and death.

Mark Twain has indelibly shaped our views of who and what the United States is as a nation and of who and what we might become. He understood the nostalgia for a "simpler" past that increased as that past receded — and he saw through the nostalgia to a past that was just as complex as the present. He recognized better than we did ourselves our potential for greatness and our potential for disaster. His fictions brilliantly illuminated the world in which he lived, changing it — and us — in the process. He knew that our feet often danced to tunes that had somehow remained beyond our hearing; with perfect pitch he played them back to us.

My mother read *Tom Sawyer* to me as a bedtime story when I was eleven. I thought Huck and Tom could be a lot of fun, but I dismissed Becky Thatcher as a bore. When I was twelve I invested a nickel at a local garage sale in a book that contained short pieces by Mark Twain. That was where I met Twain's Eve. Now, *that's* more like it, I decided, pleased to meet a female character I could identify *with* instead of against. Eve had spunk. Even if she got a lot wrong, you had to give her credit for trying. "The Man That Corrupted

Hadleyburg" left me giddy with satisfaction: none of my adolescent reveries of getting even with my enemies were half as neat as the plot of the man who got back at that town. "How I Edited an Agricultural Paper" set me off in uncontrollable giggles.

People sometimes told me that I looked like Huck Finn. "It's the freckles," they'd explain — not explaining anything at all. I didn't read *Huckleberry Finn* until junior year in high school in my English class. It was the fall of 1965. I was living in a small town in Connecticut. I expected a sequel to *Tom Sawyer*. So when the teacher handed out the books and announced our assignment, my jaw dropped: "Write a paper on how Mark Twain used irony to attack racism in *Huckleberry Finn*."

The year before, the bodies of three young men who had gone to Mississippi to help blacks register to vote — James Chaney, Andrew Goodman, and Michael Schwerner — had been found in a shallow grave; a group of white segregationists (the county sheriff among them) had been arrested in connection with the murders. America's inner cities were simmering with pent-up rage that began to explode in the summer of 1965, when riots in Watts left thirty-four people dead. None of this made any sense to me. I was confused, angry, certain that there was something missing from the news stories I read each day: the why. Then I met Pap Finn. And the Phelpses.

Pap Finn, Huck tells us, "had been drunk over in town" and "was just all mud." He erupts into a drunken tirade about "a free nigger . . . from Ohio — a mulatter, most as white as a white man," with "the whitest shirt on you ever see, too, and the shiniest hat; and there ain't a man in town that's got as fine clothes as what he had."

> . . . they said he was a p'fessor in a college, and could talk all kinds of languages, and knowed everything. And that ain't the wust. They said he could *vote*, when he was at home. Well, that let me out. Thinks I, what is the country a-coming to? It was 'lection day, and I was just about to go and vote, myself, if I warn't too drunk to get there; but when they told me there was a State in this country where they'd let that nigger vote, I drawed out. I says I'll never vote agin. Them's the very words I said. . . . And to see the

cool way of that nigger — why, he wouldn't a give me the road if I hadn't shoved him out o' the way.[12]

Later on in the novel, when the runaway slave Jim gives up his freedom to nurse a wounded Tom Sawyer, a white doctor testifies to the stunning altruism of his actions. The Phelpses and their neighbors, all fine, upstanding, well-meaning, churchgoing folk,

> agreed that Jim had acted very well, and was deserving to have some notice took of it, and reward. So every one of them promised, right out and hearty, that they wouldn't curse him no more.
>
> Then they come out and locked him up. I hoped they was going to say he could have one or two of the chains took off, because they was rotten heavy, or could have meat and greens with his bread and water, but they didn't think of it.[13]

Why did the behavior of these people tell me more about why Watts burned than anything I had read in the daily paper? And why did a drunk Pap Finn railing against a black college professor from Ohio whose vote was as good as his own tell me more about white anxiety over black political power than anything I had seen on the evening news?

Mark Twain knew that there was nothing, absolutely *nothing*, a black man could do — including selflessly sacrificing his freedom, the only thing of value he had — that would make white society see beyond the color of his skin. And Mark Twain knew that depicting racists with chilling accuracy would expose the viciousness of their world view like nothing else could. It was an insight echoed some eighty years after Mark Twain penned Pap Finn's rantings about the black professor, when Malcolm X famously asked, "Do you know what white racists call black Ph.D.'s?" and answered, " '*Nigger!*' "[14]

Mark Twain taught me things I needed to know. He taught me to understand the raw racism that lay behind what I saw on the evening news. He taught me that the most well-meaning people can be hurtful and myopic. He taught me to recognize the supreme irony of a country founded in freedom that continued to deny freedom to so many of its citizens. Every time I hear of another effort to kick Huck Finn out of school somewhere, I recall everything that Mark Twain taught *this* high school junior, and I find myself jumping into the fray.[15] I remember the black high school student who called CNN during the phone-in portion of a 1985 debate between Dr. John Wallace, a black educator spearheading efforts to ban the book, and myself. She accused Dr. Wallace of insulting her and all black high school students by suggesting they weren't smart enough to understand Mark Twain's irony. And I recall the black cameraman on the *CBS Morning News* who came up to me after he finished shooting another debate between Dr. Wallace and myself. He said he had never read the book by Mark Twain that we had been arguing about — but now he really wanted to. One thing that puzzled him, though, was why a white woman was defending it and a black man was attacking it, because as far as he could see from what we'd been saying, the book made whites look pretty bad.

As I came to understand *Huckleberry Finn* and *Pudd'nhead Wilson* as commentaries on the era now known as the nadir of American race relations, those books pointed me toward the world recorded in nineteenth-century black newspapers and periodicals and in fiction by Mark Twain's black contemporaries. My investigation of the role black voices and traditions played in shaping Mark Twain's art helped make me aware of their role in shaping all of American culture.[16] My research underlined for me the importance of changing the stories we tell about who we are to reflect the realities of what we've been.[17]

Ever since our encounter in high school English, Mark Twain has shown me the potential of American literature and American history to illuminate each other. Rarely have I found a contradiction or complexity we grapple with as a nation that Mark Twain had not puzzled over as well. He insisted on taking America seriously. And he insisted on *not* taking America seriously: "I think that there is but a single specialty with us, only one thing that can be called by the wide name 'American,'" he once wrote. "That is the national devotion to ice-water."[18]

Mark Twain threw back at us our dreams and our denial of those dreams, our greed, our goodness, our ambition, and our laziness, all rattling around together in that vast echo chamber of our talk — that sharp, spunky American talk that Mark Twain figured out how to write down without robbing it of its energy and immediacy. Talk shaped by voices that the official arbiters of "culture" deemed of no importance — voices of children, voices of slaves, voices of servants, voices of ordinary people. Mark Twain listened. And he made us listen. To the stories he told us, and to the truths they conveyed. He still has a lot to say that we need to hear.

Mark Twain lives — in our libraries, classrooms, homes, theaters, movie houses, streets, and most of all in our speech. His optimism energizes us, his despair sobers us, and his willingness to keep wrestling with the hilarious and horrendous complexities of it all keeps us coming back for more. As the twenty-first century approaches, may he continue to goad us, chasten us, delight us, berate us, and cause us to erupt in unrestrained laughter in unexpected places.

NOTES

1. Ernest Hemingway, *Green Hills of Africa* (New York: Charles Scribner's Sons, 1935), 22. George Bernard Shaw to Samuel L. Clemens, July 3, 1907, quoted in Albert Bigelow Paine, *Mark Twain: A Biography* (New York: Harper and Brothers, 1912), 3:1398.

2. Allen Carey-Webb, "Racism and *Huckleberry Finn*: Censorship, Dialogue and Change," *English Journal* 82, no. 7 (November 1993):22.

3. See Louis J. Budd, "Impersonators," in J. R. LeMaster and James D. Wilson, eds., *The Mark Twain Encyclopedia* (New York: Garland Publishing Company, 1993), 389–91.

4. See Shelley Fisher Fishkin, "Ripples and Reverberations," part 3 of *Lighting Out for the Territory: Reflections on Mark Twain and American Culture* (New York: Oxford University Press, 1996).

5. There are two exceptions. Twain published chapters from his autobiography in the *North American Review* in 1906 and 1907, but this material was not published in book form in Twain's lifetime; our volume reproduces the material as it appeared in the *North American Review*. The other exception is our final volume, *Mark Twain's Speeches*, which appeared two months after Twain's death in 1910.

An unauthorized handful of copies of *1601* was privately printed by an Alexander Gunn of Cleveland at the instigation of Twain's friend John Hay in 1880. The first American edition authorized by Mark Twain, however, was printed at the United States Military Academy at West Point in 1882; that is the edition reproduced here.

It should further be noted that four volumes — *The Stolen White Elephant and Other Detective Stories, Following the Equator and Anti-imperialist Essays, The Diaries of Adam and Eve,* and *1601, and Is Shakespeare Dead?* — bind together material originally published separately. In each case the first American edition of the material is the version that has been reproduced, always in its entirety. Because Twain constantly recycled and repackaged previously published works in his collections of short pieces, a certain amount of duplication is unavoidable. We have selected volumes with an eye toward keeping this duplication to a minimum.

Even the twenty-nine-volume Oxford Mark Twain has had to leave much out. No edition of Twain can ever claim to be "complete," for the man was too prolix, and the file drawers of both ephemera and as yet unpublished texts are deep.

6. With the possible exception of *Mark Twain's Speeches.* Some scholars suspect Twain knew about this book and may have helped shape it, although no hard evidence to that effect has yet surfaced. Twain's involvement in the production process varied greatly from book to book. For a fuller sense of authorial intention, scholars will continue to rely on the superb definitive editions of Twain's works produced by the Mark Twain Project at the University of California at Berkeley as they become available. Dense with annotation documenting textual emendation and related issues, these editions add immeasurably to our understanding of Mark Twain and the genesis of his works.

7. Except for a few titles that were not in its collection. The American Antiquarian Society in Worcester, Massachusetts, provided the first edition of *King Leopold's Soliloquy*; the Elmer Holmes Bobst Library of New York University furnished the 1906-7 volumes of the *North American Review* in which *Chapters from My Autobiography* first appeared; the Harry Ransom Humanities Research Center at the University of Texas at Austin made their copy of the West Point edition of *1601* available; and the Mark Twain Project provided the first edition of *Extract from Captain Stormfield's Visit to Heaven.*

8. The specific copy photographed for Oxford's facsimile edition is indicated in a note on the text at the end of each volume.

9. All quotations from contemporary writers in this essay are taken from their introductions to the volumes of The Oxford Mark Twain, and the quotations from Mark Twain's works are taken from the texts reproduced in The Oxford Mark Twain.

10. *The Diaries of Adam and Eve*, The Oxford Mark Twain [hereafter OMT] (New York: Oxford University Press, 1996), p. 33.

11. *Tom Sawyer Abroad*, OMT, p. 74.

12. *Adventures of Huckleberry Finn*, OMT, p. 49-50.

13. Ibid., p. 358.

14. Malcolm X, *The Autobiography of Malcolm X*, with the assistance of Alex Haley (New York: Grove Press, 1965), p. 284.

15. I do not mean to minimize the challenge of teaching this difficult novel, a challenge for which all teachers may not feel themselves prepared. Elsewhere I have developed some concrete strategies for approaching the book in the classroom, including teaching it in the context of the history of American race relations and alongside books by black writers. See Shelley Fisher Fishkin, "Teaching *Huckleberry Finn*," in James S. Leonard, ed., *Making Mark Twain Work in the Classroom* (Durham: Duke University Press, forthcoming). See also Shelley Fisher Fishkin, *Was Huck Black? Mark Twain and African-American Voices* (New York: Oxford University Press, 1993), pp. 106–8, and a curriculum kit in preparation at the Mark Twain House in Hartford, containing teaching suggestions from myself, David Bradley, Jocelyn Chadwick-Joshua, James Miller, and David E. E. Sloane.

16. See Fishkin, *Was Huck Black?* See also Fishkin, "Interrogating 'Whiteness,' Complicating 'Blackness': Remapping American Culture," in Henry Wonham, ed., *Criticism and the Color Line: Desegregating American Literary Studies* (New Brunswick: Rutgers UP, 1996, pp. 251–90 and in shortened form in *American Quarterly* 47, no. 3 (September 1995):428–66.

17. I explore the roots of my interest in Mark Twain and race at greater length in an essay entitled "Changing the Story," in Jeffrey Rubin-Dorsky and Shelley Fisher Fishkin, eds., *People of the Book: Thirty Scholars Reflect on Their Jewish Identity* (Madison: U of Wisconsin Press, 1996), pp. 47–63.

18. "What Paul Bourget Thinks of Us," *How to Tell a Story and Other Essays*, OMT, p. 197.

INTRODUCTION
A Familiarity with Lightning
Lee Smith

I t is impossible for me to separate Mark Twain's *Sketches* from my memories of my father — even now, four years after his death and at least forty years after he read so many of them aloud to me as he strode back and forth in the kitchen holding that book up before him in one hand and striking any available surface from time to time with the other, for emphasis, while my mother sat in her rocker smoking cigarettes and rolling her eyes at this performance. I loved it . I loved all my father's performances, which included "The Face on the Barroom Floor" and lots of Kipling ("Gunga Din" was our favorite); Eugene Field's "The little toy dog is covered with Dust, / but sturdy and staunch he stands," which always reduced me to tears by the end; and Mary Howitt's dreaded "'Will you walk into my parlor?' said the Spider to the Fly," which produced such a delicious fear in the pit of my stomach that sometimes I had to be medicated: one tablespoon of bourbon, and lie down, and "Ernest Smith, stop it now!" from my mother.

Even when overcome, I never wanted him to stop. I was my father's perfect, ideal audience, as he was Mark Twain's. Like the great writer, my father was both sentimental and cynical, and very shrewd. He loved tall tales, practical jokes, gimmicks, and anecdotes in which the educated man is "outsharped" by a rube with the gift of gab.

I guess this is not surprising, considering he was a mountain man who came from several generations of mountain people who had always lived right there in southwest Virginia where I was growing up — a wild, isolated area which then bore about as much resemblance to the cultured Tidewater, way across the whole state, as the frontier of Mark Twain's day bore to New York.

My mother, born Virginia Marshall and called "Gig," had come there in her youth from the flat, civilized Eastern Shore of Virginia to teach school. She never got used to the mountains, and swore that they gave her migraine headaches and colitis. Mama was always lying down on the sofa all dressed up, having a headache. But there was no question that she was crazy about my father and his whole clan of whiskey-drinking, storytelling Democrats who used to sit out on my grandmother's porch every Sunday after dinner placing fifty-dollar bets on which bird would fly off the telephone wire first. This rowdy family might have given anybody colitis. Yet she had chosen Daddy over a well-bred gentleman from Richmond, a man who "went to the University of Virginia and never got over it," according to Daddy. And though she suffered from a few ideas of aristocracy herself, Mama was no slouch in the storytelling department, either.

My whole sense of story is, as a consequence, *oral*, and it comes from them. Of course it does — as writers, we cannot really choose our truest material, any more than we can choose to have, say, curly hair. Our material is given to us. It all has to do with where we are born, and the circumstances we are born into, and how we first hear language. What I hear is a *voice*, always one particular human voice, telling the story. Most often it is the first-person narrator of that story, but sometimes it seems to be the voice of the story itself. As I set to rereading Mark Twain's *Sketches*, I was struck by how much these little stories resemble the ones I grew up hearing.

In "Political Economy," for instance, the narrator is writing an essay upon that topic when he is interrupted by a man selling lightning rods. Too busy to stop writing, the essayist orders "six or eight" lightning rods just to shut the fellow up — only to be interrupted again by the persistent salesman, who has placed eight on one chimney, and now begs to "kind of touch up the other chimneys a little" in order to "add to the generous *coup d'oeil* a soothing uniformity of achievement which would allay the excitment naturally consequent upon the first *coup d'état*." The harassed essayist orders more lightning rods. At the salesman's next summons, the essayist goes flat-out berserk, giving him free rein if only he does not interrupt the lofty labor of composition again. The final bill comes to nine hundred dollars, and the essayist's "bristling premises" are the "talk and wonder of the town." In the next thunderstorm, "the lightning struck at my establishment seven hundred and sixty-four times in forty minutes" until "there was absolutely no more electricity left in the clouds above us within grappling distance of my insatiable rods."

The first irony is that the essayist, writing upon "political economy," is outsmarted in the same by the lightning rod man, who "takes" him for nine hundred dollars and makes a fool of him as well; the further irony is that the bombastic essayist never understands that he was bamboozled, but recounts the whole adventure in a straightforward though addled manner, as if any sane man would have behaved exactly as he did, given the circumstances.

As I read this sketch, one of my father's favorite stories came flooding back to me, concerning a man named Benton Powers and my great-uncle Vern Smith. The time is just prior to the First World War; the place is my hometown of Grundy, Virginia. I can hear my daddy now.

"The first thing anybody knew, Powers showed up here in a uniform, and said he was in the United States Army, and had been ordered to raise a company right here in the county, and he urged everybody to join up. Well, they did, until they had got themselves a whole army camp set up down there, and Powers had them marching and saluting and raising the flag and I don't know what-all, and every now and then he'd leave town and come back with a higher rank and a brand-new uniform, and nobody knew what to make of it.

"But of course he didn't have any money, not to pay his soldiers nor to pay the merchants over in town where he was running up some mighty big bills, as you might imagine, coming over there and commandeering his provisions, as he called them, and charging them all to the U.S. Army. Everybody was scared stiff to try and stop him, or say anything, because his men were armed to the teeth and he had so many of them camping out there in the bottom. Finally he had charged up money all over town until all the merchants felt like they were fixing to lose their shirt. So a bunch of them, the ones that Benton Powers owed the most to, got together in a body and prevailed upon Vern to go over there please and find out when it was that Benton Powers' company was going to get taken into the United States Army, and when it was that those in town were going to get paid. For it was a considerable contribution that they were making to the war effort by that time, as you might imagine. So Vern agreed to do it, and he went, but when he got over there, why, he couldn't even get to Powers, it seemed like. He had to talk to this one and then that one, Benton Powers' chain of command, don't you know. And every one of them wearing a uniform and carrying a gun.

"Finally, Vern — who was never long on patience — started to get kindly disgusted, his lunchtime having come and went. He had just about determined to give up the whole thing, and was walking back toward the bridge, when lo and behold he happened to look sideways into a tent and spied Benton Powers himself in there sitting on a stool with his pants legs rolled up and his feet in a tub of water.

"'I've got him now!' Vern thought, and went over there as fast as he was able, whereupon he proceeded to give Benton Powers what-for. Powers just sat there, calmly puffing on a big cigar while a boy washed his feet, and nodded as if he was agreeing with Vern all the while, and then the boy dried Powers' feet off good and put his socks and shoes back on him.

"'Now Vern,' Powers said. 'This here is a outstanding footbath. My boy puts something special in it. What is it that you put in here, boy?' he asked, and his orderly said, 'Epsom salts, sir.'

"'Epsom salts,' Powers said. 'I can highly recommend the use of Epsom salts in a footbath.'

"Well, the more Vern talked about money, the more Powers talked about the amazing curative and restorative powers of this particular sort of a footbath. Finally Powers asked Vern if *he* had any foot trouble, and Vern, who suffered something terrible from gout, was forced to say, 'Hell, yes! Damned if I don't!' and then one thing led to another, until before he knew it, Vern had *his* shoes and socks off, and *his* feet in the footbath, and there he stayed until Benton Powers bid him a cordial good day and walked off whistling — the boy having mysteriously disappeared, of course, along with Vern's shoes and socks. He had to walk back across the bridge and all through town barefoot, cussing every step of the way. Now Vern used to tell this story on himself, and he'd always end it up by saying, 'By God, it was one hell of a footbath nonetheless!'"

To grow up on this kind of fare and *not* become a storyteller would have been hard. For the material was all there — and the sense of language was there as well. Let's think about "Political Economy" once more. In a way it is also an essay about language. All the sages of the past (misquoted at length) cannot help our poor essayist in his battle with the glib lightning rod sales-man, who "said that his manner of speaking was not taught in books, and that nothing but familiarity with lightning could enable a man to handle his con-versational style with impunity." He simply outtalks the educated fool. The plain fact is that *big words are funny*, especially when applied to examples of egregious folly that usually don't come to our attention with big words at-tached to them, or to people of a sort that don't either, such as lightning rod salesmen.

Another anecdote of my father's concerned a new automobile parked out-side the courthouse in downtown Grundy at a time when there were very few cars at all in Buchanan County, and certainly no other flashy red cars such as this one. So it had already attracted a great deal of attention and discussion by the time Mr. Claude Pobst, the noted trial lawyer, came out of the courthouse and spied it. Mr. Pobst walked slowly all around the car once, thumbs hooked in his braces, which gave him a grave and judicious air. He looked the car over good and spat twice to the side before he spoke: "I say, fellers, is there any among you that might enlighten a man as to whose financial calamity this might be?" — a sally which was widely repeated and admired.

Language always transcends event. Most things that happen in the world are pretty boring in the first place; in the second place, most things happen again and again and again. There are no new plots to be had. But a real story-teller can make a great story out of anything, even the most trivial occurrence. This volume contains, for instance, a sketch about the difficulty of getting a pocket watch repaired properly; complaints about barbers and chambermaids and office bores; and a multitude of satirical comments upon bureau-crats, courts of law, the profession of journalism, the claims of science, the workings of government, etc. All these potentially dry and boring topics are rendered fascinating in the telling. This reminds me of something my hus-band once said about another gifted storyteller, Roy Blount, after they had been on a trip together: that Roy could wander around in the back of a drug-store someplace and come up with a great story about it—even when you'd been right there with him all along, and never realized that anything much was happening.

My mother was like that, too. She led an uneventful life by most standards —after teaching, she "just kept house," in her own words—yet she was pas-sionately interested in the news of the town and of the day and especially in the lives of the stars as reported in the tabloids we eagerly grabbed up each time we went to the Piggly Wiggly. Everything she read or heard turned into an anecdote; each little trip into the world beyond our house yielded its little story. I will always remember her recital of what another Methodist lady said to her one Sunday morning right after church let out: "I swear, Gig, you just look so good from behind!" Mama said that she didn't know whether she "ought to be mad or not."

By now it's obvious that the key element in all these stories is *human speech*: what so-and-so said when such-and-such happened. My absolute fa-vorite story of my father's turns on such a remark. It concerns Uncle Vern again, who was a member of the Virginia state legislature, which required him to drive to Richmond several times a year, a journey of several days. Now Vern didn't like to drive a car, so it fell to my daddy to drive him over there when-ever the legislature was in session, even though he was "not but a boy" and had to "lay out of school" in order to do it.

Once there, Uncle Vern took rooms in the old Hotel Jefferson, and it be-came Daddy's job to go out for whiskey or cigarettes or cigars or anything else the legislators required of an evening. Vern Smith drank only Jack Daniel's bourbon, and he drank it straight. Well, one night during a rowdy card game, Daddy seized his opportunity and got drunk himself. He claimed later not to remember the end of the card game, or who won, or how he got put to bed on the extra cot in Uncle Vern's room. But he woke up the next morning feeling "the awfullest I ever felt, and wanted to die on the spot." He opened one eye and looked around: there was Uncle Vern himself, "all spraddled out on his back, snoring like a train"; there lay the remains of the party — cigar butts, food scraps, liquor bottles . . . *liquor bottles!*

From somewhere deep inside his misery, Daddy remembered something about "the hair of the dog that bit you," that old remedy for hangover which prescribes another swig of the same. Daddy rolled out of bed and crawled over toward the gaming table, where he could scarcely summon the strength to snatch up a bottle of Uncle Vern's prize bourbon, still half full. Daddy took a long drink and vomited all over the fancy floral carpeting of the Hotel Jefferson. At length, just about to die, he finally raised his sorry head to find Vern propped up on his bed "all wild-haired and staring at me."

"Now Ernest," Vern said, "if you're just practicing, I wish to hell you'd use the other bottle!"

This story — like all these stories I heard as a child — was doubly oral. The oral remark was privileged, and the story was always told aloud. It was Mark Twain's great genius, and his great gift to all of us who grew up hearing this kind of story, that he chose to transmit the *told* story straight onto the page. This renders the material of our actual lives possible for written fiction. This makes that ear we've got good for something besides mimicking our cousins exactly.

For me, to be able to write in the vernacular is to be able to write.

I am also interested in Twain's experiments with first-person point of view, nowhere more evident than in these *Sketches*. When he is not burlesquing an existing form (such as the Sunday school pamphlet, letters to the editor, the fable, or the medieval romance), Twain invariably makes use of a first-person narrator. Occasionally the speaker is Mr. Twain himself, as in "Speech at the Scottish Banquet at London" or "After-Dinner Speech." But more often it is a persona, frequently a self-justifying fool or bumbler telling a story which he himself doesn't get the point of. "My Late Senatorial Secretaryship" is representative. Here, the narrator is "private secretary to a senator," entrusted with the business of answering the senator's mail. He does not answer it appropriately, of course; he answers it hilariously, disastrously. In response to a constituent's request for the establishment of a post office at Baldwin's Ranch, he writes, "GENTLEMEN: What the mischief do you suppose you want with a post-office at Baldwin's Ranche? It would not do you any good. If any letters came there, you couldn't read them, you know...." Etc., until at last the ruined senator is forced to shout: "Leave the house! Leave it for ever and forever, too!"

To which our hapless secretary rejoins, "I regarded that as a sort of covert intimation that my services could be dispensed with, and so I resigned. I never will be a private secretary to a senator again. You can't please that kind of people. They don't know anything. They can't appreciate a party's efforts." Of course the obtuse secretary is an unreliable narrator, and nothing is more enjoyable for the reader than an unreliable narrator, who invariably tells far more than he means to. We get to see him as he sees himself, but we understand more than he does; our position thus adds a certain irony to the proceedings — and generally, when we are reading these sketches, it affords us a lot of fun.

Sometimes there is a kind of double first-person perspective at work, as in "A Ghost Story," where our ostensible narrator is a gentleman who "took a large room, far up Broadway, in a huge old building whose upper stories had been wholly unoccupied for years, until I came." But a significant part of this sketch is told by the visiting ghost of the Cardiff Giant, so we really have *two* first-person narratives here. This is likewise true of "Cannibalism in the Cars," in which the narrator, a man from Washington, falls into conversation with a stranger who then tells his own grotesque tale.

And in this volume's version of the famous frog story — the "Jumping Frog. (In English. Then in French. Then Clawed Back into a Civilized Language Once More by Patient, Unremunerated Toil)" — we have no less than *three* storytellers, all of them playing off each other: first comes Mr. Twain himself, who makes the introductions; then the somewhat dim-witted visitor who pays a call upon "good-natured, garrulous old Simon Wheeler"; then the said Simon Wheeler; and finally Mr. Twain again, giving us his literal (and hence hysterical) translation of the French version of "Jumping Frog."

Its ending goes like this: "When Smiley recognized how it was, he was like mad. He deposited his frog by the earth and ran after that individual, but he not him caught never."

All these experiments in point of view revolve around one central truth: Twain was not interested so much in plot as in people. The story itself depends upon who is telling it. Twain's later, darker view of human nature is not much manifest in *Sketches*; these characters may be benighted or bumble-headed or boring or deluded, but they are not evil. They are comic. What fascinates Twain here is how they react to the things that happen to them, what they make of it all, how they express themselves on the subject. He lets them speak in their own voices by and large, a chorus ranging from high-flown oratory to the plain speech of working people to the almost burlesqued African-American dialect of the day. It seems generally true that the more elevated the speech, the likelier that person is to be an idiot; words of wisdom and common sense are invariably voiced by the common man.

So it follows that the most profound and moving sketch in this whole collection should be told by a freed slave, Aunt Rachel. The pathos of her "True Story" is further heightened by Twain's aforementioned use of the double narrator. It is especially ironic that the initial narrator is not even conscious that he is a racist. He simply expects Aunt Rachel, described merely as "our servant, and colored," to have had no life of her own. All he knows of her is that she is a "cheerful, hearty soul"; they tease her every evening after dinner, and believe that she enjoys it. She is "sitting respectfully below our level" when the narrator naively asks her (not out of real interest, but because the thought just "occurred" to him) the question which provokes her life story: "Aunt Rachel, how is it that you've lived sixty years and never had any trouble?"

Aunt Rachel begins by stating her pride in her own heritage; she takes after her Maryland mother, who used to say, "I wa'nt bawn in the mash to be fool' by trash! I's one o' de ole Blue Hen's Chickens, *I* is!" In other words she is an individual with a family and a past, despite the fact that she was "bawn down 'mongst de slaves." She quietly asserts her capacity for love: "my ole man — dat's my husban' — he was lovin' an' kind to me, jist as kind as you is to yo' own wife. An' we had chil'en — seven chil'en — an' we loved dem chil'en jist de same as you loves yo' chil'en." Then she goes on to assert her right to fury; when they sold off her husband and children, she says, including even her precious "little Henry," she "took and tear de clo'es mos' off of 'em an' beat 'em over de head wid my chain."

The narrator informs us that Aunt Rachel grows in the telling, until she "towered above us, black against the stars." By the end of the story, when she has gained her freedom and little Henry has found her at last, Aunt Rachel's heavy irony is eloquent: "Oh, no, Misto C——, *I* hain't had no trouble. An' no *joy!*" She has proved not only her capacity for pain and trouble, but also for joy — and claimed the full measure of her humanity.

The meaning of this sketch is deepened and universalized by Twain's use of the double narrators, for we as readers *become* the oblivious questioner, all of us, first showing our ignorant bias in even asking such a question, then forced to open our minds and hearts as we listen to the answer.

It is my belief that American writers have benefited as much from the way Mark Twain opened up the possibilities of first-person narration as we have from his use of vernacular language. Consider how much of our best writing has been done in the first person; the "I" statement may be the quintessentially American statement, as in "I can't claim to speak for anybody else, but by God I'll speak for myself!"

This heritage became particularly pertinent to me when I attempted to write a novel which I had wanted to write for a very long time, a novel which would be all about those mountains where I grew up. I felt the need to write such a novel when the first fast-food restaurants going into Buchanan County — that, and those satellite dishes sprouting on every hillside — signaled me that the end of that idiosyncratic, fiercely separate and individualistic way of life was at hand, and that I'd better start setting it all down fast. And a lot of the people I wanted to tape, such as my aunt Kate, and my daddy, were getting on in years. Aunt Kate was in her eighties then, so I felt I had to hurry. (Now she's a hundred and seven, so I really didn't, but that's another story!) Anyway, I started writing down everything I'd ever heard about how life used to be there in the early days — all the old stories, all the old songs — and taping everybody. At first I'd worried that nobody would want to talk to me; later I realized that the real problem was, nobody wanted to shut up. I went through diaries, old photographs, courthouse records. I tramped around in hilltop graveyards. Before long, I had a closetful of material — more material than I knew what to do with.

My general idea was to tell the tale of a particular holler (narrow valley) in my mountains, and of the family that had always lived there. I'd call it Hoot Owl Holler, because there was a Hoot Owl Holler right around the bend from my parents' house, and I'd show how things had changed in the past hundred years. Specifically I wanted to write about the land and how it had gone from a virgin forest full of wildlife to a disaster area, first the timber rights and then the mineral rights sold to mostly outside interests that had come in and raped the land repeatedly. I wanted to write about the character of the people and how the loss of the land had changed many of them from proud, self-sufficient pioneers (mythic in their stature in my mind) to government dependents. And finally I wanted to document that rich language I had — thank God! — grown up on, all those wonderful expressions so much more exact and robust than the TV talk now going into every mountain home. It wouldn't be long, I feared, before a boy growing up in Grundy would be much more likely to sound like Dan Rather than Uncle Vern. So I wanted to use phrases like "he's daddied more children than any other man in Buchanan County," or "the creek turkey-tails out oncet it gets down to the bottom," in what I hoped would be context, as they had been actually used.

Oh, but there I ran into trouble, though I had written a hundred pages before I realized it.

The problem was that I was writing this novel in the third person, in good standard American English, so that every time one of my characters piped up and said something like, "He's daddied more children . . . ," he sounded like he was on *Hee-Haw*. And I sounded like I was condescending to my characters — the last thing in the world I intended to do. The gap between the third-person narrative voice of the novel and the characters' own voices was simply too great.

Finally I realized that the only way I could write this novel was to use multiple narrators, allowing each one to tell a section of the story. I proceeded to do this, though my publisher was sorry to see it, explaining that the reading public wants a main character to identify with (I know this is true) and that the title of the novel, *Oral History*, made it sound like a textbook on dentistry (I know this is true, too). Nevertheless I persevered, and I still feel that the ghost of Mark Twain was hovering someplace in the background, inspiring me to write that novel in so many voices, starting off with an opinionated old granny-woman named Granny Younger.

"What you need is a girl," I says to Almarine. "What you need around here is some children on this land, and a woman's touch in the house. You better find you a girl," I says.

Then I left, off up Hurricane, how I go.

Later, I wished I'd of bit off my tongue.

Sometimes I know the future in my breast. Sometimes I see the future coming out like a picture show, acrost the trail ahead. But that night I never seed nothing atall. If I had, it would of been graves and dying, it would of been blood on the moon. And I never saw a blessed thing in the night but them lightning bugs a-rising from the sally grass along by Grassy Creek.

Because of course Almarine went right out and done it, what I said. Everybody does what I say. Almarine went a-courting. He courted on Hurricane, he courted over in Black Rock. He courted until he run acrost Isom's red-headed Emmy, and that was the end of him. I'll tell it all directly.

I'll tell it all, but don't you forget it is Almarine's story. Almarine's, and Pricey Jane's, and Lord yes, it's that red-headed Emmy's. Mought be it's her story moren the rest. Iffen twas my story, I never would tell it at all. There's tales I'll tell, and tales I won't. And iffen twas my story, why I'd be all hemmed in by the facts of it like Hoot Owl Holler is hemmed in by them three mountains. I couldn't move no way but forward. And often in my traveling over these hills I have seed that what you want the most, you find offen the beaten path. I never find nothing I need on the trace, for an instance. I never find ary a thing. But I am an old, old woman, and I have traveled a lot in these parts. I have seed folks come and I have seed them go. I have cotched more babies than I can name you; I have put the burying quilts around many a soul. I said I know moren you know and mought be I'll tell you moren you want to hear. I'll tell you a story that's truer than true, and nothing so true is so pretty. It's blood on the moon, as I said. The way I tell a story is the way I want to, and iffen you mislike it, you don't have to hear.

MARK TWAIN'S

SKETCHES,

NEW AND OLD

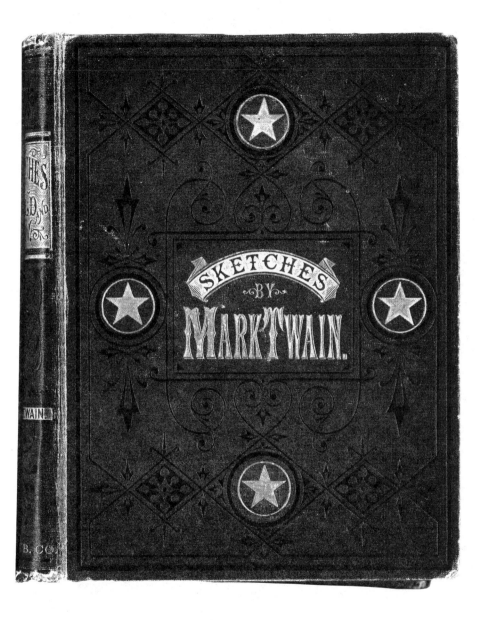

MARK TWAIN'S SKETCHES,

NEW AND OLD.

NOW FIRST PUBLISHED IN COMPLETE FORM.

SOLD ONLY BY SUBSCRIPTION.

THE AMERICAN PUBLISHING COMPANY.

HARTFORD, CONN., AND CHICAGO, ILL.

1875.

PREFACE.

———•———

I have scattered through this volume a mass of matter which has never been in print before, (such as "Learned Fables for Good Old Boys and Girls," the "Jumping Frog restored to the English tongue after martyrdom in the French," the "Membranous Croup" sketch, and many others which I need not specify): not doing this in order to make an advertisement of it, but because these things seemed instructive.

MARK TWAIN.

HARTFORD, 1875.

INDEX.

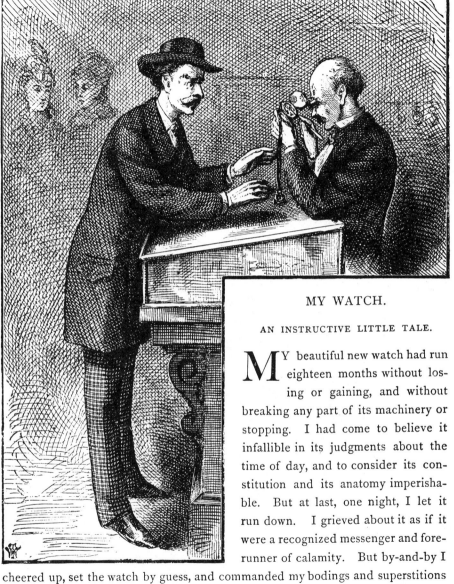

MY WATCH.

AN INSTRUCTIVE LITTLE TALE.

MY beautiful new watch had run eighteen months without losing or gaining, and without breaking any part of its machinery or stopping. I had come to believe it infallible in its judgments about the time of day, and to consider its constitution and its anatomy imperishable. But at last, one night, I let it run down. I grieved about it as if it were a recognized messenger and forerunner of calamity. But by-and-by I cheered up, set the watch by guess, and commanded my bodings and superstitions to depart. Next day I stepped into the chief jeweler's to set it by the exact time, and the head of the establishment took it out of my hand and proceeded to set it for me. Then he said, " She is four minutes slow—regulator wants pushing up." I tried to stop him—tried to make him understand that the watch kept perfect time. But no; all this human cabbage could see was that the watch was four minutes slow, and the regulator *must* be pushed up a little; and so, while I danced around him in anguish, and implored him to let the watch alone, he calmly and cruelly did the shameful deed. My watch began to gain. It gained faster and faster day by day. Within the week it sickened to a raging fever, and its pulse went up to a hundred and fifty in the shade.

At the end of two months it had left all the timepieces of the town far in the rear, and was a fraction over thirteen days ahead of the almanac. It was away into November enjoying the snow, while the October leaves were still turning. It hurried up house rent, bills payable, and such things, in such a ruinous way that I could not abide it. I took it to the watchmaker to be regulated. He asked me if I had ever had it repaired. I said no, it had never needed any repairing. He looked a look of vicious happiness and eagerly pried the watch open, and then put a small dice box into his eye and peered into its machinery. He said it wanted cleaning and oiling, besides regulating—come in a week. After being cleaned and oiled, and regulated, my watch slowed down to that degree that it ticked like a tolling bell. I began to be left by trains, I failed all appointments, I got to missing my dinner; my watch strung out three days' grace to four and let me go to protest; I gradually drifted back into yesterday, then day before, then into last week, and by-and-by the comprehension came upon me that all solitary and alone I was lingering along in week before last, and the world was out of sight. I seemed to detect in myself a sort of sneaking fellow-feeling for the mummy in the museum, and a desire to swap news with him. I went to a watchmaker again. He took the watch all to pieces while I waited, and then said the barrel was "swelled." He said he could reduce it in three days. After this the watch *averaged* well, but nothing more. For half a day it would go like the very mischief, and keep up such a barking and wheezing, and whooping and sneezing and snorting, that I could not hear myself think for the disturbance; and as long as it held out there was not a watch in the land that stood any chance against it. But the rest of the day it would keep on slowing down and fooling along until all the clocks it had left behind caught up again. So at last, at the end of twenty-four hours, it would trot up to the judges' stand all right and just in time. It would show a fair and square aver-age, and no man could say it had done more or less than its duty. But a correct average is only a mild virtue in a watch, and I took this instru-ment to another watchmaker. He said the kingbolt was broken. I said I was glad it was nothing more seri-ous. To tell the plain truth, I had no idea what the kingbolt was, but I

did not choose to appear ignorant to a stranger. He repaired the kingbolt, but what the watch gained in one way it lost in another. It would run awhile and then stop awhile, and then run awhile again, and so on, using its own discretion about the intervals. And every time it went off it kicked back like a musket. I padded my breast for a few days, but finally took the watch to another watchmaker. He picked it all to pieces, and turned the ruin over and over under his glass; and then he said there appeared to be something the matter with the hair-trigger. He fixed it, and gave it a fresh start. It did well now, except that always at ten minutes to ten the hands would shut together like a pair of scissors, and from that time forth they would travel together. The oldest man in the world could not make head or tail of the time of day by such a watch, and so I went again to have the thing repaired. This person said that the crystal had got bent, and that the mainspring was not straight. He also remarked that part of the works needed half-soling. He made these things all right, and then my timepiece performed unexceptionably, save that now and then, after working along quietly for nearly eight hours, everything inside would let go all of a sudden and begin to buzz like a bee, and the hands would straightway begin to spin round and round so fast that their individuality was lost completely, and they simply seemed a delicate spider's web over the face of the watch. She would reel off the next twenty-four hours in six or seven minutes, and then stop with a bang. I went with a heavy heart to one more watchmaker, and looked on while he took her to pieces. Then I prepared to cross-question him rigidly, for this thing was getting serious. The watch had cost two hundred dollars originally, and I seemed to have paid out two or three thousand for repairs. While I waited and looked on I presently recognized in this watchmaker an old acquaintance—a steamboat engineer of other days, and not a good engineer either. He examined all the parts carefully, just as the other watchmakers had done, and then delivered his verdict with the same confidence of manner.

He said—

"She makes too much steam—you want to hang the monkey-wrench on the safety-valve!"

I brained him on the spot, and had him buried at my own expense.

My uncle William (now deceased, alas!) used to say that a good horse was a good horse until it had run away once, and that a good watch was a good watch until the repairers got a chance at it. And he used to wonder what became of all the unsuccessful tinkers, and gunsmiths, and shoemakers, and engineers, and blacksmiths; but nobody could ever tell him.

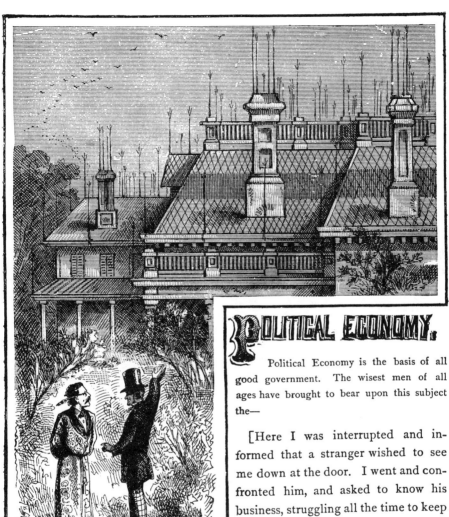

POLITICAL ECONOMY.

Political Economy is the basis of all good government. The wisest men of all ages have brought to bear upon this subject the—

[Here I was interrupted and informed that a stranger wished to see me down at the door. I went and confronted him, and asked to know his business, struggling all the time to keep a tight rein on my seething political economy ideas, and not let them break away from me or get tangled in their harness. And privately I wished the stranger was in the bottom of the canal with a cargo of wheat on top of him. I was all in a fever, but he was cool. He said he was sorry to disturb me, but

21

as he was passing he noticed that I needed some lightning-rods. I said, "Yes, yes—go on—what about it?" He said there was nothing about it, in particular—nothing except that he would like to put them up for me. I am new to housekeeping; have been used to hotels and boarding-houses all my life. Like anybody else of similar experience, I try to appear (to strangers) to be an old housekeeper; consequently I said in an off-hand way that I had been intending for some time to have six or eight lightning-rods put up, but—— The stranger started, and looked inquiringly at me, but I was serene. I thought that if I chanced to make any mistakes, he would not catch me by my countenance. He said he would rather have my custom than any man's in town. I said, "All right," and started off to wrestle with my great subject again, when he called me back and said it would be necessary to know exactly how many "points" I wanted put up, what parts of the house I wanted them on, and what quality of rod I preferred. It was close quarters for a man not used to the exigencies of housekeeping; but I went through creditably, and he probably never suspected that I was a novice. I told him to put up eight "points," and put them all on the roof, and use the best quality of rod. He said he could furnish the "plain" article at 20 cents a foot; "coppered," 25 cents; "zinc-plated spiral-twist," at 30 cents, that would stop a streak of lightning any time, no matter where it was bound, and "render its errand harmless and its further progress apocryphal." I said apocryphal was no slouch of a word, emanating from the source it did, but, philology aside, I liked the spiral-twist and would take that brand. Then he said he *could* make two hundred and fifty feet answer; but to do it right, and make the best job in town of it, and attract the admiration of the just and the unjust alike, and compel all parties to say they never saw a more symmetrical and hypothetical display of lightning-rods since they were born, he supposed he really couldn't get along without four hundred, though he was not vindictive, and trusted he was willing to try. I said, go ahead and use four hundred, and make any kind of a job he pleased out of it, but let me get back to my work. So I got rid of him at last; and now, after half-an-hour spent in getting my train of political economy thoughts coupled together again, I am ready to go on once more.]

richest treasures of their genius, their experience of life, and their learning. The great lights of commercial jurisprudence, international confraternity, and biological deviation, of all ages, all civilizations, and all nationalities, from Zoroaster down to Horace Greeley, have——

[Here I was interrupted again, and required to go down and confer further with that lightning-rod man. I hurried off, boiling and surging with prodigious thoughts wombed in words of such majesty that each one of them was in itself a straggling procession of syllables that might be fifteen minutes passing a given point, and once more I confronted him—he so calm and sweet, I so hot and frenzied. He was standing in the contemplative attitude of the Colossus of Rhodes, with one foot on my infant tuberose, and the other among my pansies, his hands on his hips, his hat-brim tilted forward, one eye shut and the other gazing critically and admiringly in the direction of my principal chimney. He said now *there* was a state of things to make a man glad to be alive; and added, " I leave it to *you* if you ever saw anything more deliriously picturesque than eight lightning-rods on one chimney?" I said I had no present recollection of anything that transcended it. He said that in his opinion nothing on earth but Niagara Falls was superior to it in the way of natural scenery. All that was needed now, he verily believed, to make my house a perfect balm to the eye, was to kind of touch up the other chimneys a little, and thus "add to the generous *coup d'œil* a soothing uniformity of achievement which would allay the excitement naturally consequent upon the first *coup d'état*." I asked him if he learned to talk out of a book, and if I could borrow it anywhere? He smiled pleasantly, and said that his manner of speaking was not taught in books, and that nothing but familiarity with lightning could enable a man to handle his conversational style with impunity. He then figured up an estimate, and said that about eight more rods scattered about my roof would about fix me right, and he guessed five hundred feet of stuff would do it; and added that the first eight had got a little the start of him, so to speak, and used up a mere trifle of material more than he had calculated on—a hundred feet or along there. I said I was in a dreadful hurry, and I wished we could get this business permanently mapped out, so that I could go on with my work. He said, " I *could* have put up those eight rods, and marched off about my business—some men *would* have done it. But no: I said to myself, this man is a stranger to me, and I will die before I'll wrong him; there ain't lightning-rods enough on that house, and for one I'll never stir out of my tracks till I've done as I would be done by, and told him so. Stranger, my duty is accomplished; if the recalcitrant and dephlogistic messenger of heaven strikes your "—— " There, now, there," I said, " put on the other eight—add five hundred feet of spiral-twist—do anything and everything you want to do; but calm your sufferings, and try to keep your feelings where you can reach them with the dictionary. Meanwhile, if we understand each other now, I will go to work again."

I think I have been sitting here a full hour, this time, trying to get back to where I was when my train of thought was broken up by the last interruption ; but I believe I have accomplished it at last, and may venture to proceed again.]

wrestled with this great subject, and the greatest among them have found it a worthy adversary, and one that always comes up fresh and smiling after every throw. The great Confucius said that he would rather be a profound political economist than chief of police. Cicero frequently said that political economy was the grandest consummation that the human mind was capable of consuming ; and even our own Greeley has said vaguely but forcibly that " *Political*——

[Here the lightning-rod man sent up another call for me. I went down in a state of mind bordering on impatience. He said he would rather have died than interrupt me, but when he was employed to do a job, and that job was expected to be done in a clean, workmanlike manner, and when it was finished and fatigue urged him to seek the rest and recreation he stood so much in need of, and he was about to do it, but looked up and saw at a glance that all the calculations had been a little out, and if a thunder storm were to come up, and that house, which he felt a personal interest in, stood there with nothing on earth to protect it but sixteen lightning-rods—— " Let us have peace !" I shrieked. " Put up a hundred and fifty ! Put some on the kitchen ! Put a dozen on the barn ! Put a couple on the cow !—Put one on the cook !—scatter them all over the persecuted place till it looks like a zinc-plated, spiral-twisted, silver-mounted cane-break ! Move ! Use up all the material you can get your hands on, and when you run out of lightning-rods put up ram-rods, cam-rods, stair-rods, piston-rods—*anything* that will pander to your dismal appetite for artificial scenery, and bring respite to my raging brain and healing to my lacerated soul !" Wholly unmoved—further than to smile sweetly—this iron being simply turned back his wristbands daintily, and said " He would now proceed to hump himself." Well, all that was nearly three hours ago. It is questionable whether I am calm enough yet to write on the noble theme of political economy, but I cannot resist the desire to try, for it is the one subject that is nearest to my heart and dearest to my brain of all this world's philosophy.]

"—— *economy is heaven's best boon to man.*" When the loose·but gifted Byron lay in his Venetian exile he observed that, if it could be granted him to go back and live his misspent life over again, he would give his lucid and unintoxicated intervals to the composition, not of frivolous rhymes, but of essays upon political economy. Washington loved this exquisite science ; such names as Baker, Beckwith, Judson, Smith, are imperishably linked with it ; and even imperial Homer, in the ninth book of the Iliad, has said :—

> Fiat justitia, ruat cœlum,
> Post mortem unum, ante bellum,
> Hic jacet hoc, ex-parte res,
> Politicum e-conomico est.

The grandeur of these conceptions of the old poet, together with the felicity of the wording which clothes them, and the sublimity of the imagery whereby they are illustrated, have singled out that stanza, and made it more celebrated than any that ever——

["Now, not a word out of you—not a single word. Just state your bill and relapse into impenetrable silence for ever and ever on these premises. Nine hundred dollars? Is that all? This check for the amount will be honored at any respectable bank in America. What is that multitude of people gathered in the street for? How?—'looking at the lightning-rods!' Bless my life, did they never see any lightning-rods before? Never saw 'such a stack of them on one establishment,' did I understand you to say? I will step down and critically observe this popular ebullition of ignorance."]

THREE DAYS LATER.—We are all about worn out. For four-and-twenty hours our bristling premises were the talk and wonder of the town. The theatres languished, for their happiest scenic inventions were tame and commonplace compared with my lightning-rods. Our street was blocked night and day with spectators, and among them were many who came from the country to see. It was a blessed relief on the second day, when a thunder-storm came up and the lightning began to " go for " my house, as the historian Josephus quaintly phrases it. It cleared the galleries, so to speak. In five minutes there was not a spectator within half a mile of my place ; but all the high houses about that distance away were full, windows, roof, and all And well they might be, for all the falling stars and Fourth-of-July fireworks of a generation, put together and rained down simultaneously out of heaven in one brilliant shower upon one helpless roof, would not have any advantage of the pyrotechnic display that was making my house so magnificently conspicuous in the general gloom of the storm. By actual count, the lightning struck at my establishment seven hundred and sixty-four times in forty minutes, but tripped on one of those faithful rods every time, and slid down the spiral twist and

shot into the earth before it probably had time to be surprised at the way the thing was done. And through all that bombardment only one patch of slates was ripped up, and that was because, for a single instant, the rods in the vicinity were transporting all the lightning they could possibly accommodate. Well, nothing was ever seen like it since the world began. For one whole day and night not a member of my family stuck his head out of the window but he got the hair snatched off it as smooth as a billiard-ball ; and if the reader will believe me, not one of us ever dreamt of stirring abroad. But at last the awful siege came to an end—because there was absolutely no more electricity left in the clouds above us within grappling distance of my insatiable rods. Then I sallied forth, and gathered daring workmen together, and not a bite or a nap did we take till the premises were utterly stripped of all their terrific armament except just three rods on the house, one on the kitchen, and one on the barn—and behold these remain there even unto this day. And then, and not till then, the people ventured to use our street again. I will remark here, in passing, that during that fearful time I did not continue my essay upon political economy. I am not even yet settled enough in nerve and brain to resume it.

To Whom it May Concern.—Parties having need of three thousand two hundred and eleven feet of best quality zinc-plated spiral-twist lightning-rod stuff, and sixteen hundred and thirty-one silver-tipped points, all in tolerable repair (and, although much worn by use, still equal to any ordinary emergency), can hear of a bargain by addressing the publisher.

THE "JUMPING FROG."

IN ENGLISH. THEN IN FRENCH. THEN CLAWED BACK INTO A CIVILIZED LANGUAGE ONCE MORE BY PATIENT, UNREMUNERATED TOIL.

EVEN a criminal is entitled to fair play; and certainly when a man who has done no harm has been unjustly treated, he is privileged to do his best to right himself. My attention has just been called to an article some three years old in a French Maga- zine entitled "Revue des Deux Mondes" (Review of Some Two Worlds), wherein the writer treats of "Les Humoristes Americaines" (These Humorists Americans). I am one of these

28

humorists Americans dissected by him, and hence the complaint I am making.

This gentleman's article is an able one (as articles go, in the French, where they always tangle up everything to that degree that when you start into a sentence you never know whether you are going to come out alive or not). It is a very good article, and the writer says all manner of kind and complimentary things about me—for which I am sure I thank him with all my heart; but then why should he go and spoil all his praise by one unlucky experiment? What I refer to is this: he says my Jumping Frog is a funny story, but still he can't see why it should ever really convulse anyone with laughter—and straightway proceeds to translate it into French in order to prove to his nation that there is nothing so very extravagantly funny about it. Just there is where my complaint originates. He has not translated it at all; he has simply mixed it all up; it is no more like the Jumping Frog when he gets through with it than I am like a meridian of longitude. But my mere assertion is not proof; wherefore I print the French version, that all may see that I do not speak falsely; furthermore, in order that even the unlettered may know my injury and give me their compassion, I have been at infinite pains and trouble to re-translate this French version back into English; and to tell the truth I have well nigh worn myself out at it, having scarcely rested from my work during five days and nights. I cannot speak the French language, but I can translate very well, though not fast, I being self-educated. I ask the reader to run his eye over the original English version of the Jumping Frog, and then read the French or my re-translation, and kindly take notice how the Frenchman has riddled the grammar. I think it is the worst I ever saw; and yet the French are called a polished nation. If I had a boy that put sentences together as they do, I would polish him to some purpose. Without further introduction, the Jumping Frog, as I originally wrote it, was as follows—[after it will be found the French version, and after the latter my re-translation from the French]:

THE NOTORIOUS JUMPING FROG OF CALAVERAS* COUNTY.

In compliance with the request of a friend of mine, who wrote me from the East, I called on good-natured, garrulous old Simon Wheeler, and inquired after my friend's friend, Leonidas

* Pronounced Cal-e-*va*-ras.

W. Smiley, as requested to do, and I hereunto append the result. I have a lurking suspicion that *Leonidas W.* Smiley is a myth; that my friend never knew such a personage; and that he only conjectured that if I asked old Wheeler about him, it would remind him of his infamous *Jim* Smiley, and he would go to work and bore me to death with some exasperating reminiscence of him as long and as tedious as it should be useless to me. If that was the design, it succeeded.

I found Simon Wheeler dozing comfortably by the bar-room stove of the dilapidated tavern in the decayed mining camp of Angel's, and I noticed that he was fat and bald-headed, and had an expression of winning gentleness and simplicity upon his tranquil countenance. He roused up, and gave me good-day. I told him a friend of mine had commissioned me to make some inquiries

about a cherished companion of his boyhood named Leondias W. Smiley—Rev. Leondias W. Smiley, a young minister of the Gospel, who he had heard was at one time a resident of Angel's Camp. I added that if Mr. Wheeler could tell me anything about this Rev. Leonidas W. Smiley, I would feel under many obligations to him. Simon Wheeler backed me into a corner and blockaded me there with his chair, and then sat down and reeled off the monotonous narrative which follows this paragraph. He never smiled, he never frowned, he never changed his voice from the gentle-flowing key to which he tuned his initial sentence, he never betrayed the slightest suspicion of enthusiasm; but all through the interminable narrative there ran a vein of impressive earnestness and sincerity, which showed me plainly that, so far from his imagining that there was anything ridiculous or funny about his story, he regarded it as a really important matter, and admired its two heroes as men of transcendent genius in *finesse.* I let him go on in his own way, and never interrupted him once.

"Rev. Leonidas W. H'm, Reverend Le—well, there was a feller here once by the name of *Jim* Smiley, in the winter of '49—or may be it was the spring of '50—I don't recollect exactly, somehow, though what makes me think it was one or the other is because I remember the big **flume** warn't finished when he first come to the camp ; but any way, he was the curiosest man about always betting on anything that turned up you ever see, if he could get anybody to bet on the other side ; and if he couldn't he'd change sides. Any way that suited the other man would suit *him*— any way just so's he got a bet, *he* was satisfied. But still he was lucky, uncommon lucky ; he most always come out winner. He was always ready and laying for a chance ; there couldn't be no soli- t'ry thing mentioned but that feller'd offer to bet on it, and take ary side you please, as I was just telling you. If there was a horse-race, you'd find him flush or you'd find him busted at the end of it ; if there was a dog-fight, he'd bet on it ; if there was a cat-fight, he'd bet on it ; if there was a chicken-fight, he'd bet on it ; why, if there was two birds setting on a fence, he would bet you which one would fly first ; or if there was a camp-meeting, he would be there reg'lar to bet on Parson Walk- er, which he judged to be the best exhort- er about here, and so he was too, and a good man. If he even see a straddle-bug start to go anywheres, he would bet you how long it would take him to get to—to wherever he was go- ing to, and if you took him up, he would fol- ler that straddle-bug to Mexico but what he would find out where he was bound for and how long he was on the road. Lots of the boys here has seen that Smiley, and can tell you about him. Why, it never made no difference to *him* —he'd bet on *any* thing — the dangdest feller. Parson Walk- er's wife laid very sick once, for a good while, and it seemed as if they warn't going to save her ; but one morning he come in,

and Smiley up and asked him how she was, and he said she was considable better—thank the Lord for his inf'nit mercy—and coming on so smart that with the blessing of Prov'dence she'd get well yet ; and Smiley, before he thought says, " Well, I'll resk two-and-a-half she don't anyway."

Thish-yer Smiley had a mare—the boys called her the fifteen-minute nag, but that was only in fun, you know, because of course she was faster than that—and he used to win money on that horse, for all she was so slow and always had the asthma, or the distemper, or the consumption, or some- thing of that kind. They used to give her two or three hundred yards' start, and then pass her under way ; but always at the fag-end of the race she'd get excited and desperate-like, and come cavorting and straddling up, and scattering her legs around limber, sometimes in the air, and sometimes out to one side amongst the fences, and kicking up m-o-r-e dust and raising m-o-r-e racket with her coughing and sneezing and blowing her nose—and *always* fetch up at the stand just about a neck ahead, as near as you could cipher it down.

And he had a little small bull-pup, that to look at him you'd think he warn't worth a cent but to set around and look ornery and lay for a chance to steal something. But as soon as money was up on him he was a different dog ; his under-jaw'd begin to stick out like the fo'castle of a steamboat, and his teeth would uncover and shine like the furnaces. And a dog might tackle him and bully-rag him, and bite him, and throw him over his shoulder two or three times, and Andrew Jackson—which was the name of the pup—Andrew Jackson would never let on but what *he* was satisfied, and hadn't expected nothing else—and the bets being doubled and doubled on the other side all the time, till the money was all up ; and then all of a sudden he would grab that other dog jest by the j'int of his hind leg and freeze to it—not chaw, you understand, but only just grip and hang on till they throwed up the sponge, if it was a year. Smiley always come out winner on that pup, till he harnessed a dog once that did'nt have no hind legs, because they'd been sawed off in a circular saw, and when the thing had gone along far enough, and the money was all up, and he come to make a snatch for his pet holt, he see in a minute how he'd been imposed on, and how the other dog had him in the door, so to speak, and he 'peared surprised, and then he looked sorter discouraged-like, and didn't try no more to win the fight, and so he got shucked out bad. He give Smiley a look, as much as to say his heart was broke, and it was *his* fault, for putting up a dog that hadn't no hind legs for him to take holt of, which was his main dependence in a fight, and then he limped off a piece and laid down and died. It was a good pup, was that Andrew Jackson, and would have made a name for hisself if he'd lived, for the stuff was in him and he had genius—I know it, because he hadn't no opportunities to speak of, and it don't stand to reason that a dog could make such a fight as he could under them circumstances if he hadn't no talent. It always makes me feel sorry when I think of that last fight of his'n, and the way it turned out.

Well, thish-yer Smiley had rat-tarriers, and chicken cocks, and tom-cats and all them kind of things, till you couldn't rest, and you couldn't fetch nothing for him to bet on but he'd match you. He ketched a frog one day, and took him home, and said he cal'lated to educate him ; and so he never done nothing for three months but-set in his back yard and learn that frog to jump. And you bet you he *did* learn him, too. He'd give him a little punch behind, and the next minute you'd see that frog whirling in the air like a doughnut—see him turn one summerset, or may be a couple, if he got a good start, and come down flat-footed and all right, like a cat. He got him up so in the matter of ketching flies, and kep' him in practice so constant, that he'd nail a fly every time as fur as he could see him. Smiley said all a frog wanted was education, and he could do 'most anything—and I believe him. Why, I've seen him set Dan'l Webster down here on this floor—Dan'l Webster was the name of the frog—and sing out, " Flies, Dan'l, flies ! " and quicker'n you could wink he'd spring straight up and snake a fly off'n the counter there, and flop down on the floor ag'in as solid as a gob of mud, and fall to scratching the side of his head with his hind foot as indifferent as as if he hadn't no idea he'd been doin' any more'n any frog might do. You never see a frog so modest and straightfor'ard as he was, for all he was so gifted. And when it come to fair and square jumping on a dead level, he could get over more ground at one straddle than any animal of his breed you ever see. Jumping on a dead level was his strong suit, you understand ; and when it come to that, Smiley would ante up money on him as long as he had a red. Smiley was monstrous

proud of his frog, and well he might be, for fellers that had traveled and been everywheres, all said he laid over any frog that ever *they* see.

Well, Smiley kep' the beast in a little lattice box, and he used to fetch him down town sometimes and lay for a bet. One day a feller—a stranger in the camp, he was—come acrost him with his box, and says :

"'What might it be that you've got in the box ?'"

And Smiley says, sorter indifferent-like, "It might be a parrot, or it might be a canary, maybe, but it ain't—it's only just a frog."

3

And the feller took it, and looked at it careful, and turned it round this way and that, and says, "II'm—so 'tis. Well, what's *he* good for?"

"Well," Smiley, says, easy and careless, "he's good enough for *one* thing, I should judge—he can outjump any frog in Calaveras county."

The feller took the box again, and took another long, particular look, and give it back to Smiley, and says, very deliberate, "Well," he says, "I don't see no p'ints about that frog that's any better'n any other frog."

"Maybe you don't," Smiley says. "Maybe you understand frogs and maybe you don't understand 'em; maybe you've had experience, and maybe you ain't only a amature, as it were. Anyways, I've got *my* opinion and I'll resk forty dollars that he can outjump any frog in Calaveras county."

And the feller studied a minute, and then says, kinder sad like, "·Well, I'm only a stranger here, and I ain't got no frog; but if I had a frog, I'd bet you."

And then Smiley says, "That's all right—that's all right—if you'll hold my box a minute, I'll go and get you a frog." And so the feller took the box, and put up his forty dollars along with Smiley's, and set down to wait.

So he set there a good while thinking and thinking to hisself, and then he got the frog out and prized his mouth open and took a teaspoon and filled him full of quail shot—filled him pretty near up to his chin—and set him on the floor. Smiley he went to the swamp and slopped around in the mud for a long time, and finally he ketched a frog, and fetched him in, and give him to this feller, and says:

"Now, if you're ready, set him alongside of Dan'l, with his fore-paws just even with Dan'l's, and I'll give the word." Then he says, "One—two—three—*git!*" and him and the feller touched up the frogs from behind, and the new frog hopped off lively, but Dan'l give a heave, and hysted up his shoulders—so—like a Frenchman, but it warn't no use—he couldn't budge; he was planted as solid as a church, and he couldn't no more stir than if he was anchored out. Smiley was a good deal surprised, and he was disgusted too, but he didn't have no idea what the matter was, of course.

The feller took the money and started away; and when he was going out at the door, he sorter jerked his thumb over his shoulder—so—at Dan'l, and says again, very deliberate, "Well," he says "*I* don't see no p'ints about that frog that's any better'n any other frog."

Smiley he stood scratching his head and looking down at Dan'l a long time, and at last he says, "I do wonder what in the nation that frog throw'd off for—I wonder if there ain't something the matter with him—he 'pears to look mighty baggy, somehow." And he ketched Dan'l by the nap of the neck, and hefted him, and says, "Why blame my cats if he don't weigh five pound!" and turned him upside down and he belched out a double handful of shot. And then he see how it was, and he was the maddest man—he set the frog down and took out after that feller, but he never ketched him. And——"

[Here Simon Wheeler heard his name called from the front yard, and got up to see what was

wanted.] And turning to me as he moved away, he said : "Just set where you are, stranger, and rest easy—I ain't going to be gone a second."

But, by your leave, I did not think that a continuation of the history of the enterprising vagabond *Jim* Smiley would be likely to afford me much information concerning the Rev. *Leonidas W.* Smiley, and so I started away.

At the door I met the sociable Wheeler returning, and he button-holed me and re-commenced :

"Well, thish-yer Smiley had a yaller one-eyed cow that didn't have no tail, only jest a short stump like a bannanner, and——"

However, lacking both time and inclination, I did not wait to hear about the afflicted cow, but took my leave.

Now let the learned look upon this picture and say if iconoclasm can further go :

[From the *Revue des Deux Mondes*, of July 15th, 1872.]

LA GRENOUILLE SANTEUSE DU COMTE DE CALAVERAS.

" —Il y avait une fois ici un individu connu sous le nom de Jim Smiley : c'était dans l'hiver de 49, peut-être bien au printemps de 50, je ne me rappelle pas exactement. Ce qui me fait croire que c'était l'un ou l'autre, c'est que je me souviens que le grand bief n'était pas achevé lorsqu'il arriva au camp pour la première fois, mais de toutes façons il était l'homme le plus friand de paris qui se pût voir, pariant sur tout ce qui se présentait, quand il pouvait trouver un adversaire, et, quand il n'en trouvait pas il passait du côté opposé. Tout ce qui convenait à l'autre lui convenait ; pourvu qu'il eût un pari, Smiley était satisfait. Et il avait une chance ! une chance inouie : presque toujours il gagnait. Il faut dire qu'il était toujours prêt à s' exposer, qu' on ne pouvait mentionner la moindre chose sans que ce gaillard offrît de parier là-dessus 'n'importe quoi et de prendre le côté que l'on voudrait, comme je vous le'disais tout à l'heure. S'il y avait des courses, vous le trouviez riche ou ruiné à la fin ; s'il y avait un combat de chiens, il apportait son enjeu ; il l'apportait pour un combat de chats, pour un combat de coqs ;—parbleu ! si vous aviez vu deux oiseaux sur une haie, il vous aurait offert de parier lequel s'envolerait le premier, et, s'il y avait *meeting* au camp, il venait parier régulièrement pour le curé Walker, qu'il jugeait être le meilleur prédicateur des environs, et qui l'était en effet, et un brave homme. Il aurait rencontré une punaise de bois en chemin, qu'il aurait parié sur le temps qu'il lui faudrait pour aller où elle voudrait aller, et, si vous l'aviez pris au mot, il aurait suivi la punaise jusqu'au Mexique, sans se soucier d'aller si loin, ni du temps qu'il y perdrait. Une fois la femme du curé Walker fut très malade pendant longtemps, il semblait qu'on ne la sauverait pas ; mais un matin le curé arrive, et Smiley lui demande comment elle va, et il dit qu'elle est bien mieux, grâce à l'infinie miséricorde, tellement mieux qu'avec la bénédiction de la Providence elle s'en tirerait, et voilà que, sans y penser, Smiley répond :—Eh bien ! je gage deux et demi qu'elle mourra tout de même.

"Ce Smiley avait une jument que les gars appelaient le bidet du quart d'heure, mais seulement pour plaisanter, vous comprenez, parce que, bien entendu, elle était plus *vite* que ça ! Et il avait coutume de gagner de l'argent avec cette bête, quoiqu'elle fût poussive, cornarde, toujours prise d'asthme, de coliques ou de consumption, ou de quelque chose d'approchant. On lui donnait 2 ou 300 *yards* au départ, puis on la dépassait sans peine ; mais jamais à la fin elle ne manquait de s'échauffer, de s' exaspérer, et elle arrivait, s'écartant, se défendant, ses jambes grêles en l'air devant les obstacles, quelquefois les évitant et faisant avec cela plus de poussière qu'aucun cheval, plus de bruit surtout avec ses éternumens et reniflemens,—crac ! elle arrivait donc toujours première d'une tête, aussi juste qu'on peut le mesurer. Et il avait un petit bouledogue qui, à le voir, ne valait pas un sou ; on aurait cru que parier contre lui c'était voler, tant il était ordinaire ; mais aussitôt les enjeux faits, il devenait un autre chien. Sa mâchoire inférieure commençait à ressortir comme un gaillard d'avant, ses dents se découvraient brillantes comme des fournaises, et un chien pouvait le taquiner, l'exciter, le mordre, le jeter deux ou trois fois par-dessus son épaule, André Jackson, c'était le nom du chien, André Jackson prenait cela tranquillement, comme s'il ne se fût jamais attendu à autre chose, et quand les paris étaient doublés et redoublés contre lui, il vous saisissait l'autre chien juste à l'articulation de la jambe de derrière, et il ne la lâchait plus, non pas qu'il la mâchât, vous concevez, mais il s'y serait tenu pendu jusqu'à ce qu'on jetât l'éponge en l'air, fallût-il attendre un an. Smiley gagnait toujours avec cette bête-là ; malheureusement ils ont fini par dresser un chien qui n'avait pas de pattes de derrière, parce qu'on les avait sciées, et quand les choses furent au point qu'il voulait, et qu'il en vint à se jeter sur son morceau favori, le pauvre chien comprit en un instant qu'on s'était moqué de lui, et que l'autre le tenait. Vous n'avez jamais vu personne avoir l'air plus penaud et plus découragé ; il ne fit aucun effort pour gagner le combat et fut rudement secoué, de sorte que, regardant Smiley comme pour lui dire :—Mon cœur est brisé, c'est ta faute ; pourquoi m'avoir livré à un chien qui n'a pas de pattes de derrière, puisque c'est par là que je les bats?— il s'en alla en clopinant, et se coucha pour mourir. Ah ! c'était un bon chien, cet André Jackson, et il se serait fait un nom, s'il avait vécu, car il y avait de l'etoffe en lui, il avait du génie, je le sais, bien que de grandes occasions lui aient manqué ; mais il est impossible de supposer qu'un chien capable de se battre comme lui, certaines circonstances étant données, ait manqué de talent. Je me sens triste toutes les fois que je pense à son dernier combat et au dénoûment qu'il a eu. Eh bien ! ce Smiley nourrissait des terriers à rats, et des coqs de combat, et des chats, et toute sorte de choses, au point qu'il était toujours en mesure de vous tenir tête, et qu'avec sa rage de paris on n'avait plus de repos. Il attrapa un jour une grenouille et l'emporta chez lui, disant qu'il prétendait faire son éducation ; vous me croirez si vous voulez, mais pendant trois mois il n'a rien fait que lui apprendre à sauter dans une cour retirée de sa maison. Et je vous réponds qu'il avait réussi. Il lui donnait un petit coup par derrière, et l'instant d'après vous voyiez la grenouille tourner en l'air comme un beignet au-dessus de la poêle, faire une culbute, quelquefois deux, lorsqu'elle était bein partie, et retomber sur ses pattes comme un chat. Il l'avait dressée dans l'art de gober des mouches, et l'y exercait continuellement, si bien qu'une mouche, du plus loin qu'elle apparaissait, était une mouche perdue. Smiley avait coutume de dire que tout ce qui manquait à une grenouille, c'était l'éducation, qu'avec l'éducation elle pouvait faire presque tout, et je le crois. Tenez, je l'ai vu poser Daniel Webster là sur ce plancher,—Daniel Webster était le nom de la grenouille,— et lui chanter :—Des mouches ! Daniel, des mouches !—En un clin d'œil, Daniel avait bondi et saisi une mouche ici sur le comptoir, puis sauté de nouveau par terre, où il restait vraiment à se gratter la tête avec sa patte de derrière, comme s'il n'avait pas eu la moindre idée de sa supériorité. Jamais vous n'avez grenouille vu de aussi modeste, aussi naturelle, douée comme elle l'était ! Et quand il s'agissait de sauter purement et simplement sur terrain plat, elle faisait plus de chemin en un saut qu'aucune bête de son espèce que vous puissiez connaître. Sauter à plat, c'était son fort ! Quand il s'agissait de cela, Smiley entassait les enjeux sur elle tant qu'il lui, restait un rouge liard. Il faut le reconnaître, Smiley était monstrueusement fier de sa grenouille, et il en avait le droit, car des gens qui avaient voyagé, qui avaient tout vu, disaient qu'on lui ferait injure de la comparer à une autre ; de façon que Smiley gardait Daniel dans une petite boîte à claire-voie qu'il emporta it parfois à la ville pour quelque pari.

"Un jour, un individu étranger au camp l'arrête avec sa boîte et lui dit :—Qu'est-ce que vous avez donc serré là dedans ?

" Smiley dit d'un air indifférent :—Cela puorrait être un perroquet ou un serin, mais ce u'est rien de pareil, ce n'est qu'une grenouille.

" L'individu la prend, la regarde avec soin, la tourne d'un côté et de l'autre puss il dit.—Tiens ! en effet ! A quoi est-elle bonne ?

"—Mon Dieu ! répond Smiley, toujours d'un air dégagé, elle est bonne pour une chose à mon avis, elle peut battre en sautant toute grenouille du comté de Calaveras.

" L'individu reprend la boîte, l'examine de uouveau longuement, et la rend à Smiley en disant d'un air délibéré :—Eh bien ! je ne vois pas que cette grenouille ait rien de mieux qu'aucune grenouille.

"—Possible que vous ne le voyiez pas, dit Smiley, possible que vous vous entendiez en gre-ouilles, possible que vous ne vous y entendez point, possible que vous ayez de l'expérience, et pos-sible que vous ne soyez qu'un amateur. De toute manière, je parie quarante dollars qu'elle battra en sautant n'importe quelle grenouille du comté de Calaveras.

" L'individu réfléchit une seconde et dit comme attristé :—Je ne suis qu'un étranger ici, je n'ai pas de grenouille ; mais, si j'en avais une, je tiendrais le pari.

"—Fort bien ! répond Smiley. Rien de plus facile. Si vous voulez tenir ma boîte une minute, j'irai vous chercher une grenouille.—Voilà donc l'individu qui garde la boîte, qui met ses quarante dollars sur ceux de Smiley et qui attend. Il attend assez longtemps, réfléchissant tout seul, et figurez-vous qu'il prend Daniel, lui ouvre la bouche de force et avec une cuiller à thé l'emplit de menu plomb de chasse, mais l'emplit jusqu'au menton, puis il le pose par terre. Smiley pendant ce temps était à barboter dans une mare. Finalement il attrape une grenouille, l'apporte à cet individu et dit :—Maintenant, si vous êtes prêt, mettez-la tout contre Daniel, avec leurs pattes de devant sur la même ligne, et je donnerai le signal ;—puis il ajoute :—Un, deux, trois, sautez !

" Lui et l'individu touchent leurs grenouilles par derrière, et la grenouille neuve se met à sautiller, mais Daniel se soulève lourdement, hausse les épaules ainsi, comme un Français ; à quoi bon ? il ne pouvait bouger, il était planté solide comme une enclume, il n'avançait pas puls que si on l'eût mis à l'ancre. Smiley fut surpris et dégoûté, mais il ne se doutait pas du tour, bien entendu. L'individu empoche l'argent, s'en va, et en s'en allant est-ce qu'il ne donne pas un coup de pouce par-dessus lé'paule, comme ça, au pauvre Daniel, en disant de son air délibéré :—Eh bien ! je ne vois pas que cette grenouille ait rien de mieux qu'une autre.

" Smiley se gratta longtemps la tête, les yeux fixés sur Daniel, jusqu'à ce qu'enfin il dit :—Je me demande comment diable il se fait que cette bête ait refusé... Est-ce qu'elle aurait quelque chose ?.. On croirait qu'elle est enflée.

" Il empoigne Daniel par la peau du cou, le soulève et dit :—Le loup me croque, s'il ne pèse pas cinq livres.

" Il le retourne; et le malheureux crache deux poignées de plomb. Quand Smiley reconnut ce qui en était, il fut comme fou. Vous le voyez d'ici poser sa grenouille par terre et courir après cet individu, mais il ne le rattrapa jamais, et...

[Translation of the above back from the French].

THE FROG JUMPING OF THE COUNTY OF CALAVERAS.

It there was one time here an individual known under the name of Jim Smiley: it was in the winter of '49, possibly well at the spring of '50, I no me recollect not exactly. This which me makes to believe that it was the one or the other, it is that I shall remember that the grand flume is not achieved when he arrives at the camp for the first time, but of all sides he was the man the most fond of to bet which one have seen, betting upon all that which is presented, when he could find an adversary; and when he not of it could not, he passed to the side opposed. All that which convenienced to the the other, to him convenienced also; seeing that he had a bet, Smiley was satisfied. And he had a chance! a chance even worthless: nearly always he gained. It must to say that he was always near to himself expose, but one no could mention the least thing without that this gaillard offered to bet the bottom, no matter what, and to take the side that one him would, as I you it said all at the hour (tout à l'heure). If it there was of races, you him find rich or ruined at the end; if it there is a combat of dogs, he bring his bet; he himself laid always for a combat of cats, for a combat of cocks;—by-blue! if you have see two birds upon a fence, he you should have offered of to bet which of those birds shall fly the first; and if there is *meeting* at the camp (*meeting* au camp) he comes to bet regularly for the curé Walker, which he judged to be the best predicator of the neighborhood (prédicateur des environs) and which he was in effect, and a brave man. He would encounter a bug of wood in the road, whom he will bet upon the time which he shall take to go where she would go—and if you him have take at the word, he will follow the bug as far as Mexique, without himself caring to go so far; neither of the time which he there lost. One time the woman of the curé Walker is very sick during long time, it seemed that one not her saved not; but one morning the curé arrives, and Smiley him demanded how she goes, and he said that she is well better, grace to the infinite misery (lui demande comment elle va, et il dit qu'elle est bien mieux, grâce à l'infinie misèricorde) so much better that with the benediction of the Providence she herself of it would pull out (elle s'en tirerait); and behold that without there thinking Smiley responds: "Well, I gage two-and-half that she will die all of same."

This Smiley had an animal which the boys called the nag of the quarter of hour, but solely for pleasantry, you comprehend, because, well understand, she was more fast as that! [Now why that exclamation?—M. T.] And it was custom of to gain of the silver with this beast, notwithstanding she was poussive, cornarde, always taken of asthma, of colics or of consumption, or something of approaching. One him would give two or three hundred yards at the departure, then one him passed without pain; but never at the last she not fail of herself èchauffer, of herself exasperate, and she arrives herself écartant, se dèfendant, her legs grêles in the air before the obstacles, sometimes them elevating and making with this more of dust than any horse, more of noise above with his éternumens and reniflemens—crac! she arrives then always first by one head, as just as one can it measure. And he had a small bull dog (boule dogue!) who, to him see, no value, not a cent; one would believe that to bet against him it was to steal, so much he was ordinary; but as soon as the game made, she becomes another dog. Her jaw inferior commence to project like a deck of before, his teeth themselves discover brilliant like some furnaces, and a dog could him tackle (le taquiner), him excite, him murder (le mordre), him throw two or three times over his shoulder, André Jackson—this was the name of the dog—André Jackson takes that tranquilly, as if he not himself was never expecting other thing, and when the bets were doubled and redoubled against him, he you sieze the other dog just at the articulation of the leg of behind, and he not it leave more, not that he it masticate, you conceive, but he himself there shall be holding during until that one throws the sponge in the air, must he wait a year. Smiley gained always with this beast-là; unhappily they have finished by elevating a dog who no had not of feet of behind, because one them had sawed; and when things were at the point that he would, and that he came to himself throw upon his morsel favorite, the poor dog comprehended in an instant that he himself was deceived in him, and that the other dog him had. You no have never see person having the air more penaud and more discouraged; he not made no effort to gain the combat, and was rudely shucked.

Eh bien! this Smiley nourished some terriers á rats, and some cocks of combat, and some cats, and all sort of things; and with his rage of betting one no had more of repose. He trapped one day a frog and him imported with him (et l'emporta chez lui) saying that he pretended to make his education. You me believe if you will, but during three months he not has nothing done but to him apprehend to jump (apprendre ă sauter) in a court retired of her mansion (de sa maison). And I you respond that he have succeeded. He him gives a small blow by behind, and the instant after you shall see the frog turn in the air like a grease-biscuit, make one summersault, sometimes two, when she was well started, and re-fall upon his feet like a cat. He him had accomplished in the art of to gobble the flies (gober des mouches), and him there exercised continually—so well that a fly at the most far that she appeared was a fly lost. Smiley had custom to say that all which lacked to a frog it was the education, but with the education she could do nearly all—and I him believe. Tenez, I him have seen pose Daniel Webster there upon this plank—Daniel Webster was the name of the frog—and to him sing, "Some flies, Daniel, some flies!"—in a flash of the eye Daniel had bounded and seized a fly here upon the counter, then jumped anew at the earth, where he rested truly to himself scratch the head with his behind-foot, as if he no had not the least idea of his superiority. Never you not have seen frog as modest, as natural, sweet as she was. And when he himself agitated to jump purely and simply upon plain earth, she does more ground in one jump than any beast of his species than you can know. To jump plain—this was his strong. When he himself agitated for that, Smiley multiplied the bets upon her as long as there to him remained a red. It must to know, Smiley was monstrously proud of his frog, and he of it was right, for some men who were traveled, who had all seen, said that they to him would be injurious to him compare to another frog. Smiley guarded Daniel in a little box latticed which he carried bytimes to the village for some bet.

One day an individual stranger at the camp him arrested with his box and him said:

"What is this that you have then shut up there within?"

Smiley said, with an air indifferent:

"That could be a paroquet, or a syringe (ou un serin), but this no is nothing of such, it not is but a frog."

The individual it took, it regarded with care, it turned from one side and from the other, then he said:

"Tiens! in effect!—At what is she good?"

"My God!" respond Smiley, always with an air disengaged, "she is good for one thing, to my notice, (à mon avis), she can batter in jumping (elle peut batter en sautant) all frogs of the county of Calaveras."

The individual re-took the box, it examined of new longly, and it rendered to Smiley in saying with an air deliberate:

"Eh bien! I no saw not that that frog had nothing of better than each frog." (Je ne vois pas que cette grenouille ait rien de mieux qu'aucune grenouille). [If that isn't grammar gone to seed, then I count myself no judge.—M. T.]

"Possible that you not it saw not," said Smiley, "possible that you—you comprehend frogs; possible that you not you there comprehend nothing; possible that you had of the experience, and possible that you not be but an amateur. Of all manner, (De toute manière) I bet forty dollars that she batter in jumping no matter which frog of the county of Calaveras."

The individual reflected a second, and said like sad:

"I not am but a stranger here, I no have not a frog; but if I of it had one, I would embrace the bet."

"Strong well!" respond Smiley; "nothing of more facility. If you will hold my box a minute, I go you to search a frog (j' irai vous chercher)."

Behold, then, the individual, who guards the box, who puts his forty dollars upon those of Smiley, and who attends, (et qui attend). He attended enough longtimes, reflecting all solely. And figure you that he takes Daniel, him opens the mouth by force and with a tea-spoon him fills with shot of the hunt, even him fills just to the chin, then he him puts by the earth. Smiley during these times was at slopping in a swamp. Finally he trapped (attrape) a frog, him carried to that individual, and said:

"Now if you be ready, put him all against Daniel, with their before-feet upon the same line, and I give the signal"—then he added: "One, two, three,—advance!"

Him and the individual touched their frogs by behind, and the frog new put to jump smartly, but Daniel himself lifted ponderously, exalted the shoulders thus, like a Frenchman—to what good? he not could budge, he is planted solid like a church, he not advance no more than if one him had put at the anchor.

Smiley was surprised and disgusted, but he not himself doubted not of the turn being intended (mais il ne se doutait pas du tour, bien entendu). The individual empocketed the silver, himself with it went, and of it himself in going is it that he no gives not a jerk of thumb over the shoulder—like that—at the poor Daniel, in saying with his air deliberate—(L' individu empoche l'argent, s'en va et en s'en allant est ce qu'il ne donne pas un coup de pouce par-dessus l'épaule, comme ca, au pauvre Daniel, endisant de son air délibéré) :

"Eh bien! *I no see not that that frog has nothing of better than another.*"

Smiley himself scratched longtimes the head, the eyes fixed upon Daniel, until that which at last he said :

"I me demand how the devil it makes itself that this beast has refused. Is it that she had something? One would believe that she is stuffed."

He grasped Daniel by the skin of the neck, him lifted and said :

"The wolf me bite if he no weigh not five pounds."

He him reversed and the unhappy belched two handfuls of shot (et le malhereus, etc).—When Smiley recognized how it was, he was like mad. He deposited his frog by the earth and ran after that individual, but he not him caught never.

Such is the Jumping Frog, to the distorted French eye. I claim that I never put together such an odious mixture of bad grammar and delirium tremens in my life. And what has a poor foreigner like me done, to be abused and misrepresented like this? When I say, "Well, I don't see no p'ints about that frog that's any better'n any other frog," is it kind, is it just, for this Frenchman to try to make it appear that I said, "Eh bien! I no saw not that that frog had nothing of better than each frog?" I have no heart to write more. I never felt so about anything before.

HARTFORD, March, 1875.

JOURNALISM IN TENNESSEE

The editor of the Memphis *Avalanche* swoops thus mildly down upon a correspondent who posted him as a Radical :—"While he was writing the first word, the middle, dotting his i's, crossing his t's, and punching his period, he knew he was concocting a sentence that was saturated with infamy and reeking with falsehood."—*Exchange*.

I WAS told by the physician that a Southern climate would improve my health, and so I went down to Tennessee, and got a berth on the *Morning Glory and Johnson County War-Whoop* as associate editor. When I went on duty I found the chief editor sitting tilted back in a three-legged chair with his feet on a pine table. There was another pine table in the room and another afflicted chair, and both were half buried under

44

newspapers and scraps and sheets of manuscript. There was a wooden box of sand, sprinkled with cigar stubs and " old soldiers," and a stove with a door hanging by its upper hinge. The chief editor had a long-tailed black cloth frock coat on, and white linen pants. His boots were small and neatly blacked. He wore a ruffled shirt, a large seal ring, a standing collar of obsolete pattern, and a checkered neckerchief with the ends hanging down. Date of costume about 1848. He was smoking a cigar, and trying to think of a word, and in pawing his hair he had rumpled his locks a good deal. He was scowling fearfully, and I judged that he was concocting a particularly knotty editorial. He told me to take the exchanges and skim through them and write up the " Spirit of the Tennessee Press," condensing into the article all of their contents that seemed of interest.

I wrote as follows :—

" SPIRIT OF THE TENNESSEE PRESS.

" The editors of the *Semi-Weekly Earthquake* evidently labor under a misapprehension with regard to the Ballyhack railroad. It is not the object of the company to leave Buzzardville off to one side. On the contrary, they consider it one of the most important points along the line, and consequently can have no desire to slight it. The gentlemen of the *Earthquake* will, of course, take pleasure in making the correction.

" John W. Blossom, Esq., the able editor of the Higginsville *Thunderbolt and Battle Cry of Freedom*, arrived in the city yesterday. He is stopping at the Van Buren House.

" We observe that our contemporary of the Mud Springs *Morning Howl* has fallen into the error of supposing that the election of Van Werter is not an established fact, but he will have discovered his mistake before this reminder reaches him, no doubt. He was doubtless misled by incomplete election returns.

" It is pleasant to note that the city of Blathersville is endeavoring to contract with some New York gentlemen to pave its well-nigh impassable streets with the Nicholson pavement. The *Daily Hurrah* urges the measure with ability, and seems confident of ultimate success."

I passed my manuscript over to the chief editor for acceptance, alteration, or destruction. He glanced at it and his face clouded. He ran his eye down the pages, and his countenance grew portentous. It was easy to see that something was wrong. Presently he sprang up and said—

" Thunder and lightning ! Do you suppose I am going to speak of those cattle that way ? Do you suppose my subscribers are going to stand such gruel as that ? Give me the pen !"

I never saw a pen scrape and scratch its way so viciously, or plough through another man's verbs and adjectives so relentlessly. While he was in the midst of his work, somebody shot at him through the open window, and marred the symmetry of my ear.

"Ah," said he, "that is that scoundrel Smith, of the *Moral Volcano*—he was due yesterday." And he snatched a navy revolver from his belt and fired. Smith dropped, shot in the thigh. The shot spoiled Smith's aim, who was just taking a second chance, and he crippled a stranger. It was me. Merely a finger shot off.

Then the chief editor went on with his erasures and interlineations. Just as he finished them a hand-grenade came down the stove pipe, and the explosion shivered the stove into a thousand fragments. However, it did no further damage, except that a vagrant piece knocked a couple of my teeth out.

"That stove is utterly ruined," said the chief editor.

I said I believed it was.

"Well, no matter—don't want it this kind of weather. I know the man that did it. I'll get him. Now, *here* is the way this stuff ought to be written."

I took the manuscript. It was scarred with erasures and interlineations till its mother wouldn't have known it if it had had one. It now read as follows:—

"SPIRIT OF THE TENNESSEE PRESS.

"The inveterate liars of the *Semi-Weekly Earthquake* are evidently endeavoring to palm off upon a noble and chivalrous people another of their vile and brutal falsehoods with regard to that most glorious conception of the nineteenth century, the Ballyhack railroad. The idea that Buzzardville was to be left off at one side originated in their own fulsome brains—or rather in the settlings which *they* regard as brains. They had better swallow this lie if they want to save their abandoned reptile carcasses the cowhiding they so richly deserve.

"That ass, Blossom, of the Higginsville *Thunderbolt and Battle Cry of Freedom*, is down here again sponging at the Van Buren.

"We observe that the besotted blackguard of the Mud Spring *Morning Howl* is giving out, with his usual propensity for lying, that Van Werter is not elected. The heaven-born mission of journalism is to disseminate truth ; to eradicate error; to educate, refine, and elevate the tone of public morals and manners, and make all men more gentle, more virtuous, more charitable, and in all ways better, and holier, and happier ; and yet this black-hearted scoundrel degrades his great office persistently to the dissemination of falsehood, calumny, vituperation, and vulgarity.

"Blathersville wants a Nicholson pavement—it wants a jail and a poorhouse more. The idea of a pavement in a one horse town composed of two gin mills, a blacksmith's shop, and that mustard-plaster of a newspaper, the *Daily Hurrah!* The crawling insect, Buckner, who edits the *Hurrah*, is braying about this business with his customary imbecility, and imagining that he is talking sense."

"Now *that* is the way to write—peppery and to the point. Mush-and-milk journalism gives me the fan-tods."

About this time a brick came through the window with a splintering crash, and gave me a considerable of a jolt in the back. I moved out of range—I began to feel in the way.

The chief said, " That was the Colonel, likely. I've been expecting him for two days. He will be up, now, right away."

He was correct. The Colonel appeared in the door a moment afterward with a dragoon revolver in his hand.

He said, "Sir, have I the honor of addressing the poltroon who edits this mangy sheet?"

"You have. Be seated, sir. Be careful of the chair, one of its legs is gone. I believe I have the honor of addressing the putrid liar, Col. Blatherskite Tecumseh ?"

"Right, sir. I have a little account to settle with you. If you are at leisure we will begin."

"I have an article on the 'Encouraging Progress of Moral and Intellectual Development in America' to finish, but there is no hurry. Begin."

Both pistols rang out their fierce clamor at the same instant. The chief lost a lock of his hair, and the Colonel's bullet ended its career in the fleshy part of my thigh. The Colonel's left shoulder was clipped a little. They fired again. Both missed their men this time, but I got my share, a shot in the arm. At the third fire both gentleman were wounded slightly, and I had a knuckle chipped. I then said, I believed I would go out and take a walk, as this was a private matter, and I had a delicacy about participating in it further. But both gentlemen begged me to keep my seat, and assured me that I was not in the way.

They then talked about the elections and the crops while they reloaded, and I fell to tying up my wounds. But presently they opened fire again with animation, and every shot took effect—but it is proper to remark that five out of the six fell to my share. The sixth one mortally wounded the Colonel, who remarked, with fine humor, that he would have to say good morning now, as he had business up town. He then inquired the way to the undertaker's and left.

The chief turned to me and said, "I am expecting company to dinner, and shall have to get ready. It will be·a favor to me if you will read proof and attend to the customers."

I winced a little at the idea of attending to the customers, but I was too bewildered by the fusilade that was still ringing in my ears to think of anything to say.

He continued, "Jones will be here at 3—cowhide him. Gillespie will call earlier, perhaps—throw him out of the window. Ferguson will be along about 4— kill him. That is all for to-day, I believe. If you have any odd time, you may write a blistering article on the police—give the Chief Inspector rats. The cowhides are under the table; weapons in the drawer—ammunition there in the corner —lint and bandages up there in the pigeon-holes. In case of accident, go to Lancet, the surgeon, down-stairs. He advertises—we take it out in trade."

He was gone. I shuddered. At the end of the next three hours I had been through perils so awful that all peace of mind and all cheerfulness were gone from me. Gillespie had called and thrown *me* out of the window. Jones arrived promptly, and when I got ready to do the cowhiding he took the job off my hands. In an encounter with a stranger, not in the bill of fare, I had lost my scalp. Another stranger, by the name of Thompson, left me a mere wreck and ruin of chaotic rags. And at last, at bay in the corner, and beset by an infuriated mob of editors, blacklegs, politicians, and desperadoes, who raved and swore and flourished their weapons about my head till the air shimmered with glancing flashes of steel, I was in the act of resigning my berth on the paper when the chief arrived, and with him a rabble of charmed and enthusiastic friends. Then ensued a scene of riot and carnage such as no human pen, or steel one either, could describe. People were shot, probed, dismembered, blown up, thrown out of the window. There was a brief tornado of murky blasphemy, with a confused and frantic war-dance glimmering through it, and then all was over. In five minutes there was silence, and the gory chief and I sat alone and surveyed the sanguinary ruin that strewed the floor around us.

He said, "You'll like this place when you get used to it."

I said, "I'll have to get you to excuse me; I think maybe I might write to suit you after a while; as soon as I had had some practice and learned the language I am confident I could. But, to speak the plain truth, that sort of energy of

expression has its inconveniences, and a man is liable to interruption. You see that yourself. Vigorous writing is calculated to elevate the public, no doubt, but, then I do not like to attract so much attention as it calls forth. I can't write with comfort when I am interrupted so much as I have been to-day. I like this berth well enough, but I don't like to be left here to wait on the customers. The experiences are novel, I grant you, and entertaining too, after a fashion, but they are not judiciously distributed. A gentleman shoots at you through the window and cripples *me;* a bomb-shell comes down the stove-pipe for your gratification and sends the stove-door down *my* throat; a friend drops in to swap compliments with you, and freckles *me* with bullet-holes till my skin won't hold my principles; you go to dinner, and Jones comes with his cowhide, Gillespie throws me out of

4

the window, Thompson tears all my clothes off, and an entire stranger takes my scalp with the easy freedom of an old acquaintance; and in less than five minutes all the blackguards in the country arrive in their war-paint, and proceed to scare the rest of me to death with their tomahawks. Take it altogether, I never had such a spirited time in all my life as I have had to-day. No; I like you, and I like your calm unruffled way of explaining things to the customers, but you see I am not used to it. The Southern heart is too impulsive; Southern hospitality is too lavish with the stranger. The paragraphs which I have written to-day, and into wnose cold sentences your masterly hand has infused the fervent spirit of Tennessean journalism, will wake up another nest of hornets. All that mob of editors will come—and they will come hungry, too, and want somebody for breakfast. I shall have to bid you adieu. I decline to be present at these festivities. I came South for my health, I will go back on the same errand, and suddenly. Tennesseean journalism is too stirring for me."

After which we parted with mutual regret, and I took apartments at the hospital.

STORY OF THE BAD LITTLE BOY.

ONCE there was a bad little boy whose name was Jim—though, if you will notice, you will find that bad little boys are nearly always called James in your Sunday-school books. It was strange, but still it was true that this one was called Jim.

He didn't have any sick mother either—a sick mother who was pious and had the consumption, and would be glad to lie down in the grave and be at rest but for the strong love she bore her boy, and the anxiety she felt that the world might be harsh and cold towards him when she was gone. Most bad boys in the Sunday-books are named James, and have sick mothers, who teach them to say, "Now, I lay me down," etc., and sing them to sleep with sweet, plaintive voices, and then kiss them good-night, and kneel down by the bedside and weep. But it was different with this fellow. He was named Jim, and there wasn't anything the matter with his mother—no consumption, nor anything of that kind. She was rather stout than otherwise, and she was not pious; moreover, she was not anxious on Jim's account. She said if he were to break his neck it wouldn't be much loss. She always spanked Jim to sleep, and she never kissed him good-night; on the contrary, she boxed his ears when she was ready to leave him.

Once this little bad boy stole the key of the pantry, and slipped in there and helped himself to some jam, and filled up the vessel with tar, so that his mother would never know the difference; but all at once a terrible feeling didn't come over him, and something didn't seem to whisper to him, "Is it right to disobey my mother? Isn't it sinful to do this? Where do bad little boys go who gobble up their good kind mother's jam?" and then he didn't kneel down all alone and promise never to be wicked any more, and rise up with a light, happy heart, and go and tell his mother all about it, and beg her forgiveness, and be blessed by her with tears of pride and thankfulness in her eyes. No; that is the way with all other bad boys in the books; but it happened otherwise with this Jim, strangely enough. He ate that jam, and said it was bully, in his sinful, vulgar way; and he put in the tar, and said that was bully also, and laughed, and observed "that the old woman would get up and snort" when she found it out; and when she did find it out, he denied knowing anything about it, and she whipped him severely, and he did the crying himself.

Everything about this boy was curious—everything turned out differently with him from the way it does to the bad Jameses in the books.

Once he climbed up in Farmer Acorn's apple-tree to steal apples, and the limb didn't break, and he didn't fall and break his arm, and get torn by the farmer's great dog, and then languish on a sick bed for weeks, and repent and become good. Oh! no; he stole as many apples as he wanted and came down all right; and he was all ready for the dog too, and knocked him endways with a brick when he came to tear him. It was very strange—nothing like it ever happened in those mild little books with marbled backs, and with pictures in them of men with swallow-tailed coats and bell-crowned hats, and pantaloons that are short in the legs, and women with the waists of their dresses under their arms, and no hoops on. Nothing like it in any of the Sunday-school books.

Once he stole the teacher's pen-knife, and, when he was afraid it would be found out and he would get whipped, he slipped it into George Wilson's cap—poor Widow Wilson's son, the moral boy, the good little boy of the village, who always obeyed his mother, and never told an untruth, and was fond of his lessons, and infatuated with Sunday-school. And when the knife dropped from the cap, and poor George hung his head and blushed, as if in conscious guilt, and the grieved teacher charged the theft upon him, and was just in the very act of bringing the switch down upon his trembling shoulders, a white-haired, improbable justice of the peace did not suddenly appear in their midst, and strike an attitude and say, "Spare this noble boy—there stands the cowering culprit! I was passing the school-door at recess, and unseen myself, I saw the theft committed!" And then Jim didn't get whaled, and the venerable justice didn't read the tearful school a homily, and take George by the hand and say such a boy deserved to be exalted, and then tell him to come and make his home with him, and sweep out the office, and make fires, and run errands, and chop wood, and study law, and help his wife do household labors, and have all the balance of the time to play, and get forty cents a month, and be happy. No; it would have happened that way in the books, but it didn't happen that way to Jim. No meddling old clam of a justice dropped in to make trouble, and so the model boy George got thrashed, and Jim was glad of it because, you know, Jim hated moral boys. Jim said he was "down on them milksops." Such was the coarse language of this bad, neglected boy.

But the strangest thing that ever happened to Jim was the time he went boating on Sunday, and didn't get drowned, and that other time that he got caught out in the storm when he was fishing on Sunday, and didn't get struck by lightning. Why, you might look, and look, all through the Sunday-school books from now till next Christmas, and you would never come across anything like this. Oh no; you would find that all the bad boys who go boating on Sunday

invariably get drowned; and all the bad boys who get caught out in storms when they are fishing on Sunday infallibly get struck by lightning. Boats with bad boys in them always upset on Sunday, and it always storms when bad boys go fishing on the Sabbath. How this Jim ever escaped is a mystery to me. This Jim bore a charmed life—that must have been the way of it. Nothing could hurt him. He even gave the elephant in the menagerie a plug of tobacco, and the elephant didn't knock the top of his head off with his trunk. He browsed around the cupboard after essence of peppermint, and didn't make a mistake and drink *aqua fortis*. He stole his father's gun and went hunting on the Sabbath, and didn't shoot three or four of his fingers off. He struck his little sister on the temple with his fist when he was angry, and she didn't linger in pain through long summer days, and die with sweet words of forgiveness upon her lips that redoubled the anguish of his breaking heart. No; she got over it. He ran off and went to sea at last, and didn't come back and find himself sad and alone in the world, his loved ones sleeping in the quiet churchyard, and the vine-embowered home of his boyhood tumbled down and gone to decay. Ah! no; he came home as drunk as a piper, and got into the station-house the first thing.

And he grew up and married, and raised a large family, and brained them all with an axe one night, and got wealthy by all manner of cheating and rascality; and now he is the infernalest wickedest scoundrel in his native village, and is universally respected, and belongs to the Legislature.

So you see there never was a bad James in the Sunday-school books that had such a streak of luck as this sinful Jim with the charmed life.

THE STORY OF THE GOOD LITTLE BOY.

ONCE there was a good little boy by the name of Jacob Blivens. He always obeyed his parents, no matter how absurd and unreasonable their demands were; and he always learned his book, and never was late at Sabbath-school. He would not play hookey, even when his sober judgment told him it was the most profitable thing he could do. None of the other boys could ever make that boy out, he acted so strangely. He wouldn't lie, no matter how convenient it was. He just said it was wrong to lie, and that was sufficient for him. And he was so honest that he was simply

56

ridiculous. The curious ways that that Jacob had, surpassed everything. He wouldn't play marbles on Sunday, he wouldn't rob birds' nests, he wouldn't give hot pennies to organ-grinders' monkeys; he didn't seem to take any interest in any kind of rational amusement. So the other boys used to try to reason it out and come to an understanding of him, but they couldn't arrive at any satisfactory conclusion. As I said before, they could only figure out a sort of vague idea that he was "afflicted," and so they took him under their protection, and never allowed any harm to come to him.

This good little boy read all the Sunday-school books; they were his greatest delight. This was the whole secret of it. He believed in the good little boys they put in the Sunday-school books; he had every confidence in them. He longed to come across one of them alive, once; but he never did. They all died before his time, maybe. Whenever he read about a particularly good one he turned over quickly to the end to see what became of him, because he wanted to travel thousands of miles and gaze on him; but it wasn't any use; that good little boy always died in the last chapter, and there was a picture of the funeral, with all his relations and the Sunday-school children standing around the grave in pantaloons that were too short, and bonnets that were too large, and everybody crying into handkerchiefs that had as much as a yard and a half of stuff in them. He was always headed off in this way. He never could see one of those good little boys on account of his always dying in the last chapter.

Jacob had a noble ambition to be put in a Sunday-school book. He wanted to be put in, with pictures representing him gloriously declining to lie to his mother, and her weeping for joy about it; and pictures representing him standing on the doorstep giving a penny to a poor beggar-woman with six children, and telling her to spend it freely, but not to be extravagant, because extravagance is a sin; and pictures of him magnanimously refusing to tell on the bad boy who always lay in wait for him around the corner as he came from school, and welted him over the head with a lath, and then chased him home, saying, "Hi! hi!" as he proceeded. That was the ambition of young Jacob Blivens. He wished to be put in a Sunday-school book. It made him feel a little uncomfortable some- times when he reflected that the good little boys always died. He loved to live, you know, and this was the most unpleasant feature about being a Sunday-school-book boy. He knew it was not healthy to be good. He knew it was more fatal than consumption to be so supernaturally good as the boys in the books were; he knew that none of them had ever been able to stand it long, and it pained him to think that if they put him in a book he wouldn't ever see it, or even if they did get the book out before he died it wouldn't be popular without any picture of his funeral in the back part of it. It couldn't be much of a Sunday-school book that couldn't tell about the advice he gave to the community when he was dying.

So at last, of course, he had to make up his mind to do the best he could under the circumstances—to live right, and hang on as long as he could, and have his dying speech all ready when his time came.

But somehow nothing ever went right with this good little boy; nothing ever turned out with him the way it turned out with the good little boys in the books. They always had a good time, and the bad boys had the broken legs; but in his case there was a screw loose somewhere, and it all happened just the other way. When he found Jim Blake stealing apples, and went under the tree to read to him about the bad little boy who fell out of a neighbor's apple-tree and broke his arm, Jim fell out of the tree too, but he fell on *him*, and broke *his* arm, and Jim wasn't hurt at all. Jacob couldn't understand that. There wasn't anything in the books like it.

And once, when some bad boys pushed a blind man over in the mud, and Jacob ran to help him up and receive his blessing, the blind man did not give him any blessing at all, but whacked him over the head with his stick and said he would like to catch him shoving *him* again, and then pretending to help him up. This was not in accordance with any of the books. Jacob looked them all over to see.

One thing that Jacob wanted to do was to find a lame dog that hadn't any place to stay, and was hungry and persecuted, and bring him home and pet him and have that dog's imperishable gratitude. And at last he found one and was happy ; and he brought him home and fed him, but when he was going to pet him the dog flew at him and tore all the clothes off him except those that were in front, and made a spectacle of him that was astonishing. He examined authorities, but he could not understand the matter. It was of the same breed of dogs that was in the books, but it acted very differently. Whatever this boy did he got into trouble. The very things the boys in the books got rewarded for turned out to be about the most unprofitable things he could invest in.

Once, when he was on his way to Sunday-school, he saw some bad boys starting off pleasuring in a sail-boat. He was filled with consternation, because he knew from his reading that boys who went sailing on Sunday invariably got drowned. So he ran out on a raft to warn them, but a log turned with him and slid him into the river. A man got him out pretty soon, and the doctor pumped the water out of him, and gave him a fresh start with his bellows, but he caught cold and lay sick a-bed nine weeks. But the most unaccountable thing about it was that the bad boys in the boat had a good time all day, and then reached home alive and well in the most surprising manner. Jacob Blivens said there was nothing like these things in the books. He was perfectly dumbfounded.

When he got well he was a little discouraged, but he resolved to keep on trying anyhow. He knew that so far his experiences wouldn't do to go in a book, but he hadn't yet reached the allotted term of life for good little boys, and he hoped to be able to make a record yet if he could hold on till his time was fully up. If everything else failed he had his dying speech to fall back on.

He examined his authorities, and found that it was now time for him to go to sea as a cabin-boy. He called on a ship captain and made his application, and when the captain asked for his recommendations he proudly drew out a tract and pointed to the words, " To Jacob Blivens, from his affectionate teacher." But the captain was a coarse, vulgar man, and he said, " Oh, that be blowed ! *that* wasn't any proof that he knew how to wash dishes or handle a slush-bucket, and he guessed he didn't want him." This was altogether the most extraordinary thing that ever happened to Jacob in all his life. A compliment from a teacher, on a tract, had never failed to move the tenderest emotions of ship captains, and open the way to all offices of honor and profit in their gift—it never had in any book that ever *he* had read. He could hardly believe his senses.

This boy always had a hard time of it. Nothing ever came out according to

the authorities with him. At last, one day, when he was around hunt- ing up bad little boys to admonish, he found a lot of them in the old iron foundry fix- ing up a little joke on fourteen or fifteen dogs, which they had tied together in long procession, and were going to ornament with empty nitro-glyc- erine cans made fast to their tails. Jacob's heart was touched. He sat down on one of those cans (for he never minded grease when duty was before him), and he took hold of the foremost dog by the collar, and turned his reproving eye upon wicked Tom Jones. But just at that moment Alderman McWelter, full of wrath, stepped in. All the bad boys ran away, but Jacob Blivens rose in conscious innocence and began one of those stately little Sunday-school-book speeches which always commence with " Oh, sir !" in dead opposition to the fact that no boy, good or bad, ever starts a remark with " Oh, sir." But the alderman never waited to hear the rest. He took Jacob Blivens by the ear and turned him around, and hit him a whack in the rear with the flat of his hand ; and in an instant that good little boy shot out through the roof and soared away towards the sun, with the fragments of those fifteen dogs stringing after him like the tail of a kite. And there wasn't a sign of that alderman or that old iron foundry left on the face of the earth; and, as for young Jacob Blivens, he never got a chance to make his last dying speech after all his trouble fixing it up, unless he made it to the birds; because, although the bulk of him came down all right in a tree-top in an adjoining county, the rest of him was apportioned around among four townships, and so they had to hold five inquests on him to find out whether he was dead or not, and how it occurred. You never saw a boy scattered so. *

Thus perished the good little boy who did the best he could, but didn't come out according to the books. Every boy who ever did as he did prospered except him. His case is truly remarkable. It will probably never be accounted for.

* This glycerine catastrophe is borrowed from a floating newspaper item, whose author's name I would give if I knew it.—[M. T.]

A COUPLE OF POEMS BY TWAIN AND MOORE.

THOSE EVENING BELLS.

BY THOMAS MOORE.

Those evening bells! those evening bells!
How many a tale their music tells
Of youth, and home, and that sweet time
When last I heard their soothing chime.

Those joyous hours are passed away;
And many a heart that then was gay,
Within the tomb now darkly dwells,
And hears no more those evening bells.

And so 'twill be when I am gone—
That tuneful peal will still ring on;
While other bards shall walk these dells,
And sing your praise, sweet evening bells.

THOSE ANNUAL BILLS.

BY MARK TWAIN.

These annual bills! these annual bills!
How many a song their discord trills
Of "truck" consumed, enjoyed, forgot,
Since I was skinned by last years lot!

Those joyous beans are passed away;
Those onions blithe, O where are they!
Once loved, lost, mourned—*now* vexing ILLS
Your shades troop back in annual bills!

And so 'twill be when I'm aground—
These yearly duns will still go round,
While other bards, with frantic quills,
Shall damn and *damn* these annual bills!

NIAGARA.

NIAGARA FALLS is a most enjoyable place of resort. The hotels are excellent, and the prices not at all exorbitant. The opportunities for fishing are not surpassed in the country; in fact, they are not even equalled elsewhere. Because, in other localities, certain places in the streams are much better than others; but at Niagara one place is just as good as another, for the reason that the fish do not bite anywhere, and so there is no use in your walking five miles to fish, when you can depend on being just as unsuccessful nearer home. The advantages of this state of things have never heretofore been properly placed before the public.

The weather is cool in summer, and the walks and drives are all pleasant and none of them fatiguing.   When you start out to "do" the Falls you first drive down about a mile, and pay a small sum for the privilege of looking down from a precipice into the narrowest part of the Niagara river.   A railway "cut" through a hill would be as comely if it had the angry river tumbling and foaming through its bottom.   You can descend a staircase here a hundred and fifty feet down, and stand at the edge of the water.   After you have done it, you will wonder why you did it; but you will then be too late.

The guide will explain to you, in his blood-curdling way, how he saw the little steamer, *Maid of the Mist*, descend the fearful rapids—how first one paddle-box was out of sight behind the raging billows, and then the other, and at what point it was that her smokestack toppled overboard, and where her planking began to break and part asunder—and how she did finally live through the trip, after accomplishing the incredible feat of travelling seventeen miles in six minutes, or six miles in seventeen minutes, I have really forgotten which.   But it was very extraordinary, anyhow.   It is worth the price of admission to hear the guide tell the story nine times in succession to different parties, and never miss a word or alter a sentence or a gesture.

Then you drive over the Suspension Bridge, and divide your misery between the chances of smashing down two hundred feet into the river below, and the chances of having the railway train overhead smashing down on to you.   Either possibility is discomforting taken by itself, but mixed together, they amount in the aggregate to positive unhappiness.

On the Canada side you drive along the chasm between long ranks of photographers standing guard behind their cameras, ready to make an ostentatious frontispiece of you and your decaying ambulance, and your solemn crate with a hide on it, which you are expected to regard in the light of a horse, and a diminished and unimportant background of sublime Niagara; and a great many people *have* the incredible effrontery or the native depravity to aid and abet this sort of crime.

Any day, in the hands of these photographers, you may see stately pictures of papa and mamma, Johnny and Bub and Sis, or a couple of country cousins, all smiling vacantly, and all disposed in studied and uncomfortable attitudes in their carriage, and all looming up in their awe-inspiring imbecility before the snubbed and diminished presentment of that majestic presence whose ministering spirits are the rainbows, whose voice is the thunder, whose awful front is veiled in clouds, who was monarch here dead and forgotten ages before this hackful of small reptiles was deemed temporarily necessary to fill a crack in the world's unnoted myriads, and will still be monarch here ages and decades of ages after they shall have gathered themselves to their blood relations, the other worms, and been mingled with the unremembering dust.

There is no actual harm in making Niagara a background whereon to display

one's marvellous insignificance in a good strong light, but it requires a sort of superhuman self-complacency to enable one to do it.

When you have examined the stupendous Horseshoe Fall till you are satisfied you cannot improve on it, you return to America by the new Suspension Bridge, and follow up the bank to where they exhibit the Cave of the Winds.

Here I followed instructions, and divested myself of all my clothing, and put on a waterproof jacket and overalls. This costume is picturesque, but not beautiful. A guide, similarly dressed, led the way down a flight of winding stairs, which wound and wound, and still kept on winding long after the thing ceased to be a

5

novelty, and then terminated long before it had begun to be a pleasure. We were then well down under the precipice, but still considerably above the level of the river.

We now began to creep along flimsy bridges of a single plank, our persons shielded from destruction by a crazy wooden railing, to which I clung with both hands—not because I was afraid, but because I wanted to. Presently the descent became steeper, and the bridge flimsier, and sprays from the American Fall began to rain down on us in fast-increasing sheets that soon became blinding, and after that our progress was mostly in the nature of groping. Now a furious wind began to rush out from behind the waterfall, which seemed determined to sweep us from the bridge, and scatter us on the rocks and among the torrents below. I remarked that I wanted to go home; but it was too late. We were almost under the monstrous wall of water thundering down from above, and speech was in vain in the midst of such a pitiless crash of sound.

In another moment the guide disappeared behind the deluge, and bewildered by the thunder, driven helplessly by the wind, and smitten by the arrowy tempest of rain, I followed. All was darkness. Such a mad storming, roaring, and bellowing of warring wind and water never crazed my ears before. I bent my head, and seemed to receive the Atlantic on my back. The world seemed going to destruction. I could not see anything, the flood poured down so savagely. I raised my head, with open mouth, and the most of the American cataract went down my throat. If I had sprung a leak now, I had been lost. And at this moment I discovered that the bridge had ceased, and we must trust for a foothold to the slippery and precipitous rocks. I never was so scared before and survived it. But we got through at last, and emerged into the open day, where we could stand in front of the laced and frothy and seething world of descending water, and look at it. When I saw how much of it there was, and how fearfully in earnest it was, I was sorry I had gone behind it.

The noble Red Man has always been a friend and darling of mine. I love to read about him in tales and legends and romances. I love to read of his inspired sagacity, and his love of the wild free life of mountain and forest, and his general nobility of character, and his stately metaphorical manner of speech, and his chivalrous love for the dusky maiden, and the picturesque pomp of his dress and accoutrements. Especially the picturesque pomp of his dress and accoutrements. When I found the shops at Niagara Falls full of dainty Indian bead-work, and stunning moccasins, and equally stunning toy figures representing human beings who carried their weapons in holes bored through their arms and bodies, and had feet shaped like a pie, I was filled with emotion. I knew that now, at last, I was going to come face to face with the noble Red Man.

A lady clerk in a shop told me, indeed, that all her grand array of curiosities were made by the Indians, and that they were plenty about the Falls, and that they were friendly, and it would not be dangerous to speak to them. And sure enough, as I approached the bridge leading over to Luna Island, I came upon a noble Son of the Forest sitting under a tree, diligently at work on a bead reticule. He wore a slouch hat and brogans, and had a short black pipe in his mouth. Thus does the baneful contact with our effeminate civilization dilute the picturesque pomp which is so natural to the Indian when far removed from us in his native haunts. I addressed the relic as follows :—

" Is the Wawhoo-Wang-Wang of the Whack-a-Whack happy? Does the great Speckled Thunder sigh for the war path, or is his heart contented with dreaming of the dusky maiden, the Pride of the Forest? Does the mighty Sachem yearn to drink the blood of his enemies, or is he satisfied to make bead reticules for the

pappooses of the paleface? Speak, sublime relic of bygone grandeur—venerable ruin, speak!"

The relic said—

"An' is it mesilf, Dennis Hooligan, that ye'd be takin' for a dirty Injin, ye drawlin', lantern-jawed, spider-legged divil! By the piper that played before Moses, I'll ate ye!"

I went away from there.

By and by, in the neighborhood of the Terrapin Tower, I came upon a gentle daughter of the aborigines in fringed and beaded buckskin moccasins and leggins, seated on a bench, with her pretty wares about her. She had just carved out a wooden chief that had a strong family resemblance to a clothes-pin, and was now boring a hole through his abdomen to put his bow through. I hesitated a moment, and then addressed her:

"Is the heart of the forest maiden heavy? Is the Laughing Tadpole lonely? Does she mourn over the extinguished council-fires of her race, and the vanished glory of her ancestors? Or does her sad spirit wander afar toward the hunting-grounds whither her brave Gobbler-of-the-Lightnings is gone? Why is my daughter silent? Has she aught against the paleface stranger?"

The maiden said—

"Faix, an' is it Biddy Malone ye dare to be callin' names? Lave this, or I'll shy your lean carcass over the cataract, ye sniveling blaggard!"

I adjourned from there also.

"Confound these Indians!" I said. " They told me they were tame; but, if appearances go for anything, I should say they were all on the war path."

I made one more attempt to fraternize with them, and only one. I came upon a camp of them gathered in the shade of a great tree, making wampum and moccasins, and addressed them in the language of friendship:

"Noble Red Men, Braves, Grand Sachems, War Chiefs, Squaws, and High Muck-a-Mucks, the paleface from the land of the setting sun greets you ! You, Beneficent Polecat—you, Devourer of Mountains—you, Roaring Thundergust—you, Bully Boy with a Glass eye—the paleface from beyond the great waters greets you all ! War and pestilence have thinned your ranks, and destroyed your once proud nation. Poker and seven-up, and a vain modern expense for soap, unknown to your glorious ancestors, have depleted your purses. Appropriating, in your simplicity, the property of others, has gotten you into trouble. Misrepresenting facts, in your simple innocence, has damaged your reputation with the soulless usurper. Trading for forty-rod whisky, to enable you to get drunk and happy and tomahawk your families, has played the everlasting mischief with the picturesque pomp of your dress, and here you are, in the broad light of the nineteenth century, gotten up like the ragtag and bobtail of the purlieus of New York. For shame! Remember your ancestors! Recall their mighty deeds! Remember Uncas!—and Red Jacket!—and Hole in the Day!—and Whoopdedoodledo! Emulate their achievements! Unfurl yourselves under my banner, noble savages, illustrious guttersnipes"——

"Down wid him!" "Scoop the blaggard!" "Burn him!" "Hang him!" "Dhround him!"

It was the quickest operation that ever was. I simply saw a sudden flash in the air of clubs, brickbats, fists, bead-baskets, and moccasins—a single flash, and they all appeared to hit me at once, and no two of them in the same place. In the next instant the entire tribe was upon me. They tore half the clothes off me; they broke my arms and legs; they gave me a thump that dented the top of my head till it would hold coffee like a saucer; and, to crown their disgraceful proceedings and add insult to injury, they threw me over the Niagara Falls, and I got wet.

About ninety or a hundred feet from the top, the remains of my vest caught on a projecting rock, and I was almost drowned before I could get loose. I finally fell, and brought up in a world of white foam at the foot of the Fall, whose celled and bubbly masses towered up several inches above my head. Of course I got into the eddy. I sailed round and round in it forty-four times—chasing a chip and gaining on it—each round trip a half mile—reaching for the same bush on the bank forty-four times, and just exactly missing it by a hair's-breadth every time.

At last a man walked down and sat down close to that bush, and put a pipe in his mouth, and lit a match, and followed me with one eye and kept the other on the match, while he sheltered it in his hands from the wind. Presently a puff of wind blew it out. The next time I swept around he said—

"Got a match?"

"Yes; in my other vest. Help me out, please."

"Not for Joe."

When I came round again, I said—

"Excuse the seemingly impertinent curiosity of a drowning man, but will you explain this singular conduct of yours?"

"With pleasure. I am the coroner. Don't hurry on my account. I can wait for you. But I wish I had a match."

I said—"Take my place, and I'll go and get you one."

He declined. This lack of confidence on his part created a coldness between us, and from that time forward I avoided him. It was my idea, in case anything happened to me, to so time the occur- rence as to throw my custom into the hands of the oppo- sition coroner over on the American side.

At last a police- man came along, and arrested me for disturbing the peace by yelling at people on shore for help. The judge fined me, but I had the advantage of him. My money was with my pant- aloons, and my pantaloons were with the Indians. Thus I escaped. I am now lying in a very critical con- dition. At least I am lying anyway — critical or not critical. I am hurt all over, but I can- not tell the full extent yet, because the doctor is not done taking inventory. He will make out my manifest this eve- ning. However, thus far he thinks only sixteen of my wounds are fatal. I don't mind the others.

Upon regaining my right mind, I said—

"It is an awful savage tribe of Indians that do the bead work and moccasins for Niagara Falls, doctor. Where are they from?"

"Limerick, my son."

Answers to Correspondents.

"MORAL STATISTICIAN."—I don't want any of your statistics; I took your whole batch and lit my pipe with it. I hate your kind of people. You are always ciphering out how much a man's health is injured, and how much his intellect is impaired, and how many pitiful dollars and cents he wastes in the course of ninety-two years' indulgence in the fatal practice of smoking; and in the equally fatal practice of drinking coffee; and in playing billiards occasionally; and in taking a glass of wine at dinner, etc. etc. etc. And you are always figuring out how many women have been burned to death because of the dangerous fashion of wearing expansive hoops, etc. etc. etc. You never see more than one side of the question. You are blind to the fact that most old men in America smoke and drink coffee, although, according to your theory, they ought to have died young; and that hearty old Englishmen drink wine and survive it, and portly old Dutchmen both drink and smoke freely, and yet grow older and fatter all the time. And you never try to find out how much solid comfort, relaxation, and enjoyment a man derives from smoking in the course of a lifetime (which is worth ten times the money he would save by letting it alone), nor the appalling aggregate of happiness lost in a lifetime by your kind of people from *not* smoking. Of course you can save money by denying yourself all those little vicious enjoyments for fifty years; but then what can you do

72

with it? What use can you put it to? Money can't save your infinitesimal soul. All the use that money can be put to is to purchase comfort and enjoyment in this life; therefore, as you are an enemy to comfort and enjoyment, where is the use of accumulating cash? It won't do for you to say that you can use it to better purpose in furnishing a good table, and in charities, and in supporting tract societies, because you know yourself that you people who have no petty vices are never known to give away a cent, and that you stint yourselves so in the matter of food that you are always feeble and hungry. And you never dare to laugh in the daytime for fear some poor wretch, seeing you in a good humor, will try to borrow a dollar of you; and in church you are always down on your knees, with your eyes buried in the cushion, when the contribution-box comes around; and you never give the revenue officers a full statement of your income. Now you know all these things yourself, don't you? Very well, then, what is the use of your stringing out your miserable lives to a lean and withered old age? What is the use of your saving money that is so utterly worthless to you? In a word, why don't you go off somewhere and die, and not be always trying to seduce people into becoming as "ornery" and unloveable as you are yourselves, by your villainous "moral statistics?" Now, I don't approve of dissipation, and I don't indulge in it either; but I haven't a particle of confidence in a man who has no redeeming petty vices, and so I don't want to hear from you any more. I think you are the very same man who read me a long lecture last week about the degrading vice of smoking cigars, and then came back, in my absence, with your reprehensible fire-proof gloves on, and carried off my beautiful parlor stove.

"YOUNG AUTHOR."—Yes, Agassiz *does* recommend authors to eat fish, because the phosphorus in it makes brains. So far you are correct. But I cannot help you to a decision about the amount you need to eat—at least, not with certainty. If the specimen composition you send is about your fair usual average, I should judge that perhaps a couple of whales would be all you would want for the present. Not the largest kind, but simply good, middling-sized whales.

"SIMON WHEELER," *Sonora.*—The following simple and touching remarks and accompanying poem have just come to hand from the rich gold-mining region of Sonora :—

To Mr. Mark Twain: The within parson, which I have set to poetry under the name and style of " He Done His Level Best," was one among the whitest men I ever see, and it an't every man that knowed him that can find it in his heart to say he's glad the poor cuss is busted and gone home to the States. He was here in an early day, and he was the handyest man about takin' holt of anything that come along you most ever see, I judge. He was a cheerful, stirrin' cretur, always doin' somethin', and no man can say he ever see him do anything by halvers. Preachin' was his nateral gait, but he warn't a man to lay back and twidle his thumbs because there didn't happen to be nothin' doin' in his own especial line—no, sir, he was a man who would meander forth and stir up something for hisself. His last acts was to go his pile on " kings-*and* " (calklatin' to fill, but which he didn't fill), when there was a " flush " out agin him, and naterally, you see, he went under. And so he was cleaned out, as you may say, and he struck the home-trail, cheerful but flat broke. I knowed this talonted man in Arkansaw, and if you would print this humbly tribute to his gorgis abilities, you would greatly obleege his onhappy friend.

HE DONE HIS LEVEL BEST.

Was he a mining on the flat—
     He done it with a zest ;
Was he a leading of the choir—
     He done his level best.

If he'd a reg'lar task to do,
     He never took no rest ;
Or if 'twas off-and-on—the same—
     He done his level best.

If he was preachin' on his beat,
     He'd tramp from east to west,
And north to south—in cold and heat
     He done his level best.

He'd yank a sinner outen (Hades), *
     And land him with the blest ;
Then snatch a prayer'n waltz in again,
     And do his level best.

---

* Here I have taken a slight liberty with the original MS. " Hades " does not make such good metre as the other word of one syllable, but it sounds better.

> He'd cuss and sing and howl and pray,
> And dance and drink and jest,
> And lie and steal—all one to him—
> He done his level best.
>
> Whate'er this man was sot to do,
> He done it with a zest ;
> No matter *what* his contract was,
> HE'D DO HIS LEVEL BEST.

Verily, this man *was* gifted with "gorgis abilities," and it is a happiness to me to embalm the memory of their lustre in these columns. If it were not that the poet crop is unusually large and rank in California this year, I would encourage you to continue writing, Simon Wheeler; but, as it is, perhaps it might be too risky in you to enter against so much opposition.

"PROFESSIONAL BEGGAR." No ; you are not obliged to take greenbacks at par.

"MELTON MOWBRAY,"* *Dutch Flat.*—This correspondent sends a lot of dog-gerel, and says it has been regarded as very good in Dutch Flat. I give a specimen verse :—

> "The Assyrian came down like a wolf on the fold,
> And his cohorts were gleaming with purple and gold ;
> And the sheen of his spears was like stars on the sea ;
> When the blue wave rolls nightly on deep Galilee."

There, that will do. That may be very good Dutch Flat poetry, but it won't do in the metropolis. It is too smooth and blubbery; it reads like buttermilk gurgling from a jug. What the people ought to have is something spirited—something like "Johnny Comes Marching Home." However, keep on practising, and you may succeed yet. There is genius in you, but too much blubber.

"ST. CLAIR HIGGINS." *Los Angeles.*—"My life is a failure ; I have adored, wildly, madly, and

---

*This piece of pleasantry, published in a San Francisco paper, was mistaken by the country journals for seriousness, and many and loud were the denunciations of the ignorance of author and editor, in not knowing that the lines in question were "written by Byron."

she whom I love has turned coldly from me and shed her affections upon another. What would you advise me to do?"

You should set your affections on another, also—or on several, if there are enough to go round. Also, do everything you can to make your former flame unhappy. There is an absurd idea disseminated in novels, that the happier a girl is with another man, the happier it makes the old lover she has blighted. Don't allow yourself to believe any such nonsense as that. The more cause that girl finds to regret that she did not marry you, the more comfortable you will feel over it. It isn't poetical, but it is mighty sound doctrine.

"ARITHMETICUS." *Virginia, Nevada.*—"If it would take a cannon ball 3 1-3 seconds to travel four miles, and 3 3-8 seconds to travel the next four, and 3 5-8 to travel the next four, and if its rate of progress continued to diminish in the same ratio, how long would it take it to go fifteen hundred millions of miles?

I don't know.

"AMBITIOUS LEARNER," *Oakland.*—Yes; you are right—America was not discovered by Alexander Selkirk.

"DISCARDED LOVER."—I loved, and still love, the beautiful Edwitha Howard, and intended to marry her. Yet, during my temporary absence at Benicia, last week, alas! she married Jones. Is my happiness to be thus blasted for life? Have I no redress?"

Of course you have. All the law, written and unwritten, is on you side. The *intention* and not the *act* constitutes crime—in other words, constitutes the *deed*. If you call your bosom friend a fool, and *intend* it for an insult, it *is* an insult; but if you do it playfully, and meaning no insult, it is *not* an insult. If you discharge a pistol *accidentally*, and kill a man, you can go free, for you have done no murder; but if you try to kill a man, and manifestly *intend* to kill him, but fail utterly to do it, the law still holds that the *intention* constituted the crime, and you are guilty of murder. Ergo, if you had married Edwitha *accidentally*, and without really *intending* to do it, you would not actually be married to her at all, because the *act* of marriage could not be complete without the *intention*. And ergo, in the strict spirit of the law, since you deliberately *intended* to marry Edwitha, and didn't do it, you are married to her all the same—because, as I said before, the *intention* constitutes the crime. It is as clear as day that Edwitha is your wife, and your redress lies in taking a club and mutilating Jones with it as much as you can. Any man has a right to protect his own wife from the advances of other men. But you have another alternative—you were married to Edwitha *first*, because of your deliberate intention, and now you can prosecute her for bigamy, in subsequently marrying Jones. But there is another phase in this complicated case: You *intended* to marry Edwitha, and consequently, according to law, she is your wife—there is no getting around that; but she didn't marry you, and if she *never intended* to marry you, *you are not her husband*, of course. Ergo, in marrying Jones, she was guilty of bigamy, because she was the wife of another man at the time; which is all very well as far as it goes—but then, don't you see, she had no other *husband* when she married Jones, and consequently she was *not* guilty of bigamy. Now, according to this view of the case, Jones married a *spinster*, who was a *widow* at the same time and another man's *wife* at the same time, and yet who had no *husband* and *never had one*, and never had any *intention* of getting married, and therefore, of course, *never had* been married; and by the same reasoning you are a *bachelor*, because you have never been any one's *husband;* and a *married man*, because you have a wife living; and to all intents and purposes a *widower*, because you have been deprived of that wife; and a consummate *ass* for going off to Benicia in the first place, while things were so mixed. And by this time I have got myself so tangled up in the intricacies of this extraordinary case that I shall have to give up any further attempt to advise you—I might get confused and fail to make myself understood. I think I could take up the argument where I left off, and by following it closely awhile, perhaps I could prove to your satisfaction, either that you never existed at all, or that you are dead now, and consequently don't need the faithless Edwitha—I think I could do that, if it would afford you any comfort.

"ARTHUR AUGUSTUS."—No ; you are wrong; that is the proper way to throw a brickbat or a tomahawk; but it doesn't answer so well for a bouquet; you will hurt somebody if you keep it up. Turn your nosegay upside down, take it by the stems, and toss it with an upward sweep. Did you ever pitch quoits ? that is the idea. The practice of recklessly heaving immense solid bouquets, of the general size and weight of prize cabbages, from the dizzy altitude of the galleries, is dangerous and very reprehensible. Now, night before last, at the Academy of Music, just after Signorina —— had finished that exquisite melody, "The Last Rose of Summer," one of these floral pile-drivers came cleaving down through the atmosphere of applause, and if she hadn't deployed suddenly to the right, it would have driven her into the floor like a shingle-nail. Of course that bouquet was well meant; but how would you like to have been the target? A sincere compliment is always grateful to a lady, so long as you don't try to knock her down with it.

"Young Mother."—And so you think a baby is a thing of beauty and a joy forever? Well, the idea is pleasing, but not original; every cow thinks the same of its own calf. Perhaps the cow may not think it so elegantly, but still she thinks it nevertheless. I honor the cow for it. We all honor this touching maternal instinct wherever we find it, be it in the home of luxury or in the humble cow-shed. But really, madam, when I come to examine the matter in all its bearings, I find that the correctness of your assertion does not assert itself in all cases. A soiled baby, with a neglected nose, cannot be conscientiously regarded as a thing of beauty; and inasmuch as babyhood spans but three short years, no baby is competent to be a joy "forever." It pains me thus to demolish two-thirds of your pretty sentiment in a single sentence; but the position I hold in this chair requires that I shall not permit you to deceive and mislead the public with your plausible figures of speech. I know a female baby, aged eighteen months, in this city, which cannot hold out as a "joy" twenty-four hours on a stretch, let alone "forever." And it possesses some of the most remarkable eccentricities of character and appetite that have ever fallen under my notice. I will set down here a statement of this infant's operations (conceived, planned, and carried out by itself, and without suggestion or assistance from its mother or any one else), during a single day; and what I shall say can be substantiated by the sworn testimony of witnesses.

It commenced by eating one dozen large blue-mass pills, box and all; then it fell down a flight of stairs, and arose with a blue and purple knot on its forehead, after which it proceeded in quest of further refreshment and amusement. It found a glass trinket ornamented with brass-work—smashed up and ate the glass, and then swallowed the brass. Then it drank about twenty drops of laudanum, and more than a dozen tablespoonfuls of strong spirits of camphor. The reason why it took no more laudanum was because there was no more to take. After this it lay down on its back, and shoved five or six inches of a silver-headed whale-bone cane down its throat; got it fast there, and it was all its mother could do to pull the cane out again, without pulling out some of the child with it. Then, being hungry for glass again, it broke up several wine-glasses, and fell to eating and swallowing the fragments, not minding a cut or two. Then it ate a quantity of butter, pepper, salt, and California matches, actually taking a spoonful of butter, a spoonful of salt, a spoonful of pepper, and three or four lucifer matches at each mouthful. (I will remark here that this thing of beauty likes painted German lucifers, and eats all she can get of them; but she prefers California matches, which I regard as a compliment to our home manufactures of more than ordinary value, coming, as it does, from one who is too young to flatter.) Then she washed her head with soap and water, and afterwards ate what soap was left, and drank as much of the suds as she had room for; after which she sallied forth and took the cow familiarly by the tail, and got kicked heels over head. At odd times during the day, when this joy for ever happened to have nothing particular on hand, she put in the time by climbing up on places, and falling down off them, uniformly damaging herself in the operation. As young as she is, she speaks many words tolerably distinctly; and being plain-spoken in other respects, blunt and to the point, she opens conversation with all strangers, male or female, with the same formula, " How do, Jim ?" Not being familiar with the ways of children, it is possible that I have been magnifying into matter of surprise things which may not strike any one who is familiar with infancy as being at all astonishing. However, I cannot believe that such is the case, and so I repeat that my report of this baby's performances is strictly true ; and if any one doubts it, I can produce the child. I will further engage that she will devour anything that is given her (reserving to myself only the right to exclude anvils), and fall down from any place to which she may be elevated (merely stipulating that her preference for alighting on her head shall be respected, and, therefore, that the elevation chosen shall be high enough to enable her to accomplish this to her satisfaction.) But I find I have wandered from my subject; so, without further argument, I will reiterate my conviction that not *all* babies are things of beauty and joys forever.

"Arithmeticus." *Virginia, Nevada.*—"I am an enthusiastic student of mathematics, and it is so vexatious to me to find my progress constantly impeded by these mysterious arithmetical technicalities. Now do tell me what the difference is between geometry and conchology?"

Here *you* come again with your arithmetical conundrums, when I am suffering death with a cold in the head. If you could have seen the expression of scorn that darkened my countenance a moment ago, and was instantly split from the centre in every direction like a fractured looking-glass by my last sneeze, you never would have written that disgraceful question. Conchology is a science which has nothing to do with mathematics: it relates only to shells. At the same time, however, a man who opens oysters for a hotel, or shells a fortified town, or sucks eggs, is not, strictly speaking, a conchologist—a fine stroke of sarcasm that, but it will be lost on such an unintellectual clam as you. Now compare conchology and geometry together, and you will see what the difference is, and your question will be answered. But don't torture me with any more arithmetical horrors until you know I am rid of my cold. I feel the bitterest animosity towards you at this moment—bothering me in this way, when I can do nothing but sneeze and rage and snort pocket-handkerchiefs to atoms. If I had you in range of my nose, now, I would blow your brains out.

TO RAISE POULTRY.

Seriously, from early youth I have taken an especial interest in the subject of poultry-raising, and so this membership touches a ready sympathy in my breast. Even as a schoolboy, poultry-raising was a study with me, and I may say without egotism that as early as the age of seventeen I was acquainted with all the best and speediest methods of raising chickens, from raising them off a roost by burning lucifer matches under their noses, down to lifting them off a fence on a frosty night by insinuating the end of a warm board under their heels. By the time I was twenty years old, I

* Being a letter written to a Poultry Society that had conferred a complimentary membership upon the author.

6   81

really suppose I had raised more poultry than any one individual in all the section round about there. The very chickens came to know my talent, by and by. The youth of both sexes ceased to paw the earth for worms, and old roosters that came to crow, " remained to pray," when I passed by.

I have had so much experience in the raising of fowls that I cannot but think that a few hints from me might be useful to the Society. The two methods I have already touched upon are very simple, and are only used in the raising of the commonest class of fowls; one is for summer, the other for winter. In the one case you start out with a friend along about eleven o'clock on a summer's night (not later, because in some States—especially in California and Oregon—chickens always rouse up just at midnight and crow from ten to thirty minutes, according to the ease or difficulty they experience in getting the public waked up), and your friend carries with him a sack. Arrived at the hen-roost (your neighbor's, not your own), you light a match and hold it under first one and then another pullet's nose until they are willing to go into that

bag without making any trouble about it. You then return home, either taking the bag with you or leaving it behind, according as circumstances shall dictate. *N. B.* I *have* seen the time when it was eligible and appropriate to leave the sack behind and walk off with considerable velocity, without ever leaving any word where to send it.

In the case of the other method mentioned for raising poultry, your friend takes along a covered vessel with a charcoal fire in it, and you carry a long slender plank. This is a frosty night, understand. Arrived at the tree, or fence, or other hen-roost (your own if you are an idiot), you warm the end of your plank in your friend's fire vessel, and then raise it aloft and ease it up gently against a slumbering chicken's foot. If the subject of your attentions is a true bird, he will infallibly return thanks with a sleepy cluck or two, and step out and take up quarters on the plank, thus becoming so conspicuously accessory before the fact to his own murder as to make it a grave question in our minds, as it once was in the mind of Black-stone, whether he is not really and deliberately committing suicide in the second degree. [But you enter into a contemplation of these legal refinements subsequently —not then].

When you wish to raise a fine, large, donkey-voiced Shanghai rooster, you do it with a lasso, just as you would a bull. It is because he must be choked, and choked effectually, too. It is the only good, certain way, for whenever he mentions a matter which he is cordially interested in, the chances are ninety-nine in a hundred that he secures somebody else's immediate attention to it too, whether it be day or night.

The Black Spanish is an exceedingly fine bird and a costly one. Thirty-five dollars is the usual figure, and fifty a not uncommon price for a specimen. Even its eggs are worth from a dollar to a dollar and a half a-piece, and yet are so unwholesome that the city physician seldom or never orders them for the workhouse. Still I have once or twice procured as high as a dozen at a time for nothing, in the dark of the moon. The best way to raise the Black Spanish fowl is to go late in the evening and raise coop and all. The reason I recommend this method is, that the birds being so valuable, the owners do not permit them to roost around pro-miscuously, but put them in a coop as strong as a fire-proof safe, and keep it in the kitchen at night. The method I speak of is not always a bright and satisfying success, and yet there are so many little articles of *vertu* about a kitchen, that if you fail on the coop you can generally bring away something else. I brought away a nice steel trap one night, worth ninety cents.

But what is the use in my pouring out my whole intellect on this subject? I have shown the Western New York Poultry Society that they have taken to their bosom a party who is not a spring chicken by any means, but a man who knows all about poultry, and is just as high up in the most efficient methods of raising it as the President of the institution himself. I thank these gentlemen for the honorary membership they have conferred upon me, and shall stand at all times ready and willing to testify my good feeling and my official zeal by deeds as well as by this hastily penned advice and information. Whenever they are ready to go to raising poultry, let them call for me any evening after eleven o'clock, and I shall be on hand promptly.

EXPERIENCE OF THE McWILLIAMSES
WITH MEMBRANOUS CROUP.

*[As related to the author of this book by Mr.
McWilliams, a pleasant New York gentleman
whom the said author met by chance on a
journey.]*

WELL, to go back to where I was before
I digressed to explain to you how that
frightful and incurable disease, membranous croup, was ravaging the town and
driving all mothers mad with terror, I called
Mrs. McWilliams's attention to little Penelope
and said:

"Darling, I wouldn't let that child be chewing that pine stick if I were you."

"Precious, where is the harm in it?" said she, but at the same time preparing to take away the stick—for women cannot receive even the most palpably judicious suggestion without arguing it; that is, married women.

I replied:

"Love, it is notorious that pine is the least nutritious wood that a child can eat."

My wife's hand paused, in the act of taking the stick, and returned itself to her lap. She bridled perceptibly, and said:

"Hubby, you know better than that. You know you do. Doctors *all* say that the turpentine in pine wood is good for weak back and the kidneys."

"Ah—I was under a misapprehension. I did not know that the child's kidneys and spine were affected, and that the family physician had recommended—"

"Who said the child's spine and kidneys were affected?"

"My love, you intimated it."

"The idea! I never intimated anything of the kind."

"Why my dear, it hasn't been two minutes since you said—"

"Bother what I said! I don t care what I did say. There isn't any harm in the child's chewing a bit of pine stick if she wants to, and you know it perfectly well. And she *shall* chew it, too. So there, now!"

"Say no more, my dear. I now see the force of your reasoning, and I will go and order two or three cords of the best pine wood to-day. No child of mine shall want while I—"

"O *please* go along to your office and let me have some peace. A body can never make the simplest remark but you must take it up and go to arguing and arguing and arguing till you don't know what you are talking about, and you *never* do."

"Very well, it shall be as you say. But there is a want of logic in your last remark which—"

However, she was gone with a flourish before I could finish, and had taken the child with her. That night at dinner she confronted me with a face as white as a sheet:

"O, Mortimer, there's another! Little Georgie Gordon is taken."

"Membranous croup?"

"Membranous croup."

"Is there any hope for him?"

"None in the wide world. O, what is to become of us!"

By and by a nurse brought in our Penelope to say good-night and offer the customary prayer at the mother's knee. In the midst of "Now I lay me down to sleep," she gave a slight cough! My wife fell back like one stricken with death. But the next moment she was up and brimming with the activities which terror inspires.

She commanded that the child's crib be removed from the nursery to our bed-room; and she went along to see the order executed. She took me with her, of course. We got matters arranged with speed. A cot bed was put up in my

wife's dressing room for the nurse. But now Mrs. McWilliams said we were too far away from the other baby, and what if *he* were to have the symptoms in the night—and she blanched again, poor thing.

We then restored the crib and the nurse to the nursery and put up a bed for ourselves in a room adjoining.

Presently, however, Mrs. McWilliams said suppose the baby should catch it from Penelope? This thought struck a new panic to her heart, and the tribe of us could not get the crib out of the nursery again fast enough to satisfy my wife, though she assisted in her own person and well nigh pulled the crib to pieces in her frantic hurry.

We moved down stairs; but there was no place there to stow the nurse, and Mrs. McWilliams said the nurse's experience would be an inestimable help. So we returned, bag and baggage, to our own bed-room once more, and felt a great gladness, like storm-buffeted birds that have found their nest again.

Mrs. McWilliams sped to the nursery to see how things were going on there. She was back in a moment with a new dread. She said:

"What *can* make Baby sleep so?"

I said:

"Why, my darling, Baby *always* sleeps like a graven image."

"I know. I know; but there's something peculiar about his sleep, now. He seems to—to—he seems to breathe so *regularly*. O, this is dreadful."

"But my dear he always breathes regularly."

"Oh, I know it, but there's something frightful about it now. His nurse is too young and inexperienced. Maria shall stay there with her, and be on hand if anything happens."

"That is a good idea, but who will help *you?*"

"You can help me all I want. I wouldn't allow anybody to do anything but myself, any how, at such a time as this."

I said I would feel mean to lie abed and sleep, and leave her to watch and toil over our little patient all the weary night.—But she reconciled me to it. So old Maria departed and took up her ancient quarters in the nursery.

Penelope coughed twice in her sleep.

"Oh, why *don't* that doctor come! Mortimer, this room is too warm. This room is certainly too warm. Turn off the register—quick!"

I shut it off, glancing at the thermometer at the same time, and wondering to myself if 70 *was* too warm for a sick child.

The coachman arrived from down town, now, with the news that our physician was ill and confined to his bed.—Mrs. McWilliams turned a dead eye upon me, and said in a dead voice:

"There is a Providence in it. It is foreordained. He never was sick before.— Never. We have not been living as we ought to live, Mortimer. Time and time again I have told you so. Now you see the result. Our child will never get well. Be thankful if you can forgive yourself; I never can forgive *my*self."

I said, without intent to hurt, but with heedless choice of words, that I could not see that we had been living such an abandoned life.

"*Mortimer!* Do you want to bring the judgment upon Baby, too!"

Then she began to cry, but suddenly exclaimed:

"The doctor must have sent medicines!"

I said:

"Certainly. They are here. I was only waiting for you to give me a chance."

"Well do give them to me! Don't you know that every moment is precious now? But what was the use in sending medicines, when he *knows* that the disease is incurable?"

I said that while there was life there was hope.

"Hope! Mortimer, you know no more what you are talking about than the child unborn. If you would—. As I live, the directions say give one teaspoonful once an hour! Once an hour!—as if we had a whole year before us to save the child in! Mortimer, please hurry. Give the poor perishing thing a table-spoonful, and *try* to be quick!"

"Why, my dear, a table-spoonful might—"

"*Don't* drive me frantic!.....There, there, there, my precious, my own; it's nasty bitter stuff, but it's good for Nelly—good for Mother's precious darling; and it will make her well. There, there, there, put the little head on Mamma's breast and go to sleep, and pretty soon—Oh, I know she can't live till morning! Mortimer, a table-spoonful every half hour will—. Oh, the child needs belladonna too; I know she does—and aconite. Get them, Mortimer. Now do let me have my way. You know nothing about these things."

We now went to bed, placing the crib close to my wife's pillow. All this turmoil had worn upon me, and within two minutes I was something more than half asleep. Mrs. McWilliams roused me:

"Darling, is that register turned on?"

"No."

" I thought as much. Please turn it on at once. This room is cold."

I turned it on, and presently fell asleep again. I was aroused once more:

"Dearie, would you mind moving the crib to your side of the bed? It is nearer the register."

I moved it, but had a collision with the rug and woke up the child. I dozed off once more, while my wife quieted the sufferer. But in a little while these words came murmuring remotely through the fog of my drowsiness:

"Mortimer, if we only had some goose-grease—will you ring?"

I climbed dreamily out, and stepped on a cat, which responded with a protest and would have got a convincing kick for it if a chair had not got it instead.

"Now, Mortimer, why do you want to turn up the gas and wake up the child again?"

"Because I want to see how much I am hurt, Caroline."

"Well look at the chair, too—I have no doubt it is ruined. Poor cat, suppose you had—

"Now I am not going to suppose anything about the cat. It never would have occurred if Maria had been allowed to remain here and attend to these duties which are in her line and are not in mine."

"Now Mortimer, I should think you would be ashamed to make a remark like that. It is a pity if you cannot do the few little things I ask of you at such an awful time as this when our child—"

"There, there, I will do anything you want. But I can't raise anybody with this bell. They're all gone to bed. Where is the goose-grease?"

"On the mantel piece in the nursery. If you'll step there and speak to Maria—"

I fetched the goose-grease and went to sleep again: Once more I was called:

"Mortimer, I so hate to disturb you, but the room is still too cold for me to try to apply this stuff. Would you mind lighting the fire? It is all ready to touch a match to."

I dragged myself out and lit the fire, and then sat down disconsolate.

"Mortimer, don't sit there and catch your death of cold. Come to bed."

"As I was stepping in, she said:

"But wait a moment. Please give the child some more of the medicine."

Which I did. It was a medicine which made a child more or less lively; so my wife made use of its waking interval to strip it and grease it all over with the goose-oil. I was soon asleep once more, but once more I had to get up.

"Mortimer, I feel a draft. I feel it distinctly. There is nothing so bad for this disease as a draft. Please move the crib in front of the fire."

I did it; and collided with the rug again, which I threw in the fire. Mrs. Mc Williams sprang out of bed and rescued it and we had some words. I had another trifling interval of sleep, and then got up, by request, and constructed a flax-seed poul- tice. This was placed upon the child's breast and left there to do its healing work.

A wood fire is not a perma- nent thing. I got up every twenty minutes and renewed ours, and this gave Mrs. Mc Williams the op- portunity to shorten the times of giving the medicines by ten minutes, which was a great sat- isfaction to her. Now and then, between times, I reorganized the the flax-seed poultices, and applied sinapisms and other sorts of blisters where unoccupied places could be found upon the child. Well, toward morning the wood gave out and my wife wanted me to go down cellar and get some more. I said:

"My dear, it is a laborious job, and the child must be nearly warm enough, with her extra clothing. Now mightn't we put on another layer of poultices and—"

I did not finish, because I was interrupted. I lugged wood up from below for some little time, and then turned in and fell to snoring as only a man can whose strength is all gone and whose soul is worn out. Just at broad daylight I felt a grip on my shoulder that brought me to my senses suddenly.—My wife was glaring down upon me and gasping. As soon as she could command her tongue she said:

"It is all over! All over! The child's perspiring! What *shall* we do?

"Mercy, how you terrify me! *I* don't know what we ought to do. Maybe if we scraped her and put her in the draft again—"

"O, idiot! There is not a moment to lose! Go for the doctor. Go yourself. Tell him he *must* come, dead or alive."

I dragged that poor sick man from his bed and brought him. He looked at the child and said she was not dying. This was joy unspeakable to me, but it made my wife as mad as if he had offered her a personal affront. Then he said the child's cough was only caused by some trifling irritation or other in the throat. At this I thought my wife had a mind to show him the door.—Now the doctor said he would make the child cough harder and dislodge the trouble. So he gave her something that sent her into a spasm of coughing, and presently up came a little wood splinter or so.

"This child has no membranous croup," said he. "She has been chewing a bit of pine shingle or something of the kind, and got some little slivers in her throat. They won't do her any hurt."

"No," said I, "I can well believe that. Indeed the turpentine that is in them is very good for certain sorts of diseases that are peculiar to children. My wife will tell you so."

But she did not. She turned away in disdain and left the room; and since that time there is one episode in our life which we never refer to. Hence the tide of our days flows by in deep and untroubled serenity.

[Very few married men have such an experience as McWilliams's, and so the author of this book thought that maybe the novelty of it would give it a passing interest to the reader.]

MY FIRST LITERARY VENTURE.

I WAS a very smart child at the age of thirteen—an unusually smart child, I thought at the time. It was then that I did my first newspaper scribbling, and most unexpectedly to me it stirred up a fine sensation in the community. It did, indeed, and I was very proud of it, too. I was a printer's " devil," and a progressive and aspiring one. My uncle had me on his paper (the *Weekly Hanni-bal Journal*, two dollars a year in advance—five hundred subscribers, and they paid in cordwood, cabbages, and unmarketable turnips), and on a lucky summer's day he left town to be gone a week, and asked me if I thought I could edit one issue of the paper judiciously. Ah! didn't I want to try! Higgins was the editor on the rival paper. He had lately been jilted, and one night a friend found an open note on the poor fellow's bed, in which he stated that he could no longer endure life and had drowned himself in Bear Creek. The friend ran down there and discovered Higgins wading back to shore! He had concluded he wouldn't. The village was full of it for several days, but Higgins did not suspect it. I thought this was a fine opportunity. I wrote an elaborately wretched account of the whole matter, and then illustrated it with villainous cuts engraved on the bottoms of wooden type with a jack-knife—one of them a picture of Higgins wading out into the creek in his shirt, with a lantern, sounding the depth of the water with a walking-stick. I thought it was desperately funny, and was densely unconscious that there was any moral obliquity about such a publication. Being satisfied with this effort I looked around for other worlds to conquer, and it struck me that it would make good, interesting matter to charge the editor of a neighboring country

paper with a piece of gratuitous rascality and "see him squirm."

I did it, putting the article into the form of a parody on the Burial of "Sir John Moore"—and a pretty crude parody it was, too.

Then I lampooned two prominent citizens outrageously—not because they had done anything to deserve it, but merely because I thought it was my duty to make the paper lively.

Next I gently touched up the newest stranger—the lion of the day, the gorgeous journeyman tailor from Quincy. He was a simpering coxcomb of the first water, and the "loudest" dressed man in the State. He was an inveterate woman-killer. Every week he wrote lushy "poetry" for the "Journal," about his newest conquest. His rhymes for my week were headed, "To MARY IN H—— L," meaning to Mary in Hannibal, of course. But while setting up the piece I was suddenly riven from head to heel by what I regarded as a perfect thunderbolt of humor, and I compressed it into a snappy foot-note at the bottom—thus :—"We will let this thing pass, just this once; but we wish Mr. J. Gordon Runnels to understand distinctly that we have a character to sustain, and from this time forth when he wants to commune with his friends in h—l, he must select some other medium than the columns of this journal!"

The paper came out, and I never knew any little thing attract so much attention as those playful trifles of mine.

For once the Hannibal Journal was in demand—a novelty it had not experienced before. The whole town was stirred. Higgins dropped in with a double-barrelled shot-gun early in the forenoon. When he found that it was an infant (as he called me) that had done him the damage, he simply pulled my ears and went away; but he threw up his situation that night and left town for good. The tailor came with his goose and a pair of shears; but he despised me too, and departed for the South that night. The two lampooned citizens came with threats of libel, and went away incensed at my insignificance. The country editor pranced in with a warwhoop next day, suffering for blood to drink; but he ended by forgiving me cordially and inviting me down to the drug store to wash away all animosity in a friendly bumper of " Fahnestock's Vermifuge." It was his little joke. My uncle was very angry when he got back—unreasonably so, I thought, considering what an impetus I had given the paper, and considering also that gratitude for his preservation ought to have been uppermost in his mind, inasmuch as by his delay he had so wonderfully escaped dissection, tomahawking, libel, and getting his head shot off. But he softened when he looked at the accounts and saw that I had actually booked the unparalleled number of thirty-three new subscribers, and had the vegetables to show for it, cordwood, cabbage, beans, and unsalable turnips enough to run the family for two years!

How the Author was Sold in Newark.

IT is seldom pleasant to tell on one's self, but sometimes it is a sort of relief to a man to make a confession. I wish to unburden my mind now, and yet I almost believe that I am moved to do it more because I long to bring censure upon another man than because I desire to pour balm upon my wounded heart. (I don't know what balm is, but I believe it is the correct expression to use in this connection—never having seen any balm.) You may remember that I lectured in Newark lately for the young gentlemen of the ——— Society? I did at any rate. During the afternoon of that day I was talking with one of the young gentlemen just referred to, and he said he had an uncle who, from some cause or other, seemed to have grown permanently bereft of all emotion. And with tears in his eyes, this young man said, "Oh, if I could only see him laugh once more! Oh, if I could only see him weep!" I was touched. I could never withstand distress.

I said: "Bring him to my lecture. I'll start him for you."

"Oh, if you could but do it! If you could but do it, all our family would bless you for evermore—for he is so very dear to us. Oh, my benefactor, can you make him laugh? can you bring soothing tears to those parched orbs?"

I was profoundly moved. I said: "My son, bring the old party round. I have got some jokes in that lecture that will make him laugh if there is any laugh in him; and if they miss fire, I have got some others that will make him cry or kill him, one or the other." Then the young man blessed me, and wept on my neck, and went after his uncle. He placed him in full view, in the second row of benches that night, and I began on him. I tried him with mild jokes, then with severe ones; I dosed him with bad jokes and riddled him with good ones; I fired old stale jokes into him, and peppered him fore and aft with red-hot new ones; I warmed up to my work, and assaulted him on the right and left, in front and behind; I fumed and sweated and charged and ranted till I was hoarse and sick, and frantic and furious; but I never moved him once—I never started a smile or a tear! Never a ghost of a smile, and never a suspicion of moisture! I was astounded. I closed the lecture at last with one despairing shriek—with one wild burst of humor, and hurled a joke of supernatural atrocity full at him!

Then I sat down bewildered and exhausted.

The president of the society came up and bathed my head with cold water, and said: "What made you carry on so towards the last?"

I said: "I was trying to make that confounded old fool laugh, in the second row."

And he said: "Well, you were wasting your time, because he is deaf and dumb, and as blind as a badger!"

Now, was that any way for that old man's nephew to impose on a stranger and orphan like me? I ask you as a man and brother, if that was any way for him to do?

7

THE OFFICE BORE.

H E arrives just as regularly as the clock strikes nine in the morning. And so he even beats the editor sometimes, and the porter must leave his work and climb two or three pair of stairs to unlock the "Sanctum" door and let him in. He lights one of the office pipes—not reflecting, perhaps, that the editor may be one of those "stuck-up" people who would as soon have a stranger defile his tooth-

brush as his pipe-stem. Then he begins to loll—for a person who can consent to loaf his useless life away in ignominious indolence has not the energy to sit up straight. He stretches full length on the sofa awhile; then draws up to half-length; then gets into a chair, hangs his head back and his arms abroad, and stretches his legs till the rims of his boot-heels rest upon the floor; by and by sits up and leans forward, with one leg or both over the arm of the chair. But it is still observable that with all his changes of position, he never assumes the upright or a fraudful affectation of dignity. From time to time he yawns, and stretches, and scratches himself with a tranquil, mangy enjoyment, and now and then he grunts a kind of stuffy, overfed grunt, which is full of animal contentment. At rare and long intervals, however, he sighs a sigh that is the eloquent expression of a secret confession, to wit: "I am useless and a nuisance, a cumberer of the earth." The bore and his comrades—for there are usually from two to four on hand, day and night—mix into the conversation when men come in to see the editors for a moment on business; they hold noisy talks among themselves about politics in particular, and all other subjects in general —even warming up, after a fashion, sometimes, and seeming to take almost a real interest in what they are discussing. They ruthlessly call an editor from his work with such a remark as: "Did you see this, Smith, in the 'Gazette?'" and proceed to read the paragraph while the sufferer reins in his impatient pen and listens: they often loll and sprawl round the office hour after hour, swapping anecdotes, and relating personal experiences to each other— hairbreadth escapes, social encounters with distinguished men, election reminiscences, sketches of odd characters, etc. And through all those hours they never seem to comprehend that they are robbing the editors of their time, and the public of journalistic excellence in next day's paper. At other times they drowse, or dreamily pore over exchanges, or droop limp and pensive over the chair-arms for an hour. Even this solemn silence is small respite to the editor, for the next uncomfortable thing to having people look over his shoulders, perhaps, is to have them sit by in silence and listen to the scratching of his pen. If a body desires to talk private business with one of the editors, he must call him outside, for no hint milder than blasting powder or nitro-glycerine would be likely to move the bores out of listening distance. To have to sit and endure the presence of a bore day after day; to feel your cheerful spirits begin to sink as his footstep sounds on the stair, and utterly vanish away as his tiresome form

enters the door; to suffer through his anecdotes and die slowly to his reminiscences; to feel always the fetters of his clogging presence; to long hopelessly for
one single day's privacy; to note with a shudder, by and by, that to contemplate
his funeral in fancy has ceased to soothe, to imagine him undergoing in strict
and fearful detail the tortures of the ancient Inquisition has lost its power to
satisfy the heart, and that even to wish him millions and millions and millions
of miles in Tophet is able to bring only a fitful gleam of joy; to have to endure
all this, day after day, and week after week, and month after month, is an affliction that transcends any other that men suffer. Physical pain is pastime to it,
and hanging a pleasure excursion.

JOHNNY GREER.

"THE church was densely crowded that lovely summer Sabbath," said
the Sunday-school superintendent, "and all, as their eyes rested upon
the small coffin, seemed impressed by the poor black boy's fate.
Above the stillness the pastor's voice rose, and chained the interest of every ear
as he told, with many an envied compliment, how that the brave, noble, daring
little Johnny Greer, when he saw the drowned body sweeping down toward the
deep part of the river whence the agonized parents never could have recovered
it in this world, gallantly sprang into the stream, and at the risk of his life
towed the corpse to shore, and held it fast till help came and secured it. Johnny
Greer was sitting just in front of me. A ragged street boy, with eager eye,
turned upon him instantly, and said in a hoarse whisper—

"'No; but did you, though?'

"'Yes.'

"'Towed the carkiss ashore and saved it yo'self?'

"'Yes.'

"'Cracky! What did they give you?'

"'Nothing.'

"'W-h-a-t! [with intense disgust.] D'you know what I'd a done? I'd a
anchored him out in the stream, and said, *Five dollars, gents, or you carn't have yo'
nigger.*'"

HE FACTS IN THE CASE OF THE GREAT BEEF CONTRACT.

In as few words as possible I wish to lay before the nation what share, howsoever small, I have had in this matter—this matter which has so exercised the public mind, engendered so much ill-feeling, and so filled the newspapers of both continents with distorted statements and extravagant comments.

The origin of this distressful thing was this—and I assert here that every fact in the following *résumé* can be amply proved by the official records of the General Government:—

John Wilson Mackenzie, of Rotterdam, Chemung county, New Jersey, deceased, contracted with the General Government, on or about the 10th day of October, 1861, to furnish to General Sherman the sum total of thirty barrels of beef.

Very well.

He started after Sherman with the beef, but when he got to Washington Sherman had gone to Manassas; so he took the beef and followed him there, but arrived too late; he followed him to Nashville, and from Nashville to Chattanooga, and from Chattanooga to Atlanta—but he never could overtake him. At Atlanta he took a fresh start and followed him clear through his march to the sea. He arrived too late again by a few days; but hearing that Sherman was going out in the *Quaker City* excursion to the Holy Land, he took shipping for B e i r u t, calculating to head off the other vessel. When he arrived in Jerusalem with his beef, he learned that Sherman had not sailed in the *Quaker City*, but had gone to the Plains to fight the Indians. He returned to America, and started for the Rocky Mountains. After sixty-eight days of arduous travel on the Plains, and when he had got within four miles of Sherman's head-quarters, he was tomahawked and scalped, and the Indians got the beef.

They got all of it but one barrel. Sherman's army captured that, and so even in death, the bold navigator partly fulfilled his contract. In his will, which he had kept like a journal, he bequeathed the contract to his son Bartholomew W. Bartholomew W. made out the following bill, and then died:—

THE UNITED STATES
      In account with JOHN WILSON MACKENSIE, of New Jersey, deceased.... Dr.
To thirty barrels of beef for General Sherman, at $100......................$3,000
To traveling expenses and transportation................................14,000
                          Total...........$17,000
              Rec'd Pay't.

He died then; but he left the contract to Wm. J. Martin, who tried to collect it, but died before he got through. *He* left it to Barker J. Allen, and he tried to collect it also. He did not survive. Barker J. Allen left it to Anson G. Rogers, who attempted to collect it, and got along as far as the Ninth Auditor's Office, when Death the great Leveller, came all unsummoned, and foreclosed on *him* also. He left the bill to a relative of his in Connecticut, Vengeance Hopkins by name, who lasted four weeks and two days, and made the best time on record, coming within one of reaching the Twelfth Auditor. In his will he gave the contract bill to his uncle, by the name of O-be-joyful Johnson. It was too undermining for Joyful. His last words were: "Weep not for me—*I* am willing to go."

And so he was, poor soul. Seven people inherited the contract after that; but they all died. So it came into my hands at last. It fell to me through a relative by the name of Hubbard—Bethlehem Hubbard, of Indiana. He had had a grudge against me for a long time; but in his last moments he sent for me, and forgave me everything, and, weeping gave me the beef contract. This ends the history of it up to the time that I succeeded to the property. I will now endeavor to set myself straight before the nation in everything that concerns my share in the matter. I took this beef contract, and the bill for mileage and transportation, to the President of the United States.

He said, "Well, sir, what can I do for you?"

I said, "Sire, on or about the 10th day of October, 1861, John Wilson Mackenzie, of Rotterdam, Chemung county, New Jersey, deceased, contracted with the General Government to furnish to General Sherman the sum total of thirty barrels of beef——"

He stopped me there, and dismissed me from his presence—kindly, but firmly. The next day I called on the Secretary of State.

He said, " Well, sir ? "

I said, " Your Royal Highness: on or about the 10th day of October, 1861, John Wilson Mackenzie, of Rotterdam, Chemung county, New Jersey, deceased, contracted with the General Government to furnish to General Sherman the sum total of thirty barrels of beef——"

" That will do, sir—that will do; this office has nothing to do with contracts for beef."

" I was bowed out. I thought the matter all over, and finally, the following day, I visited the Secretary of the Navy, who said, " Speak quickly, sir; do not keep me waiting."

I said, " Your Royal Highness, on or about the 10th day of October, 1861, John Wilson Mackenzie, of Rotterdam, Chemung county, New Jersey, deceased, contracted with the General Government to furnish to General Sherman the sum total of thirty barrels of beef——"

Well, it was as far as I could get. *He* had nothing to do with beef contracts for General Sherman either. I began to think it was a curious kind of a Government. It looks somewhat as if they wanted to get out of paying for that beef. The following day I went to the Secretary of the Interior.

I said, " Your Imperial Highness, on or about the 10th day of October—"

" That is sufficient, sir. I have heard of you before. Go, take your infamous beef contract out of this establishment. The Interior Department has nothing whatever to do with subsistence for the army."

I went away. But I was exasperated now. I said I would haunt them; I would infest every department of this iniquitous Government till that contract business was settled. I would collect that bill, or fall, as fell my predecessors, trying. I assailed the Postmaster-General; I besieged the Agricultural Department; I waylaid the Speaker of the House of Representatives. *They* had nothing to do with army contracts for beef. I moved upon the Commissioner of the Patent Office.

I said, " Your August Excellency, on or about——"

" Perdition ! have you got *here* with your incendiary beef contract, at last ? We have *nothing* to do with beef contracts for the army, my dear sir."

" Oh, that is all very well—but *somebody* has got to pay for that beef. It has got to be paid *now*, too, or I'll confiscate this old Patent Office and everything in it."

" But, my dear sir——"

" It don't make any difference, sir. The Patent Office is liable for that beef, I reckon ; and, liable or not liable, the Patent Office has got to pay for it."

Never mind the details. It ended in a fight. The Patent Office won. But I found out something to my advantage. I was told that the Treasury Department was the proper place for me to go to. I went there. I waited two hours and a half, and then I was admitted to the First Lord of the Treasury.

I said, " Most noble, grave, and reverend Signor, on or about the 10th day of October, 1861, John Wilson Macken——"

" That is sufficient, sir. I have heard of you. Go to the First Auditor of the Treasury."

I did so. He sent me to the Second Auditor. The Second Auditor sent me to the Third, and the Third sent me to the First Comptroller of the Corn-Beef Division. This began to look like business. He examined his books and all his loose papers, but found no minute of the beef contract. I went to the Second Comptroller of the Corn-Beef Division. He examined his books and his loose papers, but with no success. I was encouraged. During that week I got as far as the Sixth Comptroller in that division ; the next week I got through the Claims Department ; the third week I began and completed the Mislaid Contracts Department, and got a foothold in the Dead Reckoning Department. I finished that in three days. There was only one place left for it now. I laid siege to the Commissioner of Odds and Ends. To his clerk, rather—he was not there himself. There were sixteen beautiful young ladies in the room, writing in books, and there were seven well-favored young clerks showing them how. The young women smiled up over their shoulders, and the clerks smiled back at them, and all went merry as a marriage bell. Two or three clerks that were reading the newspapers looked at me rather hard, but went on reading, and nobody said anything. However, I had been used to this kind of alacrity from Fourth-Assistant-Junior Clerks all through my eventful career, from the very day I entered the first office of the Corn-Beef Bureau clear till I passed out of the last one in the Dead Reckoning Division. I had got so accomplished by this time that I could stand on one foot from the moment I entered an office till a clerk spoke to me, without changing more than two, or maybe three times.

So I stood there till I had changed four different times. Then I said to one of the clerks who was reading—

"Illustrious Vagrant, where is the Grand Turk?"

"What do you mean, sir? whom do you mean? If you mean the Chief of the Bureau, he is out."

"Will he visit the harem to-day?"

The young man glared upon me awhile, and then went on reading his paper. But I knew the ways of those clerks. I knew I was safe if he got through before another New York mail arrived. He only had two more papers left. After awhile he finished them, and then he yawned and asked me what I wanted.

"Renowned and honored Imbecile: On or about——"

"You are the beef contract man. Give me your papers."

He took them, and for a long time he ransacked his odds and ends. Finally he found the North-West Passage, as *I* regarded it—he found the long-lost record of that beef contract—he found the rock upon which so many of my ancestors had split before they ever got to it. I was deeply moved. And yet I rejoiced—for I had survived. I said with emotion, "Give it me. The Government will settle now." He waved me back, and said there was something yet to be done first.

"Where is this John Wilson Mackenzie?" said he.

"Dead."

"When did he die?"

"He didn't die at all—he was killed."

"How?"

"Tomahawked."

"Who tomahawked him?"

" Why, an Indian, of course. You didn't suppose it was the superintendent of a Sunday-school, did you? "

" No. An Indian, was it? "

" The same."

" Name of the Indian? "

" His name? *I* don't know his name."

" *Must* have his name. Who saw the tomahawking done? "

" I don't know."

" You were not present yourself, then? "

" Which you can see by my hair. I was absent."

" Then how do you know that Mackenzie is dead? "

" Because he certainly died at that time, and I have every reason to believe that he has been dead ever since. I *know* he has, in fact."

" We must have proofs. Have you got the Indian? "

" Of course not."

" Well, you must get him. Have you got the tomahawk? "

" I never thought of such a thing."

" You must get the tomahawk. You must produce the Indian and the tomahawk. If Mackenzie's death can be proven by these, you can then go before the commission appointed to audit claims with some show of getting your bill under such headway that your children may possibly live to receive the money and enjoy it. But that man's death *must* be proven. However, I may as well tell you that the Government will never pay that transportation and those traveling expenses of the lamented Mackenzie. It *may* possibly pay for the barrel of beef that Sherman's soldiers captured, if you can get a relief bill through Congress making an appropriation for that purpose; but it will not pay for the twenty-nine barrels the Indians ate."

" Then there is only a hundred dollars due me, and *that* isn't certain! After all Mackenzie's travels in Europe, Asia, and America with that beef; after all his trials and tribulations and transportation; after the slaughter of all those innocents that tried to collect that bill! Young man, why didn't the First Comptroller of the Corn-Beef Division tell me this."

" He didn't know anything about the genuineness of your claim."

" Why didn't the Second tell me ? why didn't the Third ? why didn't all those divisions and departments tell me ? "

" None of them knew. We do things by routine here. You have followed the routine and found out what you wanted to know. It is the best way. It is the only way. It is very regular, and very slow, but it is very certain."

" Yes, certain death. It has been, to the most of our tribe. I begin to feel that I, too, am called. Young man, you love the bright creature yonder with the gentle blue eyes and the steel pens behind her ears—I see it in your soft glances ; you wish to marry her—but you are poor. Here, hold out your hand —here is the beef contract ; go, take her and be happy ! Heaven bless you, my children ! "

This is all I know about the great beef contract, that has created so much talk in the community. The clerk to whom I bequeathed it died. I know nothing further about the contract, or any one connected with it. I only know that if a man lives long enough he can trace a thing through the Circumlocution Office of Washington, and find out, after much labor and trouble and delay, that which he could have found out on the first day if the business of the Circumlocution Office were as ingeniously systematized as it would be if it were a great private mercantile institution.

The Case of Geo. Fisher.

THE CASE OF GEORGE FISHER.*

THIS is history. It is not a wild extravaganza, like "John Williamson Mackenzie's Great Beef Contract," but is a plain statement of facts and circumstances with which the Congress of the United States has interested itself from time to time during the long period of half a century.

I will not call this matter of George Fisher's a great deathless and unrelenting swindle upon the Government and people of the United States—for

* Some years ago, when this was first published, few people believed it, but considered it a mere extravaganza. In these latter days it seems hard to realize that there was ever a time when the

109

it has never been so decided, and I hold that it is a grave and solemn wrong for a writer to cast slurs or call names when such is the case—but will simply present the evidence and let the reader deduce his own verdict. Then we shall do nobody injustice, and our consciences shall be clear.

On or about the 1st day of September 1813, the Creek war being then in progress in Florida, the crops, herds, and houses of Mr. George Fisher, a citizen, were destroyed, either by the Indians or by the United States troops in pursuit of them. By the terms of the law, if the *Indians* destroyed the property, there was no relief for Fisher; but if the *troops* destroyed it, the Government of the United States was debtor to Fisher for the amount involved.

George Fisher must have considered that the *Indians* destroyed the property, because, although he lived several years afterward, he does not appear to have ever made any claim upon the Government.

In the course of time Fisher died, and his widow married again. And by and by, nearly twenty years after that dimly-remembered raid upon Fisher's cornfields, *the widow Fisher's new husband* petitioned Congress for pay for the property, and backed up the petition with many depositions and affidavits which purported to prove that the troops, and not the Indians, destroyed the property; that the troops, for some inscrutable reason, deliberately burned down "houses" (or cabins) valued at $600, the same belonging to a peaceable private citizen, and also destroyed various other property belonging to the same citizen. But Congress declined to believe that the troops were such idiots (after overtaking and scattering a band of Indians proved to have been found destroying Fisher's property) as to calmly continue the work of destruction themselves, and make a complete job of what the Indians had only commenced. So Congress denied the petition of the heirs of George Fisher in 1832, and did not pay them a cent.

We hear no more from them officially until 1848, sixteen years after their first attempt on the Treasury, and a full generation after the death of the man whose

_____

robbing of our government was a novelty. The very man who showed me where to find the documents for this case was at that very time spending hundreds of thousands of dollars in Washington for a mail steamship concern, in the effort to procure a subsidy for the company—a fact which was a long time in coming to the surface, but leaked out at last and underwent Congressional investigation.

fields were destroyed. The new generation of Fisher heirs then came forward and put in a bill for damages. The Second Auditor awarded them $8,873, being half the damage sustained by Fisher. The Auditor said the testimony showed that at least half the destruction was done by the Indians "*before the troops started in pursuit,*" and of course the Government was not responsible for that half.

2. That was in April, 1848. In December 1848, the heirs of George Fisher, deceased, came forward and pleaded for a "revision" of their bill of damages. The revision was made, but nothing new could be found in their favor except an error of $100 in the former calculation. However, in order to keep up the spirits of the Fisher family, the Auditor concluded to go back and allow *interest* from the date of the first petition (1832) to the date when the bill of damages was awarded. This sent the Fishers home happy with sixteen years' interest on $8,873—the same amounting to $8,997.94. Total, $17,870.94.

3. For an entire year the suffering Fisher family remained quiet—even satisfied, after a fashion. Then they swooped down upon Government with their wrongs once more. That old patriot, Attorney-General Toucey, burrowed through the musty papers of the Fishers and discovered one more chance for the desolate orphans—interest on that original award of $8,873 from date of destruction of the property (1813) up to 1832! Result, $10,004.89 for the indigent Fishers. So now we have:—First, $8,873 damages; second, interest on it from 1832 to 1848, $8,997.94; third, interest on it dated back to 1813, $10,004.89. Total, $27,875.83! What better investment for a great-grandchild than to get the Indians to burn a cornfield for him sixty or seventy years before his birth, and plausibly lay it on lunatic United States troops?

4. Strange as it may seem, the Fishers let Congress alone for five years—or, what is perhaps more likely, failed to make themselves heard by Congress for that length of time. But at last in 1854, they got a hearing. They persuaded Congress to pass an act requiring the Auditor to re-examine their case. But this time they stumbled upon the misfortune of an honest Secretary of the Treasury (Mr. James Guthrie), and he spoiled everything. He said in very plain language that the Fishers were not only not entitled to another cent, but that those children of many sorrows and acquainted with grief *had been paid too much already.*

5. Therefore another interval of rest and silence ensued—an interval which lasted four years—viz., till 1858. The "right man in the right place" was then Secretary of War—John B. Floyd, of peculiar renown! Here was a master intellect; here was the very man to succor the suffering heirs of dead and forgotten Fisher. They came up from Florida with a rush—a great tidal wave of Fishers freighted with the same old musty documents about the same immortal cornfields of their ancestor. They straightway got an Act passed transferring the Fisher matter from the dull Auditor to the ingenious Floyd. What did Floyd do? He said, "IT WAS PROVED *that the Indians destroyed everything they could before the troops entered in pursuit.*" He considered, therefore, that what they destroyed must have consisted of "*the houses with all their contents, and the liquor*" (the most trifling part of the destruction, and set down at only $3200 all told), and that the Government troops then drove them off and calmly proceeded to destroy—

Two hundred and twenty acres of corn in the field, thirty-five acres of wheat, and nine hundred and eighty-six head of live stock! [What a singularly intelligent army we had in those days, according to Mr. Floyd—though not according to the Congress of 1832.]

So Mr. Floyd decided that the Government was not responsible for that $3200 worth of rubbish which the Indians destroyed, but was responsible for the property destroyed by the troops—which property consisted of (I quote from the printed United States Senate document)—

	DOLLARS.
Corn at Bassett's Creek	3,000
Cattle	5,000
Stock hogs	1.050
Drove hogs	1,204
Wheat	350
Hides	4,000
Corn on the Alabama River	3,500
Total	18,104

That sum, in his report, Mr. Floyd calls the "*full value* of the property destroyed by the troops." He allows that sum to the starving Fishers, TOGETHER WITH

INTEREST FROM 1813. From this new sum total the amounts already paid to the Fishers were deducted, and then the cheerful remainder (a fraction under *forty thousand dollars*) was handed to them, and again they retired to Florida in a condition of temporary tranquility. Their ancestor's farm had now yielded them, altogether, nearly *sixty-seven thousand dollars* in cash.

6. Does the reader suppose that that was the end of it? Does he suppose those diffident Fishers were satisfied? Let the evidence show. The Fishers were quiet just two years. Then they came swarming up out of the fertile swamps of Florida with their same old documents, and besieged Congress once more. Congress

capitulated on the first of June, 1860, and instructed Mr. Floyd to overhaul those papers again and pay that bill. A Treasury clerk was ordered to go through those papers and report to Mr. Floyd what amount was still due the emaciated Fishers. This clerk (I can produce him whenever he is wanted) discovered what was apparently a glaring and recent forgery in the papers, whereby a witness's testimony as

8

to the price of corn in Florida in 1813 was made to name double the amount which that witness had originally specified as the price! The clerk not only called his superior's attention to this thing, but in making up his brief of the case called particular attention to it in writing. That part of the brief *never got before Congress,* nor has Congress ever yet had a hint of a forgery existing among the Fisher papers. Nevertheless, on the basis of the double prices (and totally ignoring the clerk's assertion that the figures were manifestly and unquestionably a recent forgery), Mr. Floyd remarks in his new report that "the testimony, *particularly in regard to the corn crops* DEMANDS A MUCH HIGHER ALLOWANCE than any *heretofore* made by the Auditor or myself." So he estimates the crop at *sixty bushels* to the acre (double what Florida acres produce), and then virtuously allows pay for only half the crop, *but* allows *two dollars and a half* a bushel for that half, when there are rusty old books and documents in the Congressional library to show just what the Fisher testimony showed before the forgery—viz., that in the fall of 1813 corn was only worth from $1.25 to $1.50 a bushel. Having accomplished this, what does Mr. Floyd do next? Mr. Floyd ("with an earnest desire to execute truly the legislative will," as he piously remarks) goes to work and makes out an entirely new bill of Fisher damages, and in this new bill he placidly *ignores the Indians* altogether— puts no particle of the destruction of the Fisher property upon them, but, even repenting him of charging them with burning the cabins and drinking the whisky and breaking the crockery, lays the *entire* damage at the door of the imbecile United States troops, down to the very last item! And not only that, but uses the forgery to double the loss of corn at "Bassett's Creek," and uses it again to absolutely *treble* the loss of corn on the "Alabama River." This new and ably conceived and executed bill of Mr. Floyd's figures up as follows (I copy again from the printed U. S. Senate document) :—

The United States in account with the legal representatives of George Fisher, deceased.

		Dol. C.
1813.—To 550 head of cattle, at 10 dollars	. . .	5,500 00
To 86 head of drove hogs		1,204 00
To 350 head of stock hogs		1,750 00
To 100 ACRES OF CORN ON BASSETT'S CREEK . . .		6,000 00
To 8 barrels of whisky		350 00

To 2 barrels of brandy	280 00
To 1 barrel of rum	70 00
To dry goods and merchandise in store	1,100 00
To 35 acres of wheat	350 00
To 2,000 hides	4,000 00
To furs and hats in store	600 00
To crockery ware in store	100 00
To smiths' and carpenters' tools	250 00
To houses burned and destroyed	600 00
To 4 dozen bottles of wine	48 00
1814.—To 120 acres of corn on Alabama River	9,500 00
To crops of peas, fodder, etc.	3,250 00
Total	34,952 00
To interest on $22,202, from July 1813 to November 1860, 47 years and 4 months	63,053 68
To interest on $12,750, from September 1814 to November 1860, 46 years and 2 months	35,317 50
Total	133,323 18

He puts everything in this time. He does not even allow that the Indians destroyed the crockery or drank the four dozen bottles of (currant) wine. When it came to supernatural comprehensiveness in "gobbling," John B. Floyd was without his equal, in his own or any other generation. Subtracting from the above total the $67,000 already paid to George Fisher's implacable heirs, Mr. Floyd announced that the Government was still indebted to them in the sum of *sixty-six thousand five hundred and nineteen dollars and eighty-five cents,* "which," Mr. Floyd complacently remarks, "will be paid, accordingly, to the administrator of the estate of George Fisher, deceased, or to his attorney in fact."

But, sadly enough for the destitute orphans, a new President came in just at this time, Buchanan and Floyd went out, and they never got their money. The first thing Congress did in 1861 was to rescind the resolution of June 1, 1870, under which Mr. Floyd had been ciphering. Then Floyd (and doubtless the heirs of George Fisher likewise) had to give up financial business for a while, and go into the Confederate army and serve their country.

Were the heirs of George Fisher killed? No. They are back now at this very time (July 1870), beseeching Congress through that blushing and diffident creature, Garrett Davis, to commence making payments again on their interminable and insatiable bill of damages for corn and whisky destroyed by a gang of irresponsible Indians, so long ago that even government red-tape has failed to keep consistent and intelligent track of it.

Now, the above are facts. They are history. Any one who doubts it can send to the Senate Document Department of the Capitol for H. R. Ex. Doc. No. 21, 36th Congress, 2nd Session, and for S. Ex. Doc. No. 106, 41st. Congress 2nd Session, and satisfy himself. The whole case is set forth in the first volume of the Court of Claims Reports.

It is my belief that as long as the continent of America holds together, the heirs of George Fisher, deceased, will still make pilgrimages to Washington from the swamps of Florida, to plead for just a little more cash on their bill of damages (even when they received the last of that sixty-seven thousand dollars, they said it was only *one-fourth* what the Government owed them on that fruitful corn-field), and as long as they choose to come, they will find Garrett Davises to drag their vampire schemes before Congress. This is not the only hereditary fraud (if fraud it is—which I have before repeatedly remarked is not proven) that is being quietly handed down from generation to generation of fathers and sons, through the persecuted Treasury of the United States.

DISGRACEFUL PERSECUTION OF A BOY.

IN San Francisco, the other day, "A well-dressed boy, on his way to Sunday-school, was arrested and thrown into the city prison for stoning Chinamen." What a commentary is this upon human justice! What sad prominence it gives to our human disposition to tyrannize over the weak! San Francisco has little right to take credit to herself for her treatment of this poor boy. What had the child's education been? How should he suppose it was wrong to stone a Chinamen? Before we side against him, along with outraged San Francisco, let us give him a chance—let us hear the testimony for the defence.

He was a "well-dressed" boy, and a Sunday-school scholar, and therefore, the chances are that his parents were intelligent, well-to-do people, with just enough natural villainy in their composition to make them yearn after the daily papers, and enjoy them; and so this boy had opportunities to learn all through the week how to do right, as well as on Sunday.

It was in this way that he found out that the great commonwealth of California imposes an unlawful mining-tax upon John the foreigner, and allows Patrick the foreigner to dig gold for nothing—probably because the degraded Mongol is at no expense for whisky, and the refined Celt cannot exist without it.

It was in this way that he found out that a respectable number of the tax-gatherers—it would be unkind to say all of them—collect the tax twice, instead of once; and that, inasmuch as they do it solely to discourage Chinese immigration into the mines, it is a thing that is much applauded, and likewise regarded as being singularly facetious.

It was in this way that he found out that when a white man robs a sluice-box (by the term white man is meant Spaniards, Mexicans, Portuguese, Irish, Hondurans, Peruvians, Chileans, &c., &c.), they make him leave the camp; and when a Chinaman does that thing, they hang him.

It was in this way that he found out that in many districts of the vast Pacific coast, so strong is the wild, free love of justice in the hearts of the people, that whenever any secret and mysterious crime is committed, they say, "Let justice be done, though the heavens fall," and go straightway and swing a Chinaman.

It was in this way that he found out that by studying one half of each day's "local items," it would appear that the police of San Francisco were either asleep or dead, and by studying the other half it would seem that the reporters were gone mad with admiration of the energy, the virtue, the high effectiveness, and the dare-devil intrepidity of that very police—making exultant mention of how "the Argus-eyed officer So-and-so," captured a wretched knave of a Chinaman who was stealing chickens, and brought him gloriously to the city prison; and how "the gallant officer Such-and-such-a-one," quietly kept an eye on the movements of an "unsuspecting, almond-eyed son of Confucius" (your reporter is nothing if not facetious), following him around with that far-off look of vacancy and unconsciousness always so finely affected by that inscrutible being, the forty-dollar policeman, during a waking interval, and captured him at last in the very act of placing his hands in a suspicious manner upon a paper of tacks, left by the owner in an exposed situation; and how one officer performed this prodigious thing, and another officer that, and another the other—and pretty 'much every one of these performances having for a dazzling central incident a Chinaman guilty of a shilling's worth of crime, an unfortunate, whose misdemeanor must be hurraed into something enormous in order to keep the public from noticing how many really important rascals went uncaptured in the meantime, and how overrated those glorified policemen actually are.

It was in this way that the boy found out that the Legislature, being aware that the Constitution has made America an asylum for the poor and the oppressed of all nations, and that, therefore, the poor and oppressed who fly to our shelter must not be charged a disabling admission fee, made a law that every Chinman, upon landing, must be *vaccinated* upon the wharf, and pay to the State's appointed officer *ten dollars* for the service, when there are plenty of doctors in San Francisco who would be glad enough to do it for him for fifty cents.

It was in this way that the boy found out that a Chinaman had no rights that any man was bound to respect; that he had no sorrows that any man was bound to pity; that neither his life nor his liberty was worth the purchase of a penny when a white man needed a scapegoat; that nobody loved Chinamen, nobody befriended them, nobody spared them suffering when it was convenient to inflict it; everybody, individuals, communities, the majesty of the State itself, joined in hating, abusing, and persecuting these humble strangers.

And, therefore, what *could* have been more natural than for this sunny-hearted boy, tripping along to Sunday-school, with his mind teeming with freshly-learned incentives to high and virtuous action, to say to himself—

"Ah, there goes a Chinaman! God will not love me if I do not stone him."

And for this he was arrested and put in the city jail.

Everything conspired to teach him that it was a high and holy thing to stone a Chinaman, and yet he no sooner attempts to do his duty that he is punished for it—he, poor chap, who has been aware all his life that one of the principal recreations of the police, out toward the Gold Refinery, is to look on with tranquil enjoyment while the butchers of Brannan Street set their dogs on unoffending Chinamen, and make them flee for their lives. *

Keeping in mind the tuition in the humanities which the entire "Pacific coast" gives its youth, there is a very sublimity of incongruity in the virtuous flourish with which the good city fathers of San Francisco proclaim (as they

---

* I have many such memories in my mind, but am thinking just at present of one particular one, where the Brannan Street butchers set their dogs on a Chinaman who was quietly passing with a basket of clothes on his head ; and while the dogs mutilated his flesh, a butcher increased the hilarity of the occasion by knocking some of the Chinaman's teeth down his throat with half a brick. This incident sticks in my memory with a more malevolent tenacity, perhaps, on account of the fact that I was in the employ of a San Francisco journal at the time, and was not allowed to publish it because it might offend some of the peculiar element that subscribed for the paper.

have lately done) that " The police are positively ordered to arrest all boys, of every description and wherever found, who engage in assaulting Chinamen."

Still, let us be truly glad they have made the order, notwithstanding its inconsistency; and let us rest perfectly confident the police are glad, too. Because there is no personal peril in arresting boys, provided they be of the small kind, and the reporters will have to laud their performances just as loyally as ever, or go without items.

The new form for local items in San Francisco will now be:—"The ever vigilant and efficient officer So-and-so succeeded, yesterday afternoon, in arresting Master Tommy Jones, after a determined resistance," etc., etc., followed by the customary statistics and final hurrah, with its unconscious sarcasm: " We are happy in being able to state that this is the forty-seventh boy arrested by this gallant officer since the new ordinance went into effect. The most extraordinary activity prevails in the police department. Nothing like it has been seen since we can remember."

THE JUDGE'S "SPIRITED WOMAN."

"I WAS sitting here," said the judge, "in this old pulpit, holding court, and we were trying a big, wicked-looking Spanish desperado for killing the husband of a bright, pretty Mexican woman. It was a lazy summer day, and an awfully long one, and the witnesses were tedious. None of us took any interest in the trial except that nervous, uneasy devil of a Mexican woman—because you know how they love and how they hate, and this one had loved her husband with all her might, and now she had boiled it all down into hate, and stood here spitting it at that Spaniard with her eyes; and I tell you she would stir *me* up, too, with a little of her summer lightning, occasionally. Well, I had my coat off and my heels up, lolling and sweating, and smoking one of those cabbage cigars the San Francisco people used to think were good enough for us in those times; and the lawyers they all had their coats off, and were smoking and whittling, and the witnesses the same, and so was the prisoner. Well, the fact is, there warn't any interest in a murder trial then, because the fellow was always brought in "not guilty," the jury expecting him to do as much for them some time; and, although the evidence was straight and square against this Spaniard, we knew we could not convict him without seeming to be rather high-handed and sort of reflecting on every gentleman in the community; for there warn't any carriages and liveries then, and so the only 'style' there was, was to keep your private graveyard. But that woman seemed to have her heart set on hanging that Spaniard; and you'd ought to have seen how she would glare on him a minute, and then look up at me in her pleading way, and then turn and for the next five minutes search the jury's faces, and by and by drop her face in her hands for just a little while as if she was most ready to give up; but out she'd come again directly, and be as live and anxious as ever. But when the jury announced the verdict—Not Guilty, and I told the prisoner he was acquitted and free to go, that woman rose up till she appeared to be as tall and grand as a seventy-four-gun-ship, and says she—

" ' Judge, do I understand you to say that this man is not guilty, that murdered my husband without any cause before my own eyes and my little children's, and that all has been done to him that ever justice and the law can do ? "

" ' The same,' says I.

" And then what do you reckon she did ? Why, she turned on that smirking Spanish fool like a wild cat, and out with a ' navy ' and shot him dead in open court !"

" That *was* spirited, I am willing to admit."

" Wasn't it, though ? " said the judge admiringly. " I wouldn't have missed it for anything. I adjourned court right on the spot, and we put on our coats and went out and took up a collection for her and her cubs, and sent them over the mountains to their friends. Ah, she was a spirited wench ! "

INFORMATION WANTED.

"WASHINGTON, *December* 10, 1867.

"COULD you give me any information respecting such islands, if any, as the Government is going to purchase?"

It is an uncle of mine that wants to know. He is an industrious man and well-disposed, and wants to make a living in an honest, humble way, but more especially he wants to be quiet. He wishes to settle down, and be quiet and unostentatious. He has been to the new island St. Thomas, but he says he thinks things are unsettled there. He went there early with an *attaché* of the State department, who was sent down with money to pay for the island. My uncle had his money in the same

123

box, and so when they went ashore, getting a receipt, the sailors broke open the box and took all the money, not making any distinction between Government money, which was legitimate money to be stolen, and my uncle's, which was his own private property, and should have been respected. But he came home and got some more and went back. And then he took the fever. There are seven kinds of fever down there, you know; and, as his blood was out of order by reason of loss of sleep and general wear and tear of mind, he failed to cure the first fever, and then somehow he got the other six. He is not a kind of man that enjoys fevers, though he is well-meaning and always does what he thinks is right, and so he was a good deal annoyed when it appeared he was going to die.

But he worried through, and got well and started a farm. He fenced it in, and the next day that great storm came on and washed the most of it over to Gibralter, or around there somewhere. He only said, in his patient way, that it was gone, and he wouldn't bother about trying to find out where it went to, though it was his opinion it went to Gibralter.

Then he invested in a mountain, and started a farm up there, so as to be out of the way when the sea came ashore again. It was a good mountain, and a good farm, but it wasn't any use; an earthquake came the next night and shook it all down. It was all fragments, you know, and so mixed up with another man's property, that he could not tell which were his fragments without going to law; and he would not do that, because his main object in going to St. Thomas was to be quiet. All that he wanted was to settle down and be quiet.

He thought it all over, and finally he concluded to try the low ground again, especially as he wanted to start a brickyard this time. He bought a flat, and put out a hundred thousand bricks to dry preparatory to baking them. But luck appeared to be against him. A volcano shoved itself through there that night, and elevated his brickyard about two thousand feet in the air. It irritated him a good deal. He has been up there, and he says the bricks are all baked right enough, but he can't get them down. At first, he thought maybe the Government would get the bricks down for him, because since Government bought the island, it ought to protect the property where a man has invested in good faith; but all he wants is quiet, and so he is not going to apply for the subsidy he was thinking about.

He went back there last week in a couple of ships of war, to prospect around the coast for a safe place for a farm where he could be quiet; but a great " tidal wave " came, and hoisted both of the ships out into one of the interior counties, and he came near losing his life. So he has given up prospecting in a ship, and is discouraged.

Well, now, he don't know what to do. He has tried Alaska; but the bears kept after him so much, and kept him so much on the jump, as it were, that he had to leave the country. He could not be quiet there with those bears prancing after him all the time. That is how he came to go to the new island we have bought— St. Thomas. But he is getting to think St. Thomas is not quiet enough for a man of his turn of mind, and that is why he wishes me to find out if Government is likely to buy some more islands shortly. He has heard that Government is thinking about buying Porto Rico. If that is true, he wishes to try Porto Rico, if it is a quiet place. How is Porto Rico for his style of man ? Do you think the Government will buy it?

SOME LEARNED FABLES,
FOR GOOD OLD BOYS AND GIRLS.

IN THREE PARTS.

PART FIRST.

HOW THE ANIMALS OF THE WOOD SENT OUT A SCIENTIFIC EXPEDITION.

ONCE the creatures of the forest held a great convention and appointed a commission consisting of the most illustrious scientists among them to go forth, clear beyond the forest and out into the unknown and unexplored world, to verify the truth of the matters already taught in

their schools and colleges and also to make discoveries. It was the most imposing enterprise of the kind the nation had ever embarked in. True, the government had once sent Dr. Bull Frog, with a picked crew, to hunt for a north-westerly passage through the swamp to the right-hand corner of the wood, and had since sent out many expeditions to hunt for Dr. Bull Frog; but they never could find him, and so government finally gave him up and ennobled his mother to show its gratitude for the services her son had rendered to science. And once government sent Sir Grass Hopper to hunt for the sources of the rill that emptied into the swamp; and afterwards sent out many expeditions to hunt for Sir Grass, and at last they were successful—they found his body, but if he had discovered the sources meantime, he did not let on. So government acted handsomely by deceased, and many envied his funeral.

But these expeditions were trifles compared with the present one; for this one comprised among its servants the very greatest among the learned; and besides it was to go to the utterly unvisited regions believed to lie beyond the mighty forest —as we have remarked before. How the members were banqueted, and glorified, and talked about! Everywhere that one of them showed himself, straightway there was a crowd to gape and stare at him.

Finally they set off, and it was a sight to see the long procession of dry-land Tortoises heavily laden with savans, scientific instruments, Glow-Worms and Fire-Flies for signal-service, provisions, Ants and Tumble-Bugs to fetch and carry and delve, Spiders to carry the surveying chain and do·other engineering duty, and so forth and so on; and after the Tortoises came another long train of iron-clads— stately and spacious Mud Turtles for marine transportation service; and from every Tortoise and every Turtle flaunted a flaming gladiolus or other splendid banner; at the head of the column a great band of Bumble-Bees, Mosquitoes, Katy-Dids and Crickets discoursed martial music; and the entire train was under the escort and protection of twelve picked regiments of the Army Worm.

At the end of three weeks the expedition emerged from the forest and looked upon the great Unknown World. Their eyes were greeted with an impressive spectacle. A vast level plain stretched before them, watered by a sinuous stream; and beyond, there towered up against the sky a long and lofty barrier of some kind, they did not know what. The Tumble-Bug said he believed it was simply land tilted up on its edge, because he knew he could see trees on it. But Prof. Snail and the others said:

"You are hired to dig, sir—that is all. We need your muscle, not your brains. When we want your opinion on scientific matters, we will hasten to let you know. Your coolness, is intolerable, too—loafing about here meddling with august matters of learning, when the other laborers are pitching camp. Go along and help handle the baggage."

The Tumble-Bug turned on his heel uncrushed, unabashed, observing to himself, "If it isn't land tilted up, let me die the death of the unrighteous."

Professor Bull Frog, (nephew of the late explorer,) said he believed the ridge was the wall that enclosed the earth. He continued:

"Our fathers have left us much learning, but they had not traveled far, and so we may count this a noble new discovery. We are safe for renown, now, even though our labors began and ended with this single achievement. I wonder what this wall is built of? Can it be fungus? Fungus is an honorable good thing to build a wall of."

Professor Snail adjusted his field-glass and examined the rampart critically. Finally he said:

"The fact that it is not diaphanous, convinces me that it is a dense vapor formed by the calorification of ascending moisture dephlogisticated by refraction. A few endiometrical experiments would confirm this, but it is not necessary.—The thing is obvious."

So he shut up his glass and went into his shell to make a note of the discovery of the world's end, and the nature of it.

"Profound mind!" said Professor Angle-Worm to Professor Field-Mouse; "profound mind! nothing can long remain a mystery to that august brain."

Night drew on apace, the sentinel crickets were posted, the Glow Worm and Fire-Fly lamps were lighted, and the camp sank to silence and sleep. After breakfast in the morning, the expedition moved on. About noon a great avenue was reached, which had in it two endless parallel bars of some kind of hard black substance, raised the height of the tallest Bull Frog above the general level. The scientists climbed up on these and examined and tested them in various ways. They walked along them for a great distance, but found no end and no break in them. They could arrive at no decision. There was nothing in the records of science that mentioned anything of this kind. But at last the bald and venerable geographer, Professor Mud Turtle, a person who, born poor, and of a drudging low family, had, by his own native force raised himself to the headship of the geographers of his generation, said:

"My friends, we have indeed made a discovery here. We have found in a pal-

pable, compact and imperishable state what the wisest of our fathers always regarded as a mere thing of the imagination. Humble yourselves, my friends, for we stand in a majestic presence. These are parallels of latitude!"

Every heart was bowed, so awful, so sublime was the magnitude of the discovery. Many shed tears. The camp was pitched and the rest of the day given up to writing voluminous accounts of the marvel, and correcting astronomical tables to fit it. Toward midnight a demoniacal shriek was heard, then a clattering and rumbling noise, and the next instant a vast terrific eye shot by, with a long tail attached, and disappeared in the gloom, still uttering triumphant shrieks.

The poor camp laborers were stricken to the heart with fright, and stampeded for the high grass in a body. But not the scientists. They had no superstitions. They calmly proceeded to exchange theories. The ancient geographer's opinion was asked. He went into his shell and deliberated long and profoundly. When he came out at last, they all knew by his worshiping countenance that he brought light. Said he:

9

"Give thanks for this stupendous thing which we have been permitted to witness. —It is the Vernal Equinox!"

There were shoutings and great rejoicings.

"But," said the Angle-worm, uncoiling after reflection, "this is dead summer time."

"Very well," said the Turtle, "we are far from our region; the season differs with the difference of time between the two points."

"Ah, true. True enough. But it is night. How should the sun pass in the night?"

"In these distant regions he doubtless passes always in the night at this hour."

"Yes, doubtless that is true. But it being night, how is it that we could see him?"

"It is a great mystery. I grant that. But I am persuaded that the humidity of the atmosphere in these remote regions is such that particles of daylight adhere to the disk and it was by aid of these that we were enabled to see the sun in the dark."

This was deemed satisfactory, and due entry was made of the decision.

But about this moment those dreadful shriekings were heard again; again the rumbling and thundering came speeding up out of the night; and once more a flaming great eye flashed by and lost itself in gloom and distance.

The camp laborers gave themselves up for lost. The savants were sorely perplexed. Here was a marvel hard to account for. They thought and they talked, they talked and they thought.—Finally the learned and aged Lord Grand-Daddy-Longlegs, who had been sitting, in deep study, with his slender limbs crossed and his stemmy arms folded, said:

"Deliver your opinions, brethren, and then I will tell my thought—for I think I have solved this problem."

"So be it, good your lordship," piped the weak treble of the wrinkled and withered Professor Woodlouse, "for we shall hear from your lordship's lips naught but wisdom."—[Here the speaker threw in a mess of trite, threadbare, exasperating quotations from the ancient poets and philosophers, delivering them with unction in the sounding grandeurs of the original tongues, they being from the Mastodon, the Dodo, and other dead languages]. "Perhaps I ought not to presume to meddle with matters pertaining to astronomy at all, in such a presence as this, I who have made it the business of my life to delve only among the riches of the extinct languages and unearth the opulence of their ancient lore; but still, as unacquainted as I am with the noble science of astronomy, I beg with deference and humility to suggest that inasmuch as the last of these wonderful apparitions proceeded in exactly the opposite direction from that pursued by the first, which you decide to be the Vernal Equinox, and greatly resembled it in all particulars, is it not possible, nay certain, that this last is the *Autumnal* Equi——"

"O-o-o!" "O-o-o! go to bed! go to bed!" with annoyed derision from everybody. So the poor old Woodlouse retreated out of sight, consumed with shame.

Further discussion followed, and then the united voice of the commission begged Lord Longlegs to speak. He said:

"Fellow-scientists, it is my belief that we have witnessed a thing which has occurred in perfection but once before in the knowledge of created beings. It is a phenomenon of inconceivable importance and interest, view it as one may, but its interest to us is vastly heightened by an added knowledge of its nature which no scholar has heretofore possessed or even suspected. This great marvel which we have just witnessed, fellow-savants, (it almost takes my breath away!) is nothing less than the transit of Venus!"

Every scholar sprang to his feet pale with astonishment. Then ensued tears, hand-shakings, frenzied embraces, and the most extravagant jubilations of every sort. But by and by, as emotion began to retire within bounds, and reflection to return to the front, the accomplished Chief Inspector Lizard observed:

"But how is this?— Venus should traverse the sun's surface, not the earth's."

The arrow went home. It carried sorrow to the breast of every apostle of learning there, for none could deny that this was a formidable criticism. But tranquilly the venerable Duke crossed his limbs behind his ears and said:

"My friend has touched the marrow of our mighty discovery. Yes—all that have lived before us thought a transit of Venus consisted of a flight across the sun's face; they thought it, they maintained it, they honestly believed it, simple hearts, and were justified in it by the limitations of their knowledge; but to us has been granted the inestimable boon of proving that the transit occurs across the earth's face, *for we have* SEEN *it*!"

The assembled wisdom sat in speechless adoration of this imperial intellect. All doubts had instantly departed, like night before the lightning.

The Tumble-Bug had just intruded, unnoticed. He now came reeling forward among the scholars, familiarly slapping first one and then another on the shoulder, saying "Nice ('ic!) nice old boy!" and smiling a smile of elaborate content. Arrived at a good position for speaking, he put his left arm akimbo with his knuckles planted in his hip just under the edge of his cut-away coat, bent his right leg, placing his toe on the ground and resting his heel with easy grace against his left shin, puffed out his aldermanic stomach, opened his lips, leaned his right elbow on Inspector Lizard's shoulder, and—

But the shoulder was indignantly withdrawn and the hard-handed son of toil went to earth. He floundered a bit but came up smiling, arranged his attitude with the same careful detail as before, only choosing Professor Dogtick's shoulder for a support, opened his lips and—

Went to earth again. He presently scrambled up once more, still smiling, made a loose effort to brush the dust off his coat and legs, but a smart pass of his hand missed entirely and the force of the unchecked impulse slewed him suddenly around, twisted his legs together, and projected him, limber and sprawling, into the lap of the Lord Longlegs. Two or three scholars sprang forward, flung the low creature head over heels into a corner and reinstated the patrician, smoothing his ruffled dignity with many soothing and regretful speeches. Professor Bull Frog roared out:

"No more of this, sirrah Tumble-Bug! Say your say and then get you about your business with speed!—Quick—what is your errand? Come—move off a trifle; you smell like a stable; what have you been at?"

"Please ('ic!) please your worship I chanced to light upon a find. But no m (*e-uck!*) matter 'bout that. There's b ('ic!) been another find which— —beg pardon, your honors, what was that th ('ic!) thing that ripped by here first?"

"It was the Vernal Equinox."

"Inf ('ic!) fernal equinox. 'At's all right.—D ('ic!) Dunno *him.* What's other one?"

"The transit of Venus."

"G ('ic!) Got me again. No matter. Las' one dropped something."

"Ah, indeed! Good luck! Good news! Quick—what is it?"

"M ('ic!) Mosey out 'n' see. It'll pay."

No more votes were taken for four and twenty hours. Then the following entry was made:

"The commission went in a body to view the find. It was found to consist of a hard, smooth, huge object with a rounded summit surmounted by a short upright projection resembling a section of a cabbage stalk divided transversely—This projection was not solid, but was a hollow cylinder plugged with a soft woody substance unknown to our region—that is, it had been so plugged, but unfortunately this obstruction had been heedlessly removed by Norway Rat, Chief of the Sappers and Miners, before our arrival. The vast object before us, so mysteriously conveyed from the glittering domains of space, was found to be hollow and nearly filled with a pungent liquid of a brownish hue, like rain-water that has stood for some time. And such a spectacle as met our view! Norway Rat was perched upon the summit engaged in thrusting his tail into the cylindrical projection, drawing it out dripping, permitting the struggling multitude of laborers to suck the end of it, then straightway reinserting it and delivering the fluid to the mob as before. Evidently this liquor had strangely potent qualities; for all that partook of it were immediately exalted with great and pleasurable emotions, and went staggering about singing ribald songs, embracing, fighting, dancing, discharging irruptions of profanity, and defying all authority. Around us struggled a massed and uncontrolled mob—uncontrolled and likewise uncontrollable, for the whole army, down to the very sentinels, were mad like the rest, by reason of the drink. We were seized upon by these reckless creatures, and within the hour we, even we, were undistinguishable from the rest—the demoralization was complete and universal. In time the camp wore itself out with its orgies and sank into a stolid and pitiable stupor, in whose mysterious bonds rank was forgotten and strange bed-fellows made, our eyes, at the resurrection, being blasted and our souls petrified with the incredible spectacle of that intolerable stinking scavenger, the Tumble-Bug, and the illustrious patrician my lord Grand Daddy, Duke of Longlegs, lying soundly steeped in sleep, and clasped lovingly in each other's arms, the like whereof hath not been seen in all the ages that tradition compasseth, and doubtless none shall ever in this world find faith to master the belief of it save only we that have beheld the damnable and unholy vision. Thus inscrutable be the ways of God, whose will be done!

"This day, by order, did the Engineer-in-Chief, Herr Spider, rig the necessary tackle for the overturning of the vast reservoir, and so its calamitous contents were discharged in a torrent upon the thirsty earth, which drank it up and now there is no more danger, we reserving but a few drops for experiment and scrutiny, and to exhibit to the king and subsequently preserve among the wonders of the museum. What this liquid is, has been determined. It is without question that fierce and most destructive fluid called lightning. It was wrested, in its container, from its store-house in the clouds, by the resistless might of the flying planet, and hurled at our feet as she sped by. An interesting discovery here results. Which is, that lightning, kept to itself, is quiescent; it is the assaulting contact of the thunderbolt that releases it from captivity, ignites its awful fires and so produces an instantaneous combustion and explosion which spread disaster and desolation far and wide in the earth."

After another day devoted to rest and recovery, the expedition proceeded upon its way. Some days later it went into camp in a pleasant part of the plain, and the savants sallied forth to see what they might find. Their reward was at hand. Professor Bull Frog discovered a strange tree, and called his comrades. They inspected it with profound interest.—It was very tall and straight, and wholly devoid of bark, limbs or foliage. By triangulation Lord Longlegs determined its altitude; Herr Spider measured its circumference at the base and computed the circumference at its top by a mathematical demonstration based upon the warrant furnished by the uniform degree of its taper upward. It was considered a very extraordinary find; and since it was a tree of a hitherto unknown species, Professor Woodlouse gave it a name of a learned sound, being none other than that of Professor Bull Frog translated into the ancient Mastodon language, for it had always been the custom with discoverers to perpetuate their names and honor themselves by this sort of connection with their discoveries.

Now, Professor Field-Mouse having placed his sensitive ear to the tree, detected a rich, harmonious sound issuing from it. This surprising thing was tested and enjoyed by each scholar in turn and great was the gladness and astonishment of all. Professor Woodlouse was requested to add to and extend the tree's name so as to make it suggest the musical quality it possessed— which he did, furnishing the addition *Anthem Singer*, done into the Mastodon tongue.

By this time Professor Snail was making some telescopic inspections. He discovered a great number of these trees, extending in a single rank, with wide intervals between, as far as his instrument would carry, both southward and northward. He also presently discovered that all these trees were bound together, near their tops, by fourteen great ropes, one above another, which ropes were continuous, from tree to tree, as far as his vision could reach. This was surprising. Chief

Engineer Spider ran aloft and soon reported that these ropes were simply a web hung there by some colossal member of his own species, for he could see its prey dangling here and there from the strands, in the shape of mighty shreds and rags that had a woven look about their texture and were no doubt the discarded skins of prodigious insects which had been caught and eaten. And then he ran along one of the ropes to make a closer inspection, but felt a smart sudden burn on the soles of his feet, accompanied by a paralyzing shock, wherefore he let go and swung himself to the earth by a thread of his own spinning, and advised all to hurry at once to camp, lest the monster should appear and get as much interested in the savants as they were in him and his works. So they departed with speed, making notes about the gigantic web as they went. And that evening the naturalist of the expedition built a beautiful model of the colossal spider, having no need to see it in order to do this, because he had picked up a fragment of its vertebræ by the tree, and so knew exactly what the creature looked like and what its habits and its preferences were, by this simple evidence alone. He built it with a tail, teeth, fourteen legs and a snout, and said it ate grass, cattle, pebbles and dirt with equal enthusiasm. This animal was regarded as a very precious addition to science. It was hoped a dead one might be found, to stuff. Professor Woodlouse thought that he and his brother scholars, by lying hid and being quiet, might maybe catch a live one. He was advised to try it. Which was all the attention that was paid to his suggestion. The conference ended with the naming the monster after the naturalist, since he, after God, had created it.

"And improved it, mayhap," muttered the Tumble-Bug, who was intruding again, according to his idle custom and his unappeasable curiosity.

END OF PART FIRST.

SOME FABLES FOR GOOD OLD BOYS AND GIRLS.

PART SECOND.

HOW THE ANIMALS OF THE WOOD COMPLETED THEIR SCIENTIFIC LABORS.

A week later the expedition camped in the midst of a collection of wonderful curiosities. These were a sort of vast caverns of stone that rose singly and in bunches out of the plain by the side of the river which they had first seen when they emerged from the forest. These caverns stood in long straight rows on opposite sides of broad aisles that were bordered with single ranks of trees. The summit of each cavern sloped sharply both ways. Several horizontal rows of great square holes, obstructed by a thin, shiny, transparent substance, pierced the frontage of each cavern. Inside were caverns within caverns; and one might ascend and visit these minor compartments by means of curious winding ways consisting of continuous regular terraces raised one above another. There were many huge shapeless objects in each compartment which were considered to have been living creatures at one time, though now the thin brown skin was shrunken and loose, and rattled when disturbed. Spiders were here in great number, and their cob-webs, stretched in all directions and wreathing the great skinny dead together, were a pleasant spectacle, since they inspired with life and wholesome cheer a scene which would otherwise have brought to the mind only a sense of forsakenness and desolation. Information was sought of these spiders, but in vain. They were of a different nationality from those with the expedition and their language seemed but a musical, meaningless jargon. They were a timid, gentle race, but ignorant, and heathenish worshipers of unknown gods. The expedition detailed a great detachment of missionaries to teach them the true religion, and in a week's time a precious work had been wrought among those darkened creatures, not three families being by that time at peace with each other or having a settled belief in any system of religion whatever. This encouraged the expedition to establish a colony of missionaries there permanently, that the work of grace might go on.

But let us not outrun our narrative. After close examination of the fronts of the caverns, and much thinking and exchanging of theories, the scientists determined the nature of these singular formations. They said that each belonged mainly to the Old Red Sandstone period; that the cavern fronts rose in innumerable and wonderfully regular strata high in the air, each stratum about five frog-spans thick, and that in the present discovery lay an overpowering refutation of all received geology: for between every two layers of Old Red Sandstone reposed a thin layer of decomposed limestone; so instead of there having been but one Old Red Sandstone period there had certainly been not less than a hundred and seventy-five! And by the same token it was plain that there had also been a hundred and seventy-five floodings of the earth and depositings of limestone strata! The unavoidable deduction from which pair of facts, was, the overwhelming truth that the world, instead of being only two hundred thousand years old, was older by millions upon millions of years! And there was another curious thing: every stratum of Old Red Sandstone was pierced and divided at mathematically regular intervals by vertical strata of limestone. Up-shootings of igneous rock through fractures in water formations were common; but here was the first instance where water-formed rock had been so projected. It was a great and noble discovery and its value to science was considered to be inestimable.

A critical examination of some of the lower strata demonstrated the presence of fossil ants and tumble-bugs (the latter accompanied by their peculiar goods), and with high gratification the fact was enrolled upon the scientific record; for this was proof that these vulgar laborers belonged to the first and lowest orders of created beings, though at the same time there was something repulsive in the reflection that the perfect and exquisite creature of the modern uppermost order owed its origin to such ignominious beings through the mysterious law of Development of Species.

The Tumble-Bug, overhearing this discussion, said he was willing that the parvenus of these new times should find what comfort they might in their wise-drawn theories, since as far as he was concerned he was content to be of the old first families and proud to point back to his place among the old original aristocracy of the land.

"Enjoy your mushroom dignity, stinking of the varnish of yesterday's veneering, since you like it," said he; "suffice it for the Tumble-Bugs that they come of a race that rolled their fragrant spheres down the solemn aisles of antiquity, and left their imperishable works embalmed in the Old Red Sandstone to proclaim it to the

wasting centuries as they file along the highway of Time!"

"O, take a walk!" said the chief of the expedition, with derision.

The summer passed, and winter approached. In and about many of the caverns were what seemed to be inscriptions. Most of the scientists said they were inscriptions, a few said they were not. The chief philologist, Professor Woodlouse, maintained that they were writings, done in a character utterly unknown to scholars, and in a language equally unknown. He had early ordered his artists and draughtsmen to make fac-similes of all that were discovered; and had set himself about finding the key to the hidden tongue. In this work he had followed the method which had always been used by decipherers previously. That is to say, he placed a number of copies of inscriptions before him and studied them both collectively and in detail. To begin with, he placed the following copies together:

THE AMERICAN HOTEL.	MEALS AT ALL HOURS.
THE SHADES.	NO SMOKING.
BOATS FOR HIRE CHEAP.	UNION PRAYER MEETING, 4 P. M.
BILLIARDS.	THE WATERSIDE JOURNAL.
THE A 1 BARBER SHOP.	TELEGRAPH OFFICE.

KEEP OFF THE GRASS.　　　　　TRY BRANDRETH'S PILLS.
COTTAGES FOR RENT DURING THE WATERING SEASON.
FOR SALE CHEAP.　　　　　　　FOR SALE CHEAP.
FOR SALE CHEAP.　　　　　　　FOR SALE CHEAP.

At first it seemed to the Professor that this was a sign-language, and that each word was represented by a distinct sign; further examination convinced him that it was a written language, and that every letter of its alphabet was represented by a character of its own; and finally, he decided that it was a language which conveyed itself partly by letters, and partly by signs or hieroglyphics. This conclusion was forced upon him by the discovery of several specimens of the following nature:

He observed that certain inscriptions were met with in greater frequency than others. Such as "FOR SALE CHEAP;" "BILLIARDS;" "S. T.—1860—X;" "KENO;" "ALE ON DRAUGHT." Naturally, then, these must be religious maxims. But this idea was cast aside, by and by, as the mystery of the strange alphabet began to clear itself. In time, the Professor was enabled to translate several of the inscriptions with considerable plausibility, though not to the perfect satisfaction of all the scholars. Still, he made constant and encouraging progress.

Finally a cavern was discovered with these inscriptions upon it:

WATERSIDE MUSEUM.

Open at all Hours.　　　　　*Admission 50 cents.*

WONDERFUL COLLECTION OF WAX-WORKS, ANCIENT FOSSILS, ETC.

Professor Woodlouse affirmed that the word "Museum" was equivalent to the phrase "*lumgath molo*," or "Burial-Place." Upon entering, the scientists were well astonished. But what they saw may be best conveyed in the language of their own official report:

"Erect, and in a row, were a sort of rigid great figures which struck us instantly as belonging to the long extinct species of reptile called MAN, described in our ancient records. This was a peculiarly gratifying discovery, because of late times it has become fashionable to regard this creature as a myth and a superstition, a work of the inventive imaginations of our remote ancestors. But here, indeed, was Man, perfectly preserved, in a fossil state. And this was his burial place, as already ascertained by the inscription. And now it began to be suspected that the caverns we had been inspecting had been his ancient haunts in that old time that he roamed the earth—for upon the breast of each of these tall fossils was an inscription in the character heretofore noticed. One read, 'CAPTAIN KIDD, THE PIRATE;' another 'QUEEN VICTORIA;' another, 'ABE LINCOLN;' another, 'GEORGE WASHINGTON,' etc.

"With feverish interest we called for our ancient scientific records to discover if perchance the description of Man there set down would tally with the fossils before us. Professor Woodlouse read it aloud in its quaint and musty phraseology, to wit:

"'In ye time of our fathers Man still walked ye earth, as by tradition we know. It was a creature of exceeding great size, being compassed about with a loose skin, sometimes of one color, sometimes of many, the which it was able to cast at will; which being done, the hind legs were discovered to be armed with short claws like to a mole's but broader, and ye fore-legs with fingers of a curious slimness and a length much more prodigious than a frog's, armed also with broad talons for scratching in ye earth for its food. It had a sort of feathers upon its head such as hath a rat, but longer, and a beak suitable for seeking its food by ye smell thereof. When it was stirred with happiness, it leaked water from its eyes; and when it suffered or was sad, it manifested it with a horrible hellish cackling clamor that was exceeding dreadful to hear and made one long that it might rend itself and perish, and so end its troubles. Two Mans being together, they uttered noises at each other like to this: 'Haw-haw-haw—dam good, dam good,' together with other sounds of more or less likeness to these, wherefore yᵉ poets conceived that they talked, but poets be always ready to catch at any frantic folly, God he knows. Sometimes this creature goeth about with a long stick yᵉ which it putteth to its face and bloweth fire and smoke through yᵉ same with a sudden and most damnable bruit and noise that doth fright its prey to death, and so seizeth it in its talons and walketh away to its habitat, consumed with a most fierce and devilish joy.'

"Now was the description set forth by our ancestors wonderfully endorsed and confirmed by the fossils before us, as shall be seen. The specimen marked 'Cap-tain Kidd' was examined in de-tail. Upon its head and part of its face was a sort of fur like that upon the tail of a horse. With great labor its loose skin was removed, whereupon its body was dis-covered to be of a polished white texture, thor-oughly petrified. The straw it had eaten, so many ages gone by, was still in its body, undigest-ed—and even in its legs.

" Surrounding these fossils were objects that would mean nothing to the ignorant, but to the eye of science they were a revelation. They laid bare the secrets of dead ages. These musty Memorials told us when Man lived, and what were his habits. For here, side by side with Man, were the evidences that he had lived in the earliest ages of creation, the companion of the other low orders of life that belonged to that forgotten time.—Here was the fossil nautilus that sailed the primeval seas; here was the skeleton of the mastodon, the ichthyosaurus, the cave bear, the prodigious elk.

Here, also, were the charred bones of some of these extinct animals and of the young of Man's own species, split lengthwise, showing that to his taste the marrow was a toothsome luxury. It was plain that Man had robbed those bones of their contents, since no tooth-mark of any beast was upon them—albeit the Tumble-Bug intruded the remark that " no beast could mark a bone with its teeth, anyway." Here were proofs that Man had vague, groveling notions of art; for this fact was conveyed by certain things marked with the untranslatable words, 'FLINT HATCHETS, KNIVES, ARROW-HEADS, AND BONE-ORNAMENTS OF PRIMEVAL MAN.' Some of these seemed to be rude weapons chipped out of flint, and in a secret place was found some more in process of construction, with this untranslatable legend, on a thin, flimsy material, lying by :

" *Jones, if you don't want to be discharged from the Musseum, make the next primeaveal weppons more careful—you couldn't even fool one of these sleapy old syentiffic grannys from the Coledge with the last ones. And mind you the animles you carved on some of the Bone Ornaments is a blame sight too good for any primeaveal man that was ever fooled.—Varnum, Manager.*"

" Back of the burial place was a mass of ashes, showing that Man always had a feast at a funeral—else why the ashes in such a place ? and showing, also, that he believed in God and the immortality of the soul—else why these solemn ceremonies ?

To sum up.—We believe that man had a written language. We *know* that he indeed existed at one time, and is not a myth; also, that he was the companion of the cave bear, the mastodon, and other extinct species; that he cooked and ate them and likewise the young of his own kind; also, that he bore rude weapons, and knew something of art; that he imagined he had a soul, and pleased himself with the fancy that it was immortal. But let us not laugh; there may be creatures in existence to whom we and our vanities and profundities may seem as ludicrous."

END OF PART SECOND.

SOME FABLES FOR GOOD OLD BOYS AND GIRLS.

PART THIRD.

Near the margin of the great river the scientists presently found a huge, shapely stone, with this inscription:

"*In 1847, in the spring, the river overflowed its banks and covered the whole township. The depth was from two to six feet. More than 900 head of cattle were lost, and many homes destroyed. The Mayor ordered this memorial to be erected to perpetuate the event. God spare us the repetition of it!*"

With infinite trouble, Professor Woodlouse succeeded in making a translation of this inscription, which was sent home and straightway an enormous excitement was created about it. It confirmed, in a remarkable way, certain treasured traditions of the ancients. The translation was slightly marred by one or two untranslatable

144

words, but these did not impair the general clearness of the meaning. It is here presented:

"*One thousand eight hundred and forty-seven years ago, the (fires?) descended and consumed the whole city. Only some nine hundred souls were saved, all others destroyed. The (king?) commanded this stone to be set up to . . . . . (untranslatable) . . . . . prevent the repetition of it.*"

This was the first successful and satisfactory translation that had been made of the mysterious character left behind him by extinct man, and it gave Professor Woodlouse such reputation that at once every seat of learning in his native land conferred a degree of the most illustrious grade upon him, and it was believed that if he had been a soldier and had turned his splendid talents to the extermination of a remote tribe of reptiles, the king would have ennobled him and made him rich. And this, too, was the origin of that school of scientists called Manologists, whose specialty is the deciphering of the ancient records of the extinct bird termed Man. [For it is now decided that Man was a bird and not a reptile]. But Professor Woodlouse began and remained chief of these, for it was granted that no translations were ever so free from error as his. Others made mistakes—he seemed incapable of it. Many a memorial of the lost race was afterward found, but none ever attained to the renown and veneration achieved by the "Mayoritish Stone"—it being so called from the word "Mayor" in it, which, being translated "King," "Mayoritish Stone" was but another way of saying "King Stone."

Another time the expedition made a great "find." It was a vast round flattish mass, ten frog-spans in diameter and five or six high. Professor Snail put on his spectacles and examined it all around, and then climbed up and inspected the top. He said:

"The result of my perlustration and perscontation of this isoperimetrical protuberance is a belief that it is one of those rare and wonderful creations left by the Mound Builders. The fact that this one is lamellibranchiate in its formation, simply adds to its interest as being possibly of a different kind from any we read of in the records of science, but yet in no manner marring its authenticity. Let the megalophonous grasshopper sound a blast and summon hither the perfunctory and circumforaneous Tumble-Bug, to the end that excavations may be made and learning gather new treasures."

10

Not a Tumble-Bug could be found on duty, so the Mound was excavated by a working party of Ants. Nothing was discovered. This would have been a great disappointment, had not the venerable Longlegs explained the matter.—He said:

"It is now plain to me that the mysterious and forgotten race of Mound Builders did not always erect these edifices as mausoleums, else in this case as in all previous cases, their skeletons would be found here, along with the rude implements which the creatures used in life. Is not this manifest?"

"True! true!" from everybody.

"Then we have made a discovery of peculiar value here; a discovery which greatly extends our knowledge of this creature in place of diminishing it; a discovery which will add lustre to the achievements of this expedition and win for us the commendations of scholars everywhere. For the absence of the customary relics here means nothing less than this: The Mound Builder, instead of being the ignorant, savage reptile we have been taught to consider him, was a creature of cultivation and high intelligence, capable of not only appreciating worthy achievements of the great and noble of his species, but of commemorating them! Fellow-scholars, this stately Mound is not a sepulchre, it is a monument!"

A profound impression was produced by this.

But it was interrupted by rude and derisive laughter—and the Tumble-Bug appeared.

"A monument!" quoth he. "A monument set up by a Mound Builder! Aye, so it is! So it is, indeed, to the shrewd keen eye of science; but to an ignorant poor devil who has never seen a college, it is not a Monument, strictly speaking, but is yet a most rich and noble property; and with your worships' good permission I will proceed to manufacture it into spheres of exceeding grace and—"

The Tumble-Bug was driven away with stripes, and the draughtsmen of the expedition were set to making views of the Monument from different standpoints, while Professor Woodlouse, in a frenzy of scientific zeal, traveled all over it and all around it hoping to find an inscription. But if there had ever been one it had decayed or been removed by some vandal as a relic.

The views having been completed, it was now considered safe to load the precious Monument itself upon the backs of four of the largest Tortoises and send it home to the King's museum, which was done; and when it arrived it was received with enormous *éclat* and escorted to its future abiding-place by thousands of enthusiastic citizens, King Bullfrog XVI. himself attending and condescending to sit enthroned upon it throughout the progress.

The growing rigor of the weather was now admonishing the scientists to close their labors for the present, so they made preparations to journey homeward. But even their last day among the Caverns bore fruit; for one of the scholars found in an out-of-the-way corner of the Museum or "Burial-Place" a most strange and extraordinary thing. It was nothing less than a double Man-Bird lashed together breast to breast by a natural ligament, and labelled with the untranslatable words, "*Siamese Twins*" The official report concerning this thing closed thus:

appears that there were in old times two distinct species of this majestic fowl, the one being single and the other double. Nature has a reason for all things.—It is plain to the eye of science that the Double-Man originally inhabited a region where dangers abounded; hence he was paired together to the end that while one part slept the other might watch; and likewise that, danger being discovered, there might always be a double instead of a single power to oppose it. All honor to the mystery-dispelling eye of godlike Science!"

And near the Double Man-Bird was found what was plainly an ancient record of his, marked upon numberless sheets of a thin white substance and bound together. Almost the first glance that Professor Woodlouse threw into it revealed this following sentence, which he instantly translated and laid before the scientists, in a tremble, and it uplifted every soul there with exultation and astonishment:

"*In truth it is believed by many that the lower animals reason and talk together.*"

When the great official report of the expedition appeared, the above sentence bore this comment:

"Then there are lower animals than Man! This remarkable passage can mean nothing else. Man himself is extinct, but *they* may still exist. What can they be? Where do they inhabit? One's enthusiasm bursts all bounds in the contemplation of the brilliant field of discovery and investigation here thrown open to science. We close our labors with the humble prayer that your Majesty will immediately appoint a commission and command it to rest not nor spare expense until the search for this hitherto unsuspected race of the creatures of God shall be crowned with success."

The expedition then journeyed homeward after its long absence and its faithful endeavors, and was received with a mighty ovation by the whole grateful country.

There were vulgar, ignorant carpers, of course, as there always are and always will be; and naturally one of these was the obscene Tumble-Bug. He said that all he had learned by his travels was that science only needed a spoonful of supposition to build a mountain of demonstrated fact out of; and that for the future he meant to be content with the knowledge that nature had made free to all creatures and not go prying into the august secrets of the Deity.

MY LATE SENATORIAL SECRETARYSHIP.

I AM not a private secretary to a senator any more, now. I held the berth two months in security and in great cheerfulness of spirit, but my bread began to return from over the waters, then—that is to say, my works came back and revealed themselves. I judged it best to resign. The way of it was this. My employer sent for me one morning tolerably early, and, as soon as I had finished inserting some conundrums clandestinely into his last great speech upon finance, I entered the presence. There was something portentous in his appearance. His cravat was untied, his hair was in a state of disorder, and his countenance bore about it the signs of a suppressed storm. He held a package of letters in his tense grasp, and I knew that the dreaded Pacific mail was in. He said—

"I thought you were worthy of confidence."

I said, "Yes, sir."

He said, "I gave you a letter from certain of my constituents in the State of Nevada, asking the establishment of a post-office at Baldwin's Ranch, and told you to answer it, as ingeniously as you could, with arguments which should persuade them that there was no real necessity for an office at that place."

I felt easier. "Oh, if that is all, sir, I *did* do that."

"Yes, you *did.* I will read your answer, for your own humiliation:

"WASHINGTON, Nov. 24.

"'*Messrs. Smith, Jones, and others.*

"'GENTLEMEN: What the mischief do you suppose you want with a post-office at Baldwin's Ranche? It would not do you any good. If any letters came there, you couldn't read them, you know; and, besides, such letters as ought to pass through, with money in them, for other localities, would not be likely to *get* through, you must perceive at once; and that would make trouble for us all. No, don't bother about a post-office in your camp. I have your best interests at heart, and feel that it would only be an ornamental folly. What you want is a nice jail, you know—a nice, substantial jail and a free school. These will be a lasting benefit to you. These will make you really contented and happy. I will move in the matter at once.

"'Very truly, etc.,
"'MARK TWAIN,
"'For James W. N**, U. S. Senator.'

"That is the way you answered that letter. Those people say they will hang me, if I ever enter that district again; and I am perfectly satisfied they *will*, too."

"Well, sir, I did not know I was doing any harm. I only wanted to convince them."

"Ah. Well you *did* convince them, I make no manner of doubt. Now, here is another specimen. I gave you a petition from certain gentlemen of Nevada, praying that I would get a bill through Congress incorporating the Methodist Episcopal Church of the State of Nevada. I told you to say, in reply, that the creation of such a law came more properly within the province of the State Legislature; and to endeavor to show them that, in the present feebleness of the religious element in that new commonwealth, the expediency of incorporating the church was questionable. What did you write?

"'WASHINGTON, Nov. 24.

"'*Rev. John Halifax and others.*

"'GENTLEMEN: You will have to go to the State Legislature about that speculation of yours—Congress don't know anything about religion. But don't you hurry to go there, either ; because this thing you propose to do out in that new country isn't expedient—in fact, it is ridiculous. Your religious people there are too feeble, in intellect, in morality, in piety—in everything, pretty much. You had better drop this—you can't make it work. You can't issue stock on an incorporation like that—or if you could, it would only keep you in trouble all the time. The other denominations would abuse it, and "bear" it, and "sell it short," and break it down. They would do with it just as they would with one of your silver mines out there—they would try to make all the world believe it was "wildcat." You ought not to do anything that is calculated to bring a sacred thing into disrepute. You ought to be ashamed of yourselves—that is what *I* think about it. You close your petition with the words: "And we will ever pray." I think you had better—you need to do it.

"'Very truly, etc.,

"'MARK TWAIN,

"'For James W. N**, U. S. Senator.'

"*That* luminous epistle finishes me with the religious element among my constituents. But that my political murder might be made sure, some evil instinct prompted me to hand you this memorial from the grave company of elders composing the Board of Aldermen of the city of San Francisco, to try your hand upon—a memorial praying that the city's right to the water-lots upon the city front might be established by law of Congress. I told you this was a dangerous matter to move in. I told you to write a non-committal letter to the Aldermen—an ambiguous letter—a letter that should avoid, as far as possible, all real consideration and discussion of the water-lot question. If there is any feeling left in you—any shame—surely this letter you wrote, in obedience to that order, ought to evoke it, when its words fall upon your ears:

"'WASHINGTON, Nov. 27.

"' *The Hon. Board of Aldermen, etc.*

"'GENTLEMEN: George Washington, the revered Father of his Country is dead. His long and brilliant career is closed, alas! forever. He was greatly respected in this section of the country, and his untimely decease cast a gloom over the whole community. He died on the 14th day of December, 1799. He passed peacefully away from the scene of his honors and his great achievements, the most lamented hero and the best beloved that ever earth hath yielded unto Death. At such a time as this, *you* speak of water-lots!—what a lot was his!

"'What is fame! Fame is an accident. Sir Isaac Newton discovered an apple falling to the ground—a trivial discovery, truly, and one which a million men had made before him—but his parents were influential, and so they tortured that small circumstance into something wonderful, and, lo! the simple world took up the shout and, in almost the twinkling of an eye, that man was famous. Treasure these thoughts.

"'Poesy, sweet poesy, who shall estimate what the world owes to thee!

"Mary had a little lamb, its fleece was white as snow—
And everywhere that Mary went, the lamb was sure to go."

"Jack and Gill went up the hill
To draw a pail of water;
Jack fell down and broke his crown,
And Gill came tumbling after."

For simplicity, elegance of diction, and freedom from immoral tendencies, I regard those two poems in the light of gems. They are suited to all grades of intelligence, to every sphere of life— to the field, to the nursery, to the guild. Especially should no Board of Aldermen be without them.

"'Venerable fossils! write again. Nothing improves one so much as friendly correspondence. Write again—and if there is anything in this memorial of yours that refers to anything in particular, do not be backward about explaining it. We shall always be happy to hear you chirp.

"'Very truly, etc.

"'MARK TWAIN,

"'For James W. N**, U. S. Senator.

"That is an atrocious, a ruinous epistle! Distraction!"

"Well, sir, I am really sorry if there is anything wrong about it—but—but it appears to me to dodge the water-lot question."

"Dodge the mischief! Oh!—but never mind. As long as destruction must come now, let it be complete. Let it be complete—let this last of your performances, which I am about to read, make a finality of it. I am a ruined man. I *had* my misgivings when I gave you the the letter from Humboldt, asking that the post route from Indian Gulch to Shakespeare Gap and intermediate points, be changed partly to the old Mormon trail. But I told you it was a delicate question, and warned you to deal with it deftly—to answer it dubiously, and leave them a little in the dark. And your fatal imbecility impelled you to make *this* disastrous reply. I should think you would stop your ears, if you are not dead to all shame :

" ' WASHINGTON, Nov. 30.

    " ' *Messrs. Perkins, Wagner, et al.*

    " ' GENTLEMEN: It is a delicate question about this Indian trail, but, handled with proper deftness and dubiousness, I doubt not we shall succeed in some measure or otherwise, because the place where the route leaves the Lassen Meadows, over beyond where those two Shawnee chiefs, Dilapidated-Vengeance and Biter-of-the-Clouds, were scalped last winter, this being the favorite direction to some, but others preferring something else in consequence of things, the Mormon trail leaving Mosby's at three in the morning, and passing through Jawbone Flat to Blucher, and then down by Jug-Handle, the road passing to the right of it, and naturally leaving it on the right, too, and Dawson's on the left of the trail where it passes to the left of said Dawson's and onward thence to Tomahawk, thus making the route cheaper, easier of access to all who can get at it, and compassing all the desirable objects so considered by others, and, therefore, conferring the most good upon the greatest number, and, consequently, I am encouraged to hope we shall. However, I shall be ready, and happy, to afford you still further information upon the subject, from time to time, as you may·desire it and the Post-office Department be enabled to furnish it to me.

" ' Very truly, etc.
" ' MARK TWAIN,
" ' For James W. N**, U. S. Senator.'

"There—now *what* do you think of that?"

"Well, I don't know, sir. It—well, it appears to me—to be dubious enough."

"Du—leave the house! I am a ruined man. Those Humboldt savages never will forgive me for tangling their brains up with this inhuman letter. I have lost the respect of the Methodist Church, the Board of Aldermen——"

"Well, I haven't anything to say about that, because I may have missed it a little in their cases, but I *was* too many for the Baldwin's Ranch people, General!"

"Leave the house! Leave it for ever and for ever, too!"

I regarded that as a sort of covert intimation that my service could be dispensed with, and so I resigned. I never will be a private secretary to a senator again. You can't please that kind of people. They don't know anything. They can't appreciate a party's efforts.

A FASHION ITEM.

AT General G——'s reception the other night, the most fashionably dressed lady was Mrs. G. C. She wore a pink satin dress, plain in front but with a good deal of rake to it—to the train, I mean; it was said to be two or three yards long. One could see it creeping along the floor some little time after the woman was gone. Mrs. C. wore also a white bodice, cut bias, with Pompadour sleeves, flounced with ruches; low neck, with the inside handkerchief not visible, with white kid gloves. She had on a pearl necklace, which glinted lonely, high up the midst of that barren waste of neck and shoulders. Her hair was frizzled into a tangled chapparel, forward of her ears, aft it was drawn together, and compactly bound and plaited into a stump like a pony's tail, and furthermore was canted upward at a sharp angle, and ingeniously supported by a red velvet crupper, whose forward extremity was made fast with a half-hitch around a hairpin on the top of her head. Her whole top hamper was neat and becoming. She had a beautiful complexion when she first came, but it faded out by degrees in an unaccountable way. However, it is not lost for good. I found the most of it on my shoulder afterwards. (I stood near the door when she squeezed out with the throng.) There were other ladies present, but I only took notes of one as a specimen. I would gladly enlarge upon the subject were I able to do it justice.

153

RILEY—NEWSPAPER CORRE-
SPONDENT.

ONE of the best men in Washington — or elsewhere — is RILEY, correspondent of one of the great San Francisco dailies.

Riley is full of humor, and has an unfailing vein of irony, which makes his conversation to the last degree entertaining (as long as the remarks are about somebody else). But, notwithstanding the possession of·these qualities, which should enable a man to write a happy and an appetizing letter, Riley's newspaper letters often display a more than earthly solemnity, and likewise an unimaginative devotion to petrified facts, which surprise and distress all men who know him in his unofficial character. He explains this curious thing by saying that his employers sent him to Washington to write facts, not fancy, and that several times he has come near losing his situation by inserting humorous remarks which, not being looked for at headquarters, and consequently not understood, were thought to be dark and bloody speeches intended to convey signals and warnings to murderous secret societies, or something of that kind, and so were scratched out with a shiver and a prayer and cast into the stove. Riley says that sometimes he is so afflicted with a yearning to write a sparkling and absorbingly readable letter that he simply cannot resist it, and so he goes to his den and revels in the delight of untramelled scribbling; and then, with suffering such as only a mother can know, he destroys the pretty children of his fancy and reduces his letter to the required dismal accuracy. Having seen Riley do this very thing more than once, I know whereof I speak. Often I have laughed with him over a happy passage, and grieved to see him plough his pen through it. He would say, " I had to write that or die; and I've got to scratch it out or starve. *They* wouldn't stand it, you know."

I think Riley is about the most entertaining company I ever saw. We lodged together in many places in Washington during the winter of '67-8, moving comfortably from place to place, and attracting attention by paying our board—a course which cannot fail to make a person conspicuous in Washington. Riley would tell all about his trip to California in the early days, by way of the Isthmus and the San Juan river; and about his baking bread in San Francisco to gain a living, and setting up ten-pins, and practising law, and opening oysters, and delivering lectures, and teaching French, and tending bar, and reporting for the newspapers, and keeping dancing-schools, and interpreting Chinese in the courts—which latter was lucrative, and Riley was doing handsomely and laying up a little money when people began to find fault because his translations were too "free," a thing for which Riley considered he ought not to be held responsible, since he did not know a word of the Chinese tongue, and only adopted interpreting as means of gaining an honest livelihood. Through the machinations of enemies he was removed from the position of official interpreter, and a man put in his place who was familiar with the Chinese language, but did not know any English. And Riley used to tell about publishing a newspaper up in what is Alaska now, but was only an iceberg then, with a population composed of bears, walruses, Indians, and other animals; and how the iceberg got adrift at last, and left all his paying subscribers behind, and as soon as the commonwealth floated out of the jurisdiction of Russia the people rose and threw off their allegiance and ran up the English flag, calculating to hook on and become an English colony as they drifted along down the British Possessions; but a land breeze and a crooked current carried them by, and they ran up the Stars and Stripes and steered for California, missed the connection again and swore allegiance to Mexico, but it wasn't any use; the anchors came home every time, and away they went with the north-east trades drifting off side-ways toward the Sandwich Islands, whereupon they ran up the Cannibal flag and had a grand human barbecue in honor of it, in which it was noticed that the better a man liked a friend the better he enjoyed him; and as soon as they got fairly within the tropics the weather got so fearfully hot that the iceberg began to melt, and it got so sloppy under foot that it was almost impossible for ladies to get about at all; and at last, just as they came in sight of the islands, the melancholy remnant of the once majestic iceberg canted first to one side and then to the other, and then plunged under for ever, carrying the national archives along with it—and not only the archives and the populace, but some eligible town lots which had increased in value as fast as they diminished in size in the tropics, and which Riley could have sold at thirty cents a pound and made himself rich if he could have kept the province afloat ten hours longer and got her into port.

Riley is very methodical, untiringly accommodating, never forgets anything that is to be attended to, is a good son, a staunch friend, and a permanent reliable enemy. He will put himself to any amount of trouble to oblige a body, and therefore always has his hands full of things to be done for the helpless and the shiftless. And he knows how to do nearly everything, too. He is a man whose native benevolence is a well-spring that never goes dry. He stands always ready to help whoever needs help, as far as he is able—and not simply with his money, for that is a cheap and common charity, but with hand and brain, and fatigue of limb and sacrifice of time. This sort of men is rare.

Riley has a ready wit, a quickness and aptness at selecting and applying quotations, and a countenance that is as solemn and as blank as the back side of a tombstone when he is delivering a particularly exasperating joke. One night a negro woman was burned to death in a house next door to us, and Riley said that our landlady would be oppressively emotional at breakfast, because she generally made use of such opportunities as offered, being of a morbidly sentimental turn, and so we should find it best to let her talk along and say nothing back—it was the only way to keep her tears out of the gravy. Riley said there never was a funeral in the neighborhood but that the gravy was watery for a week.

And, sure enough, at breakfast the landlady was down in the very sloughs of woe —entirely broken-hearted. Everything she looked at reminded her of that poor old negro woman, and so the buckwheat cakes made her sob, the coffee forced a groan, and when the beefsteak came on she fetched a wail that made our hair rise. Then she got to talking about deceased, and kept up a steady drizzle till both of us were soaked through and through. Presently she took a fresh breath and said, with a world of sobs—

" Ah, to think of it, only to think of it !—the poor old faithful creature. For she was *so* faithful. Would you believe it, she had been a servant in that self-same house and that self-same family for twenty-seven years come Christmas, and never a cross word and never a lick ! And, oh, to think she should meet such a death at last !—a-sitting over the red-hot stove at three o'clock in the morning and went to sleep and fell on it and was actually *roasted !* Not just frizzled up a bit, but literally roasted to a crisp ! Poor faithful creature, how she *was* cooked ! I am but a poor woman, but even if I have to scrimp to do it, I will put up a tombstone over that lone sufferer's grave—and Mr. Riley if you would have the goodness to think up a little epitaph to put on it which would sort of describe the awful way in which she met her "—

" Put it, ' *Well done*, good and faithful servant,' " said Riley, and never smiled.

A FINE OLD MAN.

JOHN WAGNER, the oldest man in Buffalo—one hundred and four years old—recently walked a mile and a half in two weeks.

He is as cheerful and bright as any of these other old men that charge around so persistently and tiresomely in the newspapers, and in every way as remarkable.

Last November he walked five blocks in a rain-storm, without any shelter but an umbrella, and cast his vote for Grant, remarking that he had voted for forty-seven presidents—which was a lie.

His "second crop" of rich brown hair arrived from New York yesterday, and he has a new set of teeth coming—from Philadelphia.

He is to be married next week to a girl one hundred and two years old, who still takes in washing.

They have been engaged eighty years, but their parents persistently refused their consent until three days ago.

John Wagner is two years older than the Rhode Island veteran, and yet has never tasted a drop of liquor in his life —unless—unless you count whisky.

158

AT that time, in Kentucky (said the Hon. Mr. K———), the law was very strict against what is termed "games of chance." About a dozen of the boys were detected playing "seven-up" or "old sledge" for money, and the grand jury found a true bill against them. Jim Sturgis was retained to defend them when the case came up, of course. The more he studied over the matter, and looked into the evidence, the plainer it was that he must lose a case at last—there was no getting around that painful fact. Those boys had certainly been betting money on a game of chance. Even public sympathy was roused in behalf of Sturgis. People said it was a pity to see him mar his successful career with a big prominent case like this, which must go against him.

But after several restless nights an inspired idea flashed upon Sturgis, and he sprang out of bed delighted. He thought he saw his way through. The next day he whispered around a' little among his clients and a few friends, and then when the case came up in court he acknowledged the seven-up and the betting, and, as his sole defence, had the astounding effrontery to put in the plea that old sledge was not a game of chance! There was the broadest sort of a smile all over the faces of that sophisticated audience. The judge smiled with the rest. But Sturgis maintained a countenance whose earnestness was even severe. The opposite counsel tried to ridicule him out of his position, and did not succeed. The judge jested in a ponderous judicial way about the thing, but did not move him. The matter was becoming grave. The judge lost a little of his patience, and said the joke had gone far enough. Jim Sturgis said he knew of no joke in the matter—his clients could not be punished for indulging in what some people chose to consider a game of chance until it was *proven* that it was a game of chance. Judge and counsel said that would be an easy matter, and forthwith called Deacons Job, Peters, Burke, and Johnson, and Dominies Wirt and Miggles, to testify; and they unanimously and with strong feeling put down the legal quibble of Sturgis by pronouncing that old sledge *was* a game of chance.

"What do you call it *now?*" said the judge.

"I call it a game of science!" retorted Sturgis; "and I'll prove it, too!"

They saw his little game.

He brought in a cloud of witnesses, and produced an overwhelming mass of testimony, to show that old sledge was not a game of chance but a game of science.

Instead of being the simplest case in the world, it had somehow turned out to be an excessively knotty one. The judge scratched his head over it a while, and said there was no way of coming to a determination, because just as many men could be brought into court who would testify on one side as could be found to testify on the other. But he said he was willing to do the fair thing by all parties, and would act upon any suggestion Mr. Sturgis would make for the solution of the difficulty.

Mr. Sturgis was on his feet in a second.

"Impanel a jury of six of each, Luck *versus* Science. Give them candles and a couple of decks of cards. Send them into the jury room, and just abide by the result!"

There was no disputing the fairness of the proposition. The four deacons and the two dominies were sworn in as the "chance" jurymen, and six inveterate old seven-up professors were chosen to represent the "science" side of the issue. They retired to the jury room.

In about two hours Deacon Peters sent into court to borrow three dollars from a friend. [Sensation.] In about two hours more Dominie Miggles sent into court to borrow a "stake" from a friend. [Sensation.] During the next three or four hours the other dominie and the other deacons sent into court for small loans. And still the packed audience waited, for it was a prodigious occasion in

Bull's Corners, and one in which every father of a family was necessarily interested.

The rest of the story can be told briefly. About daylight the jury came in, and Deacon Job, the foreman, read the following

VERDICT.

We, the jury in the case of the Commonwealth of Kentucky vs. John Wheeler *et al.*, have carefully considered the points of the case, and tested the merits of the several theories advanced, and do hereby unanimously decide that the game commonly known as old sledge or seven-up is eminently a game of science and not of chance. In demonstration whereof it is hereby and herein stated, iterated, reiterated, set forth, and made manifest that, during the entire night, the "chance" men never won a game or turned a jack, although both feats were common and frequent to the opposition ; and furthermore, in support of this our verdict, we call attention to the significant fact that the "chance" men are all busted, and the "science" men have got the money. It is the deliberate opinion of this jury, that the "chance" theory concerning seven-up is a pernicious doctrine, and calculated to inflict untold suffering and pecuniary loss upon any community that takes stock in it.

"That is the way that seven-up came to be set apart and particularized in the statute-books of Kentucky as being a game not of chance but of science, and therefore not punishable under the law," said Mr. K——. "That verdict is of record, and holds good to this day."

II

THE KILLING OF JULIUS CÆSAR "LOCALIZED."

Being the only true and reliable account ever published ; taken from the Roman " Daily Evening Fasces," of the date of that tremendous occurrence.

NOTHING in the world affords a newspaper reporter so much satisfaction as gathering up the details of a bloody and mysterious murder, and writing them up with aggravating circumstantiality. He takes a living delight in this labor of love—for such it is to him especially if he knows that all the other papers have gone to press, and his will be the only one that will contain the dreadful intelligence. A feeling of regret has often come over me that I was not reporting in Rome when Cæsar was killed—reporting on an evening paper, and the only one in the city, and getting at least twelve hours ahead of the morning paper boys with this most magnificent "item" that ever fell to the lot of the craft. Other events have happened as startling as this, but none that possessed so peculiarly all the characteristics of the favorite "item" of the present day, magnified into grandeur and sublimity by the high rank, fame, and social and political standing of the actors in it.

However, as I was not permitted to report Cæsar's assassination in the regular way, it has at least afforded me rare satisfaction to translate the following able account of it from the original Latin of the *Roman Daily Evening Fasces* of that date—second edition.

"Our usually quiet city of Rome was thrown into a state of wild excitement yesterday by the occurrence of one of those bloody affrays which sicken the heart and fill the soul with fear, while they inspire all thinking men with forebodings for the future of a city where human life is held so cheaply, and the gravest laws are so openly set at defiance. As the result of that affray, it is our painful duty, as public journalists, to record the death of one of our most esteemed citizens—a man whose name is known wherever this paper circulates, and whose fame it has been our pleasure and our privilege to extend, and also to protect from the tongue of slander and falsehood, to the best of our poor ability. We refer to Mr. J. Cæsar, the Emperor-elect.

"The facts of the case, as nearly as our reporter could determine them from the conflicting statements of eye-witnesses, were about as follows :—The affair was an election row, of course. Nine-tenths of the ghastly butcheries that disgrace the city now-a-days grow out of the bickerings and jealousies and animosities engendered by these accursed elections. Rome would be the gainer by it if her very constables were elected to serve a century ; for in our experience we have never even been able to choose a dog-pelter without celebrating the event with a dozen knock-downs and a general cramming of the station-house with drunken vagabonds over-night. It is said that when the immense majority for Cæsar at the polls in the market was declared the other day, and the crown was offered to that gentleman, even his amazing unselfishness in refusing it three times was not sufficient to save him from the whispered insults of such men as Casca, of the Tenth Ward, and other hirelings of the disappointed candidate, hailing mostly from the Eleventh and Thirteenth and other outside districts, who were overheard speaking ironically and contemptuously of Mr. Cæsar's conduct upon that occasion.

"We are further informed that there are many among us who think they are justified in believing that the assassination of Julius Cæsar was a put-up thing—a cut-and-dried arrangement, hatched by Marcus Brutus and a lot of his hired roughs, and carried out only too faithfully according to the programme. Whether there be good grounds for this suspicion or not, we leave to the people to judge for themselves, only asking that they will read the following account of the sad occurrence carefully and dispassionately before they render that judgment.

"The Senate was already in session, and Cæsar was coming down the street towards the capitol, conversing with some personal friends, and followed as usual, by a large number of citizens. Just as he was passing in front of Demosthenes and Thucydides' drug-store, he was observing casually to a gentleman, who, our informant thinks, is a fortune-teller, that the Ides of March were come. The reply was, 'Yes, they are come, but not gone yet.' At this moment Artemidorus stepped up and passed the time of day, and asked Cæsar to read a schedule or a tract or something of the kind, which he had brought for his perusal. Mr. Decius Brutus also said something about an 'humble suit' which *he* wanted read. Artemidorus begged that attention might be paid to his first, because it was of personal consequence to Cæsar. The latter replied that what concerned himself should be read last, or words to that effect. Artemidorus begged and beseeched him to read the paper instantly. *   However. Cæsar shook him off, and refused to read any petition in the street. He then entered the capitol, and the crowd followed him.

"About this time the following conversation was overheard, and we consider that, taken in connection with the events which succeeded it, it bears an appalling significance : Mr. Papilius Lena remarked to George W. Cassius (commonly known as the 'Nobby Boy of the Third Ward'), a bruiser in the pay of the Opposition, that he hoped his enterprise to-day might thrive ; and when Cassius asked 'What enterprise ?' he only closed his left eye temporarily and said with simulated indifference, 'Fare you well,' and sauntered towards Cæsar. Marcus Brutus who is suspected of being the ringleader of the band that killed Cæsar, asked what it was that Lena had said. Cassius told him, and added in a low tone, '*I fear our purpose is discovered.*'

"Brutus told his wretched accomplice to keep an eye on Lena, and a moment after Cassius urged

that lean and hungry vagrant, Casca whose reputation here is none of the best, to be sudden for *he feared prevention*. He then turned to Brutus, apparently much excited, and asked what should be done, and swore that either he or Cæsar *should never turn back*—he would kill himself first. At this time Cæsar was talking to some of the back-country members about the approaching fall elections, and paying little attention to what was going on around him. Billy Trebonius got into

---

* Mark that : it is hinted by William Shakespeare, who saw the beginning and the end of the unfortunate affray, that this "schedule" was simply a note discovering to Cæsar that a plot was brewing to take his life.

conversation with the people's friend and Cæsar's—Mark Antony—and under some pretence or other got him away, and Brutus, Decius, Casca, Cinna, Metellus Cimber, and others of the gang of infamous desperadoes that infest Rome at present, closed around the doomed Cæsar. Then Metellus Cimber knelt down and begged that his brother might be recalled from banishment, but Cæsar rebuked him for his fawning conduct, and refused to grant his petition. Immediately, at Cimber's request, first Brutus and then Cassius begged for the return of the banished Publius; but Cæsar still refused. He said he could not be moved; that he was as fixed as the North Star, and·proceeded to speak in the most complimentary terms of the firmness of that star, and its steady character. Then he said he was like it, and he believed he was the only man in the country that was; therefore, since he was 'constant' that Cimber should be banished, he was also 'constant' that he should stay banished, and he'd be hanged if he didn't keep him so!

"Instantly seizing upon this shallow pretext for a fight, Casca sprang at Cæsar and 'struck him with a dirk, Cæsar grabbing him by the arm with his right hand, and launching a blow straight from the shoulder with his left, that sent the reptile bleeding to the earth. He then backed up against Pompey's statue, and squared himself to receive his assailants. Cassius and Cimber and Cinna rushed upon him with their daggers drawn, and the former succeeded in inflicting a wound upon his body; but before he could strike again, and before either of the others could strike at all, Cæsar stretched the three miscreants at his feet with as many blows of his powerful fist. By this time the Senate was in an indescribable uproar; the throng of citizens in the lobbies had blockaded the doors in their frantic efforts to escape from the building, the sergeant-at-arms and his assistants were struggling with the assassins, venerable senators had cast aside their encumbering robes, and were leaping over benches and flying down the aisles in wild confusion towards the shelter of the committee-rooms, and a thousand voices were shouting ' Po-lice ! Po-lice !' in discordant tones that rose above the frightful din like shrieking winds above the roaring of a tempest. And amid it all, great Cæsar stood with his back against the statue, like a lion at bay, and fought his assailants weaponless and hand to hand, with the defiant bearing and the unwavering courage which he had shown before on many a bloody field. Billy Trebonius and Caius Legarius struck him with their daggers and fell, as their brother-conspirators before them had fallen. But at last, when Cæsar saw his old friend Brutus step forward armed with a murderous knife, it is said he seemed utterly overpowered with grief and amazement, and dropping his invincible left arm by his side, he hid his face in the folds of his mantle and received the treacherous blow without an effort to stay the hand that gave it. He only said, ' *Et tu, Brute?* ' and fell lifeless, on the marble pavement.

"We learn that the coat deceased had on when he was killed was the same he wore in his tent on

the afternoon of the day he overcame the Nervii, and that when it was removed from the corpse it was found to be cut and gashed in no less than seven different places. There was nothing in the pockets. It will be exhibited at the coroner's inquest, and will be damning proof of the fact of the killing. These latter facts may be relied on, as we get them from Mark Antony, whose position enables him to learn every item of news connected with the one subject of absorbing interest of to-day.

"LATER.—While the coroner was summoning a jury, Mark Antony and other friends of the late Cæsar got hold of the body, and lugged it off to the Forum, and at last accounts Antony and Brutus were making speeches over it and raising such a row among the people that, as we go to press, the chief of police is satisfied there is going to be a riot, and is taking measures accordingly."

THE WIDOW'S PROTEST.

ONE of the saddest things that ever came under my notice (said the banker's clerk) was there in Corning, during the war. Dan Murphy enlisted as a private, and fought very bravely. The boys all liked him, and when a wound by-and-by weakened him down till carrying a musket was too heavy work for him, they clubbed together and fixed him up as a sutler. He made money then, and sent it always to his wife to bank for him. She was a washer and ironer, and knew enough by hard experience to keep money when she got it. She didn't waste a penny. On the contrary, she began to get miserly as her bank account grew. She grieved to part with a cent, poor creature, for twice in her hard-working life she had known what it was to be hungry, cold, friendless, sick, and without a dollar in the world, and she had a haunting dread of suffering so again. Well, at last Dan died; and the boys, in testimony of their esteem and respect for him, telegraphed to Mrs. Murphy to know if she would like to have him embalmed and sent home; when you know the usual custom was to dump a poor devil like him into a shallow hole, and *then* inform his friends what had become of him. Mrs. Murphy jumped to the conclusion that it would only cost two or three dollars to embalm her dead husband, and so she telegraphed "Yes." It was at the "wake" that the bill for embalming arrived and was presented to the widow.

She uttered a wild sad wail that pierced every heart, and said, "Sivinty-foive dollars for stooffin' Dan, blister their sowls! Did thim divils suppose I was goin' to stairt a Museim, that I'd be dalin' in such expinsive curiassities!"

The banker's clerk said there was not a dry eye in the house.

MR. BLOKE'S ITEM.

OUR esteemed friend, Mr. John William Bloke, of Virginia City, walked into the office where we are sub-editor at a late hour last night, with an expression of profound and heartfelt suffering upon his countenance, and sighing heavily, laid the following item reverently upon the desk, and walked slowly out again. He paused a moment at the door, and seemed struggling to command his feelings sufficiently to enable him to speak, and then, nodding his head towards his manuscript, ejaculated in a broken voice, "Friend of mine—oh! how sad!" and burst into tears. We were so moved at his distress that we did not think to call him back and endeavor to comfort him until he was gone, and it was too late. The paper had already gone to press, but knowing that our friend would consider the publication of this item important, and cherishing the hope that to print it would afford a melancholy satisfaction to his sorrowing heart, we stopped the press at once and inserted it in our columns :—

DISTRESSING ACCIDENT.—Last evening, about six o'clock, as Mr. William Schuyler, an old and respectable citizen of South Park, was leaving his residence to go down town, as has been his usual custom for many years with the exception only of a short interval in the spring of 1850, during which he was confined to his bed by injuries received in attempting to stop a runaway horse by thoughtlessly placing himself directly in its wake and throwing up his hands and shouting, which if he had done so even a single moment sooner, must inevitably have frightened the animal still more instead of checking its speed, although disastrous enough to himself as it was, and rendered more melancholy and distressing by reason of the presence of his wife's mother, who was there and saw the sad occurrence, notwithstanding it is at least likely, though not necessarily so, that she should be reconnoitering in another direction when incidents occur, not being vivacious and on the look out, as a general thing, but even the reverse, as her own mother is said to have stated, who is no more, but died in the full hope of a glorious resurrection, upwards of three years ago, aged eighty-six, being a Christian woman and without guile, as it were, or property, in consequence of the fire of 1849, which destroyed every single thing she had in the world. But such is life. Let us all take warning by this solemn occurrence, and let us endeavor so to conduct ourselves that when we come to die we can do it. Let us place our hands upon our heart, and say with earnestness and sincerity that from this day forth we will beware of the intoxicating bowl.—*First Edition of the Californian.*

The head editor has been in here raising the mischief, and tearing his hair and kicking the furniture about, and abusing me like a pick-pocket. He says that every time he leaves me in charge of the paper for half an hour, I get imposed upon by the first infant or the first idiot that comes along. And he says that that distressing item of Mr. Bloke's is nothing but a lot of distressing bosh, and has no point to it, and no sense in it, and no information in it, and that there was no sort of necessity for stopping the press to publish it.

Now all this comes of being good-hearted. If I had been as unaccommodating and unsympathetic as some people, I would have told Mr. Bloke that I wouldn't receive his communication at such a late hour; but no, his snuffling distress touched my heart, and I jumped at the chance of doing something to modify his misery. I never read his item to see whether there was anything wrong about it, but hastily wrote the few lines which preceded it, and sent it to the printers. And what has my kindness done for me? It has done nothing but bring down upon me a storm of abuse and ornamental blasphemy.

Now I will read that item myself, and see if there is any foundation for all this fuss. And if there is, the author of it shall hear from me.

   *   *   *   *   *   *   *   *   *   *

I have read it, and I am bound to admit that it seems a little mixed at a first glance. However, I will peruse it once more.

   *   *   *   *   *   *   *   *   *   *

I have read it again, and it does really seem a good deal more mixed than ever.

   *   *   *   *   *   *   *   *   *   *

I have read it over five times, but if I can get at the meaning of it, I wish I

may get my just deserts. It won't bear analysis. There are things about it which I cannot understand at all. It don't say whatever became of William Schuyler. It just says enough about him to get one interested in his career, and then drops him. Who is William Schuyler, anyhow, and what part of South Park did he live in, and if he started down town at six o'clock, did he ever get

there, and if he did, did anything happen to him? Is *he* the individual that met
with the "distressing accident?" Considering the elaborate circumstantiality
of detail observable in the item, it seems to me that it ought to contain more
information than it does. On the contrary, it is obscure—and not only obscure,
but utterly incomprehensible. Was the breaking of Mr. Schuyler's leg, fifteen
years ago, the "distressing accident" that plunged Mr. Bloke into unspeakable
grief, and caused him to come up here at dead of night and stop our press to
acquaint the world with the circumstance? Or did the "distressing accident"
consist in the destruction of Schuyler's mother-in-law's property in early times?
Or did it consist in the death of that person herself three years ago? (albeit it
does not appear that she died by accident.) In a word, what *did* that "distressing accident" consist in? What did that drivelling ass of a Schuyler stand *in
the wake* of a runaway horse for, with his shouting and gesticulating, if he
wanted to stop him? And how the mischief could he get run over by a
horse that had already passed beyond him? And what are we to take "warning"
by? and how is this extraordinary chapter of incomprehensibilities going to be
a "lesson" to us? And, above all, what has the intoxicating "bowl" got to do
with it, anyhow? It is not stated that Schuyler drank, or that his wife drank,
or that his mother-in-law drank, or that the horse drank—wherefore, then, the
reference to the intoxicating bowl? It does seem to me that if Mr. Bloke had
let the intoxicating bowl alone himself, he never would have got into so much
trouble about this exasperating imaginary accident. I have read this absurd
item over and over again, with all its insinuating plausibility, until my head
swims; but I can make neither head nor tail of it. There certainly seems to
have been an accident of some kind or other, but it is impossible to determine
what the nature of it was, or who was the sufferer by it. I do not like to do it,
but I feel compelled to request that the next time anything happens to one of
Mr. Bloke's friends, he will append such explanatory notes to his account of it
as will enable me to find out what sort of an accident it was and whom it happened to. I had rather all his friends should die than that I should be driven
to the verge of lunacy again in trying to cipher out the meaning of another
such production as the above.

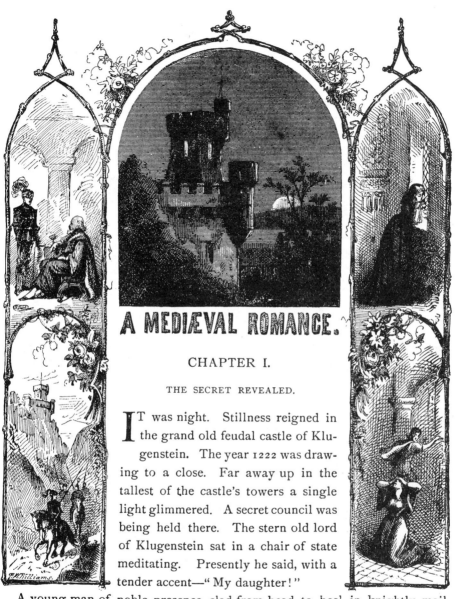

A MEDIÆVAL ROMANCE.

CHAPTER I.

THE SECRET REVEALED.

IT was night. Stillness reigned in the grand old feudal castle of Klugenstein. The year 1222 was drawing to a close. Far away up in the tallest of the castle's towers a single light glimmered. A secret council was being held there. The stern old lord of Klugenstein sat in a chair of state meditating. Presently he said, with a tender accent—" My daughter!"

A young man of noble presence, clad from head to heel in knightly mail, answered—" Speak, father!"

"My daughter, the time is come for the revealing of the mystery that hath puzzled all your young life. Know, then, that it had its birth in the matters which I shall now unfold. My brother Ulrich is the great Duke of Brandenburgh. Our father, on his deathbed, decreed that if no son were born to Ulrich the succession should pass to my house, provided a *son* were born to me. And further, in case no son were born to either, but only daughters, then the succession should pass to Ulrich's daughter if she proved stainless; if she did not, my daughter should succeed if she retained a blameless name. And so I and my old wife here prayed fervently for the good boon of a son, but the prayer was vain. You were born to us. I was in despair. I saw the mighty prize slipping from my grasp—the splendid dream vanishing away! And I had been so hopeful! Five years had Ulrich lived in wedlock, and yet his wife had borne no heir of either sex.

"'But hold,' I said, 'all is not lost.' A saving scheme had shot athwart my brain. You were born at midnight. Only the leech, the nurse, and six waiting-women knew your sex. I hanged them every one before an hour sped. Next morning all the barony went mad with rejoicing over the proclamation that a *son* was born to Klugenstein—an heir to mighty Brandenburgh! And well the secret has been kept. Your mother's own sister nursed your infancy, and from that time forward we feared nothing.

"When you were ten years old a daughter was born to Ulrich. We grieved, but hoped for good results from measles, or physicians, or other natural enemies of infancy, but were always disappointed. She lived, she throve—Heaven's malison upon her! But it is nothing. We are safe. For, ha! ha! have we not a son? And is not our son the future Duke? Our well-beloved Conrad, is it not so?—for woman of eight-and-twenty years as you are, my child, none other name than that hath ever fallen to *you!*

"Now it hath come to pass that age hath laid its hand upon my brother, and he waxes feeble. The cares of state do tax him sore, therefore he wills that you shall come to him and be already Duke in act, though not yet in name. Your servitors are ready—you journey forth to-night.

"Now listen well. Remember every word I say. There is a law as old as Germany, that if any woman sit for a single instant in the great ducal chair before she hath been absolutely crowned in presence of the people—SHE SHALL DIE! So heed my words. Pretend humility. Pronounce your judgments from the Premier's chair, which stands at the *foot* of the throne. Do this until you are crowned and safe. It is not likely that your sex will ever be discovered, but still it is the part of wisdom to make all things as safe as may be in this treacherous earthly life."

"O my father! is it for this my life hath been a lie? Was it that I might cheat my unoffending cousin of her rights? Spare me, father, spare your child!"

"What, hussy! Is this my reward for the august fortune my brain has wrought for thee? By the bones of my father, this puling sentiment of thine but ill accords with my humor. Betake thee to the Duke instantly, and beware how thou meddlest with my purpose!"

Let this suffice of the conversation. It is enough for us to know that the prayers, the entreaties, and the tears of the gentle-natured girl availed nothing. Neither they nor anything could move the stout old lord of Klugenstein. And so, at last, with a heavy heart, the daughter saw the castle gates close behind her, and found herself riding away in the darkness surrounded by a knightly array of armed vassals and a brave following of servants.

The old baron sat silent for many minutes after his daughter's departure, and then he turned to his sad wife, and said—

"Dame, our matters seem speeding fairly. It is full three months since I sent the shrewd and handsome Count Detzin on his devilish mission to my brother's daughter Constance. If he fail we are not wholly safe, but if he do succeed no power can bar our girl from being Duchess, e'en though ill fortune should decree she never should be Duke!"

"My heart is full of bodings; yet all may still be well."

"Tush, woman! Leave the owls to croak. To bed with ye, and dream of Brandenburgh and grandeur!"

CHAPTER II.

FESTIVITY AND TEARS.

SIX days after the occurrences related in the above chapter, the brilliant capital of the Duchy of Brandenburgh was resplendent with military pageantry, and noisy with the rejoicings of loyal multitudes, for Conrad, the young heir to the crown, was come. The old Duke's heart was full of happiness, for Conrad's handsome person and graceful bearing had won his love at once. The great halls of the palace were thronged with nobles, who welcomed Conrad bravely; and so bright and happy did all things seem, that he felt his fears and sorrows passing away, and giving place to a comforting contentment.

But in a remote apartment of the palace a scene of a different nature was transpiring. By a window stood the Duke's only child, the Lady Constance. Her eyes were red and swollen, and full of tears. She was alone. Presently she fell to weeping anew, and said aloud—

"The villain Detzin is gone—has fled the dukedom! I could not believe it at first, but, alas! it is too true. And I loved him so. I dared to love him though I knew the Duke my father would never let me wed him. I loved him—but now I hate him! With all my soul I hate him! Oh, what is to become of me? I am lost, lost, lost! I shall go mad!"

CHAPTER III.

THE PLOT THICKENS.

A FEW months drifted by. All men published the praises of the young Conrad's government, and extolled the wisdom of his judgments, the mercifulness of his sentences, and the modesty with which he bore himself in his great office. The old Duke soon gave everything into his hands, and sat apart and listened with proud satisfaction while his heir delivered the decrees of the crown from the seat of the Premier. It seemed plain that one so loved and praised and honored of all men as Conrad was could not be otherwise than happy. But, strangely enough, he was not. For he saw with dismay that the Princess Constance had begun to love him! The love of the rest of the world was happy fortune for him, but this was freighted with danger! And he saw, moreover, that the delighted Duke had discovered his daughter's passion likewise, and was already dreaming of a marriage. Every day somewhat of the deep sadness that had been in the princess's face faded away; every day hope and animation beamed brighter from her eye; and by and by even vagrant smiles visited the face that had been so troubled.

Conrad was appalled. He bitterly cursed himself for having yielded to the instinct that had made him seek the companionship of one of his own sex when he was new and a stranger in the palace—when he was sorrowful and yearned for a sympathy such as only women can give or feel. He now began to avoid his cousin. But this only made matters worse, for naturally enough, the more he avoided her the more she cast herself in his way. He marvelled at this at first, and next it startled him. The girl haunted him; she hunted him; she happened upon him at all times and in all places, in the night as well as in the day. She seemed singularly anxious. There was surely a mystery somewhere.

This could not go on for ever. All the world was talking about it. The Duke was beginning to look perplexed. Poor Conrad was becoming a very ghost through dread and dire distress. One day as he was emerging from a private ante-room attached to the picture gallery Constance confronted him, and seizing both' his hands in hers, exclaimed—

"Oh, why do you avoid me? What have I done—what have I said, to lose your kind opinion of me—for surely I had it once? Conrad, do not despise me, but pity a tortured heart? I cannot, cannot hold the words unspoken longer, lest they kill me—I LOVE YOU, CONRAD! There, despise me if you must, but they *would* be uttered!"

Conrad was speechless. Constance hesitated a moment, and then, misinterpreting his silence, a wild gladness flamed in her eyes, and she flung her arms about his neck and said—

"You relent! you relent! You *can* love me—you *will* love me! Oh, say you will, my own, my worshipped Conrad!"

Conrad groaned aloud. A sickly pallor overspread his countenance, and he trembled like an aspen. Presently, in desperation, he thrust the poor girl from him, and cried—

"You know not what you ask! It is for ever and ever impossible!" And then he fled like a criminal, and left the princess stupefied with amazement. A minute afterward she was crying and sobbing there, and Conrad was crying and sobbing in his chamber. Both were in despair. Both saw ruin staring them in the face.

By and by Constance rose slowly to her feet and moved away, saying—

"To think that he was despising my love at the very moment that I thought it was melting his cruel heart! I hate him! He spurned me—did this man—he spurned me from him like a dog!"

CHAPTER IV.

THE AWFUL REVELATION.

TIME passed on. A settled sadness rested once more upon the countenance of the good Duke's daughter. She and Conrad were seen together no more now. The Duke grieved at this. But as the weeks wore away Conrad's color came back to his cheeks, and his old-time vivacity to his eye, and he administered the government with a clear and steadily ripening wisdom.

Presently a strange whisper began to be heard about the palace. It grew louder; it spread farther. The gossips of the city got hold of it. It swept the dukedom. And this is what the whisper said—

"The Lady Constance hath given birth to a child!"

When the lord of Klugenstein heard it he swung his plumed helmet thrice around his head and shouted—

"Long live Duke Conrad!—for lo, his crown is sure from this day forward! Detzin has done his errand well, and the good scoundrel shall be rewarded!"

And he spread the tidings far and wide, and for eight-and-forty hours no soul in all the barony but did dance and sing, carouse and illuminate, to celebrate the great event, and all at proud and happy old Klugenstein's expense.

CHAPTER V.

THE FRIGHTFUL CATASTROPHE.

THE trial was at hand. All the great lords and barons of Brandenburgh were assembled in the Hall of Justice in the ducal palace. No space was left unoccupied where there was room for a spectator to stand or sit. Conrad, clad in purple and ermine, sat in the Premier's chair, and on either side sat the great judges of the realm. The old Duke had sternly commanded that the trial of his daughter should proceed without favor, and then had taken to his bed broken-hearted. His days were numbered. Poor Conrad had begged, as for his very life, that he might be spared the misery of sitting in judgment upon his cousin's crime, but it did not avail.

The saddest heart in all that great assemblage was in Conrad's breast.

The gladdest was in his father's, for, unknown to his daughter " Conrad," the old Baron Klugenstein was come, and was among the crowd of nobles triumphant in the swelling fortunes of his house.

After the heralds had made due proclamation and the other preliminaries had followed, the venerable Lord Chief-Justice said—" Prisoner, stand forth !"

The unhappy princess rose, and stood unveiled before the vast multitude. The Lord Chief-Justice continued—

" Most noble lady, before the great judges of this realm it hath been charged and proven that out of holy wedlock your Grace hath given birth unto a child, and by our ancient law the penalty is death excepting in one sole contingency, whereof his Grace the acting Duke, our good Lord Conrad, will advertise you in his solemn sentence now ; wherefore give heed."

Conrad stretched forth his reluctant sceptre, and in the self-same moment the womanly heart beneath his robe yearned pityingly toward the doomed prisoner, and the tears came into his eyes. He opened his lips to speak, but the Lord Chief-Justice said quickly—

" Not there, your Grace, not there ! It is not lawful to pronounce judgment upon any of the ducal line SAVE FROM THE DUCAL THRONE !"

A shudder went to the heart of poor Conrad, and a tremor shook the iron frame of his old father likewise. CONRAD HAD NOT BEEN CROWNED—dared he profane the throne ? He hesitated and turned pale with fear. But it must be done. Wondering eyes were already upon him. They would be suspicious eyes if he hesitated longer. He ascended the throne. Presently he stretched forth the sceptre again, and said—

" Prisoner, in the name of our sovereign Lord Ulrich, Duke of Brandenburgh, I proceed to the solemn duty that hath devolved upon me. Give heed to my words. By the ancient law of the land, except you produce the partner of your guilt and deliver him up to the executioner you must surely die. Embrace this opportunity —save yourself while yet you may. Name the father of your child !"

12

A solemn hush fell upon the great court—a silence so profound that men could hear their own hearts beat. Then the princess slowly turned, with eyes gleaming with hate, and pointing her finger straight at Conrad, said—

" Thou art the man !"

An appalling conviction of his helpless, hopeless peril struck a chill to Conrad's

heart like the chill of death itself. What power on earth could save him ! To disprove the charge he must reveal that he was a woman, and for an uncrowned woman to sit in the ducal chair was death ! At one and the same moment he and his grim old father swooned and fell to the ground.

*   *   *   *   *   *   *   *   *   *

The remainder of this thrilling and eventful story will NOT be found in this or any other publication, either now or at any future time.

The truth is, I have got my hero (or heroine) into such a particularly close place that I do not see how I am ever going to get him (or her) out of it again, and therefore I will wash my hands of the whole business, and leave that person to get out the best way that offers—or else stay there. I thought it was going to be easy enough to straighten out that little difficulty, but it looks different now.

PETITION CONCERNING COPYRIGHT.

TO THE HONORABLE THE SENATE AND HOUSE OF REPRESENTATIVES IN CONGRESS ASSEMBLED:

Whereas, The Constitution guarantees equal rights to all, backed by the Declaration of Independence; and

Whereas, Under our laws, the right of property in real estate is perpetual; and

Whereas, Under our laws, the right of property in the literary result of a citizen's intellectual labor is restricted to forty-two years; and

Whereas, Forty-two years seems an exceedingly just and righteous term, and a sufficiently long one for the retention of property:

Therefore, Your petitioner, having the good of his country solely at heart, humbly prays that "equal rights" and fair and equal treatment may be meted out to all citizens, by the restriction of rights in *all* property, real estate included, to the beneficent term of forty-two years. Then shall all men bless your honorable body and be happy. And for this will your petitioner ever pray.

MARK TWAIN.

A PARAGRAPH NOT ADDED TO THE PETITION.

The charming absurdity of restricting property-rights in books to forty-two years sticks prominently out in the fact that hardly any man's books ever *live* forty-two years, or even the half of it; and so, for the sake of getting a shabby advantage of the heirs of about one Scott or Burns or Milton in a hundred years, the law makers of the "Great" Republic are content to leave that poor little pilfering edict upon the statute books. It is like an emperor lying in wait to rob a phenix's nest, and waiting the necessary century to get the chance.

AFTER-DINNER SPEECH.

MR. CHAIRMAN AND LADIES AND GENTLEMEN: I thank you for the compliment which has just been tendered me, and to show my appreciation of it I will not afflict you with many words. It is pleasant to celebrate in this peaceful way, upon this old mother soil, the anniversary of an experiment which was born of war with this same land so long ago, and wrought out to a successful issue by the devotion of our ancestors. It has taken nearly a hundred years to bring the English and Americans into kindly and mutually appreciative relations, but I believe it has been accomplished at last. It was a great step when the two last misunderstandings were settled by arbitration instead of cannon. It is another great step when England adopts our sewing machines without claiming the invention—as usual. It was another when they imported one of our sleeping cars the other day. And it warmed my heart more than I can tell, yesterday, when I witnessed the spectacle of an Englishman ordering an American sherry cobbler of his own free will and accord—and not only that but with a great brain and a level head reminding the bar-keeper not to forget the strawberries. With a common origin, a common language, a common literature, a common religion and—common drinks, what is longer needful to the cementing of the two nations together in a permanent bond of brotherhood?

This is an age of progress, and ours is a progressive land. A great and glorious land, too—a land which has developed a Washington, a Franklin, a Wm. M. Tweed, a Longfellow, a Motley, a Jay Gould, a Samuel C. Pomeroy, a recent Congress which has never had its equal—(in some respects) and a United States Army which conquered sixty Indians in eight months by tiring them out—which is much better than uncivilized slaughter, God knows. We have a criminal jury system which is superior to any in the world; and its efficiency is only marred by the difficulty of finding twelve men every day who don't know anything and can't read. And I may observe that we have an insanity plea that would have saved Cain. I think I can say, and say with pride, that we have some legislatures that bring higher prices than any in the world.

I refer with effusion to our railway system, which consents to let us live, though it might do the opposite, being our owners. It only destroyed three thousand and seventy lives last year by collisions, and twenty-seven thousand two hundred and sixty by running over heedless and unnecessary people at crossings. The companies seriously regretted the killing of these thirty thousand people, and went so far as to pay for some of them—voluntarily, of course, for the meanest of us would not claim that we possess a court treacherous enough to enforce a law against a railway company. But thank Heaven the railway companies are generally disposed to do the right and kindly thing without compulsion. I know of an instance which greatly touched me at the time. After an accident the company sent home the remains of a dear distant old relative of mine in a basket, with the remark, "Please state what figure you hold him at—and return the basket." Now there couldn't be anything friendlier than that.

But I must not stand here and brag all night. However, you won't mind a body bragging a little about his country on the fourth of July. It is a fair and legitimate time to fly the eagle. I will say only one more word of brag—and a hopeful one. It is this. We have a form of government which gives each man a fair chance and no favor. With us no individual is born with a right to look down upon his neighbor and hold him in contempt. Let such of us as are not dukes find our consolation in that. And we may find hope for the future in the fact that as unhappy as is the condition of our political morality to-day, England has risen up out of a far fouler since the days when Charles I. ennobled courtezans and all political place was a matter of bargain and sale. There is hope for us yet. *

---

* At least the above is the speech which I was *going* to make, but our minister, Gen. Schenck, presided, and after the blessing, got up and made a great long inconceivably dull harangue, and wound up by saying that inasmuch as speech-making did not seem to exhilarate the guests much, all further oratory would be dispensed with, during the evening. and we could just sit and talk privately to our elbow-neighbors and have a good sociable time. It is known that in consequence of that remark forty-four perfected speeches died in the womb. The depression, the gloom, the solemnity that reigned over the banquet from that time forth will be a lasting memory with many that were there. By that one thoughtless remark Gen. Schenck lost forty-four of the best friends he had in England. More than one said that night, "And this is the sort of person that is sent to represent us in a great sister empire!"

LIONISING MURDERERS.

I HAD heard so much about the celebrated fortune-teller Madame ——, that I went to see her yesterday. She has a dark complexion naturally, and this effect is heightened by artificial aids which cost her nothing. She wears curls— very black ones, and I had an impression that she gave their native attractiveness a lift with rancid butter. She wears a reddish check handkerchief, cast loosely around her neck, and it was plain that her other one is slow getting back from the wash. I presume she takes snuff. At any rate, something resembling it had lodged among the hairs sprouting from her upper lip. I know she likes garlic—I knew that as soon as she sighed. She looked at me searchingly for nearly a minute, with her black eyes, and then said—

" It is enough. Come ! "

She started down a very dark and dismal corridor—I stepping close after her. Presently she stopped, and said that, as the way was so crooked and dark, perhaps she had better get a light. But it seemed ungallant to allow a woman to put herself to so much trouble for me, and so I said—

" It is not worth while, madam. If you will heave another sigh, I think I can follow it."

So we got along all right. Arrived at her official and mysterious den, she asked me to tell her the date of my birth, the exact hour of that occurrence, and the color of my grandmother's hair. I answered as accurately as I could. Then she said—

" Young man, summon your fortitude—do not tremble. I am about to reveal the past."

Information concerning the *future* would be in a general way, more "——

" Silence ! You have had much trouble, some joy, some good fortune, some bad. Your great grandfather was hanged."

" That is a l—."

" Silence ! Hanged sir. But it was not his fault. He could not help it."

" I am glad you do him justice."

" Ah—grieve, rather, that the jury did. He was hanged. His star crosses yours in the fourth division, fifth sphere. Consequently you will be hanged also."

" In view of this cheerful "——

" I *must* have silence. Yours was not, in the beginning, a criminal nature, but circumstances changed it. At the age of nine you stole sugar. At the age of fifteen you stole money. At twenty you stole horses. At twenty-five you committed arson. At thirty, hardened in crime, you became an editor.

You are now a public lecturer. Worse things are in store for you. You will be sent to Congress. Next, to the penitentiary. Finally, happiness will come again—all will be well—you will be hanged."

I was now in tears. It seemed hard enough to go to Congress; but to be hanged—this was too sad, too dreadful. The woman seemed surprised at my grief. I told her the thoughts that were in my mind. Then she comforted me.

" Why, man," * she said, "hold up your head—*you* have nothing to grieve about. Listen. You will live in New Hampshire. In your sharp need and distress the Brown family will succor you—such of them as Pike the assassin left alive. They will be benefactors to· you. When you shall have grown fat upon their bounty, and are grateful and happy, you will desire to make some modest return for these things, and so you will go to the house some night and brain the whole family with an axe. You will rob the dead bodies of your benefactors, and disburse your gains in riotous living among the rowdies and courtesans of Boston. Then you will be arrested, tried, condemned to be hanged, thrown into prison. Now is your happy day. You will be converted —you will be converted just as soon as every effort to compass pardon, commutation, or reprieve has failed—and then! Why, then, every morning and every

---

* In this paragraph the fortune-teller details the exact history of the Pike-Brown assassination case in New Hampshire, from the succoring and saving of the stranger Pike by the Browns, to the subsequent hanging and coffining of that treacherous miscreant. She adds nothing, invents nothing, exaggerates nothing (see any New England paper for November 1869). This Pike-Brown case is selected merely as a type, to illustrate a custom that prevails, not in New Hampshire alone, but in every State in the union—I mean the sentimental custom of visiting, petting, glorifying, and snuffling over murderers like this Pike, from the day they enter the jail under sentence of death until they swing from the gallows. The following extract from the *Temple Bar* (1866) reveals the fact that this custom is not confined to the United States :—"On December 31st, 1841, a man named John Johnes, a shoemaker, murdered his sweetheart, Mary Hallam, the daughter of a respectable laborer, at Mansfield, in the county of Nottingham. He was executed on March 23d, 1842. He was a man of unsteady habits, and gave way to violent fits of passion. The girl declined his addresses, and he said if he did not have her no one else should. After he had inflicted the first wound, which was not immediately fatal, she begged for her life, but seeing him resolved, asked for time to pray. He said that he would pray for both, and completed the crime. The wounds were inflicted by a shoemaker's knife, and her throat was cut barbarously. After this he dropped on his knees some time, and prayed God to have mercy on two unfortunate lovers. He made no attempt to escape, and confessed the crime. After his imprisonment he behaved in the most decorous manner ; he won upon the good opinion of the jail chaplain, and he was visited by the Bishop of Lincoln. It does not appear that he expressed any contrition for the crime, but seemed to pass away with triumphant certainty that he was going to rejoin his victim in heaven. *He was visited by some pious and benevolent ladies of Nottingham, some of whom declared he was a child of God, if ever there was one. One of the ladies sent him a white camelia to wear at his execution.*"

afternoon, the best and purest young ladies of the village will assemble in your cell and sing hymns.   This will show that assassination is respectable.   Then you will write a touching letter, in which you will forgive all those recent Browns.   This will excite the public admiration.   No public can withstand magnanimity.   Next, they will take you to the scaffold, with great *éclat*, at the head of an imposing procession composed of clergymen, officials, citizens generally, and young ladies walking pensively two and two, and bearing bouquets

and immortelles.   You will mount the scaffold, and while the great concourse stand uncovered in your presence, you will read your sappy little speech which the minister has written for you.   And then, in the midst of a grand and impressive silence, they will swing you into per—— Paradise, my son.   There will not be a dry eye on the ground.   You will be a hero!   Not a rough there but will envy you.   Not a rough there but will resolve to emulate you.   And next, a great procession will follow you to the tomb—will weep over your remains—

the young ladies will sing again the hymns made dear by sweet associations connected with the jail, and, as a last tribute of affection, respect, and appreciation of your many sterling qualities, they will walk two and two around your bier, and strew wreaths of flowers on it. And lo! you are canonized. Think of it, son—ingrate, assassin, robber of the dead, drunken brawler among thieves and harlots in the slums of Boston one month, and the pet of the pure and innocent daughters of the land the next! A bloody and hateful devil—a bewept, bewailed, and sainted martyr—all in a month! Fool!—so noble a fortune, and yet you sit here grieving!"

"No, madame," I said, "you do me wrong, you do indeed. I am perfectly satisfied. I did not know before that my great-grandfather was hanged, but it is of no consequence. He has probably ceased to bother about it by this time— and I have not commenced yet. I confess, madame, that I do something in the way of editing and lecturing, but the other crimes you mention have escaped my memory. Yet I must have committed them—you would not deceive a stranger. But let the past be as it was, and let the future be as it may—these are nothing. I have only cared for one thing. I have always felt that I should be hanged some day, and somehow the thought has annoyed me considerably; but if you can only assure me that I shall be hanged in New Hampshire"——

"Not a shadow of a doubt!"

"Bless you, my benefactress!—excuse this embrace—you have removed a great load from my breast. To be hanged in New Hampshire is happiness—it leaves an honored name behind a man, and introduces him at once into the best New Hampshire society in the other world."

I then took leave of the fortune-teller. But, seriously, is it well to glorify a murderous villain on the scaffold, as Pike was glorified in New Hampshire? Is it well to turn the penalty for a bloody crime into a reward? Is it just to do it? Is it safe?

A NEW CRIME.

LEGISLATION NEEDED.

THIS country, during the last thirty or forty years, has produced some of the most remarkable cases of insanity of which there is any mention in history. For instance, there was the Baldwin case, in Ohio, twenty-two years ago. Baldwin, from his boyhood up, had been of a vindictive, malignant, quarrelsome nature. He put a boy's eye out once, and never was heard upon any occasion to utter a regret for it. He did many such things. But at last he did something that was serious. He called at a house just after dark, one evening, knocked, and when the occupant came to the door, shot him dead, and then tried to escape,

187

but was captured. Two days before, he had wantonly insulted a helpless cripple, and the man he afterward took swift vengeance upon with an assassin bullet had knocked him down. Such was the Baldwin case. The trial was long and exciting: the community was fearfully wrought up. Men said this spiteful, bad-hearted villain had caused grief enough in his time, and now he should satisfy the law. But they were mistaken; Baldwin was *insane* when he did the deed—they had not thought of that. By the arguments of counsel it was shown that at half-past ten in the morning on the day of the murder, Baldwin became insane, and remained so for eleven hours and a half exactly. This just covered the case comfortably, and he was acquitted. Thus, if an unthinking and excited community had been listened to instead of the arguments of counsel, a poor crazy creature would have been held to a fearful responsibility for a mere freak of madness. Baldwin went clear, and although his relatives and friends were naturally incensed against the community for their injurious suspicions and remarks, they said let it go for this time, and did not prosecute. The Baldwins were very wealthy. This same Baldwin had momentary fits of insanity twice afterward, and on both occasions killed people he had grudges against. And on both these occasions the circumstances of the killing were so aggravated, and the murders so seemingly heartless and treacherous, that if Baldwin had not been insane he would have been hanged without the shadow of a doubt. As it was, it required all his political and family influence to get him clear in one of the cases, and cost him not less than 10,000 dollars to get clear in the other. One of these men he had notoriously been threatening to kill for twelve years. The poor creature happened, by the merest piece of ill fortune, to come along a dark alley at the very moment that Baldwin's insanity came upon him, and so he was shot in the back with a gun loaded with slugs.

Take the case of Lynch Hackett, of Pennsylvania. Twice, in public, he attacked a German butcher by the name of Bemis Feldner, with a cane, and both times Feldner whipped him with his fists. Hackett was a vain, wealthy, violent gentleman, who held his blood and family in high esteem, and believed that a reverent respect was due to his great riches. He brooded over the shame of his chastisement for two weeks, and then, in a momentary fit of insanity, armed himself to the teeth, rode into town, waited a couple of hours until he saw Feldner coming down the street with his wife on his arm, and then, as the couple passed the doorway in which he had partially concealed himself, he drove a knife into Feldner's neck, killing him instantly. The widow caught the limp form and eased it to the earth. Both were drenched with blood. Hackett jocosely remarked to her that as a professional butcher's recent wife she could appreciate the artistic neatness of the job that left her in condition to marry again, in case she wanted to. This remark, and another which he made to a friend, that his position in society made the killing of an obscure citizen simply an " eccentricity " instead of a crime, were shown to be evidences of insanity, and so Hackett escaped punishment. The jury were hardly inclined to accept these as proofs, at first, inasmuch as the prisoner had never been insane before the murder, and under the tranquilizing effect of the butchering had immediately regained his right mind; but when the defence came to show that a third cousin of Hackett's wife's stepfather was insane, and not only insane, but had a nose the very counterpart of Hackett's, it was plain that insanity was hereditary in the family, and Hackett had come by it by legitimate inheritance. Of course the jury then acquitted him. But it was a merciful providence that Mrs. H.'s people had been afflicted as shown, else Hackett would certainly have been hanged.

However, it is not possible to recount all the marvellous cases of insanity that have come under the public notice in the last thirty or forty years. There was the Durgin case in New Jersey three years ago. The servant girl, Bridget Durgin, at dead of night, invaded her mistress' bedroom and carved the lady literally to pieces with a knife. Then she dragged the body to the middle of the floor, and beat and banged it with chairs and such things. Next she opened the feather beds, and strewed the contents around, saturated everything with kerosene, and set fire to the general wreck. She now took up the young child of the murdered woman in her blood-smeared hands, and walked off, through the snow, with no shoes on, to a neighbor's house a quarter of a mile off, and told a string of wild, incoherent stories about some men coming and setting fire to the house; and then she cried piteously, and without seeming to think there was anything suggestive about the blood upon her hands, her clothing, and the baby, volunteered the remark that she was afraid those men had murdered her mistress! Afterward, by her own confession and other testimony, it was proved that the mistress had always been kind to the girl, consequently there was no revenge in the murder; and it was also shown that the girl took nothing away from the burning house, not even her own shoes, and consequently robbery was not the motive. Now, the reader says, "Here comes that same old plea of insanity again." But the reader has deceived himself this time. No such plea was offered in her defence. The judge sentenced her, nobody persecuted the Governor with petitions for her pardon and she was promptly hanged.

There was that youth in Pennsylvania, whose curious confession was published some years ago. It was simply a conglomeration of incoherent drivel from beginning to end, and so was his lengthy speech on the scaffold afterward. For a whole year he was haunted with a desire to disfigure a certain young woman, so that no one would marry her. He did not love her himself, and did not want to marry her, but he did not want anybody else to do it. He would not go anywhere with her, and yet was opposed to anybody else's escorting her. Upon one occasion he declined to go to a wedding with her, and when she got other company, lay in wait for the couple by the road, intending to make them go back or kill the escort. After spending sleepless nights over his ruling desire for a full year, he at last attempted its execution—that is, attempted to disfigure the young woman. It was a success. It was permanent. In trying to shoot her cheek (as she sat at the supper table with her parents and brothers and sisters) in such a manner as to mar its comeliness, one of his bullets wandered a little out of the course, and she dropped dead. To the very last moment of his life he bewailed the ill luck that made her move her face just at the critical moment. And so he died, apparently about half persuaded that somehow it was chiefly her own fault that she got killed. This idiot was hanged. The plea of insanity was not offered.

Insanity certainly is on the increase in the world, and crime is dying out. There are no longer any murders—none worth mentioning, at any rate. Formerly, if you killed a man, it was possible that you were insane—but now, if you, having friends and money, kill a man it is *evidence* that you are a lunatic. In these days, too, if a person of good family and high social standing steals anything, they call it *kleptomania*, and send him to the lunatic asylum. If a person of high standing squanders his fortune in dissipation, and closes his career with strychnine or a bullet, " Temporary Aberration " is what was the trouble with *him*.

Is not this insanity plea becoming rather common ? Is it not so common that the reader confidently expects to see it offered in every criminal case that comes before the courts ? And is it not so cheap, and so common, and often so trivial, that the reader smiles in derision when the newspaper mentions it ? And is it not curious to note how very often it wins acquittal for the prisoner ? Of late years it does not seem possible for a man to so conduct himself, before killing another man, as not to be manifestly insane. If he talks about the stars, he is insane. If he appears nervous and uneasy an hour before the killing, he is insane. If he weeps over a great grief, his friends shake their heads, and fear that he is "not right." If, an hour after the murder, he seems ill at ease, pre-occupied and excited, he is unquestionably insane.

Really, what we want now, is not laws against crime, but a law against *insanity*. There is where the true evil lies.

A CURIOUS DREAM.

CONTAINING A MORAL.

NIGHT before last I had a singular dream. I seemed to be sitting on a door-step (in no particular city perhaps), ruminating, and the time of night appeared to be about twelve or one o'clock. The weather was balmy and delicious. There was no human sound in the air, not even a footstep. There was no sound of any kind to emphasize the dead stillness, except the occasional hollow barking of a dog in the distance and the fainter answer of a further dog. Presently up the street I heard a bony clack-clacking, and guessed it was the castanets of a serenading party. In a minute more a tall skeleton, hooded, and half-clad in a tattered and mouldy shroud, whose shreds were flapping about the ribby lattice-work of its person swung by me with a stately stride, and disappeared in the grey gloom of the starlight. It had a broken and worm-eaten coffin on its shoulder and a bundle of something in its hand. I knew what the clack-clacking was then; it was this party's joints working together, and his elbows knocking against his sides as he walked. I may say I was surprised. Before I could collect my thoughts and enter upon any speculations as to what this apparition might portend, I heard another one coming—for I recognized his clack-clack. He had two-thirds of a coffin on his shoulder, and some foot- and head-boards under his arm. I mightily wanted to peer under his hood and speak to him, but when he turned and smiled upon me with his cavernous sockets and his projecting grin as he went by, I thought I would not detain him. He was hardly gone when I heard the clacking again, and another one issued from the shadowy half-light. This one was bending under a heavy gravestone, and dragging a shabby coffin after him by a string. When he got to me he gave me a steady look for a moment or two, and then rounded to and backed up to me, saying:

"Ease this down for a fellow, will you?"

I eased the gravestone down till it rested on the ground, and in doing so noticed that it bore the name of "John Baxter Copmanhurst," with "May, 1839," as the date of his death. Deceased sat wearily down by me, and wiped his os frontis with his major maxillary—chiefly from former habit I judged, for I could not see that he brought away any perspiration.

"It is too bad, too bad," said he, drawing the remnant of the shroud about him and leaning his jaw pensively on his hand. Then he put his left foot up on his knee and fell to scratching his ankle bone absently with a rusty nail which he got out of his coffin.

"What is too bad, friend?"

"Oh, everything, everything. I almost wish I never had died."

"You surprise me. Why do you say this? Has anything gone wrong? What is the matter?"

"Matter! Look at this shroud—rags. Look at this gravestone, all battered up. Look at that disgraceful old coffin. All a man's property going to ruin and destruction before his eyes, and ask him if anything is wrong? Fire and brimstone!"

13

"Calm yourself, calm yourself," I said. "It *is* too bad—it is certainly too bad, but then I had not supposed that you would much mind such matters, situated as you are."

"Well, my dear sir, I *do* mind them. My pride is hurt, and my comfort is impaired—destroyed, I might say. I will state my case—I will put it to you in such a way that you can comprehend it, if you will let me," said the poor skeleton, tilting the hood of his shroud back, as if he were clearing for action, and thus unconsciously giving himself a jaunty and festive air very much at variance with the grave character of his position in life—so to speak—and in prominent contrast with his distressful mood.

"Proceed," said I.

"I reside in the shameful old graveyard a block or two above you here, in this street—there, now, I just expected that cartilage would let go!—third rib from the bottom, friend, hitch the end of it to my spine with a string, if you have got such a thing about you, though a bit of silver wire is a deal pleasanter, and more durable and becoming, if one keeps it polished—to think of shredding out and going to pieces in this way, just on account of the indifference and neglect of one's poster- ity!"—and the poor ghost grated his teeth in a way that give me a wrench and a shiver—for the effect is mightily increased by the absence of muffling flesh and cuticle. "I reside in that old graveyard, and have for these thirty years; and I tell you things are changed since I first laid this old tired frame there, and turned over, and stretched out for a long sleep, with a delicious sense upon me of being *done* with bother, and grief, and anxiety, and doubt, and fear, for ever and ever, and listening with comfortable and increasing satisfaction to the sexton's work, from the startling clatter of his first spadeful on my coffin till it dulled away to the faint patting that shaped the roof of my new home—delicious! My! I wish you could try it to-night!" and out of my reverie deceased fetched me with a rattling slap with a bony hand.

"Yes, sir, thirty years ago I laid me down there, and was happy. For it was out in the country, then—out in the breezy, flowery, grand old woods, and the lazy winds gossiped with the leaves, and the squirrels capered over us and around us, and the creeping things visited us, and the birds filled the tranquil solitude with music. Ah, it was worth ten years of a man's life to be dead then! Everything was pleasant. I was in a good neighborhood, for all the dead people that lived near me belonged to the best families in the city. Our posterity appeared to think the world of us. They kept our graves in the very best condition; the fences were always in faultless repair, head-boards were kept painted or whitewashed, and were replaced with new ones as soon as they began to look rusty or decayed; monuments were kept upright, railings intact and bright, the rosebushes and shrubbery trimmed, trained, and free from blemish, the walks clean and smooth and gravelled. But that day is gone by. Our descendants have forgotten us. My grandson lives in a stately house built with money made by these old hands of mine, and I sleep in a neglected grave with invading vermin that gnaw my shroud to build them nests

withal! I and friends that lie with me founded and secured the prosperity of this fine city, and the stately bantling of our loves leaves us to rot in a dilapidated cemetery which neighbors curse and strangers scoff at. See the difference between the old time and this—for instance: Our graves are all caved in, now; our head-boards have rotted away and tumbled down; our railings reel this way and that, with one foot in the air, after a fashion of unseemly levity; our monuments lean wearily, and our gravestones bow their heads discouraged; there be no adornments any more—no roses, nor shrubs, nor gravelled walks, nor anything that is a comfort to the eye; and even the paintless old board fence that did make a show of holding us sacred from companionship with beasts and the defilement of heedless feet, has tottered till it overhangs the street, and only advertises the presence of our dismal resting-place and invites yet more derision to it.   And now we cannot hide our poverty and tatters in the friendly woods, for the city has stretched its withering arms abroad and taken us in, and all that remains of the cheer of our old home is the cluster of lugubrious forest trees that stand, bored and weary of a city life, with their feet in our coffins, looking into the hazy distance and wishing they were there. I tell you it is disgraceful!

"You begin to comprehend—you begin to see how it is.   While our descendants are living sumptuously on our money, right around us in the city, we have to fight hard to keep skull and bones together.   Bless you, there isn't a grave in our cemetery that doesn't leak—not one.   Every time it rains in the night we have to climb out and roost in the trees—and sometimes we are wakened suddenly by the chilly water trickling down the back of our necks.   Then I tell you there is a general heaving up of old graves and kicking over of old monuments, and scamp-ering of old skeletons for the trees!   Bless me, if you had gone along there some such nights after twelve you might have seen as many as fifteen of us roosting on one limb, with our joints rattling drearily and the wind wheezing through our ribs! Many a time we have perched there for three or four dreary hours, and then come down, stiff and chilled through and drowsy, and borrowed each other's skulls to bale out our graves with—if you will glance up in my mouth, now as I tilt my head back, you can see that my head-piece is half full of old dry sediment—how top-heavy and stupid it makes me sometimes!   Yes, sir, many a time if you had happened to come along just before the dawn you'd have caught us baling out the graves and hanging our shrouds on the fence to dry.   Why, I had an elegant shroud stolen from there one morning—think a party by the name of Smith took it, that resides in a plebeian graveyard over yonder—I think so because the first time I ever saw him he hadn't anything on but a check-shirt, and the last time I saw him, which was at a social gathering in the new cemetery, he was the best dressed corpse in the company—and it is a significant fact that he left when he saw me; and presently an old woman from here missed her coffin—she generally took it with her when she went anywhere, because she was liable to take cold and bring on the spasmodic rheumatism that originally killed her if she exposed herself to the night air much. She was named Hotchkiss—Anna Matilda Hotchkiss—you might know her? She has two upper front teeth, is tall, but a good deal inclined to stoop, one rib on the left side gone, has one shred of rusty hair hanging from the left side of her head, and one little tuft just above and a little forward of her right ear, has her under jaw wired on one side where it had worked loose, small bone of left forearm gone—lost in a fight—has a kind of swagger in her gait and a 'gallus' way of going with her arms akimbo and her nostrils in the air—has been pretty free and easy, and is all damaged and battered up till she looks like a queensware crate in ruins—maybe you have met her?"

"God forbid!" I involuntarily ejaculated, for somehow I was not looking for that form of question, and it caught me a little off my guard. But I hastened to make amends for my rudeness, and say, "I simply meant I had not had the honor—for I would not deliberately speak discourteously of a friend of yours. You were saying that you were robbed—and it was a shame, too—but it appears by what is left of the shroud you have on that it was a costly one in its day. How did——"

A most ghastly expression began to develop among the decayed features and shrivelled integuments of my guest's face, and I was beginning to grow uneasy and distressed, when he told me he was only working up a deep, sly smile, with a wink in it, to suggest that about the time he acquired his present garment a ghost in a neighboring cemetery missed one. This reassured me, but I begged him to confine himself to speech thenceforth, because his facial expression was uncertain. Even

with the most elaborate care it was liable to miss fire.   Smiling should especially be
avoided.   What *he* might honestly consider a shining success was likely to strike
me in a very different light.   I said I liked to see a skeleton cheerful, even decor-
ously playful, but I did not think smiling was a skeleton's best hold.

"Yes, friend," said the poor skeleton, "the facts are just as I have given them to
you.   Two of these old graveyards—the one that I resided in and one further along
—have been deliberately neglected by our descendants of to-day until there is no
occupying them any longer.   Aside from the osteological discomfort of it—and that
is no light matter this rainy weather—the present state of things is ruinous to
property.   We have got to move or be content to see our effects wasted away and
utterly destroyed.   Now, you will hardly believe it, but it is true, nevertheless,
that there isn't a single coffin in good repair among all my acquaintance—now that
is an absolute fact.   I do not refer to low people who come in a pine box mounted
on an express wagon, but I am talking about your high-toned, silver mounted
burial-case, your monumental sort, that travel under black plumes at the head of a
procession and have choice of cemetery lots—I mean folks like the Jarvises, and
the Bledsoes and Burlings, and such.   They are all about ruined.   The most
substantial people in our set, they were.   And now look at them—utterly used up
and poverty-stricken.   One of the Bledsoes actually traded his monument to a late
bar-keeper for some fresh shavings to put under his head.   I tell you it speaks
volumes, for there is nothing a corpse takes so much pride in as his monument.   He
loves to read the inscription.   He comes after awhile to believe what it says himself, and then you may see him sitting on the fence night after night enjoying it.
Epitaphs are cheap, and they do a poor chap a world of good after he is dead,
especially if he had hard luck while he was alive.   I wish they were used more.
Now, I don't complain, but confidentially I *do* think it was a little shabby in my
descendants to give me nothing but this old slab of a gravestone—and all the more
that there isn't a compliment on it.   It used to have

'GONE TO HIS JUST REWARD'

on it, and I was proud when I first saw it, but by-and-by I noticed that whenever
an old friend of mine came along he would hook his chin on the railing and pull a

long face and read along down till he came to that, and then he would chuckle to himself and walk off, looking satisfied and comfortable. So I scratched it off to get rid of those fools. But a dead man always takes a deal of pride in his monument. Yonder goes half-a-dozen of the Jarvises, now, with the family monument along. And Smithers and some hired spectres went by with his a while ago. Hello, Higgins, good-bye, old friend! That's Meredith Higgins—died in '44—belongs to our set in the cemetery—fine old family—great-grandmother was an Injun—I am on the most familiar terms with him—he didn't hear me was the reason he didn't answer me. And I am sorry, too, because I would have liked to introduce you. You would admire him. He is the most disjointed, sway-backed, and generally distorted old skeleton you ever saw, but he is full of fun. When he laughs it sounds like rasping two stones together, and he always starts it off with a cheery screech like raking a nail across a window-pane. Hey, Jones! That is old Columbus Jones—shroud cost four hundred dollars—entire trousseau, including monument, twenty-seven hundred. This was in the Spring of '26. It was enormous style for those days. Dead people came all the way from the Alleghanies to see his things—the party that occupied the grave next to mine remembers it well. Now do you see that individual going along with a piece of a head-board under his arm, one leg-bone below his knee gone, and not a thing in the world on? That is Barstow Dalhousie, and next to Columbus Jones he was the most sumptuously outfitted person that ever entered our cemetery. We are all leaving. We cannot tolerate the treatment we are receiving at the hands of our descendants. They open new cemeteries, but they leave us to our ignominy. They mend the streets, but they never mend anything that is about us or belongs to us. Look at that coffin of mine—yet I tell you in its day it was a piece of furniture that would have attracted attention in any drawing-room in this city. You may have it if you want it—I can't afford to repair it. Put a new bottom in her, and part of a new top, and a bit of fresh lining along the left side, and you'll find her about as comfortable as any receptacle of her species you ever tried. No thanks—no, don't mention it—you have been civil to me, and I would give you all the property I have got before I would seem ungrateful. Now this winding-sheet is a kind of a sweet thing in its way, if you would like to ——. No? Well, just as you say, but

I wished to be fair and liberal—there's nothing mean about *me*. Good-by, friend, I must be going. I may have a good way to go to-night—don't know. I only know one thing for certain, and that is, that I am on the emigrant trail, now, and I'll never sleep in that crazy old cemetery again. I will travel till I find respectable quarters, if I have to hoof it to New Jersey. All the boys are going. It was decided in public conclave, last night, to emigrate, and by the time the sun rises there won't be a bone left in our old habitations. Such cemeteries may suit my surviving friends, but they do not suit the remains that have the honor to make these remarks. My opinion is the general opinion. If you doubt it, go and see how the departing ghosts upset things before they started. They were almost riotous in their demonstrations of distaste. Hello, here are some of the Bledsoes, and if you will give me a lift with this tombstone I guess I will join company and jog along with them—mighty respectable old family, the Bledsoes, and used to always come out in six-horse hearses, and all that sort of thing fifty years ago when I walked these streets in daylight. Good-by, friend."

And with his gravestone on his shoulder he joined the grisly procession, dragging his damaged coffin after him, for notwithstanding he pressed it upon me so earnestly, I utterly refused his hospitality. I suppose that for as much as two hours these sad outcasts went clacking by, laden with their dismal effects, and all that time I sat pitying them. One or two of the youngest and least dilapidated among them inquired about midnight trains on the railways, but the rest seemed unacquainted with that mode of travel, and merely asked about common public roads to various towns and cities, some of which are not on the map now, and vanished from it and from the earth as much as thirty years ago, and some few of them never *had* existed anywhere but on maps, and private ones in real estate agencies at that. And they asked about the condition of the cemeteries in these towns and cities, and about the reputation the citizens bore as to reverence for the dead.

This whole matter interested me deeply, and likewise compelled my sympathy for these homeless ones. And it all seeming real, and I not knowing it was a dream, I mentioned to one shrouded wanderer an idea that had entered my head to publish an account of this curious and very sorrowful exodus, but said also that I could not describe it truthfully, and just as it occurred, without seeming to trifle with a grave subject and exhibit an irreverence for the dead that would shock and distress their surviving friends. But this bland and stately remnant of a former citizen leaned him far over my gate and whispered in my ear, and said :—

"Do not let that disturb you. The community that can stand such graveyards as those we are emigrating from can stand anything a body can say about the neglected and forsaken dead that lie in them."

At that very moment a cock crowed, and the weird procession vanished and left not a shred or a bone behind. I awoke, and found myself lying with my head out of the bed and "sagging" downwards considerably—a position favorable to dreaming dreams with morals in them, maybe, but not poetry.

NOTE.—The reader is assured that if the cemeteries in his town are kept in good order, this Dream is not levelled at his town at all, but is levelled particularly and venomously at the *next* town.

It's one o' de ole Blue Hen's chickens, I is.

A TRUE STORY.

IT was summer time, and twilight. We were sitting on the porch of the farm-house, on the summit of the hill, and "Aunt Rachel" was sitting respectfully below our level, on the steps,—for she was our servant, and colored. She was of mighty frame and stature; she was sixty years old, but her eye was undimmed and her strength unabated. She was a cheerful, hearty soul, and it was no more trouble for her to laugh than it is for a bird to sing. She was under fire, now, as usual when the day was done. That is to say, she was being chaffed without mercy, and was enjoying it. She would let off peal after peal of laughter, and then sit with her face in her hands and shake with throes of enjoyment which she could no longer get breath enough to express. At such a moment as this a thought occurred to me, and I said:

"Aunt Rachel, how is it that you've lived sixty years and never had any trouble?"

She stopped quaking. She paused, and there was a moment of silence.

202

She turned her face over her shoulder toward me, and said, without even a smile in her voice :—

"Misto C——, is you in 'arnest?"

It surprised me a good deal; and it sobered my manner and my speech, too. I said :—

"Why, I thought—that is, I meant—why, you *can't* have had any trouble. I've never heard you sigh, and never seen your eye when there wasn't a laugh in it."

She faced fairly around, now, and was full of earnestness.

"Has I had any trouble? Misto C——, I's gwyne to tell you, den I leave it to you. I was bawn down 'mongst de slaves; I knows all 'bout slavery, 'case I ben one of 'em my own se'f. Well, sah, my ole man—dat's my husban'—he was lovin' an' kind to me, jist as kind as you is to yo' own wife. An' we had chil'en —seven chil'en—an' we loved dem chil'en jist de same as you loves yo' chil'en. Dey was black, but de Lord can't make no chil'en so black but what dey mother loves 'em an' wouldn't give 'em up, no, not for anything dat's in dis whole world.

"Well sah, I was raised in ole Fo'ginny, but my mother she was raised in Maryland; an' my *souls!* she was turrible when she'd git started! My *lan'!* but she'd make de fur fly! When she'd git into dem tantrums, she always had one word dat she said. She'd straighten herse'f up an' put her fists in her hips an' say, ' I want you to understan' dat I wa'nt bawn in the mash to be fool' by trash! I's one o' de ole Blue Hen's Chickens, *I* is!' 'Ca'se, you see, dat's what folks dat's bawn in Maryland calls deyselves, an' dey's proud of it. Well, dat was her word. I don't ever forgit it, beca'se she said it so much, an' beca'se she said it one day when my little Henry tore his wris' awful, and most busted his head, right up at de top of his forehead, an' de niggers didn't fly aroun' fas' enough to 'tend to him. An' when dey talk' back at her, she up an' she says, ' Look-a-heah!' she says, ' I want you niggers to understan' dat I wa'nt bawn in de mash to be fool' by trash! I's one o' de ole Blue Hen's Chickens, *I* is!' an' den she clar' dat kitchen an' bandage' up de chile herse'f. So I says dat word, too, when I's riled.

"Well, bymeby my ole mistis say she's broke, an' she' got to sell all the niggers on de place. An' when I heah dat dey gwyne to sell us all off at oction in Richmon', oh de good gracious! I know what dat mean!"

Aunt Rachel had gradually risen, while she warmed to her subject, and now she towered above us, black against the stars.

"Dey put chains on us an' put us on a stan' as high as dis po'ch,—twenty foot high,—an' all de people stood aroun', crowds an' crowds. An' dey'd come up dah an' look at us all roun', an' squeeze our arm, an' make us git up an' walk, an' den say, 'Dis one too ole,' or 'Dis one lame,' or 'Dis one don't 'mount to much.' An' dey sole my ole man, an' took him away, an' dey begin to sell my chil'en an' take *dem* away, an' I begin to cry; an' de man say, 'Shet up yo' dam blubberin',' an' hit me on de mouf wid his han'. An' when de las' one was gone but my little Henry, I grab' *him* clost up to my breas' so, an' I ris up an' says, 'You shan't take him away,' I says; 'I'll kill de man dat tetches him!' I says. But my little Henry whisper an' say, 'I gwyne to run away, an' den I work an' buy yo' freedom.' Oh, bless de chile, he always so good! But dey got him —dey got him, de men did; but I took and tear de clo'es mos' off of 'em an' beat 'em over de head wid my chain; an' *dey* give it to *me*, too, but I didn't mine dat.

"Well, dah was my ole man gone, an' all my chil'en, all my seven chil'en— an' six of 'em I hain't set eyes on ag'in to dis day, an' dat's twenty-two year ago las' Easter. De man dat bought me b'long' in Newbern, an' he took me dah. Well, bymeby de years roll on an' de waw come. My marster he was a Confedrit colonel, an' I was his family's cook. So when de Unions took dat town, dey all run away an' lef' me all by myse'f wid de other niggers in dat mons'us big house. So de big Union officers move in dah, an' dey ask me would I cook for *dem*. 'Lord bless you,' says I, 'dat's what I's *for.*'

"Dey wa'nt no small-fry officers, mine you, dey was de biggest dey *is ;* an' de way dey made dem sojers mosey roun'! De Gen'l he tole me to boss dat kitchen; an' he say, 'If anybody come meddlin' wid you, you jist make 'em walk chalk; don't you be afeared,' he say; 'you's 'mong frens, now.'

"Well, I thinks to myse'f, if my little Henry ever got a chance to run away, he'd make to de Norf, o' course. So one day I comes in dah whar de big officers was, in de parlor, an' I drops a kurtchy, so, an' I up an' tole 'em 'bout my Henry, dey a-listenin' to my troubles jist de same as if I was white folks; an' I says, 'What I come for is beca'se if he got away and got up Norf whar you gemmen comes from, you might 'a' seen him, maybe, an' could tell me so as I could fine him ag'in; he was very little, an' he had a sk-yar on his lef' wris', an' at de top of his forehead.' Den dey look mournful, an' de Gen'l say, 'How long sence you los' him?' an' I say, 'Thirteen year.' Den de Gen'l say, 'He wouldn't be little no mo', now—he's a man!'

"I never thought o' dat befo'! He was only dat little feller to *me*, yit. I never thought 'bout him growin' up an' bein' big. But I see it den. None o' de gemmen had run acrost him, so dey couldn't do nothin' for me. But all dat time, do' *I* didn't know it, my Henry *was* run off to de Norf, years an' years, an, he was a barber, too, an' worked for hisse'f. An' bymeby, when de waw come' he ups an' he says: ' I's done barberin',' he says, ' I's gwyne to fine my ole mammy, less'n she's dead.' So he sole out an' went to whar dey was recruitin', an' hired hisse'f out to de colonel for his servant; an' den he went all froo de battles everywhah, huntin' for his ole mammy; yes indeedy, he'd hire to fust one officer an' den another, tell he'd ransacked de whole Souf; but you see *I* didn't know nuffin 'bout *dis*. How was *I* gwyne to know it?

"Well, one night we had a big sojer ball; de sojers dah at Newbern was always havin' balls an' carryin' on. Dey had 'em in my kitchen, heaps o' times, 'ca'se it was so big. Mine you, I was *down* on sich doin's; beca'se my place was wid de officers, an' it rasp me to have dem common sojers cavortin' roun' my kitchen like dat. But I alway' stood aroun' an' kep' things straight, I did; an' sometimes dey'd git my dander up, an' den I'd make 'em clar dat kitchen, mine I *tell* you!

"Well, one night—it was a Friday night—dey comes a whole plattoon f'm a *nigger* ridg ment dat was on guard at de house,—de house was head-quarters, you know,—an' den I was jist a-*bilin'*! Mad? I was jist a-*boomin'*! I swelled aroun', an' swelled aroun'; I jist was a-itchin' for 'em to do somefin for to start me. *An'* dey was a-waltzin' an' a-dancin'! *my!* but dey was havin' a time! an'

I jist a-swellin' an' a-swellin' up! Pooty soon, 'long comes *sich* a spruce young nigger a-sailin' down de room wid a yaller wench roun' de wais'; an' roun' an' roun' an' roun' dey went, enough to make a body drunk to look at 'em; an' when dey got abreas' o' me, dey went to kin' o' balancin' aroun' fust on one leg an' den on t'other, an' smilin' at my big red turban, an' makin' fun, an' I ups an' says '*Git* along wid you!—rubbage!' De young man's face kin' o' changed, all of a sudden, for 'bout a second, but den he went to smilin' ag'in, same as he

was befo'. Well, 'bout dis time, in comes some nig-gers dat played music and b'long' to de ban', an' dey never could git along widout put-tin' on airs. An' de very fust air dey put on dat night, I lit into 'em! Dey laughed, an' dat made me wuss. De res' o' de niggers got to laughin', an' den my soul alive but I was hot! My eye was jist a-blazin'! I jist straightened my-self up, so,—jist as I is now, plum to de ceilin', mos',—an' I digs my fists into my hips, an' I says, 'Look-a-heah!' I says, 'I want you niggers to understan' dat I wa'nt bawn in de mash to be fool' by trash! I's one o' de ole Blue Hen's Chickens, *I* is!' an' den I see dat young man stan' a-starin' an' stiff, lookin' kin' o' up at de ceilin' like he fo'got somefin, an' couldn't 'member it no mo'. Well, I jist march' on dem niggers,—so, lookin' like a gen'l,—an' dey jist cave' away befo' me an' out at de do'. An' as dis young man was a-goin' out, I heah him say to another nigger, 'Jim,' he says, 'you go 'long an' tell de cap'n I be on han' 'bout eight o'clock in de mawnin'; dey's somefin on my mine,' he says; 'I don't sleep no mo' dis night. You go 'long, he says, 'an' leave me by my own se'f.'

"Dis was 'bout one o'clock in de mawnin'. Well, 'bout seven, I was up an' on han', gittin' de officers' breakfast. I was a-stoopin' down by de stove,—jist so, same as if yo' foot was de stove,—an' I'd opened de stove do' wid my right han',—so, pushin' it back, jist as I pushes yo' foot,—an' I'd jist got de pan o' hot biscuits in my han' an' was 'bout to raise up, when I see a black face come aroun' under mine, an' de eyes a-lookin' up into mine, jist as I's a-lookin' up clost under yo' face now; an' I jist stopped *right dah*, an' never budged! jist gazed , an' gazed, so; an' de pan begin to tremble, an' all of a sudden I *knowed!* De pan drop' on de flo' an' I grab his lef' han' an' shove back his sleeve,—jist so, as I's doin' to you,—an' den I goes for his forehead an' push de hair back, so, an' 'Boy!' I says, 'if you an't my Henry, what is you doin' wid dis welt on yo' wris' an' dat sk-yar on yo' forehead? De Lord God ob heaven be praise', I got my own ag'in!'

"Oh, no, Misto C——, *I* hain't had no trouble. An' no *joy!*"

THE SIAMESE TWINS.

I DO not wish to write of the personal *habits* of these strange creatures solely, but also of certain curious details of various kinds concerning them, which belonging only to their private life, have never crept into print. Knowing the Twins intimately, I feel that I am peculiarly well qualified for the task I have taken upon myself.

The Siamese Twins are naturally tender and affectionate in disposition, and have clung to each other with singular fidelity throughout a long and eventful life. Even as children they were inseparable companions; and it was noticed that they always seemed to prefer each other's society to that of any other persons. They nearly always played together; and, so accustomed was their mother to this peculiarity, that, whenever both of them chanced to be lost, she usually only hunted for one of them—satisfied that when she found that one she would find his brother somewhere in the immediate neighborhood. And yet these creatures were ignorant and unlettered—barbarians themselves and the offspring of barbarians, who knew not the light of philosophy and science. What a withering rebuke is this to our boasted civilization, with its quarrelings, its wranglings, and its separations of brothers!

As men, the Twins have not always lived in perfect accord; but still there has always been a bond between them which made them unwilling to go away from each other and dwell apart. They have even occupied the same house, as a general thing, and it is believed that they have never failed to even sleep together on any night since they were born. How surely do the habits of a lifetime become second nature to us! The Twins always go to bed at the same time; but Chang usually gets up about an hour before his brother. By an understanding between themselves, Chang does all the in-door work and Eng runs all the errands. This is because Eng likes to go out; Chang's habits are sedentary. However, Chang always goes along. Eng is a Baptist, but Chang is a Roman Catholic; still, to please his brother, Chang consented to be baptized at the same time that Eng was, on condition that it should not "count." During the War they were strong partizans, and both fought gallantly all through the great struggle—Eng on the Union side and Chang on the Confederate. They took each other prisoners at Seven Oaks, but the proofs of capture were so evenly balanced in favor of each, that a general army court had to be assembled to determine which one was properly the captor, and which the captive. The jury was unable to agree for a long time; but the vexed question was finally decided by agreeing to consider them both prisoners, and then exchanging them. At one time Chang was convicted of disobedience of orders, and sentenced to ten days in the guard-house, but Eng, in spite of all arguments, felt obliged to share his imprisonment, notwithstanding he himself was entirely innocent; and so, to save the blameless brother from suffering, they had to discharge both from custody—the just reward of faithfulness.

14

Upon one occasion the brothers fell out about something, and Chang knocked Eng down, and then tripped and fell on him, whereupon both clinched and began to beat and gouge each other without mercy. The bystanders interferred, and tried to separate them, but they could not do it, and so allowed them to fight it out. In the end both were disabled, and were carried to the hospital on one and the same shutter.

Their ancient habit of going always together had its drawbacks when they reached man's estate, and entered upon the luxury of courting. Both fell in love with the same girl. Each tried to steal clandestine interviews with her, but at the critical moment the other would always turn up. By and by Eng saw, with distraction, that Chang had won the girl's affections; and, from that day forth, he had to bear with the agony of being a witness to all their dainty billing and cooing. But with a magnanimity that did him infinite credit, he succumbed to his fate, and gave countenance and encouragement to a state of things that bade fair to sunder his generous heart-strings. He sat from seven every evening until two in the morning, listening to the fond foolishness of the two lovers, and to the concussion of hundreds of squandered kisses—for the privilege of sharing only one of which he would have given his right hand. But he sat patiently, and waited, and gaped, and yawned, and stretched, and longed for two o'clock to come. And he took long walks with the lovers on moonlight evenings—sometimes traversing ten miles, notwithstanding he was usually suffering from rheumatism. He is an inveterate smoker; but he could not smoke on these occasions, because the young lady was painfully sensitive to the smell of tobacco. Eng cordially wanted them married, and done with it; but although Chang often asked the momentous question, the young lady could not gather sufficient courage to answer it while Eng was by. However, on one occasion, after having walked some sixteen miles, and sat up till nearly daylight, Eng dropped asleep, from sheer exhaustion, and then the question was asked and answered. The lovers were married. All acquainted with the circumstance applauded the noble brother-in-law. His unwavering faithfulness was the theme of every tongue. He had stayed by them all through their long and arduous courtship; and when at last they were married, he lifted his hands above their heads, and said with impressive unction, " Bless ye, my children I will never desert ye ! " and he kept his word. Fidelity like this is all too rare in this cold world.

By and by Eng fell in love with his sister-in-law's sister, and married her, and since that day they have all lived together, night and day, in an exceeding sociability which is touching and beautiful to behold, and is a scathing rebuke to our boasted civilization.

The sympathy existing between these two brothers is so close and so refined that the feelings, the impulses, the emotions of the one are instantly experienced by the other. When one is sick, the other is sick; when one feels pain, the other feels it; when one is angered, the other's temper takes fire. We have already seen with what happy facility they both fell in love with the same girl. Now, Chang is bitterly opposed to all forms of intemperance, on principle; but Eng is the reverse—for, while these men's feelings and emotion are so closely wedded, their reasoning faculties are unfettered; their *thoughts* are free. Chang belongs to the Good Templars, and is a hard working, enthusiastic supporter of all temperance reforms. But, to his bitter distress, every now and then Eng gets drunk, and, of course, that makes Chang drunk too. This unfortunate thing has been a great sorrow to Chang, for it almost destroys his usefulness in his favorite field of effort. As sure as he is to head a great temperance procession Eng ranges up alongside of him, prompt to the minute, and drunk as a lord; but yet no more dismally and hopelessly drunk than his brother, who has not tasted a drop. And so the two begin to hoot and yell, and throw mud and bricks at the Good Templars; and of course they break up the procession. It would be manifestly wrong to punish Chang for what Eng does, and, therefore, the Good Templars accept the untoward situation, and suffer in silence and sorrow. They have officially and deliberately examined into the matter, and find Chang blameless. They have taken the two brothers and filled Chang full of warm water and sugar and Eng full of whisky, and in twenty-five minutes it was not possible to tell which was the drunkest. Both were as drunk as loons—and on hot whisky punches, by the smell of their breath. Yet all the while Chang's moral principles were unsullied, his conscience clear; and so all just men were forced to confess that he was not morally, but only physically drunk. By every right and by every moral evidence the man was strictly sober; and, therefore, it caused his friends all the more anguish to see him shake hands with the pump, and try to wind his watch with his night-key.

There is a moral in these solemn warnings—or, at least, a warning in these solemn morals; one or the other. No matter, it is somehow. Let us heed it; let us profit by it.

I could say more of an instructive nature about these interesting beings, but let what I have written suffice.

Having forgotton to mention it sooner, I will remark in conclusion, that the ages of the Siamese Twins are respectively fifty-one and fifty-three years.

SPEECH AT THE SCOTTISH BANQUET IN LONDON.

A T the anniversary festival of the Scottish Corporation of London on Monday evening, in response to the toast of "The Ladies," MARK TWAIN replied. The following is his speech as reported in the *London Observer:*—

"I am proud, indeed, of the distinction of being chosen to respond to this especial toast, to ' The Ladies,' or to women if you please, for that is the preferable term, perhaps ; it is certainly the older, and therefore the more entitled to reverence. (Laughter.) I have noticed that the Bible, with that plain, blunt honesty which is such a conspicuous characteristic of the Scriptures, is always particular to never refer to even the illustrious mother of all mankind herself as a ' lady,' but speaks of her as a woman. (Laughter.) It is odd, but you will find it is so. I am peculiarly proud of this honor, because I think that the toast to women is one which, by right and by every rule of gallantry, should take precedence of all others—of the army, of the navy, of even royalty itself—perhaps, though the latter is not necessary in this day and in this land, for the reason that, tacitly, you do drink a broad general health to all good women when you drink the health of the Queen of England and the Princess of Wales. (Loud cheers.) I have in mind a poem just now which is familiar to you all, familiar to everybody. And what an inspiration that was (and how instantly the present toast recalls the verses to all our minds) when the most noble, the most gracious, the purest, and sweetest of all poets says :—

> "'Woman ! O woman !—er——
> Wom——'

(Laughter.) However, you remember the lines ; and you remember how feelingly, how daintily, how almost imperceptibly the verses raise up before you, feature by feature, the ideal of a true and perfect woman ; and how, as you contemplate the finished marvel, your homage grows into worship of the intellect that could create so fair a thing out of mere breath, mere words. And you call to mind now, as I speak, how the poet, with stern fidelity to the history of all humanity, delivers this beautiful child of his heart and his brain over to the trials and the sorrows that must come to all, sooner or later, that abide in the earth, and how the pathetic story culminates in that apostrophe—so wild, so regretful, so full of mournful retrospection. The lines run thus :—

> "' Alas !—alas !—a—alas !
> ——Alas !—— — —alas !'

—and so on. (Laughter.) I do not remember the rest ; but, taken altogether, it seems to me that poem is the noblest tribute to woman that human genius has ever brought forth—(laughter)—and I feel that if I were to talk hours I could not do my great theme completer or more graceful justice than I have now done in simply quoting that poet's matchless words. (Renewed laughter.) The phases of the womanly nature are infinite in their variety. Take any type of woman, and you shall find in it something to respect, something to admire, something to love. And you shall find the whole joining you heart and hand. Who was more patriotic than Joan of Arc ? Who was braver? Who has given us a grander instance of self-sacrificing devotion ? Ah ! you remember, you remember well, what a throb of pain, what a great tidal wave of grief swept over us all when Joan of Arc fell at Waterloo. (Much laughter.) Who does not sorrow for the loss of Sappho, the sweet singer of Israel? (Laughter.) Who among us does not miss the gentle ministrations, the softening influences, the humble piety of Lucretia Borgia ? (Laughter.) Who can join in the heartless libel that says woman is extravagant in dress when he can look back and call to mind our simple and lowly mother Eve arrayed in her modification of the Highland costume. (Roars of laughter.) Sir, women have been soldiers, women have been painters, women have been poets. As long as language lives the name of Cleopatra will live. And, not because she conquered George III.—(laughter)—but because she wrote those divine lines—

> " ' Let dogs delight to bark and bite,
> For God hath made them so.'

(More laughter.) The story of the world is adorned with the names of illustrious ones of our own sex—some of them sons of St. Andrew, too—Scott, Bruce, Burns, the warrior Wallace, Ben Nevis—(laughter)—the gifted Ben Lomond, and the great new Scotchman, Ben Disraeli.* (Great laughter.) Out of the great plains of history tower whole mountain ranges of sublime women—the Queen of Sheba, Josephine, Semiramis, Sairey Gamp ; the list is endless—(laughter)—but I will not call the mighty roll, the names rise up in your own memories at the mere suggestion, luminous with the glory of deeds that cannot die, hallowed by the loving worship of the good and the true of all epochs and all climes. (Cheers.) Suffice it for our pride and our honor that we in our day have added to it such names as those of Grace Darling and Florence Nightingale. (Cheers.) Woman is all that she should be—gentle, patient, long suffering, trustful, unselfish, full of generous impulses. It is her blessed mission to comfort the sorrowing, plead for the erring, encourage the faint of purpose, succor the distressed, uplift the fallen, befriend the friendless—in a word, afford the healing of her sympathies and a home in her heart for all the bruised and persecuted children of misfortune that knock at its hospitable door. (Cheers.) And when I say, God bless her, there is none among us who has known the ennobling affection of a wife, or the steadfast devotion of a mother but in his heart will say, Amen ! (Loud and prolonged cheering.)

---

* Mr. Benjamin Disraeli, at that time Prime Minister of England, had just been elected Lord Rector of Glasgow University, and had made a speech which gave rise to a world of discussion.

A GHOST STORY.

I TOOK a large room, far up Broadway, in a huge old building whose upper stories had been wholly unoccupied for years, until I came. The place had long been given up to dust and cobwebs, to solitude and silence. I seemed groping among the tombs and invading the privacy of the dead, that first night I climbed up to my quarters. For the first time in my life a superstitious dread came over me; and as I turned a dark angle of the stairway and an invisible cobweb swung its slazy woof in my face and clung there, I shuddered as one who had encountered a phantom.

I was glad enough when I reached my room and locked out the mould and the darkness. A cheery fire was burning in the grate, and I sat down before it with a comforting sense of relief. For two hours I sat there, thinking of bygone times; recalling old scenes, and summoning half-forgotten faces out of the mists of the past; listening, in fancy, to voices that long ago grew silent for all time, and to once familiar songs that nobody sings now. And as my reverie softened down to a sadder and sadder pathos, the shrieking of the winds outside softened to a wail, the angry beating of the rain against the panes diminished to a tranquil patter, and one by one the noises in the street subsided, until the hurrying footsteps of the last belated straggler died away in the distance and left no sound behind.

The fire had burned low. A sense of loneliness crept over me. I arose and undressed, moving on tip-toe about the room, doing stealthily what I had to do, as if I were environed by sleeping enemies whose slumbers it would be fatal to break. I covered up in bed, and lay listening to the rain and wind and the faint creaking of distant shutters, till they lulled me to sleep.

I slept profoundly, but how long I do not know. All at once I found myself awake, and filled with a shuddering expectancy. All was still. All but my own heart—I could hear it beat. Presently the bed clothes began to slip away slowly toward the foot of the bed, as if some one were pulling them! I could not stir; I could not speak. Still the blankets slipped deliberately away, till my breast was uncovered. Then with a great effort I seized them and drew them over my head. I waited, listened, waited. Once more that steady pull began, and once more I lay torpid a century of dragging seconds till my breast was naked again. At last I roused my energies and snatched the covers back to their place and held them with a strong grip. I waited. By and bye I felt a faint tug, and took a fresh grip. The tug strengthened to a steady strain—it grew stronger and stronger. My hold parted, and for the third time the blankets slid away. I groaned. An answering groan came from the foot of the bed! Beaded drops of sweat stood upon my forehead. I was more dead than alive. Presently I heard a heavy footstep in my room—the step of an elephant, it seemed to me—it was not like anything human. But it was moving *from* me—there was relief in that. I heard it approach the door—pass out without moving bolt or lock—and wander away among the dismal corridors, straining the floors and joists till they creaked again as it passed—and then silence reigned once more.

When my excitement had calmed, I said to myself, "This is a dream—simply a hideous dream." And so I lay thinking it over until I convinced myself that it *was* a dream, and then a comforting laugh relaxed my lips and I was happy again. I got up and struck a light; and when I found that the locks and bolts were just as I had left them, another soothing laugh welled in my heart and rippled from my lips. I took my pipe and lit it, and was just sitting down before the fire, when—— down went the pipe out of my nerveless fingers, the blood forsook my cheeks, and my placid breathing was cut short with a gasp! In the ashes on the hearth, side by side with my own bare footprint, was another, so vast that in comparison mine was but an infant's! Then I had *had* a visitor, and the elephant tread was explained.

I put out the light and returned to bed, palsied with fear. I lay a long time, peering into the darkness, and listening. Then I heard a grating noise overhead, like the dragging of a heavy body across the floor; then the throwing down of the body, and the shaking of my windows in response to the concussion. In distant parts of the building I heard the muffled slamming of doors. I heard, at intervals, stealthy footsteps creeping in and out among the corridors, and up and down the stairs. Sometimes these noises approached my door, hesitated, and went away again. I heard the clanking of chains faintly, in remote passages, and listened while the clanking grew nearer—while it wearily climbed the stairways, marking each move by the loose surplus of chain that fell with an accented rattle upon each succeeding step as the goblin that bore it advanced. I heard muttered sentences; half-uttered screams that seemed smothered violently; and the swish of invisible garments, the rush of invisible wings. Then I became conscious that my chamber was invaded— that I was not alone. I heard sighs and breathings about my bed, and mysterious whisperings. Three little spheres of soft phosphorescent light appeared on the ceiling directly over my head, clung and glowed there a moment, and then dropped —two of them upon my face and one upon the pillow. They spattered, liquidly, and felt warm. Intuition told me they had turned to gouts of blood as they fell— I needed no light to satisfy myself of that. Then I saw pallid faces, dimly luminous, and white uplifted hands, floating bodiless in the air,—floating a moment and then disappearing. The whispering ceased, and the voices and the sounds, and a solemn stillness followed. I waited, and listened. I felt that I must have light, or die. I was weak with fear. I slowly raised myself toward a sitting posture, and my face came in contact with a clammy hand! All strength went from me, apparently, and I fell back like a stricken invalid. Then I heard the rustle of a garment—it seemed to pass to the door and go out.

When everything was still once more, I crept out of bed, sick and feeble, and lit the gas with a hand that trembled as if it were aged with a hundred years. The light brought some little cheer to my spirits. I sat down and fell into a dreamy contemplation of that great footprint in the ashes. By and bye its outlines began to waver and grow dim. I glanced up and the broad gas flame was slowly wilting away. In the same moment I heard that elephantine tread again. I noted its approach, nearer and nearer, along the musty halls, and dimmer and dimmer the light waned. The tread reached my very door and paused—the light had dwindled to a sickly blue, and all things about me lay in a spectral twilight. The door did not open, and yet I felt a faint gust of air fan my cheek, and presently was conscious of a huge, cloudy presence before me. I watched it with fascinated eyes. A pale glow stole over the Thing; gradually its cloudy folds took shape—an arm appeared, then legs, then a body, and last a great sad face looked out of the vapor. Stripped of its filmy housings, naked, muscular and comely, the majestic Cardiff Giant loomed above me!

All my misery vanished—for a child might know that no harm could come with that benignant countenance. My cheerful spirits returned at once, and in sympathy with them the gas flamed up brightly again. Never a lonely outcast was so glad to welcome company as I was to greet the friendly giant. I said :

" Why, is it nobody but you? Do you know, I have been scared to death for the last two or three hours? I am most honestly glad to see you. I wish I had a chair———.Here, here, don't try to sit down in that thing ! "

But it was too late. He was in it before I could stop him, and down he went—I never saw a chair shivered so in my life.

" Stop, stop, you'll ruin ev——"

Too late again. There was another crash, and another chair was resolved into its original elements.

"Confound it, haven't you got any judgment at all?   Do you want to ruin all the furniture on the place?   Here, here, you petrified fool——"

But it was no use.   Before I could arrest him he had sat down on the bed, and it was a melancholy ruin.

"Now what sort of a way is that to do?   First you come lumbering about the place bringing a legion of vagabond goblins along with you to worry me to death, and then when I overlook an indelicacy of costume which would not be tolerated anywhere by cultivated people except in a respectable theatre, and not even there if the nudity were of *your* sex, you repay me by wreck-ing all the furni-ture you can find to sit d o w n on. And why will you? You damage your-self as much as you do me.   You have broken off the end of your spinal col-umn, and littered up the floor with chips off your hams till the place looks like a marble-yard. You ought to be ashamed of your-self—you are big enough t o know better."

"Well, I will not break any m o r e furniture.   But what am I to do? I have not had a chance to sit down for a c e n t u r y." And the tears came into his eyes.   "Poor devil," I said, "I should not have been so harsh with you.   And you are an orphan, too, no doubt.   But sit down on the floor here —nothing else can stand your weight—and besides, we cannot be sociable with you away up there above me; I want you down where I can perch on this high counting-house stool and gossip with you face to face."

So he sat down on the floor, and lit a pipe which I gave him, threw one of my red blankets over his shoulders, inverted my sitz-bath on his head, helmet fashion, and made himself picturesque and comfortable.   Then he crossed his ancles, while

I renewed the fire, and exposed the flat, honey-combed bottoms of his prodigious feet to the grateful warmth.

"What is the matter with the bottom of your feet and the back of your legs, that they are gouged up so?"

"Infernal chilblains—I caught them clear up to the back of my head, roosting out there under Newell's farm. But I love the place; I love it as one loves his old home. There is no peace for me like the peace I feel when I am there."

We talked along for half an hour, and then I noticed that he looked tired, and spoke of it.

"Tired?" he said. "Well I should think so. And now I will tell you all about it, since you have treated me so well. I am the spirit of the Petrified Man that lies across the street there in the Museum. I am the ghost of the Cardiff Giant. I can have no rest, no peace, till they have given that poor body burial again. Now what was the most natural thing for me to do, to make men satisfy this wish? Terrify them into it!—haunt the place where the body lay! So I haunted the museum night after night. I even got other spirits to help me. But it did no good, for nobody ever came to the museum at midnight. Then it occurred to me to come over the way and haunt this place a little. I felt that if I ever got a hearing I must succeed, for I had the most efficient company that perdition could furnish. Night after night we have shivered around through these mildewed halls, dragging chains, groaning, whispering, tramping up and down stairs, till to tell you the truth I am almost worn out. But when I saw a light in your room to-night I roused my energies again and went at it with a deal of the old freshness. But I am tired out—entirely fagged out. Give me, I beseech you, give me some hope!"

I lit off my perch in a burst of excitement, and exclaimed:

"This transcends everything! everything that ever did occur! Why you poor blundering old fossil, you have had all your trouble for nothing—you have been haunting a *plaster cast* of yourself—the real Cardiff Giant is in Albany!* Confound it, don't you know your own remains?"

---

*A fact. The original fraud was ingeniously and fraudfully duplicated, and exhibited in New York as the "only genuine" Cardiff Giant, (to the unspeakable disgust of the owners of the real colossus,) at the very same time that the latter was drawing crowds at a museum in Albany.

I never saw such an eloquent look of shame, of pitiable humiliation, overspread a countenance before.

The Petrified Man rose slowly to his feet, and said :

" Honestly, *is* that true ?"

" As true as I am sitting here."

He took the pipe from his mouth and laid it on the mantel, then stood irresolute a moment, (unconsciously, from old habit, thrusting his hands where his pantaloons pockets should have been, and meditatively dropping his chin on his breast,) and finally said :

" Well—I *never* felt so absurd before. The Petrified Man has sold every body else, and now the mean fraud has ended by selling its own ghost! My son, if there is any charity left in your heart for a poor friendless phantom like me, don't let this get out. Think how *you* would feel if you had made such an ass of yourself."

I heard his stately tramp die away, step by step down the stairs and out into the deserted street, and felt sorry that he was gone, poor fellow—and sorrier still that he had carried off my red blanket and my bath-tub.

THE CAPITOLINE VENUS.

CHAPTER I.

[Scene—An Artist's Studio in Rome.]

"OH, George, I *do* love you!"

"Bless your dear heart, Mary, I know that—*why* is your father so obdurate?"

"George, he means well, but art is folly to him—he only understands groceries. He thinks you would starve me."

"Confound his wisdom—it savors of inspiration. Why am I not a money-making, bowelless grocer, instead of a divinely-gifted sculptor with nothing to eat?"

"Do not despond, Georgy, dear—all his prejudices will fade away as soon as you shall have acquired fifty thousand dol——"

222

"Fifty thousand demons! Child, I am in arrears for my board!"

CHAPTER II.

[Scene—A Dwelling in Rome.]

"My dear sir, it is useless to talk. I haven't anything against you, but I can't let my daughter marry a hash of love, art, and starvation—I believe you have nothing else to offer."

"Sir, I am poor, I grant you. But is fame nothing? The Hon. Bellamy Foodle, of Arkansas, says that my new statue of America is a clever piece of sculpture, and he is satisfied that my name will one day be famous."

"Bosh! What does that Arkansas ass know about it? Fame's nothing—the market price of your marble scare-crow is the thing to look at. It took you six months to chisel it, and you can't sell it for a hundred dollars. No, sir! Show me fifty thousand dollars and you can have my daughter—otherwise she marries young Simper. You have just six months to raise the money in. Good morning, sir."

"Alas! Woe is me!"

CHAPTER III.

[Scene—The Studio.]

"Oh, John, friend of my boyhood, I am the unhappiest of men."

"You're a simpleton!"

"I have nothing left to love but my poor statue of America—and see, even she has no sympathy for me in her cold marble countenance—so beautiful and so heartless!"

"You're a dummy!"

"Oh, John!"

"Oh, fudge! Didn't you say you had six months to raise the money in?"

"Don't deride my agony, John. If I had six centuries what good would it do? How could it help a poor wretch without name, capital or friends?"

"Idiot! Coward! Baby! Six months to raise the money in—and five will do!"

"Are you insane?"

"Six months—an abundance. Leave it to me. I'll raise it."

"What do you mean, John? How on earth can you raise such a monstrous sum for *me*?"

"*Will* you let that be *my* business, and not meddle? Will you leave the thing in my hands? Will you swear to submit to whatever I do? Will you pledge me to find no fault with my actions?"

"I am dizzy—bewildered—but I swear."

John took up a hammer and deliberately smashed the nose of America! He

made another pass and two of her fingers fell to the floor—another, and part of an ear came away—another, and a row of toes was mangled and dismembered—another, and the left leg, from the knee down, lay a fragmentary ruin!

John put on his hat and departed.

George gazed speechless upon the battered and grotesque nightmare before him for the space of thirty seconds, and then wilted to the floor and went into convulsions.

John returned presently with a carriage, got the broken-hearted artist and the broken-legged statue aboard, and drove off, whistling low and tranquilly. He left the artist at his lodgings, and drove off and disappeared down the *Via Quirinalis* with the statue.

CHAPTER IV.

[*Scene—The Studio.*]

"The six months will be up at two o'clock to-day! Oh, agony! My life is blighted. I would that I were dead. I had no supper yesterday. I have had no breakfast to-day. I dare not enter an eating-house. And hungry?—don't mention it! My bootmaker duns me to death—my tailor duns me—my landlord haunts me. I am miserable. I haven't seen John since that awful day. *She* smiles on me tenderly when we meet in the great thoroughfares, but her old flint of a father makes her look in the other direction in short order. Now who is knocking at that door? Who is come to persecute me? That malignant villain the bootmaker, I'll warrant. *Come in!*"

"Ah, happiness attend your highness—Heaven be propitious to your grace! I have brought my lord's new boots—ah, say nothing about the pay, there is no hurry, none in the world. Shall be proud if my noble lord will continue to honor me with his custom—ah, adieu!"

"Brought the boots himself! Don't want his pay! Takes his leave with a bow and a scrape fit to honor majesty withal! Desires a continuance of my custom! Is the world coming to an end? Of all the——*come in!*"

"Pardon, signor, but I have brought your new suit of clothes for——"

"*Come in!!*"

"A thousand pardons for this intrusion, your worship! But I have prepared the beautiful suite of rooms below for you—this wretched den is but ill suited to——"

"*Come in!!!*"

"I have called to say that your credit at our bank, sometime since unfortunately interrupted, is entirely and most satisfactorily restored, and we shall be most happy if you will draw upon us for any——"

"COME IN!!!!"

15

" My noble boy, she is yours! She'll be here in a moment! Take her—marry her—love her—be happy!—God bless you both! Hip, hip, hur——"

"COME IN!!!!!"

" Oh, George, my own darling, we are saved!"

" Oh, Mary, my own darling, we *are* saved—but I'll swear I don't know why nor how!"

CHAPTER V.

[*Scene—A Roman Café.*]

One of a group of Amercan gentlemen reads and translates from the weekly edition of *Il Slangwhanger di Roma* as follows:

"WONDERFUL DISCOVERY !—Some six months ago Signor John Smitthe, an American gentleman now some years a resident of Rome, purchased for a trifle a small piece of ground in the Campagna, just beyond the tomb of the Scipio family, from the owner, a bankrupt relative of the Princess Borghese. Mr. Smitthe afterwards went to the Minister of the Public Records and had the piece of ground transferred to a poor American artist named George Arnold, explaining that he did it as payment and satisfaction for pecuniary damage accidentally done by him long since upon property belonging to Signor Arnold, and further observed that he would make additional satisfaction by improving the ground for Signor A., at his own charge and cost. Four weeks ago, while making some necessary excavations upon the property, Signor Smitthe unearthed the most remarkable ancient statue that has ever been added to the opulent art treasures of Rome. It was an exquisite figure of a woman, and though sadly stained by the soil and the mould of ages, no eye can look unmoved upon its ravishing beauty. The nose, the left leg from the knee down, an ear, and also the toes of the right foot and two fingers of one of the hands, were gone, but otherwise the noble figure was in a remarkable state of preservation. The government at once took military possession of the statue, and appointed a commission of art critics, antiquaries and cardinal princes of the church to assess its value and determine the remuneration that must go to the owner of the ground in which it was found. The whole affair was kept a profound secret until last night. In the meantime the commission sat with closed doors, and deliberated. Last night they decided unanimously that the statue is a Venus, and the work of some unknown but sublimely gifted artist of the third century before Christ. They consider it the most faultless work of art the world has any knowledge of.

" At midnight they held a final conference and decided that the Venus was worth the enormous sum of *ten million francs!* In accordance with Roman law and Roman usage, the government being half owner in all works of art found in the Campagna, the State has naught to do but pay five million francs to Mr. Arnold and take permanent possession of the beautiful statue. This morning the Venus will be removed to the Capitol, there to remain, and at noon the commission will wait upon Signor Arnold with His Holiness the Pope's order upon the Treasury for the princely sum of five million francs in gold."

Chorus of Voices.—" Luck ! It's no name for it !"

Another Voice.—" Gentlemen, I propose that we immediately form an American joint-stock company for the purchase of lands and excavations of statues, here, with proper connections in Wall Street to bull and bear the stock."

All.—"Agreed."

CHAPTER VI.

[*Scene—The Roman Capitol Ten Years Later.*]

"Dearest Mary, this is the most celebrated statue in the world. This is the renowned 'Capitoline Venus' you've heard so much about. Here she is with her little blemishes 'restored' (that is, patched) by the most noted Roman artists— and the mere fact that they did the humble patching of so noble a creation will make their names illustrious while the world stands. How strange it seems—this

place! The day before I last stood here, ten happy years ago, I wasn't a rich man —bless your soul, I hadn't a cent. And yet I had a good deal to do with making Rome mistress of this grandest work of ancient art the world contains."

"The worshipped, the illustrious Capitoline Venus—and what a sum she is valued at! Ten millions of francs!"

"Yes—*now* she is."

"And oh, Georgy, how divinely beautiful she is!"

"Ah, yes—but nothing to what she was before that blessed John Smith broke her leg and battered her nose. Ingenious Smith!—gifted Smith—noble Smith! Author of all our bliss! Hark! Do you know what that wheeze means? Mary, that cub has got the whooping cough. Will you *never* learn to take care of the children!"

THE END.

The Capitoline Venus is still in the Capitol at Rome, and is still the most charming and most illustrious work of ancient art the world can boast of. But if ever it shall be your fortune to stand before it and go into the customary ecstacies over it, don't permit this true and secret history of its origin to mar your bliss—and when you read about a gigantic Petrified Man being dug up near Syracuse, in the State of New York, or near any other place, keep your own counsel,—and if the Barnum that buried him there offers to sell to you at an enormous sum, don't you buy. Send him to the Pope!"

NOTE.—The above sketch was written at the time the famous swindle of the "Petrified Giant" was the sensation of the day in the United States.

SPEECH ON ACCIDENT INSURANCE.

DELIVERED IN HARTFORD, AT A DINNER TO CORNELIUS WALFORD, OF LONDON.

GENTLEMEN: I am glad indeed to assist in welcoming the distinguished guest of this occasion to a city whose fame as an insurance center has extended to all lands, and given us the name of being a quadruple band of brothers working sweetly hand in hand,—the Colt's arms company making the destruction of our race easy and convenient, our life insurance citizens paying for the victims when they pass away, Mr. Batterson perpetuating their memory with his stately monuments, and our fire insurance comrades taking care of their hereafter. I am glad to assist in welcoming our guest—first, because he is an Englishman, and I owe a heavy debt of hospitality to certain of his fellow-countrymen; and secondly, because he is in sympathy with insurance and has been the means of making many other men cast their sympathies in the same direction.

Certainly there is no nobler field for human effort than the insurance line of business—especially accident insurance. Ever since I have been a director in an accident insurance company I have felt that I am a better man. Life has seemed more precious. Accidents have assumed a kindlier aspect. Distressing special providences have lost half their horror. I look upon a cripple, now, with affectiontionate interest—as an advertisement. I do not seem to care for poetry any more. I do not care for politics—even agriculture does not excite me. But to me, now, there is a charm about a railway collision that is unspeakable.

There is nothing more beneficent than accident insurance. I have seen an entire family lifted out of poverty and into affluence by the simple boon of a broken leg. I have had people come to me on crutches, with tears in their eyes, to bless this beneficent institution. In all my experience of life, I have seen nothing so seraphic as the look that comes into a freshly mutilated man's face when he feels in his vest pocket with his remaining hand and finds his accident ticket all right. And I have seen nothing so sad as the look that came into another splintered customer's face, when he found he couldn't collect on a wooden leg.

I will remark here, by way of advertisement, that that noble charity which we have named the HARTFORD ACCIDENT INSURANCE COMPANY,* is an institution which is peculiarly to be depended upon. A man is bound to prosper who gives it his custom. No man can take out a policy in it and not get crippled before the year is out. Now there was one indigent man who had been disappointed so often with other companies that he had grown disheartened, his appetite left him, he ceased to smile—said life was but a weariness. Three weeks ago I got him to insure with us, and now he is the brightest, happiest spirit in this land—has a good steady income and a stylish suit of new bandages every day, and travels around on a shutter.

I will say, in conclusion, that my share of the welcome to our guest is none the less hearty because I talk so much nonsense, and I know that I can say the same for the rest of the speakers.

---

* The speaker is a director of the company named.

JOHN CHINAMAN IN NEW YORK.

A S I passed along by one of those monster American tea-stores in New York, I found a Chinaman sitting before it acting in the capacity of a sign. Everybody that passed by gave him a steady stare as long as their heads would twist over their shoulders without dislocating their necks, and a group had stopped to stare deliberately.

Is it not a shame that we, who prate so much about civilization and humanity, are content to degrade a fellow-being to such an office as this? Is it not time for reflection when we find ourselves willing to see in such a being, matter for frivolous curiosity instead of regret and grave reflection?

Here was a poor creature whom hard fortune had exiled from his natural home beyond the seas, and whose troubles ought to have touched these idle strangers that thronged about him; but did it? Apparently not. Men calling themselves the superior race, the race of culture and of gentle blood, scanned his quaint Chinese hat, with peaked roof and ball on top, and his long queue dangling down his back; his short silken blouse, curiously frogged and figured (and, like the rest of his raiment, rusty, dilapidated, and awkwardly put on); his blue cotton, tight-legged pants, tied close around the ankles; and his clumsy blunt-toed shoes with thick cork soles; and having so scanned him from head to foot, cracked some unseemly joke about his outlandish attire or his melancholy face, and passed on. In my heart I pitied the friendless Mongol. I wondered what was passing behind his sad face, and what distant scene his vacant eye was dreaming of. Were his thoughts with his heart, ten thousand miles away, beyond the billowy wastes of the Pacific? among the rice-fields and the plumy palms of China? under the shadows of remembered mountain-peaks, or in groves of bloomy shrubs and strange forest-trees unknown to climes like ours? And now and then, rippling among his visions and his dreams, did he hear familiar laughter and half-forgotten voices, and did he catch fitful glimpses of the friendly faces of a bygone time? A cruel fate it is, I said, that is befallen this bronzed wanderer. In order that the group of idlers might be touched at least by the words of the poor fellow, since the appeal of his pauper dress and his dreary exile was lost upon them, I touched him on the shoulder and said—

"Cheer up—don't be down-hearted. It is not America that treats you in this way, it is merely one citizen, whose greed of gain has eaten the humanity out of his heart. America has a broader hospitality for the exiled and oppressed. America and Americans are always ready to help the unfortunate. Money shall be raised—you shall go back to China—you shall see your friends again. What wages do they pay you here?"

"Divil a cint but four dollars a week and find meself; but it's aisy, barrin the troublesome furrin clothes that's so expinsive."

The exile remains at his post. The New York tea-merchants who need picturesque signs are not likely to run out of Chinamen.

HOW I EDITED AN AGRICULTURAL PAPER.

I DID not take temporary editorship of an agricultural paper without misgivings. Neither would a landsman take command of a ship without misgivings. But I was in circumstances that made the salary an object. The regular editor of the paper was going off for a holiday, and I accepted the terms he offered, and took his place.

The sensation of being at work again was luxurious, and I wrought all the week with unflagging pleasure. We went to press, and I waited a day with some solicitude to see whether my effort was going to attract any notice. As I left the office, toward sundown, a group of men and boys at the foot of the stairs dispersed with one impulse, and gave me passage-way, and I heard one or two of them say: "That's him!" I was naturally pleased by this incident. The next morning I found a similar group at the foot of the stairs, and scattering couples and individuals standing here and there in the street, and over the way, watching me with interest. The group separated and fell back as I approached, and I heard a man say, "Look at his eye!" I pretended not to observe the notice I was attracting, but secretly I was pleased with it, and was purposing to write an account of it to my aunt. I went up the short flight of stairs, and heard cheery voices and a ringing laugh as I drew near the door, which I opened, and caught a glimpse of two young rural-looking men, whose faces blanched and lengthened when they saw me, and then they both plunged through the window with a great crash. I was surprised.

In about half an hour an old gentleman, with a flowing beard and a fine but rather austere face, entered, and sat down at my invitation. He seemed to have something on his mind. He took off his hat and set it on the floor, and got out of it a red silk handkerchief and a copy of our paper.

He put the paper on his lap, and while he polished his spectacles with his handkerchief, he said, "Are you the new editor?"

I said I was.

"Have you ever edited an agricultural paper before?"

"No," I said; "this is my first attempt."

"Very likely. Have you had any experience in agriculture practically?"

"No; I believe I have not."

"Some instinct told me so," said the old gentleman, putting on his spectacles, and looking over them at me with asperity, while he folded his paper into a convenient shape. "I wish to read you what must have made me have that instinct. It was this editorial. Listen, and see if it was you that wrote it:—

'Turnips should never be pulled, it injures them. It is much better to send a boy up and let him shake the tree."

"Now, what do you think of that?—for I really suppose you wrote it?"

"Think of it? Why, I think it is good. I think it is sense. I have no doubt that every year millions and millions of bushels of turnips are spoiled in this township alone by being pulled in a half-ripe condition, when, if they had sent a boy up to shake the tree"——

"Shake your grandmother! Turnips don't grow on trees!"

"Oh, they don't, don't they? Well, who said they did? The language was intended to be figurative, wholly figurative. Anybody that knows anything will know that I meant that the boy should shake the vine."

Then this old person got up and tore his paper all into small shreds, and stamped on them, and broke several things with his cane, and said I did not know as much as a cow; and then went out and banged the door after him, and, in short, acted in such a way that I fancied he was displeased about something. But not knowing what the trouble was, I could not be any help to him.

Pretty soon after this a long cadaverous creature, with lanky locks hanging down to his shoulders, and a week's stubble bristling from the hills and valleys of his face, darted within the door, and halted, motionless, with finger on lip, and head and body bent in listening attitude. No sound was heard. Still he listened. No sound. Then he turned the key in the door, and came elaborately tiptoeing toward me till he was within long reaching distance of me, when he stopped, and after scanning my face with intense interest for a while, drew a folded copy of our paper from his bosom, and said—

"There, you wrote that. Read it to me—quick? Relieve me. I suffer."

I read as follows; and as the sentences fell from my lips I could see the relief come, I could see the drawn muscles relax, and the anxiety go out of the face, and rest and peace steal over the features like the merciful moonlight over a desolate landscape:

"The guano is a fine bird, but great care is necessary in rearing it. It should not be imported earlier than June or later than September. In the winter it should be kept in a warm place, where it can hatch out its young.

"It is evident that we are to have a backward season for grain. Therefore it will be well for the farmer to begin setting out his cornstalks and planting his buckwheat cakes in July instead of August.

"Concerning the pumpkin.—This berry is a favorite with the natives of the interior of New England, who prefer it to the gooseberry for the making of fruit-cake, and who likewise give it the preference over the raspberry for feeding cows, as being more filling and fully as satisfying. The pumpkin is the only esculent of the orange family that will thrive in the North, except the gourd and one or two varieties of the squash. But the custom of planting it in the front yard with the shrubbery is fast going out of vogue, for it is now generally conceded that the pumpkin as a shade tree is a failure.

"Now, as the warm weather approaches, and the ganders begin to spawn"——

The excited listener sprang toward me to shake hands, and said—

"There, there—that will do. I know I am all right now, because you have read it just as I did, word for word. But, stranger, when I first read it this morning, I said to myself, I never, never believed it before, notwithstanding my friends kept me under watch so strict, but now I believe I *am* crazy; and with that I fetched a howl that you might have heard two miles, and started out to kill somebody—because, you know, I knew it would come to that sooner or later, and so I might as well begin. I read one of them paragraphs over again, so as to be certain, and then I burned my house down and started. I have crippled several people, and have got one fellow up a tree, where where I can get him if I want him. But I thought I would call in here as I passed along and make the thing perfectly certain; and now it *is* certain, and I tell you it is lucky for the chap that is in the tree. I should have killed him, sure, as I went back. Good-bye, sir, good-bye; you have taken a great load off my mind. My reason has stood the strain of one of your agricultural articles, and I know that nothing can ever unseat it now. *Good*-bye, sir."

I felt a little uncomfortable about the cripplings and arsons this person had been entertaining himself with, for I could not help feeling remotely accessory to them. But these thoughts were quickly banished, for the regular editor walked in! [I thought to myself, Now if you had gone to Egypt as I recommended you to, I might have had a chance to get my hand in; but you wouldn't do it, and here you are. I sort of expected you.]

The editor was looking sad and perplexed and dejected.

He surveyed the wreck which that old rioter and these two young farmers had made, and then said, "This is a sad business—a very sad business. There is the mucilage bottle broken, and six panes of glass, and a spittoon and two candlesticks. But that is not the worst. The reputation of the paper is injured—and permanently, I fear. True, there never was such a call for the paper before, and it never sold such a large edition or soared to such celebrity;—but does one want to be famous for lunacy, and prosper upon the infirmities of his mind? My friend, as I am an honest man, the street out here is full of people, and others are roosting on the fences, waiting to get a glimpse of you, because they think you are crazy. And well they might after reading your editorials. They are a disgrace to journalism. Why, what put it into your head that you could edit a paper of this nature? You do not seem to know the first rudiments of agriculture. You speak of a furrow and a harrow as being the same thing; you talk of the moulting season for cows; and you recommend the domestication of the pole-cat on account of its playfulness and its excellence as a ratter! Your remark that clams will lie quiet if music be played to them was superfluous—entirely superfluous. Nothing disturbs clams. Clams *always* lie quiet. Clams care nothing whatever about music. Ah, heavens and earth, friend! if you had made the acquiring of ignorance the study of your life, you could not have graduated with higher honor than you could to-day. I never saw anything like it. Your observation that the horse-chestnut as an article of commerce is steadily gaining in favor, is simply calculated to destroy this journal. I want you to throw up your situation and go. I want no more holiday—I could not enjoy it if I had it. Certainly not with you in my chair. I would always stand in dread of what you might be going to recommend next. It makes me lose all patience every time I think of your discussing oyster-beds under the head of "Landscape Gardening." I want you to go. Nothing on earth could persuade me to take another holiday. Oh! why didn't you *tell* me you didn't know anything about agriculture?"

"*Tell* you, you cornstalk, you cabbage, you son of a cauliflower? It's the first time I ever heard such an unfeeling remark. I tell you I have been in the editorial business going on fourteen years, and it is the first time I ever heard of a man's having to know anything in order to edit a newspaper. You turnip! Who write the dramatic critiques for the second-rate papers? Why, a parcel of promoted shoemakers and apprentice apothecaries, who know just as much about good acting as I do about good farming and no more. Who review the books? People who never wrote one. Who do up the heavy leaders on finance? Parties who have had the largest opportunities for knowing nothing about it. Who criticise the Indian campaigns? Gentlemen who do not know a war-whoop from a wigwam, and who never have had to run a foot race with a tomahawk, or pluck arrows out of the several members of their families to build the evening camp-fire with. Who write the temperance appeals, and clamor about the flowing bowl? Folks who will never draw another sober breath till they do it in the grave. Who edit the agricultural papers, you—yam? Men, as general thing, who fail in the poetry line, yellow-colored novel line, sensation-drama line, city-editor line, and finally fall back on agriculture as a temporary reprieve from the poorhouse. *You* try to tell *me* anything about the newspaper business! Sir, I have been through it from Alpha to Omaha, and I tell you that the less a man knows the bigger the noise he makes and the higher the salary he commands. Heaven knows if I had but been ignorant instead of cultivated, and impudent instead of diffident, I could have made a name for myself in this cold selfish world. I take my leave, sir. Since I have been treated as you have treated me, I am perfectly willing to go. But I have done my duty. I have fulfilled my contract as far as I was permitted to do it. I said I could make your paper of interest to all classes—and I have. I said I could run your circulation up to twenty thousand copies, and if I had had two more weeks I'd have done it. And I'd have given you the best class of readers that ever an agricultural paper had—not a farmer in it, nor a solitary individual who could tell a water-melon tree trom a peach-vine to save his life. *You* are the loser by this rupture, not me, Pie-plant. Adios."

I then left.

THE PETRIFIED MAN.

NOW, to show how really hard it is to foist a moral or a truth upon an unsuspecting public through a burlesque without entirely and absurdly missing one's mark, I will here set down two experiences of my own in this thing. In the fall of 1862, in Nevada and California, the people got to running wild about extraordinary petrifications and other natural marvels. One could scarcely pick up a paper without finding in it one or two glorified discoveries of this kind. The mania was becoming a little ridiculous. I was a bran-new local editor in Virginia City, and I felt called upon to destroy this growing evil; we all have our benignant fatherly moods at one time or another, I suppose. I chose to kill the petrifaction mania with a delicate, a very delicate satire. But maybe it was altogether too delicate, for nobody ever perceived the satire part of it at all. I put my scheme in the shape of the discovery of a remarkably petrified man.

I had had a temporary falling out with Mr. ——, the new coroner and justice of the peace of Humboldt, and thought I might as well touch him up a little at the same time and make him ridiculous, and thus combine pleasure with business. So

I told, in patient belief-compelling detail, all about the finding of a petrified man at Gravelly Ford (exactly a hundred and twenty miles, over a breakneck mountain trail, from where —— lived); how all the savants of the immediate neighborhood had been to examine it (it was notorious that there was not a living creature within fifty miles of there, except a few starving Indians, some crippled grasshoppers, and four or five buzzards out of meat and too feeble to get away); how those savants all pronounced the petrified man to have been in a state of complete petrifaction for over ten generations; and then, with a seriousness that I ought to have been ashamed to assume, I stated that as soon as Mr. —— heard the news he summoned a jury, mounted his mule, and posted off, with noble reverence for official duty, on that awful five days' journey, through alkali, sage-brush, peril of body, and imminent starvation, to *hold an inquest* on this man that had been dead and turned to everlasting stone for more than three hundred years! And then, my hand being " in," so to speak, I went on, with the same unflinching gravity, to state that the jury returned a verdict that deceased came to his death from *protracted exposure*. This only moved me to higher flights of imagination, and I said that the jury, with that charity so characteristic of pioneers, then dug a grave, and were about to give the petrified man Christian burial, when they found that for ages a limestone sediment had been trickling down the face of the stone against which he was sitting, and this stuff had run under him and cemented him fast to the "bed-rock;" that the jury (they were all silver-miners) canvassed the difficulty a moment, and then got out their powder and fuse, and proceeded to drill a hole under him, in order to *blast him from his position*, when Mr. ——, "with that delicacy so characteristic of him, forbade them, observing that it would be little less than sacrilege to do such a thing."

From beginning to end the "Petrified Man" squib was a string of roaring absurdities, albeit they were told with an unfair pretence of truth that even imposed upon me to some extent, and I was in some danger of believing in my own fraud. But I really had no desire to deceive anybody, and no expectation of doing it. I depended on the way the petrified man was *sitting* to explain to the public that he was a swindle. Yet I purposely mixed that up with other things, hoping to make it obscure—and I did. I would describe the position of one foot, and then say his right thumb was against the side of his nose; then talk about his other foot, and presently come back and say the fingers of his right hand were spread apart; then talk about the back of his head a little, and return and say the left thumb was hooked into the right little finger; then ramble off about something else, and by and by drift back again and remark that the fingers of the left hand were spread like those of the right. But I was too ingenious. I mixed it up rather too much; and so all that description of the attitude, as a key to the humbuggery of the article, was entirely lost, for nobody but me ever discovered and comprehended the peculiar and suggestive position of the petrified man's hands.

As a *satire* on the petrifaction mania, or anything else, my Petrified Man was a disheartening failure; for everybody received him in innocent good faith, and I was stunned to see the creature I had begotten to pull down the wonder-business with, and bring derision upon it, calmly exalted to the grand chief place in the list of the genuine marvels our Nevada had produced. I was so disappointed at the curious miscarriage of my scheme, that at first I was angry, and did not like to think about it; but by and by, when the exchanges began to come in with the

16

Petrified Man copied and guilelessly glorified, I began to feel a soothing secret satisfaction; and as my gentleman's field of travels broadened, and by the exchanges I saw that he steadily and implacably penetrated territory after territory, State after State, and land after land, till he swept the great globe and culminated in sublime and unimpeached legitimacy in the august London *Lancet*, my cup was full, and I said I was glad I had done it. I think that for about eleven months, as nearly as I can remember, Mr. ——'s daily mail-bag continued to be swollen by the addition of half a bushel of newspapers hailing from many climes with the Petrified Man in them, marked around with a prominent belt of ink. I sent them to him. I did it for spite, not for fun. He used to shovel them into his back yard and curse. And every day during all those months the miners, his constituents (for miners never quit joking a person when they get started), would call on him and ask if he could tell them where they could get hold of a paper with the Petrified Man in it. He could have accommodated a continent with them. I hated —— in those days, and these things pacified me and pleased me. I could not have gotten more real comfort out of him without killing him.

MY BLOODY MASSACRE.

THE other burlesque I have referred to was my fine satire upon the financial expedients of "cooking dividends," a thing which became shamefully frequent on the Pacific coast for a while. Once more, in my self-complacent simplicity, I felt that the time had arrived for me to rise up and be a reformer. I put this reformatory satire in the shape of a fearful "Massacre at Empire City." The San Francisco papers were making a great outcry about the iniquity cf the Daney Silver-Mining Company, whose directors had declared a "cooked" or false dividend, for the purpose of increasing the value of their stock, so that they could sell out at a comfortable figure, and then scramble from under the tumbling concern. And while abusing the Daney, those papers did not forget to urge the public to get rid of all their silver stocks and invest in sound and safe San Francisco stocks, such as the Spring Valley Water Company, etc. But right at this unfortunate juncture, behold the Spring Valley cooked a dividend too! And so, under the insidious mask of an invented "bloody massacre," I stole upon the public unawares with my scathing satire upon the dividend-cooking system. In about half a column of imaginary human carnage I told how a citizen had murdered his wife and nine children, and then committed suicide. And I said slyly, at the bottom, that the sudden madness of which the this melancholy massacre was the result, had been brought about by his having allowed himself to be persuaded by the California papers to sell his sound and lucrative Nevada silver stocks, and buy into Spring Valley just in time to get cooked along with that company's fancy dividend, and sink every cent he had in the world.

Ah, it was a deep, deep satire, and most ingeniously contrived. But I made the horrible details so carefully and conscientiously interesting that the public devoured *them* greedily, and wholly overlooked the following distinctly-stated facts, to wit:—The murderer was perfectly well known to every creature in the land as a *bachelor*, and consequently he could not murder his wife and nine children; he murdered them "in his splendid dressed-stone mansion just in the edge of the great pine forest between Empire City and Dutch Nick's," when even the very pickled oysters that came on our tables knew that there was not a "dressed-stone mansion" in all Nevada Territory; also that, so far from there being a "great pine forest between Empire City and Dutch Nick's," there wasn't a solitary tree within fifteen miles of either place; and, finally, it was patent and notorious that Empire City and Dutch Nick's were one and the same place, and contained only six houses anyhow, and consequently there could be no forest *between* them; and on top of all these absurdities I stated that this diabolical murderer, after inflicting a wound upon himself that the reader ought to have seen would kill an elephant in the twinkling of an eye, jumped on his horse and rode *four miles*, waving his wife's reeking scalp in the air, and thus performing entered Carson City with tremendous *éclat*, and dropped dead in front of the chief saloon, the envy and admiration of all beholders.

Well, in all my life I never saw anything like the sensation that little satire created. It was the talk of the town, it was the talk of the Territory. Most of the citizens dropped gently into it at breakfast, and they never finished their meal. There was something about those minutely faithful details that was a sufficing substitute for food. Few people that were able to read took food that morning. Dan and I (Dan was my reportorial associate) took our seats on either side of our customary table in the "Eagle Restaurant," and, as I unfolded the shred they used to call a napkin in that establishment, I saw at the next table two stalwart innocents with that sort of vegetable dandruff sprinkled

about their clothing which was the sign and evidence that they were in from the Truckee with a load of hay. The one facing me had the morning paper folded to a long narrow strip, and I knew, without any telling, that that strip represented the column that contained my pleasant financial satire. From the way he was excitedly mumbling, I saw that the heedless son of a hay-mow was skipping with all his might, in order to get to the bloody details as quickly as possible; and so he was missing the guide-boards I had set up to warn him that the whole thing was a fraud. Presently his eyes spread wide open, just as his jaws swung asunder to take in a potato approaching it on a fork; the potato halted, the face lit up redly, and the whole man was on fire with excitement. Then he broke into a disjointed checking off of the particulars—his potato cooling in mid-air meantime, and his mouth making a reach for it occasionally, but always bringing up suddenly against a new and still more direful performance of my hero. At last he looked his stunned and rigid comrade impressively in the face, and said, with an expression of concentrated awe—

" Jim, he b'iled his baby, and he took the old 'oman's skelp.   Cuss'd if *I* want any breakfast ! "

And he laid his lingering potato reverently down, and he and his friend departed from the restaurant empty but satisfied.

He *never got down* to where the satire part of it began.   Nobody ever did. They found the thrilling particulars sufficient.   To drop in with a poor little moral at the fag-end of such a gorgeous massacre, was to follow the expiring sun with a candle, and hope to attract the world's attention to it.

The idea that anybody could ever take my massacre for a genuine occurrence never once suggested itself to me, hedged about as it was by all those tell-tale absurdities and impossibilities concerning the " great pine forest," the " dressed-stone mansion," etc..   But I found out then, and never have forgotton since, that we never *read* the dull explanatory surroundings of marvellously exciting things when we have no occasion to suppose that some irresponsible scribbler is try-ing to defraud us ; we skip all that, and hasten to revel in the blood-curdling particulars and be happy.

THE UNDERTAKER'S CHAT.

"NOW, that corpse," said the undertaker, patting the folded hands of deceased approvingly, "was a brick—every way you took him he was a brick. He was so real accommodating, and so modest-like and simple in his last moments. Friends wanted metallic burial case—nothing else would do. *I* couldn't get it. There warn't going to be time—anybody could see that.

"Corpse said never mind, shake him up some kind of a box he could stretch out in comfortable, *he* warn't particular 'bout the general style of it. Said he went more on room than style, any way in a last final container.

"Friends wanted a silver door-plate on the coffin, signifying who he was and wher' he was from. Now *you* know a fellow couldn't roust out such a gaily thing as that in a little country town like this. What did corpse say?

"Corpse said, whitewash his old canoe and dob his address and general destination onto it with a blacking brush and a stencil plate, 'long with a verse from some likely hymn or other, and p'int him for the tomb, and mark him C. O. D., and just let him flicker. *He* warn't distressed any more than you be—on the contrary just as ca'm and collected as a hearse-horse; said he judged that wher' he was going to a body would find it considerable better to attract attention by a picturesque moral character than a natty burial case with a swell door-plate on it.

"Splendid man, he was. I'd druther do for a corpse like that 'n any I've tackled in seven year. There's some satisfaction in buryin' a man like that. You feel that what you're doing is appreciated. Lord bless you, so's he got planted before he sp'iled, he was perfectly satisfied; said his relations meant well, *per*fectly well, but all them preparations was bound to delay the thing

247

more or less, and he didn't wish to be kept layin' around.   You never see such
a clear head as what he had—and so ca'm and so cool.   Just a hunk of brains—
that is what *he* was.   Perfectly awful.   It was a ripping distance from one end
of that man's head to t'other.   Often and over again he's had brain fever a-
raging in one place, and the rest of the pile didn't know anything about it—
didn't affect it any more than an Injun insurrection in Arizona affects the
Atlantic States.

" Well, the relations they wanted a big funeral, but corpse said he was down on
flummery—didn't want any procession—fill the hearse full of mourners, and get
out a stern line and tow *him* behind.   He *was* the most down on style of any
remains I ever struck.   A beautiful simple-minded creature—it was what he
was, you can depend on that.   He was just set on having things the way he
wanted them, and he took a solid comfort in laying his little plans.   He had me
measure him and take a whole raft of directions; then he had the minister stand
up behind a long box with a table-cloth over it, to represent the coffin, and
read his funeral sermon, saying 'Angcore, angcore!' at the good places, and
making him scratch out every bit of brag about him, and all the hifalutin; and
then he made them trot out the choir so's he could help them pick out the tunes
for the occasion, and he got them to sing ' Pop Goes the Weasel,' because he'd
always liked that tune when he was down-hearted, and solemn music made him
sad; and when they sung that with tears in their eyes (because they all loved
him), and his relations grieving around, he just laid there as happy as a bug,
and trying to beat time and showing all over how much he enjoyed it; and
presently he got worked up and excited, and tried to join in, for mind you he
was pretty proud of his abilities in the singing line; but the first time he opened
his mouth and was just going to spread himself his breath took a walk.

" I never see a man snuffed out so sudden.   Ah, it was a great loss—it was a
powerful loss to this poor little one-horse town.   Well, well, well, I hain't got
time to be palavering along here—got to nail on the lid and mosey along
with him; and if you'll just give me a lift we'll skeet him into the hearse and
meander along.   Relations bound to have it so—don't pay no attention to dying
injunctions, minute a corpse's gone; but, if I had *my* way, if I didn't respect his

last wishes and tow him behind the hearse *I*'ll be cuss'd. I consider that whatever a corpse wants done for his comfort is little enough matter, and a man hain't got no right to deceive him or take advantage of him; and whatever a corpse trusts me to do I'm a-going to *do*, you know, even if it's to stuff him and paint him yaller and keep him for a keepsake—you hear me *me!* "

He cracked his whip and went lumbering away with his ancient ruin of a hearse, and I continued my walk with a valuable lesson learned—that a healthy and wholesome cheerfulness is not necessarily impossible to *any* occupation. The lesson is likely to be lasting, for it will take many months to obliterate the memory of the remarks and circumstances that impressed it.

CONCERNING CHAMBERMAIDS.

AGAINST all chambermaids, of whatsoever age or nationality, I launch the curse of bachelordom! Because:

They always put the pillows at the opposite end of the bed from the gas-burner, so that while you read and smoke before sleeping (as is the ancient and honored custom of bachelors), you have to hold your book aloft, in an uncomfortable position, to keep the light from dazzling your eyes.

When they find the pillows removed to the other end of the bed in the morning, they receive not the suggestion in a friendly spirit; but, glorying in their absolute sovereignty, and unpitying your helplessness, they make the bed just as it was originally, and gloat in secret over the pang their tyranny will cause you.

Always after that, when they find you have transposed the pillows, they undo your work, and thus defy and seek to embitter the life that God has given you.

If they cannot get the light in an inconvenient position any other way, they move the bed.

If you pull your trunk out six inches from the wall, so that the lid will stay up when you open it, they always shove that trunk back again. They do it on purpose.

If you want the spittoon in a certain spot, where it will be handy, they don't, and so they move it.

They always put your other boots into inaccessible places. They chiefly enjoy depositing them as far under the bed as the wall will permit. It is because this compels you to get down in an undignified attitude and make wild sweeps for them in the dark with the boot-jack, and swear.

They always put the match-box in some other place. They hunt up a new place for it every day, and put up a bottle, or other perishable glass thing, where the box stood before. This is to cause you to break that glass thing, groping in the dark, and get yourself into trouble.

They are for ever and ever moving the furniture. When you come in, in the night, you can calculate on finding the bureau where the wardrobe was in the morning. And when you go out in the morning, if you leave the slop-bucket by the door and rocking-chair by the window, when you come in at midnight, or thereabouts, you will fall over that rocking-chair, and you will proceed toward the window and sit down in that slop-tub. This will disgust you. They like that.

No matter where you put anything, they are not going to let it stay there. They will take it and move it the first chance they get. It is their nature. And, besides, it gives them pleasure to be mean and contrary this way. They would die if they couldn't be villians.

They always save up all the old scraps of printed rubbish you throw on the floor, and stack them up carefully on the table, and start the fire with your valuable manuscripts. If there is any one particular old scrap that you are more down on than any other, and which you are gradually wearing your life out trying to get rid of, you may take all the pains you possibly can in that direction, but it won't be of any use, because they will always fetch that old scrap back and put it in the same old place again every time. It does them good.

And they use up more hair-oil than any six men. If charged with purloining the same, they lie about it. What do they care about a hereafter? Absolutely nothing.

If you leave the key in the door for convenience sake, they will carry it down to the office and give it to the clerk. They do this under the vile pretence of trying to protect your property from thieves; but actually they do it because they want to make you tramp back down-stairs after it when you come home tired, or put you to the trouble of sending a waiter for it, which waiter will expect you to pay him something. In which case I suppose the degraded creatures divide.

They keep always trying to make your bed before you get up, thus destroying your rest and inflicting agony upon you; but after you get up, they don't come any more till next day.

They do all the mean things they can think of, and they do them just out of pure cussedness, and nothing else.

Chambermaids are dead to every human instinct.

If I can get a bill through the Legislature abolishing chambermaids, I mean to do it.

AURELIA'S UNFORTUNATE YOUNG MAN.

T HE facts in the following case came to me by letter from a young lady who lives in the beautiful city of San José; she is perfectly unknown to me, and simply signs herself "Aurelia Maria," which may possibly be a fictitious name. But no matter, the poor girl is almost heart-broken by the misfortunes she has undergone, and so confused by the conflicting counsels of misguided friends and insidious enemies, that she does not know what course to pursue in order to extricate herself from the web of difficulties in which she seems almost hopelessly involved. In this dilemma she turns to me for help, and supplicates for my guidance and instruction with a moving eloquence that would touch the heart of a statue. Hear her sad story:

She says that when she was sixteen years old she met and loved, with all the devotion of a passionate nature, a young man from New Jersey, named Williamson Breckinridge Caruthers, who was some six years her senior.   They were engaged, with the free consent of their friends and relatives, and for a time it seemed as if their career was destined to be characterized by an immunity from sorrow beyond the usual lot of humanity.   But at last the tide of fortune turned ; young Caruthers became infected with small-pox of the most virulent type, and when he recovered from his illness his face was pitted like a waffle-mould, and his comeliness gone for ever.   Aurelia thought to break off the engagement at first, but pity for her unfortunate lover caused her to postpone the marriage-day for a season, and give him another trial.

The very day before the wedding was to have taken place, Breckinridge, while absorbed in watching the flight of a balloon, walked into a well and fractured one of his legs, and it had to be taken off above the knee.   Again Aurelia was moved to break the engagement, but again love triumphed, and she set the day forward and gave him another chance to reform.

And again misfortune overtook the unhappy youth.   He lost one arm by the premature discharge of a Fourth-of-July cannon, and within three months he got the other pulled out by a carding-machine.   Aurelia's heart was almost crushed by these latter calamities.   She could not but be deeply grieved to see her lover passing from her by piecemeal, feeling, as she did, that he could not last for ever under this disastrous process of reduction, yet knowing of no way to stop its dreadful career, and in her tearful despair she almost regretted, like brokers who hold on and lose, that she had not taken him at first, before he had suffered such an alarming depreciation.   Still, her brave soul bore her up, and she resolved to bear with her friend's unnatural disposition yet a little longer.

Again the wedding-day approached, and again disappointment overshadowed it : Caruthers fell ill with the erysipelas, and lost the use of one his eyes entirely. The friends and relatives of the bride, considering that she had already put up with more than could reasonably be expected of her, now came forward and insisted that the match should be broken off, but after wavering awhile, Aurelia, with a generous spirit which did her credit, said she had reflected calmly upon the matter, and could not discover that Breckinridge was to blame.

So she extended the time once more, and he broke his other leg.

It was a sad day for the poor girl when she saw the surgeons reverently bearing away the sack whose uses she had learned by previous experience, and her heart told her the bitter truth that some more of her lover was gone. She felt that the field of her affections was growing more and more circumscribed every day, but once more she frowned down her relatives and renewed her betrothal.

Shortly before the time set for the nuptials another disaster occurred. There was but one man scalped by the Owens River Indians last year. That man was Williamson Breckinridge Caruthers, of New Jersey. He was hurrying home with happiness in his heart, when he lost his hair for ever, and in that hour of bitterness he almost cursed the mistaken mercy that had spared his head.

At last Aurelia is in serious perplexity as to what she ought to do. She still loves her Breckinridge, she writes, with truly womanly feeling—she still loves what is left of him—but her parents are bitterly opposed to the match, because he has no property and is disabled from working, and she has not sufficient means to support both comfortably. "Now, what should she do?" she asks with painful and anxious solicitude.

It is a delicate question; it is one which involves the lifelong happiness of a woman, and that of nearly two-thirds of a man, and I feel that it would be assuming too great a responsiblity to do more than make a mere suggestion in the case. How would it do to build to him? If Aurelia can afford the expense, let her furnish her mutilated lover with wooden arms and wooden legs, and a glass eye and a wig, and give him another show; give him ninety days, without grace, and if he does not break his neck in the meantime, marry him and take the chances. It does not seem to me that there is much risk, any way, Aurelia, because if he sticks to his singular propensity for damaging himself every time he sees a good opportunity, his next experiment is bound to finish him, and then you are safe, married or single. If married, the wooden legs and such other valuables as he may possess revert to the widow, and you see you sustain no actual loss save the cherished fragment of a noble but most unfortunate husband, who honestly strove to do right, but whose extraordinary instincts were against him. Try it, Maria. I have thought the matter over carefully and well, and it is the only chance I see for you. It would have been a happy conceit on the part of Caruthers if he had started with his neck and broken that first; but since he has seen fit to choose a different policy and string himself out as long as possible, I do not think we ought to upbraid him for it if he has enjoyed it. We must do the best we can under the circumstances, and try not to feel exasperated at him.

"AFTER" JENKINS.

A GRAND affair of a ball—the Pioneers'—came off at the Occidental some time ago. The following notes of the costumes worn by the belles of the occasion may not be uninteresting to the general reader, and Jenkins may get an idea therefrom—

Mrs. W. M. was attired in an elegant *pâté de foie gras*, made expressly for her, and was greatly admired. Miss S. had her hair done up. She was the centre of attraction for the gentlemen and the envy of all the ladies. Mrs. G. W. was tastefully dressed in a *tout ensemble*, and was greeted with deafening applause wherever she went. Mrs. C. N. was superbly arrayed in white kid gloves. Her modest and engaging manner accorded well with the unpretending simplicity of her costume and caused her to be regarded with absorbing interest by every one.

The charming Miss M. M. B. appeared in a thrilling waterfall, whose exceeding grace and volume compelled the homage of pioneers and emigrants alike. How beautiful she was!

The queenly Mrs. L. R. was attractively attired in her new and beautiful false teeth, and the *bon jour* effect they naturally produced was heightened by her enchanting and well sustained smile.

Miss R. P., with that repugnance to ostentation in dress, which is so peculiar to her, was attired in a simple white lace collar, fastened with a neat pearl-button solitaire. The fine contrast between the sparkling vivacity of her natural optic, and the steadfast attentiveness of her placid glass eye, was the subject of general and enthusiastic remark.

Miss C. L. B. had her fine nose elegantly enamelled, and the easy grace with which she blew it from time to time, marked her as a cultivated and accomplished woman of the world; its exquisitely modulated tone excited the admiration of all who had the happiness to hear it.

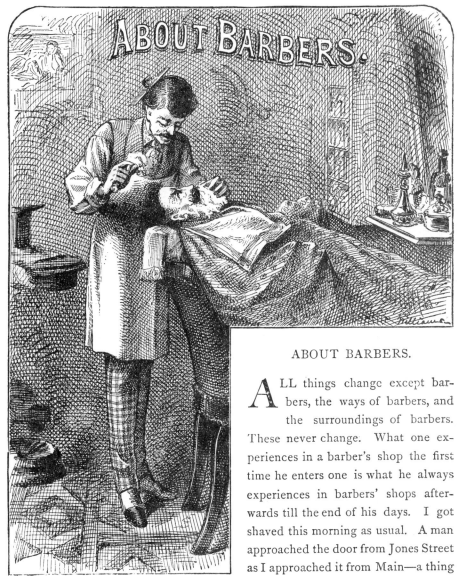

ABOUT BARBERS.

ALL things change except barbers, the ways of barbers, and the surroundings of barbers. These never change. What one experiences in a barber's shop the first time he enters one is what he always experiences in barbers' shops afterwards till the end of his days. I got shaved this morning as usual. A man approached the door from Jones Street as I approached it from Main—a thing that always happens. I hurried up, but it was of no use; he entered the door one little step ahead of me, and I followed in on his heels and saw him take the only

vacant chair, the one presided over by the best barber.   It always happens so.   I
sat down, hoping that I might fall heir to the chair belonging to the better of the
remaining two barbers, for he had already begun combing his man's hair, while his
comrade was not yet quite done rubbing up and oiling his customer's locks.   I
watched the probabilities with strong interest.   When I saw that No. 2 was gaining
on No. 1 my interest grew to solicitude.   When No. 1 stopped a moment to make
change on a bath ticket for a new comer, and lost ground in the race, my solicitude
rose to anxiety.   When No. 1 caught up again, and both he and his comrade were
pulling the towels away and brushing the powder from their customer's cheeks,
and it was about an even thing which one would say " Next!" first, my very breath
stood still with the suspense.   But when at the culminating moment No. 1 stopped
to pass a comb a couple of times through his customer's eyebrows, I saw that he
had lost the race by a single instant, and I rose indignant and quitted the shop, to
keep from falling into the hands of No. 2 ; for I have none of that enviable firmness
that enables a man to look calmly into the eyes of a waiting barber and tell him he
will wait for his fellow-barber's chair.

I stayed out fifteen minutes, and then went back, hoping for better luck.   Of
course all the chairs were occupied now, and four men sat waiting, silent, unsocia-
ble, distraught, and looking bored, as men always do who are awaiting their turn
in a barber's shop.   I sat down in one of the iron-armed compartments of an old
sofa, and put in the time for a while reading the framed advertisements of all sorts
of quack nostrums for dyeing and coloring the hair.   Then I read the greasy names
on the private bay rum bottles ; read the names and noted the numbers on the
private shaving cups in the pigeon-holes ; studied the stained and damaged cheap
prints on the walls, of battles, early Presidents, and voluptuous recumbent sultanas,
and the tiresome and everlasting young girl putting her grandfather's spectacles
on ; execrated in my heart the cheerful canary and the distracting parrot that few
barbers' shops are without.   Finally, I searched out the least dilapidated of last
year's illustrated papers that littered the foul centre-table, and conned their
unjustifiable misrepresentations of old forgotten events.

At last my turn came.   A voice said "Next!" and I surrendered to—No. 2, of
course.   It always happens so.   I said meekly that I was in a hurry, and it affected

him as strongly as if he had never heard it. He shoved up my head, and put a napkin under it. He ploughed his fingers into my collar and fixed a towel there. He explored my hair with his claws and suggested that it needed trimming. I said I did not want it trimmed. He explored again and said it was pretty long for the present style—better have a little taken off; it needed it behind especially. I said I had had it cut only a week before. He yearned over it reflectively a moment, and then asked with a disparaging manner, who cut it? I came back at him promptly with a "You did!" I had him there. Then he fell to stirring up his lather and re-garding himself in the glass, stop-ping now and then to get close and examine his chin critically or inspect a pimple. Then he lathered one side of my face thoroughly, and was about to lather the other, when a dog fight attracted his at-tention, and he ran to the win-dow and stayed and saw it out, losing two shill-ings on the result in bets with the other barbers, a thing which gave me great satisfac-tion. He finished lathering, and then began to rub in the suds with his hand.

He now began to sharpen his razor on an old suspender, and was delayed a good deal on account of a controversy about a cheap masquerade ball he had figured at the night before, in red cambric and bogus ermine, as some kind of a king. He was so gratified with being chaffed about some damsel whom he had smitten with his charms that he used every means to continue the controversy by pretending to be annoyed at the chaffings of his fellows. This matter begot more surveyings of himself in the glass, and he put down his razor and brushed his hair with elaborate care, plaster-ing an inverted arch of it down on his forehead, accomplishing an accurate "part"

behind, and brushing the two wings forward over his ears with nice exactness. In the meantime the lather was drying on my face, and apparently eating into my vitals.

Now he began to shave, digging his fingers into my countenance to stretch the skin and bundling and tumbling my head this way and that as convenience in shaving demanded. As long as he was on the tough sides of my face I did not suffer; but when he began to rake, and rip, and tug at my chin, the tears came. He now made a handle of my nose, to assist him in shaving the corners of my

upper lip, and it was by this bit of circumstantial evidence that I discovered that a part of his duties in the shop was to clean the kerosene lamps. I had often wondered in an indolent way whether the barbers did that, or whether it was the boss. About this time I was amusing myself trying to guess where he would be most likely to cut me this time, but he got ahead of me, and sliced me on the end of the chin before I had got my mind made up. He immediately sharpened his razor—he might have done it before. I do not like a close shave, and would not let him go over me a

second time. I tried to get him to put up his razor, dreading that he would make for the side of my chin, my pet tender spot, a place which a razor cannot touch twice without making trouble; but he said he only wanted to just smooth off one little roughness, and in the same moment he slipped his razor along the forbidden ground, and the dreaded pimple-signs of a close shave rose up smarting and answered to the call. Now he soaked his towel in bay rum, and slapped it all over my face nastily; slapped it over as if a human being ever yet washed his face in that way. Then he dried it by slapping with the dry part of the towel, as if a human being ever dried his face in such a fashion; but a barber seldom rubs you like a Christian. Next he poked bay rum into the cut place with his towel, then choked the wound with powdered starch, then soaked it with bay rum again, and would have gone on soaking and powdering it for evermore, no doubt, if I had not rebelled and begged off. He powdered my whole face now, straightened me up, and began to plough my hair thoughtfully with his hands. Then he suggested a shampoo, and said my hair needed it badly, very badly. I observed that I shampooed it myself very thoroughly in the bath yesterday. I "had him" again. He next recommended some of "Smith's Hair Glorifier," and offered to sell me a bottle. I declined. He praised the new perfume, "Jones' Delight of the Toilet," and proposed to sell me some of that. I declined again. He tendered me a toothwash atrocity of his own invention, and when I declined offered to trade knives with me.

He returned to business after the miscarriage of this last enterprise, sprinkled me all over, legs and all, greased my hair in defiance of my protest against it, rubbed and scrubbed a good deal of it out by the roots, and combed and brushed the rest, parting it behind, and plastering the eternal inverted arch of hair down on my forehead, and then, while combing my scant eyebrows and defiling them with pomade, strung out an account of the achievements of a six-ounce black and tan terrier of his till I heard the whistles blow for noon, and knew I was five minutes too late for the train. Then he snatched away the towel, brushed it lightly about my face, passed his comb through my eyebrows once more, and gaily sang out " Next!"

This barber fell down and died of apoplexy two hours later. I am waiting over a day for my revenge—I am going to attend his funeral.

"PARTY CRIES" IN IRELAND.

BELFAST is a peculiarly religious community. This may be said of the whole of the north of Ireland. About one half of the people are Protestants and the other half Catholics. Each party does all it can to make its own doctrines popular and draw the affections of the irreligious toward them. One hears constantly of the most touching instances of this zeal. A week ago a vast concourse of Catholics assembled at Armagh to dedicate a new Cathedral; and when they started home again the roadways were lined with groups of meek and lowly Protestants who stoned them till all the region round about was marked with blood. I thought that only Catholics argued in that way, but it seems to be a mistake.

Every man in the community is a missionary and carries a brick to admonish the erring with. The law has tried to break this up, but not with perfect success. It has decreed that irritating "party cries" shall not be indulged in, and that persons uttering them shall be fined forty shillings and costs. And so, in the police court reports, every day, one sees these fines recorded. Last week a girl twelve years old was fined the usual forty shillings and costs for proclaiming in the public streets that she was "a Protestant." The usual cry is, "To hell with the Pope!" or "To hell with the Protestants!" according to the utterer's system of salvation.

One of Belfast's local jokes was very good. It referred to the uniform and inevitable fine of forty shillings and costs for uttering a party cry—and it is no economical fine for a poor man, either, by the way. They say that a policeman found a drunken man lying on the ground, up a dark alley, entertaining himself with shouting, "To *hell* with!" "To *hell* with!" The officer smelt a fine —informers get half:

"What's that you say?"

"To *hell* with!"

"To hell with *who?* To hell with *what?*"

"Ah, bedad ye can finish it yourself—it's too expinsive for me!"

I think the seditious disposition, restrained by the economical instinct is finely put, in that.

THE FACTS CONCERNING THE RECENT RESIGNATION.

WASHINGTON, *Dec.* 2, 1867.

I HAVE resigned. The Government appears to go on much the same, but there is a spoke out of its wheel, nevertheless. I was clerk of the Senate Committee on Conchology, and I have thrown up the position. I could see the plainest disposition on the part of the other members of the Government to debar me from having any voice in the counsels of the nation, and so I could no longer hold office and retain my self-respect. If I were to detail all the outrages that were heaped upon me during the six days that I was connected with the Government in an official capacity, the narrative would fill a volume. They appointed me clerk of that Committee on Conchology, and then allowed me no amanuensis to play billiards with. I would have borne that, lonesome as it was, if I had met with that courtesy from the other members of the Cabinet which was my due. But I did not. Whenever I observed that the head of a department was pursuing a wrong course, I laid down everything and went and tried to set him right, as it was my duty to do; and I never was thanked for it in a single instance. I went, with the best intentions in the world, to the Secretary of the Navy, and said—

"Sir, I cannot see that Admiral Farragut is doing anything but skirmishing around there in Europe, having a sort of pic-nic. Now, that may be all very well, but it does not exhibit itself to me in that light. If there is no fighting for him to do, let him come home. There is no use in a man having a whole fleet for a pleasure excursion. It is too expensive. Mind, I do not object to pleasure excursions for the naval officers—pleasure excursions that are in reason—pleasure excursions that are economical. Now, they might go down the Mississippi on a raft "——

You ought to have heard him storm! One would have supposed I had committed a crime of some kind. But I didn't mind. I said it was cheap, and full of republican simplicity, and perfectly safe. I said that, for a tranquil pleasure excursion, there was nothing equal to a raft.

Then the Secretary of the Navy asked me who I was; and when I told him I was connected with the Government, he wanted to know in what capacity. I said that, without remarking upon the singularity of such a question, coming, as it did, from a member of that same Government, I would inform him that I was clerk of the Senate Committee on Conchology. Then there was a fine storm! He finished by ordering me to leave the premises, and give my attention strictly to my own business in future. My first impulse was to get him removed. However, that would harm others beside himself, and do me no real good, and so I let him stay.

I went next to the Secretary of War, who was not inclined to see me at all until he learned that I was connected with the Government. If I had not been on important business, I suppose I could not have got in. I asked him for a light (he was smoking at the time), and then I told him I had no fault to find with his defending the parole stipulations of General Lee and his comrades in arms, but that I could not approve of his method of fighting the Indians on the Plains. I said he fought too scattering. He ought to get the Indians more together—get them together in some convenient place, where he could have provisions enough for both parties, and then have a general massacre. I said there was nothing so convincing to an Indian as a general massacre. If he could not approve of the massacre, I said the next surest thing for an Indian was soap and education. Soap and education are not as sudden as a massacre, but they are more deadly in the long run; because a half-massacred Indian may recover, but if you educate him and wash him, it is bound to finish him sometime or other. It undermines his constitution; it strikes at the foundation of his being. "Sir," I said, "the time has come when blood-curdling cruelty has become necessary. Inflict soap and a spelling-book on every Indian that ravages the Plains, and let them die!"

The Secretary of War asked me if I was a member of the Cabinet, and I said I was. He inquired what position I held, and I said I was clerk of the Senate Committee on Conchology. I was then ordered under arrest for contempt of court, and restrained of my liberty for the best part of the day.

I almost resolved to be silent thenceforward, and let the Government get along the best way it could. But duty called, and I obeyed. I called on the Secretary of the Treasury. He said—

"What will *you* have?"

The question threw me off my guard. I said, "Rum punch."

He said, "If you have got any business here, sir, state it—and in as few words as possible."

I then said that I was sorry he had seen fit to change the subject so abruptly, because such conduct was very offensive to me; but under the circumstances I would overlook the matter and come to the point. I now went into an earnest expostulation with him upon the extravagant length of his report. I said it was expensive, unnecessary, and awkwardly constructed; there were no descriptive passages in it, no poetry, no sentiment—no heroes, no plot, no pictures—not even woodcuts. Nobody would read it, that was a clear case. I urged him not to ruin his reputation by getting out a thing like that. If he ever hoped to succeed in literature, he must throw more variety into his writings. He must beware of dry detail. I said that the main popularity of the almanac was derived from its poetry and conundrums, and that a few conundrums distributed around through his Treasury report would help the sale of it more than all the internal revenue he could put into it. I said these things in the kindest spirit, and yet the Secretary of the Treasury fell into a violent passion. He even said I was an ass. He abused me in the most vindictive manner, and said that if I came there again meddling with his business, he would throw me out of the window. I said I would take my hat and go, if I could not be treated with the respect due to my office, and I did go. It was just like a new author. They always think they know more than anybody else when they are getting out their first book. Nobody can tell *them* anything.

During the whole time that I was connected with the Government it seemed as if I could not do anything in an official capacity without getting myself into trouble. And yet I did nothing, attempted nothing, but what I conceived to be for the good of my country. The sting of my wrongs may have driven me to unjust and harmful conclusions, but it surely seemed to me that the Secretary of State, the Secretary of War, the Secretary of the Treasury, and others of my *confrères,* had conspired from the very beginning to drive me from the Administration. I never attended but one Cabinet meeting while I was connected with the Government. That was sufficient for me. The servant at the White House door did not seem disposed to make way for me.until I asked if the other members of the Cabinet had arrived. He said they had, and I entered. They were all there; but nobody offered me a seat. They stared at me as if I had been an intruder. The President said—·

" Well, sir, who are *you* ? "

I handed him my card, and he read—"The Hon. Mark Twain, Clerk of the Senate Committee on Conchology." Then he looked at me from head to foot, as if he had never heard of me before. The Secretary of the Treasury said—

" This is the meddlesome ass that came to recommend me to put poetry and conundrums in my report, as if it were an almanac."

The Secretary of War said—" It is the same visionary that came to me yesterday with a scheme to educate a portion of the Indians to death, and massacre the balance."

The Secretary of the Navy said—"I recognize this youth as the person who has been interfering with my business time and again during the week. He is distressed about Admiral Farragut's using a whole fleet for a pleasure excursion, as he terms it. His proposition about some insane pleasure excursion on a raft is too absurd to repeat."

I said—"Gentlemen, I perceive here a disposition to throw discredit upon every act of my official career; I perceive, also, a disposition to debar me from all voice in the counsels of the nation. No notice whatever was sent to me to-day. It was only by the merest chance that I learned that there was going to be a Cabinet meeting. But let these things pass. All I wish to know is, is this a Cabinet meeting, or is it not ? "

The President said it was.

" Then," I said, " let us proceed to business at once, and not fritter away valuable time in unbecoming fault-findings with each other's official conduct."

The Secretary of State now spoke up, in his benignant way, and said, " Young man, you are laboring under a mistake. The clerks of the Congressional committees are not members of the Cabinet. Neither are the doorkeepers of the Capitol, strange as it may seem. Therefore, much as we could desire your more than human wisdom in our deliberations, we cannot lawfully avail ourselves of it. The counsels of the nation must proceed without you; if disaster follows, as follow full well it may, be it balm to your sorrowing spirit, that by deed and voice you did what in you lay to avert it. You have my blessing. Farewell."

These gentle words soothed my troubled breast, and I went away. But the servants of a nation can know no peace. I had hardly reached my den in the capitol, and disposed my feet on the table like a representative, when one of the Senators on the Conchological Committee came in in a passion and said—

"Where have you been all day?"

I observed that, if that was anybody's affair but my own, I had been to a Cabinet meeting.

"To a Cabinet meeting? I would like to know what business you had at a Cabinet meeting?"

I said I went there to consult—allowing for the sake of argument, that he was in anywise concerned in the matter. He grew insolent then, and ended by saying he had wanted me for three days past to copy a report on bomb-shells, egg-shells, clam-shells, and I don't know what all, connected with conchology, and nobody had been able to find me.

This was too much. This was the feather that broke the clerical camel's back. I said, "Sir, do you suppose that I am going to *work* for six dollars a day? If that is the idea, let me recommend the Senate Committee on Conchology to hire somebody else. I am the slave of *no* faction! Take back your degrading commission. Give me liberty, or give me death!"

From that hour I was no longer connected with the Government. Snubbed by the department, snubbed by the Cabinet, snubbed at last by the chairman of a committee I was endeavoring to adorn, I yielded to persecution, cast far from me the perils and seductions of my great office, and forsook my bleeding country in the hour of her peril.

But I had done the State some service, and I sent in my bill:—

The United States of America in account with the Hon. Clerk of the Senate Committee on Conchology, Dr.

To consultation with Secretary of War, ...	$50
To consultation with Secretary of Navy, ...	50.

To consultation with Secretary of the Treasury, ... 50
Cabinet consultation, ... No charge.
To mileage to and from Jerusalem,* *via* Egypt, Algiers, Gibraltar, and Cadiz, 14,000
miles, at 20c. a mile, ... 2800
To salary as Clerk of Senate Committee on Conchology, six days, at $6 per day, . 36

Total, ... $2986

Not an item of this bill has been paid, except that trifle of 36 dollars for clerkship salary. The Secretary of the Treasury, pursuing me to the last, drew his pen through all the other items, and simply marked in the margin "Not allowed." So, the dread alternative is embraced at last. Repudiation has begun! The nation is lost.

I am done with official life for the present. Let those clerks who are willing to be imposed on remain. I know numbers of them, in the Departments, who are never informed when there is to be a Cabinet meeting, whose advice is never asked about war, or finance, or commerce, by the heads of the nation, any more than if they were not connected with the Government, and who actually stay in their offices day after day and work! They know their importance to the nation, and they unconsciously show it in their bearing, and the way they order their sustenance at the restaurant—but they work. I know one who has to paste all sorts of little scraps from the newspaper into a scrap-book—sometimes as many as eight or ten scraps a day. He doesn't do it well, but he does it as well as he can. It is very fatiguing. It is exhausting to the intellect. Yet he only gets 1800 dollars a year. With a brain like his, that young man could amass thousands and thousands of dollars in some other pursuit, if he chose to do it. But no—his heart is with his country, and he will serve her as long as she has got a scrap-book left. And I know clerks that don't know how to write very well, but such knowledge as they possess they nobly lay at the feet of their country, and toil on and suffer for 2500 dollars a year. What they write has to be written over again by other clerks, sometimes; but when a man has done his best for his country, should his country complain? Then there are clerks that have no clerkships, and are waiting, and waiting, and waiting, for a vacancy—waiting patiently for a chance to help their country out—

---

* Territorial delegates charge mileage both ways, although they never go back when they get here once. Why my mileage is denied me is more than I can understand.

and while they are waiting, they only get barely, 2000 dollars a year for it. It is sad—it is very, very sad. When a member of Congress has a friend who is gifted, but has no employment wherein his great powers may be brought to bear, he confers him upon his country, and gives him a clerkship in a Department. And there that man has to slave his life out, fighting documents for the benefit of a nation that never thinks of him, never sympathizes with him—and all for 2000 or 3000 dollars a year. When I shall have completed my list of all the clerks in the several departments, with my statement of what they have to do, and what they get for it, you will see that there are not half enough clerks, and that what there are do not get half enough pay.

HISTORY REPEATS ITSELF.

THE following I find in a Sandwich Island paper which some friend has sent me from that tranquil far-off retreat. The coincidence between my own experience and that here set down by the late Mr. Benton is so remarkable that I cannot forbear publishing and commenting upon the paragraph. The Sandwich Island paper says:—

"How touching is this tribute of the late Hon. T. H. Benton to his mother's influence:—'My mother asked me never to use tobacco; I have never touched it from that time to the present day. She asked me not to gamble, and I have never gambled. I cannot tell who is losing in games that are being played. She admonished me, too, against liquor-drinking, and whatever capacity for endurence I have at present, and whatever usefulness I may have attained through life, I attribute to having complied with her pious and correct wishes. When I was seven years of age she asked me not to drink, and then I made a resolution of total abstinence; and that I have adhered to it through all time I owe to my mother.'"

I never saw anything so curious. It is almost an exact epitome of my own moral career—after simply substituting a grandmother for a mother. How well I remember my grandmother's asking me not to use tobacco, good old soul! She said, "You're at it again, are you, you whelp? Now, don't ever let me catch you chewing tobacco before breakfast again, or I lay I'll black-snake you within an inch of your life!" I have never touched it at that hour of the morning from that time to the present day.

271

She asked me not to gamble. She whispered and said, "Put up those wicked cards this minute!—two pair and a jack, you numskull, and the other fellow's got a flush!"

I never have gambled from that day to this—never once—without a "cold deck" in my pocket. I cannot even tell who is going to lose in games that are being played unless I dealt myself.

When I was two years of age she asked me not to drink, and then I made a resolution of total abstinence. That I have adhered to it and enjoyed the beneficent effects of it through all time, I owe to my grandmother. I have never drunk a drop from that day to this of any kind of water.

HONOURED AS A CURIOSITY.

IF you get into conversation with a stranger in Honolulu, and experience that natural desire to know what sort of ground you are treading on by finding out what manner of man your stranger is, strike out boldly and address him as " Captain." Watch him narrowly, and if you see by his countenance that you are on the wrong track, ask him where he preaches. It is a safe bet that he is either a missionary or captain of a whaler. I became personally acquainted with seventy-two captains and ninety-six missionaries. The captains and ministers form one-half of the population ;

the third fourth is composed of common Kanakas and mercantile foreigners and their families; and the final fourth is made up of high officers of the Hawaiian Government. And there are just about cats enough for three apiece all around.

A solemn stranger met me in the suburbs one day, and said:

" Good morning, your reverence. Preach in the stone church yonder, no doubt ! "

" No, I don't. I'm not a preacher."

" Really, I beg your pardon, captain. I trust you had a good season. How much oil " ——

" Oil! Why what do you take me for? I'm not a whaler."

" Oh! I beg a thousands pardons, your Excellency. Major-General in the household troops, no doubt? Minister of the Interior, likely? Secretary of War? First Gentleman of the Bedchamber? Commissioner of the Royal "——

" Stuff! man. I'm not connected in any way with the Government."

" Bless my life! Then who the mischief are you? what the mischief are you? and how the mischief did you get here? and where in thunder did you come from ? "

" I'm only a private personage—an unassuming stranger—lately arrived from America."

" No! Not a missionary! not a whaler! not a member of his Majesty's Government! not even Secretary of the Navy! Ah! heaven! it is too blissful to be true; alas! I do but dream. And yet that noble, honest countenance— those oblique, ingenuous eyes—that massive head, incapable of—of anything; your hand; give me your hand, bright waif. Excuse these tears. For sixteen weary years I have yearned for a moment like this, and "——

Here his feeling were too much for him, and he swooned away. I pitied this poor creature from the bottom of my heart. I was deeply moved. I shed a few tears on him, and kissed him for his mother. I then took what small change he had, and " shoved."

THE LATE BENJAMIN FRANKLIN.

["Never put off till to-morrow what you can do day after to-morrow just as well."—B. F.]

THIS party was one of those persons whom they call Philosophers. He was twins, being born simultaneously in two different houses in the city of Boston. These houses remain unto this day, and have signs upon them worded in accordance with the facts. The signs are considered well enough to have, though not necessary, because the inhabitants point out the two birth-places to the stranger anyhow, and sometimes as often as several times in the same day. The subject of this memoir was of a vicious disposition, and early prostituted his talents to the invention of maxims and aphorisms

275

calculated to inflict suffering upon the rising generation of all subsequent ages. His simplest acts, also, were contrived with a view to their being held up for the emulation of boys for ever—boys who might otherwise have been happy. It was in this spirit that he became the son of a soap-boiler, and probably for no other reason than that the efforts of all future boys who tried to be anything might be looked upon with suspicion unless they were the sons of soap-boilers. With a malevolence which is without parallel in history, he would work all day, and then sit up nights, and let on to be studying algebra by the light of a

smouldering fire, so that all other boys might have to do that also, or else have Benjamin Franklin thrown up to them. Not satisfied with these proceedings, he had a fashion of living wholly on bread and water, and studying astronomy at meal time—a thing which has brought affliction to mil-lions of boys since, whose fathers had read Franklin's pernicious biogra-phy.

His maxims were full of animosity towards boys. Nowadays a boy cannot follow out a single natural instinct without tumbling over some of those everlasting aphorisms and hearing from Franklin on the spot. If he buys two cents' worth of peanuts, his father says, " Remember what Franklin has said, my son—'A groat a day's a penny a year;'" and the comfort is all gone out of those peanuts. If he wants to spin his top when he has done work, his father quotes, " Procrastination is the thief of time." If he does a virtuous action, he never gets any thing for it, because " Virtue is its own reward." And that boy is hounded to death and robbed of his natural rest, because Franklin said once, in one of his inspired flights of malignity—

" Early to bed and early to rise
Makes a man healthy and wealthy and wise."

As if it were any object to a boy to be healthy and wealthy and wise on such terms. The sorrow that that maxim has cost me through my parents' experimenting on me with it, tongue cannot tell. The legitimate result is my present state of general debility, indigence, and mental aberration. My parents used to have me up before nine o'clock in the morning, sometimes, when I was a boy. If they had let me take my natural rest, where would I have been now? Keeping store, no doubt, and respected by all.

And what an adroit old adventurer the subject of this memoir was! In order to get a chance to fly his kite on Sunday he used to hang a key on the string and let on to be fishing for lightning. And a guileless public would go home chirping about the "wisdom" and the "genius" of the hoary Sabbath-breaker. If anybody caught him playing "mumble-peg" by himself, after the age of sixty, he would immediately appear to be ciphering out how the grass grew—as if it was any of his business. My grandfather knew him well, and he says Franklin was always fixed—always ready. If a body, during his old age, happened on him unexpectedly when he was catching flies, or making mud pies, or sliding on a cellar-door, he would immediately look wise, and rip out a maxim, and walk off with his nose in the air and his cap turned wrong side before, trying to appear absent-minded and eccentric. He was a hard lot.

He invented a stove that would smoke your head off in four hours by the clock. One can see the almost devilish satisfaction he took in it by his giving it his name.

He was always proud of telling how he entered Philadelphia for the first time, with nothing in the world but two shillings in his pocket and four rolls of bread under his arm. But really, when you come to examine it critically, it was nothing. Anybody could have done it.

To the subject of this memoir belongs the honor of recommending the army to go back to bows and arrows in place of bayonets and muskets. He observed, with his customary force, that the bayonet was very well under some circumstances, but that he doubted whether it could be used with accuracy at a long range.

Benjamin Franklin did a great many notable things for his country, and made her young name to be honored in many lands as the mother of such a son. It is not the idea of this memoir to ignore that or cover it up. No; the simple idea of it is to snub those pretentious maxims of his, which he worked up with a great show of originality out of truisms that had become wearisome platitudes as early as the dispersion from Babel; and also to snub his stove, and his military inspirations, his unseemly endeavor to make himself conspicuous when he entered Philadel-

phia, and his flying his kite and fool-ing away his time in all sorts of such ways when he ought to have been foraging for soap-fat, or constructing candles. I merely desired to do away with somewhat of the prevalent calamitous idea among heads of families that Franklin *acquired* his great genius by working for noth-ing, studying by moonlight, and getting up in the night instead of waiting till morn-ing like a Chris-tian; and that this programme, rigid-ly inflicted, will make a Franklin of every father's fool. It is time these gentlemen were finding out that these execrable eccentricities of instinct and conduct are only the *evidences* of genius, not the *creators* of it. I wish I had been the father of my parents long enough to make them comprehend this truth, and thus prepare them to let their son have an easier time of it. When I was a child I had to boil soap, notwithstanding my father was wealthy, and I had to get up early and study geometry at breakfast, and peddle my own poetry, and do every-thing just as Franklin did, in the solemn hope that I would be a Franklin some day. And here I am.

To Fred Sidney Esq,
THEATRE ROYAL
STOCKTON-ON-TEES.

By whom we are Surrounded

THE "BLIND LETTER" DEPARTMENT, LONDON P. O.

ABOUT the most curious feature of the London post-office is the "Blind-Letter" Department. Only one clerk is employed in it and sometimes his place is a sinecure for a day at a time, and then again it is just the reverse. His specialty is a wonderful knack in the way of deciphering atrocious penmanship. That man can read *anything* that is done with a pen. All superscriptions are carried to him which the mighty army of his fellow clerks cannot make out, and he spells them off like print and sends them on their way. He keeps in a book, fac-similes of

279

the most astonishing specimens he comes across. He also keeps fac-similes of many of the envelopes that pass through the office with queer pictures drawn

DUNDREARY DREAMS OF HOME.

upon them. He was kind enough to have some of the picture-envelopes and

[TO THE MAJESTY THE QUEEN, AND THE PRINCESS OF WALES.]

execrable superscriptions copied for me, (the latter with "translations" added,) and I here offer them for the inspection of the curious reader.

[REV'D E. W. EDGELL,
40 YORK ST., GLOUCESTER PLACE, LONDON.]

FROM DR. LIVINGSTONE TO HIS DAUGHTER.

INTELLIGENCE OFFICE FOR MINISTERS.

SENT BY ONE CLERGYMAN TO ANOTHER.

FIRST INTERVIEW WITH ARTEMUS WARD.

I HAD never seen him before. He brought letters of introduction from mutual
friends in San Francisco, and by invitation I breakfasted with him. It was
almost religion, there in the silver mines, to precede such a meal with whiskey
cocktails. Artemus, with the true cosmopolitan instinct, always deferred to the
customs of the country he was in, and so he ordered three of those abominations.
Hingston was present. I said I would rather not drink a whiskey cocktail. I
said it would go right to my head, and confuse me so that I would be in a helpless
tangle in ten minutes. I did not want to act like a lunatic before strangers. But

283

Artemus gently insisted, and I drank the treasonable mixture under protest, and felt all the time that I was doing a thing I might be sorry for. In a minute or two I began to imagine that my ideas were clouded. I waited in great anxiety for the conversation to open, with a sort of vague hope that my understanding would prove clear, after all, and my misgivings groundless.

Artemus dropped an unimportant remark or two, and then assumed a look of superhuman earnestness, and made the following astounding speech. He said:—

"Now there is one thing I ought to ask you about before I forget it. You have been here in Silverland—here in Nevada—two or three years, and, of course, your position on the daily press has made it necessary for you to go down in the mines and examine them carefully in detail, and therefore you know all about the silver-mining business. Now, what I want to get at is—is, well, the way the deposits of ore are made, you know. For instance. Now, as I understand it, the vein which contains the silver is sandwiched in between casings of granite, and runs along the ground, and sticks up like a curb-stone. Well, take a vein forty feet thick, for example, or eighty, for that matter, or even a hundred—say you go down on it with a shaft, straight down, you know, or with what you call 'incline,' maybe you go down five hundred feet, or maybe you don't go down but two hundred—any way you go down, and all the time this vein grows narrower, when the casings come nearer or approach each other, you may say—that is, when they do approach, which of course they do not always do, particularly in cases where the nature of the formation is such that they stand apart wider than they otherwise would, and which geology has failed to account for, although everything in that science goes to prove that, all things being equal, it would if it did not, or would not certainly if it did, and then of course they are. Do not you think it is?"

I said to myself:—

"Now I just knew how it would be—that whiskey cocktail has done the business for me; I don't understand any more than a clam."

And then I said aloud—

"I—I—that is—if you don't mind, would you—would you say that over again? I ought"——

"Oh, certainly, certainly! You see I am very unfamiliar with the subject, and perhaps I don't present my case clearly, but I"——

"No, no—no, no—you state it plain enough, but that cocktail has muddled me a little. But I will—no, I do understand for that matter; but I would get the hang of it all the better if you went over it again—and I'll pay better attention this time."

He said, "Why, what I was after was this."

[Here he became even more fearfully impressive than ever, and emphasized each particular point by checking it off on his finger ends.]

"This vein, or lode, or ledge, or whatever you call it, runs along between two layers of granite, just the same as if it were a sandwich. Very well. Now, suppose you go down on that, say a thousand feet, or maybe twelve hundred (it don't really matter), before you drift, and then you start your drifts, some of them across the ledge, and others along the length of it, where the sulphurets—I believe they call them sulphurets, though why they should, considering that, so far as I can see, the main dependence of a miner does not so lie, as some suppose, but in which it cannot be successfully maintained, wherein the same should not continue, while part and parcel of the same ore not committed to either in the sense referred to, whereas, under different circumstances, the most inexperienced among us could not detect it if it were, or might overlook it if it did, or scorn the very idea of such a thing, even though it were palpably demonstrated as such. Am I not right?"

I said, sorrowfully—"I feel ashamed of myself, Mr. Ward. I know I ought to understand you perfectly well, but you see that treacherous whiskey cocktail has got into my head, and now I cannot understand even the simplest proposition. I told you how it would be."

"Oh, don't mind it, don't mind it; the fault was my own, no doubt—though I did think it clear enough for "——

"Don't say a word. Clear! Why, you stated it as clear as the sun to anybody but an abject idiot; but it's that confounded cocktail that has played the mischief."

"No; now don't say that. I'll begin it all over again, and "——

"Don't now—for goodness sake, don't do anything of the kind, because I tell you my head is in such a condition that I don't believe I could understand the most trifling question a man could ask me."

"Now, don't you be afraid. I'll put it so plain this time that you can't help but get the hang of it. We will begin at the very beginning." [Leaning far across the table, with determined impressiveness wrought upon his every feature, and fingers prepared to keep tally of each point as enumerated; and I, leaning forward with painful interest, resolved to comprehend or perish.] "You know the vein, the ledge, the thing that contains the metal, whereby it constitutes the medium between all other forces, whether of present or remote agencies, so brought to bear in favor of the former against the latter, or the latter against the former or all, or both, or compromising the relative differences existing within the radius whence culminate the several degrees of similarity to which "——

I said—"Oh, hang my wooden head, it ain't any use!—it ain't any use to try—I can't understand anything. The plainer you get it the more I can't get the hang of it."

I heard a suspicious noise behind me, and turned in time to see Hingston dodging behind a newspaper, and quaking with a gentle ecstasy of laughter. I looked at Ward again, and he had thrown off his dread solemnity and was laughing also. Then I saw that I had been sold—that I had been made the victim of a swindle in the way of a string of plausibly worded sentences that didn't mean anything under the sun. Artemus Ward was one of the best fellows in the world, and one of the most companionable. It has been said that he was not fluent in conversation, but, with the above experience in my mind, I differ.

CANNIBALISM IN THE CARS.

I VISITED St Louis lately, and on my way west, after changing cars at Terre Haute, Indiana, a mild, benevolent-looking gentleman of about forty-five, or may be fifty, came in at one of the way-stations and sat down beside me. We talked together pleasantly on various subjects for an hour, perhaps, and I found him exceedingly intelligent and entertaining. When he learned that I was from Washington, he immediately began to ask questions about various public men, and about Congressional affairs; and I saw very shortly that I was conversing with a man who was perfectly familiar with the ins and outs of political life at the Capital, even to the ways and manners, and customs of procedure of Senators and Representatives in the Chambers of the National Legislature. Presently two men halted near us for a single moment, and one said to the other:

"Harris, if you'll do that for me, I'll never forget you, my boy."

My new comrade's eyes lighted pleasantly. The words had touched upon a happy memory, I thought. Then his face settled into thoughtfulness—almost into gloom. He turned to me and said, "Let me tell you a story; let me give you a secret chapter of my life—a chapter that has never been referred to by me since its events transpired. Listen patiently, and promise that you will not interrupt me."

I said I would not, and he related the following strange adventure, speaking sometimes with animation, sometimes with melancholy, but always with feeling and earnestness.

The Stranger's Narrative.

"On the 19th of December, 1853, I started from St. Louis on the evening train bound for Chicago. There were only twenty-four passengers, all told. There were no ladies and no children. We were in excellent spirits, and pleasant acquaintanceships were soon formed. The journey bade fair to be a happy one; and no individual in the party, I think, had even the vaguest presentiment of the horrors we were soon to undergo.

"At 11 P. M. it began to snow hard. Shortly after leaving the small village of Welden, we entered upon that tremendous prairie solitude that stretches its leagues on leagues of houseless dreariness far away towards the Jubilee Settlements. The winds, unobstructed by trees or hills, or even vagrant rocks, whistled fiercely across the level desert, driving the falling snow before it like spray from the crested waves of a stormy sea. The snow was deepening fast; and we knew, by the diminished speed of the train, that the engine was ploughing through it with steadily increasing difficulty. Indeed, it almost came to a dead halt sometimes, in the midst of great drifts that piled themselves like colossal graves across the track. Conversation began to flag. Cheerfulness gave place to grave concern. The possibility of being imprisoned in the snow, on the bleak prairie, fifty miles from any house, presented itself to every mind, and extended its depressing influence over every spirit.

"At two o'clock in the morning I was aroused out of an uneasy slumber by the ceasing of all motion about me. The appalling truth flashed upon me instantly—we were captives in a snow-drift! 'All hands to the rescue!' Every man sprang to obey. Out into the wild night, the pitchy darkness, the billowy snow, the driving storm, every soul leaped, with the consciousness that a moment lost now might bring destruction to us all. Shovels, hands, boards—anything, everything that could displace snow, was brought into instant requisition. It was a weird picture, that small company of frantic men fighting the banking snows, half in the blackest shadow and half in the angry light of the locomotive's reflector.

"One short hour sufficed to prove the utter uselessness of our efforts. The storm barricaded the track with a dozen drifts while we dug one away. And worse than this, it was discovered that the last grand charge the engine had made upon the enemy had broken the fore-and-aft shaft of the driving-wheel! With a free track before us we should still have been helpless. We entered the car wearied with labor, and very sorrowful. We gathered about the stoves, and gravely canvassed our situation. We had no provisions whatever—in this lay our chief distress. We could not freeze, for there was a good supply of wood in the tender. This was our only comfort. The discussion ended at last in accepting the disheartening decision of the conductor, viz., that it would be death for any man to attempt to travel fifty miles on foot through snow like that. We could not send for help; and even if we could, it could not come. We must submit, and await, as patiently as we might, succor or starvation! I think the stoutest heart there felt a momentary chill when those words were uttered.

"Within the hour conversation subsided to a low murmur here and there about the car, caught fitfully between the rising and falling of the blast; the lamps grew dim; and the majority of the castaways settled themselves among the flickering shadows to think—to forget the present, if they could—to sleep, if they might.

"The eternal night—it surely seemed eternal, to us—wore its lagging hours away at last, and the cold grey dawn broke in the east. As the light grew stronger the passengers began to stir and give signs of life, one after another, and each in turn pushed his slouched hat up from his forehead, stretched his stiffened limbs, and glanced out at the windows upon the cheerless prospect. It was cheerless indeed!—not a living thing visible anywhere, not a human habitation; nothing but a vast

19

white desert; uplifted sheets of snow drifting hither and thither before the wind—a world of eddying flakes shutting out the firmament above.

"All day we moped about the cars, saying little, thinking much. Another lingering dreary night—and hunger.

"Another dawning—another day of silence, sadness, wasting hunger, hopeless watching for succor that could not come. A night of restless slumber, filled with dreams of feasting—wakings distressed with the gnawings of hunger.

"The fourth day came and went—and the fifth! Five days of dreadful imprisonment! A savage hunger looked out at every eye. There was in it a sign of awful import—the foreshadowing of a something that was vaguely shaping itself in every heart—a something which no tongue dared yet to frame into words.

"The sixth day passed—the seventh dawned upon as gaunt and haggard and hopeless a company of men as ever stood in the shadow of death. It must out now! That thing which had been growing up in every heart was ready to leap from every lip at last! Nature had been taxed to the utmost—she must yield. RICHARD H. GASTON, of Minnesota, tall, cadaverous, and pale, rose up. All knew what was coming. All prepared—every emotion, every semblance of excitement was smothered—only a calm, thoughtful seriousness appeared in the eyes that were lately so wild.

"'Gentlemen,—It cannot be delayed longer! The time is at hand! We must determine which of us shall die to furnish food for the rest!'

"Mr. JOHN J. WILLIAMS, of Illinois, rose and said: 'Gentlemen,—I nominate the Rev. James Sawyer, of Tennessee.'

"Mr. WM. R. ADAMS, of Indiana, said: 'I nominate Mr. Daniel Slote, of New York.'

"Mr. CHARLES J. LANGDON: 'I nominate Mr. Samuel A. Bowen, of St. Louis.'

"Mr. SLOTE: 'Gentlemen,—I desire to decline in favor of Mr. John A. Van Nostrand, Jun., of New Jersey.'

"Mr. GASTON: 'If there be no objection, the gentleman's desire will be acceded to.'

"Mr. VAN NOSTRAND objecting, the resignation of Mr. Slote was rejected. The resignations of Messrs. Sawyer and Bowen were also offered, and refused upon the same grounds.

"Mr. A. L. Bascom, of Ohio: 'I move that the nominations now close, and that the House proceed to an election by ballot.'

"Mr. Sawyer: 'Gentlemen,—I protest earnestly against these proceedings. They are, in every way, irregular and unbecoming. I must beg to move that they be dropped at once, and that we elect a chairman of the meeting and proper officers to assist him, and then we can go on with the business before us understandingly.'

"Mr. Bell, of Iowa: 'Gentlemen,—I object. This is no time to stand upon forms and ceremonious observances. For more than seven days we have been without food. Every moment we lose in idle discussion increases our distress. I am satisfied with the nominations that have been made—every gentleman present is, I believe—and I, for one, do not see why we should not proceed at once to elect one or more of them. I wish to offer a resolution——'

"Mr. Gaston: 'It would be objected to, and have to lie over one day under the rules, thus bringing about the very delay you wish to avoid. The gentleman from New Jersey——'

"Mr. Van Nostrand: 'Gentlemen,—I am a stranger among you; I have not sought the distinction that has been conferred upon me, and I feel a delicacy——'

"Mr. Morgan, of Alabama (interrupting): 'I move the previous question.'

"The motion was carried, and further debate shut off, of course. The motion to elect officers was passed, and under it Mr. Gaston was chosen chairman, Mr. Blake secretary, Messrs. Holcomb, Dyer, and Baldwin, a committee on nominations, and Mr. R. M. Howland, purveyor, to assist the committee in making selections.

"A recess of half an hour was then taken, and some little caucussing followed. At the sound of the gavel the meeting reassembled, and the committee reported in favor of Messrs. George Ferguson, of Kentucky, Lucien Herrman, of Louisiana, and W. Messick, of Colorado, as candidates. The report was accepted.

"Mr. Rogers, of Missouri: 'Mr. President,—The report being properly before the House now, I move to amend it by substituting for the name of Mr. Herrman that of Mr. Lucius Harris, of St. Louis, who is well and honorably known to us all. I do not wish to be understood as casting the least reflection upon the high character and standing of the gentleman from Louisiana—far from it. I respect and esteem him as much as any gentleman here present possibly can; but none of us can be blind to the fact that he has lost more flesh during the week that we have lain here than any among us—none of us can be blind to the fact that the committee has been derelict in its duty, either through negligence or a graver fault, in thus offering for our suffrages a gentleman who, however pure his own motives may be, has really less nutriment in him——'

"THE CHAIR: 'The gentleman from Missouri will take his seat. The Chair cannot allow the integrity of the Committee to be questioned save by the regular course, under the rules. What action will the House take upon the gentleman's motion?'

"Mr. HALLIDAY, of Virginia: 'I move to further amend the report by substituting Mr. Harvey Davis, of Oregon, for Mr. Messick. It may be urged by gentlemen that the hardships and privations of a frontier life have rendered Mr. Davis tough; but, gentlemen, is this a time to cavil at toughness? is this a time to be fastidious concerning trifles? is this a time to dispute about matters of paltry significance? No, gentlemen, bulk is what we desire—substance, weight, bulk—these are the supreme requisites now—not talent, not genius, not education. I insist upon my motion.'

"Mr. MORGAN (excitedly): 'Mr. Chairman,—I do most strenuously object to this amendment. The gentleman from Oregon is old, and furthermore is bulky only in bone—not in flesh. I ask the gentleman from Virginia if it is soup we want instead of solid sustenance? if he would delude us with shadows? if he would mock our suffering with an Oregonian spectre? I ask him if he can look upon the anxious faces around him, if he can gaze into our sad eyes, if he can listen to the beating of our expectant hearts, and still thrust this famine-stricken fraud upon us? I ask him if he can think of our desolate state, of our past sorrows, of our dark future, and still unpityingly foist upon us this wreck, this ruin, this tottering swindle, this gnarled and blighted and sapless vagabond from Oregon's inhospitable shores? Never!' (Applause.)

"The amendment was put to vote, after a fiery debate, and lost. Mr. Harris was substituted on the first amendment. The balloting then began. Five ballots were held without a choice. On the sixth, Mr. Harris was elected, all voting for him but himself. It was then moved that his election should be ratified by acclamation, which was lost, in consequence of his again voting against himself.

"Mr. RADWAY moved that the House now take up the remaining candidates, and go into an election for breakfast. This was carried.

"On the first ballot there was a tie, half the members favoring one candidate on account of his youth, and half favoring the other on account of his superior size. The President gave the casting vote for the latter, Mr. Messick. This decision created considerable dissatisfaction among the friends of Mr. Ferguson, the defeated candidate, and there was some talk of demanding a new ballot; but in the midst of it, a motion to adjourn was carried, and the meeting broke up at once.

"The preparations for supper diverted the attention of the Ferguson faction from the discussion of their grievance for a long time, and then, when they would have taken it up again, the happy announcement that Mr. Harris was ready, drove all thought of it to the winds.

"We improvised tables by propping up the backs of car-seats, and sat down with hearts full of gratitude to the finest supper that had blessed our vision for seven torturing days. How changed we were from what we had been a few short hours before! Hopeless, sad-eyed misery, hunger, feverish anxiety, desperation, then— thankfulness, serenity, joy too deep for utterance now. That I know was 'the cheeriest hour of my eventful life. The wind howled, and blew the snow wildly about our prison-house, but they were powerless to distress us any more. I liked Harris. He might have been better done, perhaps, but I am free to say that no man ever agreed with me better than Harris, or afforded me so large a degree of satisfaction. Messick was very well, though rather high-flavored, but for genuine nutritiousness and delicacy of fibre, give me Harris. Messick had his good points —I will not attempt to deny it, nor do I wish to do it—but he was no more fitted for breakfast than a mummy would be, sir—not a bit. Lean?—why, bless me!— and tough? Ah, he was very tough! You could not imagine it,—you could never imagine anything like it."

"Do you mean to tell me that——"

"Do not interrupt me, please. After breakfast we elected a man by the name of Walker, from Detroit, for supper. He was very good. I wrote his wife so afterwards. He was worthy of all praise. I shall always remember Walker. He was a little rare, but very good. And then the next morning we had Morgan, of Alabama, for breakfast. He was one of the finest men I ever sat down to,—handsome educated, refined, spoke several languages fluently—a perfect gentleman—he was a perfect gentleman, and singularly juicy. For supper we had that Oregon patriarch, and he *was* a fraud, there is no question about it—old, scraggy, tough, nobody can picture the reality. I finally said, gentlemen, you can do as you like, but *I* will wait for another election. And Grimes, of Illinois, said, 'Gentlemen, *I* will wait also. When you elect a man that has *something* to recommend him, I shall be glad to join you again.' It soon became evident that there was general dissatisfaction with Davis, of Oregon, and so, to preserve the good-will that had prevailed so pleasantly since we had had Harris, an election was called, and the result of it was that Baker, of Georgia, was chosen. He was splendid! Well, well—after that we had Doolittle and Hawkins, and McElroy (there was some complaint about McElroy, because he was uncommonly short and thin), and Penrod, and two Smiths, and Bailey (Bailey had a wooden leg, which was clear loss, but he was otherwise good), and an Indian boy, and an organ grinder, and a gentleman by the name of Buckminster—a poor stick of a vagabond that wasn't any good for company and no account for breakfast. We were glad we got him elected before relief came."

"And so the blessed relief *did* come at last?"

"Yes, it came one bright, sunny morning, just after election. John Murphy was the choice, and there never was a better, I am willing to testify; but John Murphy came home with us, in the train that came to succor us, and lived to marry the widow Harris——"

"Relict of——"

"Relict of our first choice. He married her, and is happy and respected and prosperous yet. Ah, it was like a novel, sir—it was like a romance. This is my stopping-place, sir; I must bid you good-by. Any time that you can make it convenient to tarry a day or two with me, I shall be glad to have you. I like you, sir; I have conceived an affection for you. I could like you as well as I liked Harris himself, sir. Good day, sir, and a pleasant journey."

He was gone. I never felt so stunned, so distressed, so bewildered in my life. But in my soul I was glad he was gone. With all his gentleness of manner and his soft voice, I shuddered whenever he turned his hungry eye upon me; and when I heard that I had achieved his perilous affection, and that I stood almost with the late Harris in his esteem, my heart fairly stood still!

I was bewildered beyond description. I did not doubt his word; I could not question a single item in a statement so stamped with the earnestness of truth as his; but its dreadful details overpowered me, and threw my thoughts into hopeless confusion. I saw the conductor looking at me. I said, " Who is that man?"

"He was a member of Congress once, and a good one. But he got caught in a snowdrift in the cars, and like to been starved to death. He got so frost-bitten and frozen up generally, and used up for want of something to eat, that he was sick and out of his head two or three months afterwards. He is all right now, only he is a monomaniac, and when he gets on that old subject he never stops till he has eat up that whole car-load of people he talks about. He would have finished the crowd by this time, only he had to get out here. He has got their names as pat as A, B, C. When he gets them all eat up but himself, he always says :—'Then the hour for the usual election for breakfast having arrived, and there being no opposition, I was duly elected, after which, there being no objections offered, I resigned. Thus I am here.'"

I felt inexpressibly relieved to know that I had only been listening to the harmless vagaries of a madman instead of the genuine experiences of a bloodthirsty cannibal.

The Scriptural Panoramist.

"THERE was a fellow traveling around in that country," said Mr. Nickerson, "with a moral-religious show—a sort of scriptural panorama—and he hired a wooden-headed old slab to play the piano for him. After the first night's performance the showman says—

"'My friend, you seem to know pretty much all the tunes there are, and you worry along first-rate. But then, don't you notice that sometimes last night the piece you happened to be playing was a little rough on the proprieties, so to speak—didn't seem to jibe with the general gait of the picture that was passing at the time, as it were—was a little foreign to the subject, you know—as if you didn't either trump or follow suit, you understand?'

"'Well, no,' the fellow said; 'he hadn't noticed, but it might be; he had played along just as it came handy.'

" So they put it up that the simple old dummy was to keep his eye on the panorama after that, and as soon as a stunning picture was reeled out he was to fit it to a dot with a piece of music that would help the audience to get the idea of the subject, and warm them up like a camp-meeting revival. That sort of thing would corral their sympathies, the showman said.

" There was a big audience that night—mostly middle-aged and old people who belong to the church, and took a strong interest in Bible matters, and the balance were pretty much young bucks and heifers—they always come out strong on panoramas, you know, because it gives them a chance to taste one another's complexions in the dark.

" Well, the showman began to swell himself up for his lecture, and the old mud-dobber tackled the piano and ran his fingers up and down once or twice to see that she was all right, and the fellows behind the curtain commenced to grind out the panorama. The showman balanced his weight on his right foot, and propped his hands over his hips, and flung his eyes over his shoulder at the scenery, and said—

"'Ladies and gentlemen, the painting now before you illustrates the beautiful and touching parable of the Prodigal Son. Observe the happy expression just breaking over the features of the poor, suffering youth—so worn and weary with his long march; note also the ecstasy beaming from the uplifted countenance of the aged father, and the joy that sparkles in the eyes of the excited group of youths and maidens, and seems ready to burst into the welcoming chorus from their lips. The lesson, my friends, is as solemn and instructive as the story is tender and beautiful.'

" The mud-dobber was all ready, and when the second speech was finished, struck up—

"'Oh, we'll all get blind drunk,
When Johnny comes marching home!'

"Some of the people giggled, and some groaned a little. The showman couldn't say a word; he looked at the pianist sharp, but he was all lovely and serene—*he* didn't know there was anything out of gear.

"The panorama moved on, and the showman drummed up his grit and started in fresh.

"'Ladies and gentlemen, the fine picture now unfolding itself to your gaze exhibits one of the most notable events in Bible history—our Saviour and His disciples upon the Sea of Galilee. How grand, how awe-inspiring are the reflections which the subject invokes? What sublimity of faith is revealed to us in this lesson from the sacred writings? The Saviour rebukes the angry waves, and walks securely upon the bosom of the deep!'

"All around the house they were whispering, 'Oh, how lovely, how beautiful!' and the orchestra let himself out again—

> "'A life on the ocean wave,
> And a home on the rolling deep!'

"There was a good deal of honest snickering turned on this time, and considerable groaning, and one or two old deacons got up and went out. The showman grated his teeth, and cursed the piano man to himself; but the fellow sat there like a knot on a log, and seemed to think he was doing first-rate.

"After things got quiet the showman thought he would make one more stagger at it any way, though his confidence was beginning to get mighty shaky. The supes started the panorama grinding along again, and he says—

"'Ladies and gentlemen, this exquisite painting represents the raising of Lazarus from the dead by our Saviour. The subject has been handled with marvelous skill by the artist, and such touching sweetness and tenderness of expression has he thrown into it that I have known peculiarly sensitive persons to be even affected to tears by looking at it. Observe the half-confused, half-inquiring look upon the countenance of the awakened Lazarus. Observe, also, the attitude and expression of the Saviour, who takes him gently by the sleeve of his shroud with one hand, while He points with the other towards the distant city.'

"Before anybody could get off an opinion in the case the innocent old ass at the piano struck up—

"'Come rise up, William Ri-i-ley,
And go along with me!'

"Whe-ew! All the solemn old flats got up in a huff to go, and everybody else laughed till the windows rattled.

"The showman went down and grabbed the orchestra and shook him up and says—

"'That lets you out, you know, you chowder-headed old clam: Go to the door-keeper and get your money, and cut your stick—vamose the ranche! Ladies and gentlemen, circumstances over which I have no control compel me prematurely to dismiss the house.'"

CURING A COLD.

IT is a good thing, perhaps, to
write for the amusement of the
public, but it is a far higher and
nobler thing to write for their instruction, their profit, their actual
and tangible benefit. The latter is
the sole object of this article. If it
prove the means of restoring to
health one solitary sufferer among
my race, of lighting up once more
the fire of hope and joy in his faded
eyes, of bringing back to his dead
heart again the quick, generous
impulses of other days, I shall be
amply rewarded for my labor; my
soul will be permeated with the sacred delight a Christian feels when he has
done a good, unselfish deed.

Having led a pure and blameless life, I am justified in believing that no man who knows me will reject the suggestions I am about to make, out of fear that I am trying to deceive him. Let the public do itself the honor to read my experience in doctoring a cold, as herein set forth, and then follow in my footsteps.

When the White House was burned in Virginia City, I lost my home, my happiness, my constitution, and my trunk. The loss of the two first-named articles was a matter of no great consequence, since a home without a mother or a sister, or a distant young female relative in it, to remind you, by putting your soiled linen out of sight and taking your boots down off the mantel-piece, that there are those who think about you and care for you, is easily obtained. And I cared nothing for the loss of my happiness, because not being a poet, it could not be possible that melancholy would abide with me long. But to lose a good constitution and a better trunk were serious misfortunes. On the day of the fire my constitution succumbed to a severe cold, caused by undue exertion in getting ready to do something. I suffered to no purpose, too, because the plan I was figuring at for the extinguishing of the fire was so elaborate that I never got it completed until the middle of the following week.

The first time I began to sneeze, a friend told me to go and bathe my feet in hot water and go to bed. I did so. Shortly afterwards, another friend advised me to get up and take a cold shower-bath. I did that also. Within the hour, another friend assured me that it was policy to "feed a cold and starve a fever." I had both. So I thought it best to fill myself up for the cold, and then keep dark and let the fever starve awhile.

In a case of this kind, I seldom do things by halves; I ate pretty heartily; I conferred my custom upon a stranger who had just opened his restaurant that morning: he waited near me in respectful silence until I had finished feeding my cold, when he inquired if the people about Virginia City were much afflicted with colds? I told him I thought they were. He then went out and took in his sign.

I started down toward the office, and on the way encountered another bosom friend, who told me that a quart of salt water, taken warm, would come as near curing a cold as anything in the world. I hardly thought I had room for it, but I tried it anyhow. The result was surprising. I believed I had thrown up my immortal soul.

Now, as I am giving my experience only for the benefit of those who are troubled with the distemper I am writing about, I feel that they will see the propriety of my cautioning them against following such portions of it as proved inefficient with me, and acting upon this conviction, I warn them against warm salt water. It may be a good enough remedy, but I think it is too severe. If I had another cold in the head, and there were no course left me but to take either an earthquake or a quart of warm salt water, I would take my chances on the earthquake.

After the storm which had been raging in my stomach had subsided, and no more good Samaritans happening along, I went on borrowing handkerchiefs again and blowing them to atoms, as had been my custom in the early stages of my cold, until I came across a lady who had just arrived from over the plains, and who said she had lived in a part of the country where doctors were scarce, and had from necessity acquired considerable skill in the treatment of simple "family complaints." I knew she must have had much experience, for she appeared to be a hundred and fifty years old.

She mixed a decoction composed of molasses, aquafortis, turpentine, and various other drugs, and instructed me to take a wine-glass full of it every fifteen minutes. I never took but one dose; that was enough; it robbed me of all moral principle, and awoke every unworthy impulse of my nature. Under its malign influence my brain conceived miracles of meanness, but my hands were too feeble to execute them; at that time, had it not been that my strength had surrendered to a succession of assaults from infallible remedies for my cold, I am satisfied that I would have tried to rob the graveyard. Like most other people, I often feel mean, and act accordingly; but until I took that medicine I had never revelled in such supernatural depravity, and felt proud of it. At the end of two days I was ready to go to doctoring again. I took a few more unfailing remedies, and finally drove my cold from my head to my lungs.

I got to coughing incessantly, and my voice fell below zero; I conversed in a thundering base, two octaves below my natural tone; I could only compass my regular nightly repose by coughing myself down to a state of utter exhaustion, and then the moment I began to talk in my sleep, my discordant voice woke me up again.

My case grew more and more serious every day. Plain gin was recommended; I took it. Then gin and molasses; I took that also. Then gin and onions; I added the onions, and took all three. I detected no particular result, however, except that I had acquired a breath like a buzzard's.

I found I had to travel for my health. I went to Lake Bigler with my reportorial comrade, Wilson. It is gratifying to me to reflect that we traveled in considerable style; we went in the Pioneer coach, and my friend took all his baggage with him, consisting of two excellent silk handkerchiefs and a daguerreotype of his grandmother. We sailed and hunted and fished and danced all day, and I doctored my cough all night. By managing in this way, I made out to improve every hour in the twenty-four. But my disease continued to grow worse.

A sheet-bath was recommended. I had never refused a remedy yet, and it seemed poor policy to commence then; therefore I determined to take a sheet-bath, notwithstanding I had no idea what sort of arrangement it was. It was administered at midnight, and the weather was very frosty. My breast and back were bared, and a sheet (there appeared to be a thousand yards of it) soaked in ice-water, was wound around me until I resembled a swab for a Columbiad.

It is a cruel expedient. When the chilly rag touches one's warm flesh, it makes him start with sudden violence, and gasp for breath just as men do in the death agony. It froze the marrow in my bones, and stopped the beating of my heart. I thought my time had come.

Young Wilson said the circumstance reminded him of an anecdote about a negro who was being baptized, and who slipped from the parson's grasp, and came near being drowned. He floundered around, though, and finally rose up out of the water considerably strangled, and furiously angry, and started ashore at once, spouting water like a whale, and remarking, with great asperity, that "one o' dese days some gen'l'man's nigger gwyne to get killed wid jis' such dam foolishness as dis!"

Never take a sheet-bath—never. Next to meeting a lady acquaintance, who, for reasons best known to her-self, don't see you when she looks at you, and don't know you when she does see you, it is the most un-comfortable thing in the world.

But, as I was saying, when the sheet-bath failed to cure my cough, a lady friend rec-ommended the ap-plication of a mus-tard plaster to my breast. I believe that would have cured me effectual-ly, if it had not been for young Wilson. When I went to bed, I put my mustard plas-ter—which was a very gorgeous one, eighteen inches square—where I could reach it when I was ready for it. But young Wilson got hungry in the night, and—here is food for the imagination.

After sojourning a week at Lake Bigler, I went to Steamboat Springs, and beside the steam baths, I took a lot of the vilest medicines that were ever concocted. They would have cured me, but I had to go back to Virginia City, where, notwithstanding the variety of new remedies I absorbed every day, I managed to aggravate my disease by carelessness and undue exposure.

I finally concluded to visit San Francisco, and the first day I got there, a lady at the hotel told me to drink a quart of whisky every twenty-four hours, and a friend up town recommended precisely the same course. Each advised me to take a quart; that made half a gallon. I did it, and still live.

Now, with the kindest motives in the world, I offer for the consideration of consumptive patients the variegated course of treatment I have lately gone through. Let them **try it**: if it don't cure, it can't more than kill them.

20

A CURIOUS PLEASURE
EXCURSION.*

["We have received the following advertisement, but, inasmuch as it concerns a
matter of deep and general interest, we feel
fully justified in inserting it in our reading
columns. We are confident that our conduct
in this regard needs only explanation, not
apology.—ED. N. Y. HERALD."]

ADVERTISEMENT.

THIS is to inform the public
that in connection with Mr.
Barnum I have leased the
comet for a term of years; and I
desire also to solicit the public patronage in favor of a beneficial enterprise which we have in view.
We propose to fit up comfortable, and even luxurious, accommodations in the

* Published at the time of the "Comet Scare" in the summer of 1874.

306

comet for as many persons as will honor us with their patronage, and make an extended excursion among the heavenly bodies. We shall prepare 1,000,000 state rooms in the tail of the comet (with hot and cold water, gas, looking glass, parachute, umbrella, etc., in each), and shall construct more if we meet with a sufficiently generous encouragement. We shall have billiard rooms, card rooms, music rooms, bowling alleys and many spacious theatres and free libraries; and on the main deck we propose to have a driving park, with upwards of 10,000 miles of roadway in it. We shall publish daily newspapers also.

DEPARTURE OF THE COMET.

The comet will leave New York at ten P. M. on the 20th inst., and therefore it will be desirable that the passengers be on board by eight at the latest, to avoid confusion in getting under way. It is not known whether passports will be necessary or not, but it is deemed best that passengers provide them, and so guard against all contingencies. No dogs will be allowed on board. This rule has been made in deference to the existing state of feeling regarding these animals and will be strictly adhered to. The safety of the passengers will in all ways be jealously looked to. A substantial iron railing will be put up all around the comet, and no one will be allowed to go to the edge and look over unless accompanied by either my partner or myself.

THE POSTAL SERVICE

will be of the completest character. Of course the telegraph, and the telegraph only, will be employed, consequently, friends occupying state-rooms, 20,000,000 and even 30,000,000 miles apart, will be able to send a message and receive a reply inside of eleven days. Night messages will be half rate. The whole of this vast postal system will be under the personal superintendence of Mr. Hale, of Maine. Meals served at all hours. Meals served in staterooms charged extra.

Hostility is not apprehended from any great planet, but we have thought it best to err on the safe side, and therefore have provided a proper number of mortars, siege guns and boarding pikes. History shows that small, isolated communities, such as the people of remote islands, are prone to be hostile to strangers, and so the same may be the case with

THE INHABITANTS OF STARS

of the tenth or twentieth magnitude. We shall in no case wantonly offend the people of any star, but shall treat all alike with urbanity and kindliness, never conducting ourselves toward an asteroid after a fashion which we could not venture to assume toward Jupiter or Saturn.   I repeat that we shall not wantonly offend any star; but at the same time we shall promptly resent any injury that may be done us, or any insolence offered us, by parties or governments residing in any star in the firmament.   Although averse to the shedding of blood, we shall still hold this course rigidly and fearlessly, not only toward single stars, but toward constellations.   We shall hope to leave a good impression of America behind us in every nation we visit, from Venus to Uranus.   And, at all events, if we cannot inspire love we shall, at least, compel respect for our country wherever we go.   We shall take with us, free of charge,

A GREAT FORCE OF MISSIONARIES,

and shed the true light upon all the celestial orbs which, physically aglow, are yet morally in darkness.   Sunday-schools will be established wherever practicable. Compulsory education will also be introduced.

The comet will visit Mars first, and then proceed to Mercury, Jupiter, Venus and Saturn.   Parties connected with the government of the District of Columbia and with the former city government of New York, who may desire to inspect the rings, will be allowed time and every facility.   Every star of prominent magnitude will be visited, and time allowed for excursions to points of interest inland.

THE DOG STAR

has been stricken from the programme.   Much time will be spent in the Great Bear, and, indeed, of every constellation of importance.   So, also, with the Sun and Moon and the Milky Way, otherwise the Gulf Stream of the skies.   Clothing suitable for wear in the sun should be provided.   Our programme has been so arranged that we shall seldom go more than 100,000,000 of miles at a time without stopping at some star.   This will necessarily make the stoppages frequent and preserve the interest of the tourist.   Baggage checked through to any point on the route.   Parties desiring to make only a part of the proposed tour, and thus save expense, may stop over at any star they choose and wait for the return voyage.

After visiting all the most celebrated stars and constellations in our system and personally inspecting the remotest sparks that even the most powerful telescope can now detect in the firmament, we shall proceed with good heart upon

A STUPENDOUS VOYAGE

of discovery among the countless whirling worlds that make turmoil in the mighty wastes of space that stretch their solemn solitudes, their unimaginable vastness billions upon billions of miles away beyond the farthest verge of telescopic vision, till by comparison the little sparkling vault we used to gaze at on Earth shall seem like a remembered phosphorescent flash of spangles which some tropical voyager's prow stirred into life for a single instant, and which ten thousand miles of phosphorescent seas and tedious lapse of time had since diminished to an incident utterly trivial in his recollection. Children occupying seats at the first table will be charged full fare.

FIRST CLASS FARE

from the Earth to Uranus, including visits to the Sun and Moon and all the principal planets on the route, will be charged at the low rate of $2 for every 50,000,000 miles of actual travel. A great reduction will be made where parties wish to make the round trip. This comet is new and in thorough repair.and is now on her first voyage. She is confessedly the fastest on the line. She makes 20,000,000 miles a day, with her present facilities; but, with a picked American crew and good weather, we are confident we can get 40,000,000 out of her. Still, we shall never push her to a dangerous speed, and we shall rigidly prohibit racing with other comets. Passengers desiring to diverge at any point or return will be transferred to other comets. We make close connections at all principal points with all reliable lines. Safety can be depended upon. It is not to be denied that the heavens are infested with

OLD RAMSHACKLE COMETS

that have not been inspected or overhauled in 10,000 years, and which ought long ago to have been destroyed or turned into hail barges, but with these we have no connection whatever. Steerage passengers not allowed abaft the main hatch.

Complimentary round trip tickets have been tendered to General Butler, Mr. Shepherd, Mr. Richardson and other eminent gentlemen, whose public services have entitled them to the rest and relaxation of a voyage of this kind. Parties desiring to make the round trip will have extra accommodation. The entire voyage will be completed, and the passengers landed in New York again on the 14th of December, 1991. This is, at least, forty years quicker than any other comet can do it in. Nearly all the back pay members contemplate making the round trip with us in case their constituents will allow them a holiday. Every harmless amusement will be allowed on board, but no pools permitted on the run of the comet—no gambling of any kind. All fixed stars will be respected by us, but such stars as seem to need fixing we shall fix. If it makes trouble we shall be sorry, but firm.

Mr. Coggia having leased his comet to us, she will no longer be called by his name but by my partner's. N. B.—Passengers by paying double fare will be entitled to a share in all the new stars, suns, moons, comets, meteors and magazines of thunder and lightning we may discover. Patent medicine people will take notice that

WE CARRY BULLETIN BOARDS

and a paint brush along for use in the constellations, and are open to terms. Cremationists are reminded that we are going straight to—some hot places—and are open to terms. To other parties our enterprise is a pleasure excursion, but individually we mean business. We shall fly our comet for all it is worth.

FOR FURTHER PARTICULARS,

or for freight or passage, apply on board, or to my partner, but not to me, since I do not take charge of the comet until she is under weigh. It is necessary, at a time like this, that my mind should not be burdened with small business details.

MARK. TWAIN.

"The Lie Nailed."

RUNNING FOR GOVERNOR.

A FEW months ago I was nominated for Governor of the great State of New York, to run against Mr. John T. Smith and Mr. Blank J. Blank on an independent ticket. I somehow felt that I had one prominent advantage over these gentlemen, and that was—good character. It was easy to see by the newspapers that if ever they had known what it was to bear a good name, that time had gone by. It was plain that in these latter years they had become familiar with all manner of shameful crimes. But at the very moment that I was exalting my advantage and joying in it in secret, there was a muddy undercurrent of discomfort "riling" the deeps of my happiness, and that was—the having to hear my name bandied about in familiar connection with those of such people. I grew more and more disturbed. Finally I wrote my grandmother about it. Her answer came quick and sharp. She said—

"You have never done one single thing in all your life to be ashamed of—not one. Look at the newspapers—look at them and comprehend what sort of characters Messrs. Smith and Blank are, and then see if you are willing to lower yourself to their level and enter a public canvass with them."

It was my very thought! I did not sleep a single moment that night. But after all I could not recede. I was fully committed, and must go on with the fight. As I was looking listlessly over the papers at breakfast I came across this paragraph, and I may truly say I never was so confounded before.

"PERJURY.—Perhaps, now that Mr. Mark Twain is before the people as a candidate for Governor, he will condescend to explain how he came to be convicted of perjury by thirty-four witnesses in Wakawak, Cochin China, in 1863, the intent of which perjury being to rob a poor native widow and her helpless family of a meagre plantain-patch, their only stay and support in their bereavement and desolation. Mr. Twain owes it to himself, as well as to the great people whose suffrages he asks, to clear this matter up. Will he do it?"

I thought I should burst with amazement! Such a cruel, heartless charge. I never had *seen* Cochin China! I never had *heard* of Wakawak! I didn't know a plantain-patch from a kangaroo! I did not know what to do. I was crazed and helpless. I let the day slip away without doing anything at all. The next morning the same paper had this—nothing more:—

"SIGNIFICANT.—Mr. Twain, it will be observed, is suggestively silent about the Cochin China perjury."

[*Mem.*—During the rest of the campaign this paper never referred to me in any other way than as "the infamous perjurer Twain."]

Next came the *Gazette*, with this:—

"WANTED TO KNOW.—Will the new candidate for Governor deign to explain to certain of his fellow-citizens (who are suffering to vote for him!) the little circumstance of his cabin-mates in Montana losing small valuables from time to time, until at last, these things having been invariably found on Mr. Twain's person or in his 'trunk' (newspaper he rolled his traps in), they felt compelled to give him a friendly admonition for his own good, and so tarred and feathered him, and rode him on a rail, and then advised him to leave a permanent vacuum in the place he usually occupied in the camp. Will he do this?"

Could anything be more deliberately malicious than that? For I never was in Montana in my life.

[After this, this journal customarily spoke of me as " Twain, the Montana Thief."

I got to picking up papers apprehensively—much as one would lift a desired blanket which he had some idea might have a rattlesnake under it. One day this met my eye:—

" THE LIE NAILED !—By the sworn affidavits of Michael O'Flanagan, Esq., of the Five Points, and Mr. Snub Rafferty and Mr. Catty Mulligan, of Water Street, it is established that Mr. Mark Twain's vile statement that the lamented grandfather of our noble standard-bearer, Blank J. Blank, was hanged for highway robbery, is a brutal and gratuitous LIE, without a shadow of foundation in fact. It is disheartening to virtuous men to see such shameful means resorted to to achieve political success as the attacking of the dead in their graves, and defiling their honored names with slander. When we think of the anguish this miserable falsehood must cause the innocent relatives and friends of the deceased, we are almost driven to incite an outraged and insulted public to summary and unlawful vengeance upon the traducer. But no ! let us leave him to the agony of a lacerated conscience (though if passion should get the better of the public, and in its blind fury they should do the traducer bodily injury, it is but too obvious that no jury could convict and no court punish the perpetrators of the deed)."

The ingenious closing sentence had the effect of moving me out of bed with despatch that night, and out at the back door also, while the " outraged and insulted public " surged in the front way, breaking furniture and windows in their righteous indignation as they came, and taking off such property as they could carry when they went. And yet I can lay my hand upon the Book and say that I never slandered Mr. Blank's grandfather. More: I had never even heard of him or mentioned him up to that day and date.

[I will state, in passing, that the journal above quoted from always referred to me afterward as " Twain, the Body-Snatcher."]

The next newspaper article that attracted my attention was the following :—

" A SWEET CANDIDATE.—Mr. Mark Twain, who was to make such a blighting speech at the mass meeting of the Independents last night, didn't come to time ! A telegram from his physician stated that he had been knocked down by a runaway team, and his leg broken in two places—sufferer lying in great agony, and so forth, and so forth, and a lot more bosh of the same sort. And the Independents tried hard to swallow the wretched subterfuge, and pretend that they did not know what was the *real* reason of the absence of the abandoned creature whom they denominate their standard-bearer. *A certain man was seen to reel into Mr. Twain's hotel last night in a state of beastly intoxication.* It is the imperative duty of the Independents to prove that this besotted brute was not Mark Twain himself. We have them at last ! This is a case that admits of no shirking. The voice of the people demands in thunder-tones, ' WHO WAS THAT MAN ?' "

It was incredible, absolutely incredible, for a moment, that it was really my name that was coupled with this disgraceful suspicion. Three long years had passed over my head since I had tasted ale, beer, wine, or liquor of any kind.

[It shows what effect the times were having on me when I say that I saw myself confidently dubbed "Mr. Delirium Tremens Twain" in the next issue of that journal without a pang—notwithstanding I knew that with monotonous fidelity the paper would go on calling me so to the very end.]

By this time anonymous letters were getting to be an important part of my mail matter. This form was common—

"How about that old woman you kiked of your premisers which was beging.   POL PRY."

And this—

"There is things which you have done which is unbeknowens to anybody but me. You better trot out a few dols. to yours truly, or you'll hear thro' the papers from   HANDY ANDY."

This is about the idea. I could continue them till the reader was surfeited, if desirable.

Shortly the principal Republican journal "convicted" me of wholesale bribery, and the leading Democratic paper "nailed" an aggravated case of blackmailing to me.

[In this way I acquired two additional names: "Twain the Filthy Corruptionist," and "Twain the Loathsome Embracer."]

By this time there had grown to be such a clamor for an "answer" to all the dreadful charges that were laid to me that the editors and leaders of my party said it would be political ruin for me to remain silent any longer. As if to make their appeal the more imperative, the following appeared in one of the papers the very next day :—

"BEHOLD THE MAN ! —The independent candidate still maintains silence. Because he dare not speak. Every accusation against him has been amply proved, and they have been endorsed and re-endorsed by his own eloquent silence, till at this day he stands for ever convicted. Look upon your candidate, Independents ! Look upon the Infamous Perjurer ! the Montana Thief ! the Body-Snatcher ! Contemplate your incarnate Delirium Tremens ! your Filthy Corruptionist ! your Loathsome Embracer ! Gaze upon him—ponder him well—and then say if you can give your honest votes to a creature who has earned this dismal array of titles by his hideous crimes, and dares not open his mouth in denial of any one of them !"

There was no possible way of getting out of it, and so in deep humiliation, I set about preparing to "answer" a mass of baseless charges and mean and wicked falsehoods. But I never finished the task, for the very next morning a paper came out with a new horror, a fresh malignity, and seriously charged me with burning a lunatic asylum with all its inmates, because it obstructed the view from my house. This threw me into a sort of panic. Then came the charge of poisoning my uncle to get his property, with an imperative demand that the grave should be opened. This drove me to the verge of distraction. On top of this I was accused of employing toothless and incompetent old relatives to prepare the food for the foundling hospital when I was warden. I was wavering—wavering. And at last, as a due and fitting climax to the shameless persecution that party rancor had inflicted upon me, nine little toddling children,

of all shades of color and degrees of raggedness, were taught to rush on to the platform at a public meeting, and clasp me around the legs and call me PA!

I gave it up. I hauled down my colors and surrendered. I was not equal to the requirements of a 'Gubernatorial campaign in the State of New York, and so I sent in my withdrawal from the candidacy, and in bitterness of spirit signed it, "Truly yours, *once* a decent man, but now

MARK TWAIN, I. P., M. T., B. S., D. T., F. C., and L. E."

A MYSTERIOUS VISIT.

THE first notice that was taken of me when I "settled down" recently, was by a gentleman who said he was an assessor, and connected with the U. S. Internal Revenue Department. I said I had never heard of his branch of business before, but I was very glad to see him all the same—would he sit down? He sat down. I did not know anything particular to say, and yet I felt that people who have arrived at the dignity of keeping house must be conversational, must be easy and sociable in company. So, in default of anything else to say, I asked him if he was opening his shop in our neighborhood?

He said he was. [I did not wish to appear ignorant, but I *had* hoped he would mention what he had for sale.]

I ventured to ask him "How was trade?" And he said "So-so."

I then said we would drop in, and if we liked his house as well as any other, we would give him our custom.

He said he thought we would like his establishment well enough to confine ourselves to it—said he never saw anybody who would go off and hunt up another man in his line after trading with him once.

That sounded pretty complacent, but barring that natural expression of villainy which we all have, the man looked honest enough.

I do not know how it came about exactly, but gradually we appeared to melt down and run together, conversationally speaking, and then everything went along as comfortably as clockwork.

We talked, and talked, and talked—at least I did; and we laughed, and laughed, and laughed—at least he did. But all the time I had my presence of mind about me—I had my native shrewdness turned on "full head," as the engineers say. I was determined to find out all about his business in spite of his obscure answers— and I was determined I would have it out of him without his suspecting what I was at. I meant to trap him with a deep, deep ruse. I would tell him all about my own business, and he would naturally so warm to me during this seductive burst of confidence that he would forget himself, and tell me all about *his* affairs before he suspected what I was about. I thought to myself, My son, you little know what an old fox you are dealing with. I said—

"Now you never would guess what I made lecturing this winter and last spring?"

"No—don't believe I could, to save me. Let me see—let me see. About two thousand dollars, maybe? But no; no, sir, I know you couldn't have made that much. Say seventeen hundred, maybe?"

"Ha! ha! I knew you couldn't. My lecturing receipts for last spring and this winter were fourteen thousand seven hundred and fifty dollars. What do you think of that?"

"Why, it is amazing—perfectly amazing. I will make a note of it. And you say even this wasn't all?"

"All! Why bless you, there was my income from the *Daily Warwhoop* for four months—about—about—well, what should you say to about eight thousand dollars, for instance?"

"Say! Why, I should say I should like to see myself rolling in just such another ocean of affluence. Eight thousand! I'll make a note of it. Why man!—and on top of all this I am to understand that you had still more income?"

"Ha! ha! ha! Why, you're only in the suburbs of it, so to speak. There's my book, 'The Innocents Abroad'—price $3.50 to $5.00, according to the binding. Listen to me. Look me in the eye. During the last four months and a half, saying nothing of sales before that, but just simply during the four months and a half, we've sold ninety-five thousand copies of that book. Ninety-five thousand! Think of it. Average four dollars a copy, say. It's nearly four hundred thousand dollars, my son. I get half."

"The suffering Moses! I'll set *that* down. Fourteen-seven-fifty—eight—two hundred. Total, say—well, upon my word, the grand total is about two hundred and thirteen or fourteen thousand dollars! *Is* that possible?"

"Possible! If there's any mistake it's the other way. Two hundred and fourteen thousand, cash, is my income for this year if *I* know how to cipher."

Then the gentleman got up to go. It came over me most uncomfortably that maybe I had made my revelations for nothing, besides being flattered into stretching them considerably by the stranger's astonished exclamations. But no; at the last moment the gentleman handed me a large envelope, and said it contained his advertisement; and that I would find out all about his business in it; and that he would be happy to have my custom—would in fact, be *proud* to have the custom of a man of such prodigious income; and that he used to think there were several wealthy men in the city, but when they came to trade with him, he discovered that they barely had enough to live on; and that, in truth it had been such a weary, weary age since he had seen a rich man face to face, and talked to him, and touched him with his hands, that he could hardly refrain from embracing me—in fact, would esteem it a great favor if I would *let* him embrace me.

This so pleased me that I did not try to resist, but allowed this simple-hearted stranger to throw his arms about me and weep a few tranquilizing tears down the back of my neck. Then he went his way.

As soon as he was gone I opened his advertisement. I studied it attentively for four minutes. I then called up the cook, and said—

"Hold me while I faint! Let Marie turn the griddle-cakes."

By and by, when I came to, I sent down to the rum mill on the corner and hired an artist by the week to sit up nights and curse that stranger, and give me a lift occasionally in the daytime when I came to a hard place.

Ah, what a miscreant he was! His "advertisement" was nothing in the world but a wicked tax-return—a string of impertinent questions about my private affairs, occupying the best part of four foolscap pages of fine print—questions, I may remark, gotten up with such marvelous ingenuity, that the oldest man in the world couldn't understand what the most of them were driving at—questions, too, that were calculated to make a man report about four times his actual income to keep from swearing to a falsehood. I looked for a loophole, but there did not appear to be any. Inquiry No. 1 covered my case as generously and as amply as an umbrella could cover an ant hill—

"What were your profits, during the past year, from any trade, business, or vocation, wherever carried on?"

And that inquiry was backed up by thirteen others of an equally searching nature, the most modest of which required information as to whether I had committed any burglary or highway robbery, or by any arson or other secret source of emolument, had acquired property which was not enumerated in my statement of income as set opposite to inquiry No. 1.

It was plain that that stranger had enabled me to make a goose of myself. It was very, very plain; and so I went out and hired another artist. By working on my vanity, the stranger had seduced me into declaring an income of $214,000. By law, $1000 of this was exempt from income-tax—the only relief I could see, and it was only a drop in the ocean. At the legal five per cent, I must pay to the Government the sum of ten thousand six hundred and fifty dollars, income-tax!

[I may remark, in this place, that I did not do it.]

I am acquainted with a very opulent man, whose house is a palace, whose table is regal, whose outlays are enormous, yet a man who has no income, as I have often noticed by the revenue returns; and to him I went for advice, in my distress. He took my dreadful exhibition of receipts, he put on his glasses, he took his pen, and presto!—I was a pauper! It was the neatest thing that ever was. He did it simply by deftly manipulating the bill of "DEDUCTIONS." He set down my "State, national, and municipal taxes" at so much; my "losses by shipwreck, fire, etc.," at so much; my "losses on sales of real estate"—on "live stock sold"—on payments for rent of homestead"—on "repairs, improvements, interest"—on "previously taxed salary as an officer of the United States' army, navy, revenue service," and other things. He got astonishing "deductions" out of each and every one of these matters—each and every one of them. And when he was done he handed me the paper, and I saw at a glance that during the year my income, in the way of profits, had been *one thousand two hundred and fifty dollars and forty cents.*

"Now," said he, "the thousand dollars is exempt by law. What you want to do is to go and swear this document in and pay tax on the two hundred and fifty dollars."

[While he was making this speech his little boy Willie lifted a two dollar greenback out of his vest pocket and vanished with it, and I would wager anything that if my stranger were to call on that little boy to-morrow he would make a false return of his income.]

"Do you," said I, "do you always work up the 'deductions' after this fashion in your own case, sir?"

"Well, I should say so! If it weren't for those eleven saving clauses under the head of 'Deduction' I should be beggared every year to support this hateful and wicked, this extortionate and tyrannical government."

This gentleman stands away up among the very best of the solid men of the city—the men of moral weight, of commercial integrity, of unimpeachable social spotlessness—and so I bowed to his example. I went down to the revenue office, and under the accusing eyes of my old visitor I stood up and swore to lie after lie, fraud after fraud, villainy after villainy, till my soul was coated inches and inches thick with perjury, and my self-respect gone for ever and ever.

But what of it? It is nothing more than thousands of the richest and proudest, and most respected, honored, and courted men in America do every year. And so I don't care. I am not ashamed. I shall simply, for the present, talk little, and eschew fire-proof gloves, lest I fall into certain dreadful habits irrevocably.

THE END.

AFTERWORD

Sherwood Cummings

Composed between 1863 and 1875, the sixty-three sketches in this volume[1] lead us through what might be called Mark Twain's alternate writing career. During those years he was building his mainstream career on *The Innocents Abroad*, *Roughing It*, *The Gilded Age* (with Charles Dudley Warner), and "Old Times on the Mississippi." It would continue with *The Adventures of Tom Sawyer*, published in 1876 but written from 1872 to 1875. Although these mainstream works are more or less autobiographical, the sketches are in their candor, their often outrageous ironies and petulance, indispensable to our understanding of a harried genius during thirteen quite amazing years.

Consider what Sam Clemens had been through since the Civil War blockade of the Mississippi deprived him of his career as a riverboat pilot at age twenty-five, in 1861. He had been one of the kings of the River, an "absolute monarch" of the pilothouse, and paid a "princely" salary. Besides taking away his income and the profession that (as he later declared) he loved above all others, the war threw him into an ethical dilemma. Young men of Missouri — the slave state that did not secede — volunteered in nearly equal numbers for the armies of the Union and the Confederacy. He was himself alternately strong for one side and then the other. He ended up joining the Marion Rangers, a ragtag group of Confederate volunteers, and then, after two feckless weeks, deserting.

At loose ends, and worried that he might be drafted as a Union gunboat pilot, he welcomed the opportunity to join his brother Orion on a stagecoach trip to Nevada. Orion was traveling west to assume the duties that went with his appointment, under Lincoln's new administration, as secretary of the Nevada Territory, and Sam went along for the ride, fully expecting to return within three months. Instead he stayed away for six years, from 1861 to 1867.

Paradoxically, his Western years were both exile and opportunity. That he felt cut off from his old life, unworthy to claim a past, is suggested in the fact that his public writing focused on the current scene to the neglect of his life along the Mississippi, and more surprisingly, to the neglect of the ongoing Civil War. Nevertheless, he by no means ignored the war. He avidly read war news, and his letters to his family in Missouri contain observations on the war. What he wrote indicates that his sympathies now lay with the North.

His closing the door on his past made him the readier to embrace a new life. Soon after he stepped down from the stagecoach in Carson City, Nevada, on August 14, ending nearly a month of travel, he caught the silver fever. Ever since the opulent Comstock Lode had been discovered two years previously, this western corner of Nevada had been filling up with prospectors, miners, promoters, hell-raisers, and the women who entertained them. Sam Clemens joined the crowd. He began speculating in mining stocks and prospecting the mountains for silver ore. Though by no means a drunk, he enjoyed an occasional spree, and in a letter to sister-in-law Mollie Clemens admitted to "sleeping with female servants."[2] His reply to his mother's asking if he went to church was "Scasely." To her asking if there were "many ladies in Carson?" his answer was "Multitudes — probably the handsomest in the world," and as to whether Carson City's citizens were "generally moral and religious?" it was "Prodigiously so."[3]

Six months after arriving in Nevada and still brimming with the idea of striking it rich, he gave himself another six months to make his fortune and return to Missouri. The half year wore itself out in a series of disappointed hopes, but in the meantime he amused himself by sending letters now and then to the *Carson City Silver Age* and the *Virginia City Territorial Enterprise*. On the basis of these letters, signed "Josh," he was offered a job on the *Enterprise*. Low on funds and ready to abandon prospecting, he accepted, moved to Virginia City, and assumed his duties as local reporter in September 1862 at a salary of twenty-five dollars a week.

He did not remain content with mere reporting. During his late teens and early twenties he had amused himself writing squibs like "The Dandy Frightening the Squatter" and " 'Oh, She Has a Red Head!' " for newspapers. The pieces had been gentle enough. Now he impishly entertained himself by composing for the *Enterprise* a "news item" about a petrified man found in the nearby mountains. He was delighted when editors of several California newspapers, apparently not catching the description of the "stony mummy's" thumbing his nose, reprinted the story. He survived the repercussions of that hoax, and even (just barely) those following "A Bloody Massacre Near Carson" a year later, about a crazed settler's killing his wife, seven of his nine children, and himself; but when in May 1864 he found himself facing a duel with James L. Laird, editor of the *Virginia City Union*, for writing that Laird had not made a promised charity payment, he quietly left for San Francisco.

His next two years were less than triumphant. He was often discontented with, even bitter about, his circumstances and himself. The position he took in the spring of 1864 as reporter for the *San Francisco Morning Call* galled him. He resigned in October at the suggestion of the management. He made a hand-to-mouth living for about a year freelancing for California papers and journals. Whatever dreams he might have had about establishing a literary reputation he soberly reassessed in a touching letter to his brother and sister-in-law in October 1865: He was fit only for "scribbling to excite the **laughter** of God's creatures. Poor, pitiful business!" Talent, he continued, "is a mighty engine when supplied with the steam of **education** — which I have not got."[4]

Toward the end of 1865, his income having fallen to zero and his debts mounting, he took, as he tells us in chapter 59 of *Roughing It*, to "slinking" so as to avoid creditors, and to "robbing" his landlady by eating meals he could not pay for. Very early in 1866 he put a pistol to his head "but wasn't man enough to pull the trigger."[5] In a letter to his sister-in-law the following May he summed up his Western adventure as five years of "drifting about the out-skirts of the world, battling for bread."[6]

Representing that period are twelve sketches. They are scattered through-out this volume, for Mark Twain's organizing principle was not chronology but a strategy of "beginning with his strongest and newest pieces, and con-cluding with another burst of strength."[7] That arrangement will be decon-structed here in favor of our focusing on our author's response to his Western exile. The sketches, in chronological order, are:

"Curing a Cold," *San Francisco Golden Era*, 20 September 1863 (300)

"Aurelia's Unfortunate Young Man," *Californian*, 22 October 1864 (253)

"The Killing of Julius Caesar 'Localized,' " *Californian*, 12 November 1864 (162)

"Answers to Correspondents," *Californian*, June–July 1865 (72)

"The Jumping Frog" (29–35 only), *Saturday Press* (New York), 18 November 1865 (28)

"The Scriptural Panoramist," *Californian*, 18 November 1865 (296)

" 'After' Jenkins," *Virginia City Territorial Enterprise*, 19 or 21 November 1865 (256)

"Story of the Bad Little Boy," *Californian*, 23 December 1865 (51)

"Mr. Bloke's Item," *Jumping Frog*, 1867 (167)

"Concerning Chambermaids," *Jumping Frog*, 1867 (250)

"Honored as a Curiosity," *Jumping Frog*, 1867 (273)

"First Interview with Artemus Ward," *Sunday Mercury* (New York), 7 July 1867 (283)

These pieces are perhaps offered as humor, but their expression of self-pity, vindictiveness, and desperation leaves little to chuckle at. Their overriding view is of a world turned topsy-turvy.

In "Curing a Cold" our author tries cold remedies, however torturous the treatment or hideous the taste, and not only remains uncured but through the chemical effects of the treatments becomes morally abased to a level of "su-pernatural depravity." In the next piece sixteen-year-old Aurelia loves her fiancé "with all the devotion of a passionate nature," but before the marriage can be arranged, his face is pitted with smallpox and he loses both legs, both arms, an eye, and his scalp. To the delicate question, "Now, what should she do?" the narrator's answer is that Aurelia should not upbraid her fiancé for stringing himself out "if he has enjoyed it," and should marry him, for he cannot last long, and she will be luckier than most widows in inheriting his spare parts.

In "Julius Caesar" our author describes an assassination in all its gory detail by way of spoofing sensational journalism, and in "Answers to Correspondents" he tells one correspondent to "go off somewhere and die" and advises "Young Mother" that the typical infant diet includes broken glass, laudanum, lucifer matches, and bath water. The scriptural panoramist's biblical pictures and reverent commentary are mocked by the accompanying pianist's rowdy music, and in " 'After' Jenkins" high-fashion ladies of San Francisco are described as attending a ball in varying degrees of nakedness. The "bad little boy" not only steals jam, apples, and penknives with impunity but as a grown-up brains his wife and children with an axe and is rewarded with universal respect and a seat in the legislature.

In the later items the anger abates, but the sense of life's absurdity continues. "Concerning Chambermaids" is an extravagant grumble to prove that "chambermaids are dead to every human instinct." "Mr. Bloke's Item" and "Artemus Ward" are engaging demonstrations of the precariousness of meaning: language, our principal means of communication, is liable to slip into gibberish. "Honored as a Curiosity" is in this context almost lighthearted. There is about our correspondent to the Sandwich Islands only a hint of loneliness: in his singularity he is a "bright waif."

From the dire perspective of these eleven sketches we can perhaps reassess the famous jumping frog story. It may not be fanciful to suggest that the load of quail shot that immobilized Dan'l, "for all he was so gifted," is the crippling load of alienation and anger that his author was bearing as his fortunes approached their nadir.

Sam Clemens' fortunes began to rise — and his acerbity to diminish — in 1866. His travel letters from the Sandwich Islands to the *Sacramento Union* in the spring and summer were well received, as was "Forty-three Days in an Open Boat," an account he drew from three shipwreck survivors who were his fellow passengers on his return voyage to San Francisco. That fall he discovered his lucrative talent as a platform spellbinder when he entertained a packed house in San Francisco, drolling about his Hawaiian adventures. Capitalizing on his newfound gift, he arranged a lecture tour, and before he left for the East in December he performed on eleven more platforms in California and Nevada.

His rise from the depths, both emotional and economic, continued in 1867 — and indeed would generally continue during the years he was writing these sketches. From January to May, when he was loosely based in New York City, he lectured there and, in combination with a visit to his family, in Saint Louis, Hannibal, Keokuk, and Quincy. In May his *Celebrated Jumping Frog of Calaveras County, and Other Sketches* was published, and early in June, as correspondent for the *San Francisco Alta California*, he boarded the *Quaker City*, his charge being to send the *Alta* letters describing the adventures of some seventy "pilgrims" to the countries bordering the Mediterranean, on the world's first transatlantic pleasure cruise. Returning to the States in November, he served for a few weeks as private secretary to United States senator William M. Stewart of Nevada. As a climax to his year of adventuring he met the modest and beautiful Olivia Langdon, sister of *Quaker City* passenger Charley Langdon of Elmira, New York.

His first meeting with his wife-to-be seems not to have made a strong impression on Sam Clemens, for there is scant mention of Livy in his private writing of the next several months. But when after a four-month sojourn in San Francisco in the spring and summer of 1868 he returned to New York and visited the Langdons in their Elmira home, he fell in love with Livy and almost simultaneously proposed to her. Livy was appropriately surprised and declined to say yes until November. Their engagement was formally announced the following February, and a year later, on the second of February, 1870, they were married.

Eighteen seventy also turned out to be Mark Twain's *annus mirabilis* of sketch production. During the three years since his *Jumping Frog* he had published only ten of the pieces in *Sketches*, an average of slightly more than three a year. In contrast, he produced twenty-six of these sketches in 1870, a production the more impressive considering that it was a hectic year for the newlyweds — a year that included the decline and death of Olivia's father,

Jervis, the premature birth in November of the Clemenses' son, Langdon, and Clemens' dogged effort to make progress in the writing of *Roughing It*. The sketches from the 1867–69 period, in chronological order, are:

"Information Wanted," *New York Tribune*, 18 December 1867 (123)

"The Facts Concerning the Recent Resignation," *New York Tribune*, 27 December 1867 (264)

"My Late Senatorial Secretaryship," *Galaxy*, May 1868 (149)

"Cannibalism in the Cars," *Broadway*, November 1868 (287)

"The Siamese Twins," *Packard's Monthly*, August 1869 (208)

"Niagara," *Buffalo Express*, 21 August 1869 (63)

"A Fine Old Man," *Buffalo Express*, 25 August 1869 (158)

"Journalism in Tennessee," *Buffalo Express*, 4 September 1869 (44)

"The Capitoline Venus," *Buffalo Express*, 25 August 1869 (222)

"Lionising Murderers," *Buffalo Express*, 27 November 1869 (182)

The following were published in 1870, in the *Galaxy* unless otherwise noted:

"A Medieval Romance," *Buffalo Express*, 1 January (171)

"A Ghost Story," *Buffalo Express*, 15 January (215)

"A Mysterious Visit," *Buffalo Express*, 19 March (316)

"A New Crime," *Buffalo Express*, 16 April (187)

"A Curious Dream," *Buffalo Express*, 30 April, 7 May (192)

"Disgraceful Persecution of a Boy," May (117)

"The Facts in the Case of the Great Beef Contract," May (101)

"The Story of the Good Little Boy," May (56)

"The Widow's Protest," June (166)

"To Raise Poultry," *Buffalo Express*, 4 June (81)

"My Bloody Massacre," June (243)

"The Petrified Man," June (239)

"The Judge's 'Spirited Woman,' " June (121)

"Johnny Greer," July (100)

"The Office Bore," July (98)

"How I Edited an Agricultural Paper," July (233)

"The Late Benjamin Franklin," July (275)

"Political Economy," September (21)

"John Chinaman in New York," September (231)

"Science vs. Luck," October (159)

"A Fashion Item," October (153)

"Riley — Newspaper Correspondent," November (154)

"The Undertaker's Chat," November (247)

"My Watch — An Instructive Little Tale," December (17)

"History Repeats Itself," December (271)

"Running for Governor," December (311)

In these sketches the anger and petulance are much diminished, but not the audacity of imagination or the vividness of expression. None are earthshaking and many are slight, but each preserves in printed language the ephemeral art of the platform speaker who cannot afford to lose his audience. A sampling of several of them will suggest their remarkable invention and variety.

"Cannibalism in the Cars" is a splendid high-wire act. Like a ghost story told around a campfire, it succeeds if our aroused emotions cancel reason. Mark Twain's special trick is to use "reasonableness," realism, and the dry language of parliamentary procedure to defeat reason. If his trick works, if in spite of the rickety frame which requires us to believe that there was a location in Illinois in 1853 "fifty miles from any house" or that a railroad company would fail to rescue snowbound passengers, he is indeed a spellbinder.

"The Siamese Twins" is a jocose speculation on the lives of Chang and Eng, contrasting personalities physically linked together, who were given top billing in P. T. Barnum's freak show. Linked opposites was to become a major theme in Mark Twain's work, particularly in *Pudd'nhead Wilson*, and his current circumstance as recent Wild Westerner betrothed to a delicate Eastern beauty of fine family may already have made him sensitive to the latent ironies of his new connection.

"Journalism in Tennessee" is a masterpiece of ironic narrative and black comedy. The naiveté and diffidence of the newly hired associate editor who narrates the story never waver during a day when he has two teeth knocked out, and is accidentally shot ten times, cowhided, and scalped. The ceremonious and homicidal Southern editor converses agreeably with his dueling opponent during a lull in the shooting while both men reload. The mutilated and apologetic associate editor explains his decision to resign as based on his not being used to the impulsiveness of the Southern heart, or to Southern hospitality, which is "too lavish with the stranger."

A bumptious American put-down of Mediterranean Europe's pride in its antiquity, "The Capitoline Venus" tells the "true" story of the famed and recently unearthed statue of Venus in Rome's Capitoline Museum. Not in the least ancient, nor representing Venus, it is, our author insists, actually a statue of America by a gifted American sculptor. As such it is not worth a hundred dollars, but when it is "antiqued" with hammer blows and the mud stains of a brief burial, it brings the sculptor — through the canny help of a friend — five million francs in gold. At one and the same time Mark Twain mocks effete Europe's cultural pretensions and praises America's creative vigor.

In "A Medieval Romance" our author coaxes the reader into perusing a ridiculous story about a princess raised as a prince. He uses all the devices of fairy-tale narration and antique diction to draw the reader to the climax — which is the author's admission that the plot has become so impossibly complicated that he can see no way of ending the story! His delight in the quaint and grotesque continued to be expressed in "A Curious Dream," about he exodus of skeletons from a neglected graveyard, and in "A Ghost Story," with its Poe-esque diction and its making use of all the tried and true conventions of the genre.

"The Story of the Good Little Boy" and "Disgraceful Persecution of a Boy" appeared together in the May 1870 issue of the *Galaxy* magazine, perhaps to the moral puzzlement of the issue's readers. Underneath their heavy irony the two stories seem to be at odds with each other in their view of the workings of the moral universe. Jacob Blivens, a little boy so sympathetic, honest, and good "that he was simply ridiculous," is rewarded by his author with a broken arm, a beating, an attack by a vicious dog, a near drowning, and nine weeks of illness, before he is finally blown to bits in an explosion. Ah, but who is this in "Disgraceful Persecution of a Boy" protesting the inhumanity of Brannan Street butchers who set their dogs on unoffending Chinese, and of the police who "look on with tranquil enjoyment," except our cynical creator of the Good Little Boy? That Mark Twain was beginning to develop a social conscience is further suggested in his two very brief pieces "The Judge's 'Spirited Woman,'" about an indignant widow who takes justice into her own hands, and "Johnny Greer," about a heroic ragged street boy whose bravery is worth lip service but not money.

"The Office Bore" is a slight piece made delightful through Mark Twain's virtuosity with language. Words can hardly convey more vivid imagery than this: "From time to time he yawns, and stretches, and scratches himself with a tranquil, mangy enjoyment, and now and then he grunts a kind of stuffy, overfed grunt, which is full of animal contentment"; and the next-to-last sentence, almost two hundred words long, is a masterpiece of elaborate complaint. Another masterpiece of hyper-rhetoric is the charge and counter-charge of the two editors in "How I Edited an Agricultural Paper." The permanent editor's detailed grievances, summed up with "Ah, heavens and earth, friend! if you had made the acquiring of ignorance the study of your life, you could not have graduated with higher honor than you could to-day," would seem to be rhetorically and morally overwhelming, but they are easily matched by the substitute editor's eloquent defense of ignorance, supported by the undeniable fact that in the editorial business "from Alpha to Omaha . . . the less a man knows the bigger the noise he makes and the higher the salary he commands."

"The Late Benjamin Franklin" is a thoroughly ambiguous grumble about an American hero whose early life and circumstances were much like Clemens' own. Both quit school early in favor of earning money as printer's apprentices, both became writers, both were ambitious, hardworking, and successful, and as much as Mark Twain seems to be poking fun at Franklin's maxim-making, his own style was aphoristic; in later years he would compose scores of maxims of his own, using them as chapter headings in *Pudd'nhead Wilson* and *Following the Equator*.

As a surprise wedding gift from the bride's father, Jervis Langdon, Sam and Livy Clemens were presented with a deed to a fine house at 472 Delaware Avenue in Buffalo, where the groom owned a third interest (also financed by Jervis) in the *Buffalo Express*. Living in such an abode, complete with servants, carriage house, and a stable with its team of horses was, as

Mark Twain wrote in "Political Economy," a new experience, "having been used to hotels and boarding-houses all my life." New, too, would be any dealings with lightning rod salesmen, and however accurate in detail "Political Economy" may or may not be, it was surely informed by experience. The True Williams sketch on page 21, where our author, attired in a lounging robe, pen behind his ear, has been pulled away from his desk, is a priceless pictorial commentary.

Among the last of Mark Twain's 1870 sketches are two fanciful pieces — "My Watch" and "The Undertaker's Chat" — that are quite unlike anything he had written before. That fact would hardly be remarkable except that with our foresight into his authorial future the two sketches may be seen as Clemens' first gingerly experiments in uncovering his past and recovering the Missouri vernacular of his boyhood. "My Watch" is rather eerily not about a watch's losing or gaining but about its acting as a time machine, taking the author so far into the past that "the world was out of sight." "The Undertaker's Chat" — again eerily enough — tells about a corpse that refuses to die and speaks in a vernacular uncannily like Huck's. Moreover, like Huck, whose plan for freeing Jim is simple and practical as against Tom's plan, which is absurd and cruel but strong on "style," the corpse is "the most down on style of any remains I ever struck."

The experimentation with new themes and forms would continue in the final sketches. In chronological order those sketches are:

"The Case of George Fisher," *Galaxy*, January 1871 (109)

"My First Literary Venture," *Galaxy*, April 1871 (93)

"About Barbers," *Galaxy*, August 1871 (257)

"How the Author was Sold in Newark," in *A Curious Dream and Other Sketches*, Routledge, 1872 (96)

"After-Dinner Speech," 4 July 1873 (180)

"Speech at the Scottish Banquet in London," November 1873 (213)

"A Couple of Poems by Twain and Moore," 7 January 1874 (62)

"A Curious Pleasure Excursion," *New York Herald*, 6 July 1874 (306)

"Speech on Accident Insurance," 12 October 1874 (229)

"A True Story," *Atlantic Monthly*, November 1874 (202)

"The 'Blind Letter' Department, London P.O.," *Sketches*, 1875 (279)

"Some Learned Fables, for Good Old Boys and Girls," *Sketches*, 1875 (126)

"Experience of the McWilliamses with Membranous Croup," *Sketches*, 1875 (85)

" 'Party Cries' in Ireland," *Sketches*, 1875 (262)

"Petition Concerning Copyright," *Sketches*, 1875 (179)

Up through 1875 there is nothing in Mark Twain's writing, had it ended there, that would make him more illustrious than, say, his Hartford neighbors Charles Dudley Warner or Harriet Beecher Stowe, or his Western acquaintance Bret Harte, or that other chronicler of boyhood, Thomas Bailey Aldrich. Nevertheless, we can in four of these final sketches observe a reaching out, a willingness to experiment, and a dramatic breakthrough.

"Experience of the McWilliamses with Membranous Croup" is a rare — and wry — glimpse of our author as family man. It would be sequeled in 1880 with "Mrs. McWilliams and the Lightning" and in 1882 with "The McWilliamses and the Burglar Alarm." Renamed the Edwardses, the family would appear one more time in "The Great Dark." Written in 1898 after the author's bankruptcy and the death of his daughter Susy, "The Great Dark" presents the Edwardses as undergoing surrealistic and ominous shipboard adventures.

Tumble-Bug, the modest, earthy hero of "Some Learned Fables, for Good Old Boys and Girls," is a foreshadowing, however faint, of modest, earthy Huck, just as some of the blustering, posturing scientists anticipate the King and the Duke with their fantastic self-aggrandizements.

"A Curious Pleasure Excursion" is a frolic of the imagination with no hint of the ironies and tensions that characterize the early sketches. This spacious fantasy is expressed in equally spacious prose, like the marvelous sentence (308–9) that begins, "After visiting all the most celebrated stars and constellations. . ." In concluding his spiel our author-astronaut brags that we will "fly our comet for all it is worth," promising to land his passengers back on earth on the fourteenth of December, 1991, one hundred and seventeen years after takeoff!

The distance between the bitter exile who wrote the early sketches and the exuberant author of "A Curious Pleasure Excursion" is simply astronomical. Something extraordinarily lucky and liberating has happened to him. That something was surely his being welcomed into the generous and loving ambience of the Langdon family, so unlike the austere atmosphere of his boyhood home. He had been welcomed, too, into a new way of looking at race and class. The Langdons had been active abolitionists. Samuel Clemens, whose mother had regarded slavery as a sacred institution, confessed that until he was in his thirties his attitude toward slavery had been ruled by "ignorance, intolerance, opaque perception . . . and a pathetic unconsciousness of it all,"[8] as, indeed, his unforgivable joke around the burning to death of a Negro woman in "Riley — Newspaper Correspondent" shows.

The sea-change in the author's racial attitude during his first four years as a member of the Langdon family is summed up in that shining jewel "A True Story," which is two stories in one. The sale and separation of Rachel's family followed by the joyful reunion of mother and son is one story. The other story is of Mr. C's awakening, conversion, and dedication, and it is handled with consummate delicacy.

The author presents himself as Mr. C, seated on his porch with unnamed others of an evening while his colored servant, the sixty-year-old Rachel, sits "respectfully below" on the steps. The tableau is broken when Mr. C's thoughtless remark moves Rachel to tell her story, during the course of which she rises to her feet and towers above her listeners, "black against the stars." The story of her family's being sold on the auction block — husband, wife, and seven children — and of her reunion with her youngest son is climaxed in the thrilling penultimate paragraph when she uses Mr. C's person to illustrate how she identified her son by his scars. She pushes Mr. C's foot, gazes long into his face, bares his wrist and forehead, and declares that she has got her own again. What can this astonishing ritual mean except that the author has been singled out to receive, as surrogate son to a former slave, a special understanding?

That understanding would effect a change in the subject and tone of Mark Twain's writing. There is a world of difference, for example, between Tom Sawyer's village adventures narrated by an amused and indulgent author and

Huck's account of his adventures with runaway Jim along twelve hundred miles of river. And "Aunt Rachel" — in actuality Mary Ann Cord, cook for the Langdons at their Quarry Farm home — would reappear, thinly disguised, two more times: as the admonitory Roxana in *Pudd'nhead Wilson* in 1894, when Clemens was suffering financially after unwise investments, and ten years later in *No. 44, The Mysterious Stranger*, where as Katrina she becomes poor and ragged No. 44's "majestic new friend," under whose sponsorship he realizes his full creative powers.

NOTES

1. The reader will look in vain for a sixty-fourth sketch — "From 'Hospital Days'" — indexed as appearing on page "299." The listing of this work by author Jane Stuart Woolsey was a printer's error.

2. *Mark Twain's Letters, Volume 1 (1853–1866)*, edited by Edgar Marquess Branch, Michael B. Frank, Kenneth M. Sanderson, et al. (Berkeley: University of California Press, 1988), p. 145.

3. Ibid., p. 138.

4. Ibid., p. 323.

5. Ibid., footnote 6, p. 325.

6. Ibid., p. 342.

7. *Early Tales and Sketches, Volume 1 (1851–1864)*, edited by Edgar Marquess Branch and Robert H. Hirst (Berkeley: University of California Press, 1979), p. 641.

8. *Mark Twain's Letters*, edited by Albert Bigelow Paine (New York: Harper, 1917), 1:289.

FOR FURTHER READING

Sherwood Cummings

For an overview of Mark Twain's life during the years covered by these sketches, consult Albert Bigelow Paine's *Mark Twain: A Biography* (New York: Harper, 1912), vol. 1. For a vivid record of mark Twain's thoughts during the time he was writing these sketches, the first three volumes of *Mark Twain's Letters* (Berkeley: University of California Press, 1988, 1990, 1995) are invaluable. *Mark Twain's Notebooks and Journals, Volume 1 (1855–1873)*, edited by Frederick Anderson, Michael B. Frank, and Kenneth M. Sanderson (Berkeley: University of California Press, 1975), gives further insight into the author's reactions to his early adventures. Louis J. Budd's *Mark Twain: Collected Tales, Sketches, Speeches, and Essays, 1852–1890* (New York: Library of America, 1992) includes many of the sketches along with notes and a year-by-year chronology of Mark Twain's life and writing. *The Love Letters of Mark Twain*, edited by Dixon Wecter (New York: Harper, 1949), offers a detailed and touching account of Sam and Livy's relationship from 1868 on. For a remarkable appreciation of Twain's "A True Story" by a foreign critic, see Makoto Nagawara's " 'A True Story' and Its Manuscript: Mark Twain's Image of the American Black," *Poetica: An International Journal of Linguistic Literary Studies*, xxix:xxx (Tokyo, 1989), 143–56.

ILLUSTRATORS AND ILLUSTRATIONS
IN MARK TWAIN'S FIRST AMERICAN EDITIONS

Beverly R. David & Ray Sapirstein

From the "gorgeous gold frog" stamped into the cover of *The Celebrated Jumping Frog of Calaveras County* in 1867 to the comet-riding captain on the frontispiece of *Extract from Captain Stormfield's Visit to Heaven* in 1909, illustrators and illustrations were an integral part of Mark Twain's first editions.

Twain marketed most of his major works by subscription, and illustration functioned as an important sales tool. Subscription books were packed with pictures of every type and size and were bound in brassy gold-stamped covers. The books were sold by agents who flipped through a prospectus filled with lively illustrations, selected text, and binding samples. Illustrations quickly conveyed a sense of the story, condensing the proverbial "thousand words" and outlining the scope and tone of the work, making an impression on the potential purchaser even before the full text had been printed. Book canvassers were rewarded with up to 50 percent of the selling price, which started at $3.50 and ranged as high as $7.00 for more ornate bindings. The books themselves were seldom produced until a substantial number of customers had placed orders. To justify the relatively high price and to reassure buyers that they were getting their money's worth, books published by subscription had to offer sensational volume and apparent substance. As Frank Bliss of the American Publishing Company observed, these consumers "would not pay for blank paper and wide margins. They wanted everything filled up with type or pictures." While authors of trade books generally tolerated lighter sales, gratified by attracting a "better class of readers," as Hamlin Hill put it, authors of subscription books sacrificed literary respectability for popular appeal and considerable profit.[1]

The humorist George Ade remembered Twain's books vividly, offering us a child's-eye view of the nineteenth-century subscription book market.

Just when front-room literature seemed at its lowest ebb, so far as the American boy was concerned, along came Mark Twain. His books looked at a distance, just like the other distended, diluted, and altogether tasteless volumes that had been used for several decades to balance the ends of the center table . . . so thick and heavy and emblazoned with gold that [they] could keep company with the bulky and high-priced Bible. . . . The publisher knew his public, so he gave a pound of book for every fifty cents, and crowded in plenty of wood-cuts and stamped the outside with golden bouquets and put in a steel engraving of the author, with a tissue paper veil over it, and "sicked" his multitude of broken-down clergymen, maiden ladies, grass widows, and college students on the great American public.

Can you see the boy, Sunday morning prisoner, approach the book with a dull sense of foreboding, expecting a dose of Tupper's *Proverbial Philosophy*? Can you see him a few minutes later when he finds himself linked arm-in-arm with Mulberry Sellers or Buck Fanshaw or the convulsing idiot who wanted to know if Christopher Columbus was sure-enough dead? No wonder he curled up on the hair-cloth sofa and hugged the thing to his bosom and lost all interest in Sunday school. *Innocents Abroad* was the most enthralling book ever printed until *Roughing It* appeared. Then along came *The Gilded Age*, *Life on the Mississippi*, and *Tom Sawyer*. . . . While waiting for a new one we read the old ones all over again.[2]

Publishers, editors, and Twain himself spent a good deal of time on design — choosing the most talented artists, directing their interpretations of text, selecting from the final prints, and at times removing material they deemed unfit for illustration.[3]

With the exception of *Following the Equator* (1897), books released in the twilight of Twain's career were not sold by subscription. Twain's later books, published for the trade market by Harper and Brothers, seldom contained more than a frontispiece and a dozen or so tasteful illustrations, rather than the hundreds of illustrations per volume that subscription publishing demanded. Illustration, however, remained a major component of Twain's later work in two important cases: *Extracts from Adam's Diary*, illustrated by Fred

Strothmann in 1904, and *Eve's Diary*, illustrated by Lester Ralph in 1906.

The stories behind the illustrators and illustrations of Mark Twain's first editions abound in back-room intrigue. The besotted or negligent lapses of some of the artists and the procrastinations of the engravers are legendary. The consequent production delays, mistimed releases, and copyright infringements all implied a lack of competent supervision that frequently infuriated Twain and ultimately encouraged him to launch his own publishing company.

In many cases, Twain took illustrations into account as he wrote and edited his text, using them as counterpoint and accompaniment to his words, often allowing them to inform his general narrative strategy and to influence the amount of detail he felt necessary to include in his written descriptions. In the most artful and carefully considered illustrated works, an analysis of the relationships between author and illustrator and between text and pictures illuminates key dimensions of Twain's writings and the responses they have elicited from readers. Examinations of even the most straightforward examples of decorative imagery yield insights into the publishing history of Twain's books and his attitudes toward the production process.

The original illustrations in Twain's works have often been replaced in the twentieth century by subsequent visual interpretations. But while Norman Rockwell's well-known nostalgic renderings of *Tom Sawyer* and *Huckleberry Finn* may tell us much about 1930s sensibilities, we would do well to reacquaint ourselves with the first American editions and the artwork they contained if we want to understand the books Twain wrote and the world they affected.

Illustrated books, like the illustrated weekly magazines that first appeared in the 1860s, were a significant source of visual images entering nineteenth-century homes. Because of their widespread popularity and the relative paucity of other sources of visual information, Twain's books helped to define America's perceptions of remote people, exotic scenes, and historic events. In addition to being an essential element of Mark Twain's body of work, illustrations are a documentary source in their own right, a window into Twain's world and our own.

NOTES

1. For background on subscription book publishing, see Hamlin Hill, *Mark Twain and Elisha Bliss* (Columbia: University of Missouri Press, 1964), chapter 1. See also R. Kent Rasmussen, "Subscription-book publishing" entry, *Mark Twain A to Z: The Essential Reference to His Life and Writings* (New York: Facts on File, 1995), p. 448.

2. George Ade, "Mark Twain and the Old-Time Subscription Book," *Review of Reviews* 61 (June 10, 1910): 703–4; reprinted in Frederick Anderson, ed., *Mark Twain: The Critical Heritage* (London: Routledge and Kegan Paul, 1971), pp. 337–39.

3. Beverly R. David, *Mark Twain and His Illustrators, Volume 1 (1869–1875)* (Troy, N.Y.: Whitston Publishing Company, 1986), discusses in detail Twain's involvement in the production of his early books.

READING THE ILLUSTRATIONS IN
SKETCHES, NEW AND OLD

Beverly R. David & Ray Sapirstein

Elisha Bliss, Mark Twain's publisher, was dubious about the salability of a collection of stories, an untested formula in subscription publishing. Nevertheless, he finally agreed to publish *Mark Twain's Sketches, New and Old* (1875), an amalgam of old magazine stories and a few new ones, with illustrations added to give the book bulk and to satisfy the exigencies of the subscription market. The "Sketches" in the title of the work also made illustration a virtual certainty.

When Twain first proposed the project in 1870, he specified that he wanted Edward F. Mullen to draw the illustrations. On several occasions, Twain had lobbied hard for Mullen, a recovering alcoholic "sadly in need of work and money."[1] Impressed with Mullen's illustrations in magazines and for *Artemus Ward: His Travels*, Twain had sought him out earlier for his (*Burlesque*) *Autobiography*. Mullen, however, was in the hospital drying out and was unable to do the work. Twain also mentioned him in 1871 in connection with a never realized "Noah's Ark book."[2] In the end, Mullen contributed only to *Roughing It*, supplying a handful of images. As *Sketches* came together in 1875, Bliss routinely delivered the printer's copy of Twain's manuscript to his staff artist, True Williams (1839–1897), who had worked on each of Twain's books since *Innocents Abroad* (1869).[3] Williams ultimately contributed 130 drawings to the 320-page *Sketches*.

Twain was at home in Hartford, also the home of Bliss's American Publishing Company, while Williams was working on the drawings, and he may have provided the artist with direct input. In any case, he jotted occasional directions for the illustrations in the manuscript. For example, in "The Petrified Man" he wrote, "Make a picture of him."[4] Williams responded with an image clearly detailing Twain's description of the stony corpse thumbing his nose at gullible readers (239).

Twain also instructed Williams on relevant ideas for "Some Learned Fables, for Good Old Boys and Girls." He included a doodle of the procession of animals on their expedition and the set of mysterious store signs, marking locations for the illustrations. Williams produced the whimsical parade of "creatures of the forest" for the first part of the story (126), and for the last part he reproduced Twain's signs (140), polishing the author's primitive technique but keeping the content intact.[5]

For "The 'Blind Letter' Department, London P.O." Twain had Williams invent, perhaps with his help, some of the letters that passed through the London Post Office bearing queer pictures and indecipherable addresses. Williams drew ten envelopes, "authoring" the bulk of the thin story and fulfilling Twain's promise: "I here offer them for the inspection of the curious reader" (279).

Twain was probably most invested in the illustrations for "The Jumping Frog." Since the golden frog stamped into the cover was the only artwork in his small first book, and since he had recently purchased the rights to his now famous story from the original publisher, C. H. Webb, Twain contemplated releasing a "fully illustrated" version. As early as 1871 he had wanted to republish the sketch in its own volume, against Bliss's advice. He wrote Bliss emphatically, "I want you to issue Jumping Frog *illustrated*, along with 2 other sketches for the *holidays* next year. I've paid high for the Frog & I want him to get his price back by himself."[6] Four years later, Bliss's judgment prevailed, and "The Jumping Frog" was published as part of *Sketches*. Among the illustrations, Williams made two detailed close-ups of the celebrated Dan'l Webster. In 1907, William Lyon Phelps suggested that the larger image (33) bore some resemblance to Dan'l's eminent namesake: "the intense gravity of the frog's face, with the droop at the corners of the mouth, might well be envied by an American Senator."[7]

As in *Innocents Abroad* and *Roughing It*, Williams' caricatures of Twain are scattered throughout the book. Roughly a fifth of the stories are accompanied by these rather broad interpretations of Twain's likeness. The first image in the book, the headpiece for "My Watch," presents Twain attempting to keep the jeweler from tinkering with his watch (17). A few pages further on, he has been cornered by Simon Wheeler and forced to listen to the frog tale (30), and at the end of "Journalism in Tennessee," Twain appears in the accident ward of a hospital (50). In the title heading for "Niagara," Williams shows Twain smoking a pipe and baiting a fishhook while sitting impossibly close to the falls (63). The book is full of first-person narratives, and repeatedly the illustrations emphasize Twain's "I" with his trademark features: piercing eyes, probing nose, rugged Western mustache, and thick head of unruly hair. To an extent, each facial feature denotes Twain's Western roots and skeptical outlook. Undeniably, the caricatures were self-promoting, both constructing and advertising Twain's public persona.

Williams' illustrations were a major selling point. The advertising prospectus, probably written by Bliss, read:

> Artist has vied with Author in the preparation of this book, and the result is a volume of rare beauty; THE MOST ARTISTIC ILLUSTRATIONS are profusely scattered over its pages, and the reader will often hesitate which first to enjoy — the sparkling humor of the Pen or Pencil.[8]

Unswayed by Bliss's eloquent promotional blurb, however, most appraisals of Williams' illustrations in *Sketches* have been negative, typically linking his alcoholism to careless workmanship. Albert Bigelow Paine, Twain's biographer and an authority on illustration, made the connection in 1912, hinting that Williams either had "no inspiration or he was allowed too much of another sort," and declaring the pictures "absurdly bad."[9] Hamlin Hill cites an episode in which Williams was said to have climbed a lamp post while on a drunken spree, and remarks:

> anyone familiar with his illustrations can only conclude that he worked on them while he was unable to navigate the lamp posts. Grisly, poorly executed, heavy with ink, Williams' engravings have little to recommend them except their vastness.[10]

Unfortunately, because his alcoholism apparently made a great impression on

Twain and those who knew him firsthand, little else is mentioned of him in the historical record, and these anecdotes dominate and frequently determine critiques of his work.[11]

While Williams contributed to the delayed release of several of Twain's books, frustrating Twain considerably, much of the artist's work well suits the author's literary attitude in *Sketches*. Sharing Twain's sense of the absurd, Williams exulted in the eerie and lurid, and he thumbed his nose at artistic pretension with his cartoonish style, admittedly primitive at times. He undoubtedly read the text closely and had a good grasp of the highlights to be illustrated, though the facial features and expressions of his characters tend toward awkward oversimplification. Williams' great strength, however, was his ability to invent detailed and darkly humorous landscapes, several of which prefigure the faux-Victorian Gothic horror of Edward Gorey: the electrically conductive house in "Political Economy" (26), the volcanic eruption in "Information Wanted" (123), "The Late Benjamin Franklin" flying his kite with a jug at his feet (275), and the ill-fated locomotive toiling through the snow in "Cannibalism in the Cars" (287). The ghoulish snake-entwined skull integrated into the title of "My Bloody Massacre" (243) exemplifies Williams' greatest contributions to the tenor of the book: his spooky hand-lettered chapter heads. As with many of the graphic elements of *Sketches, New and Old*, Williams carried the format over into the design of *The Adventures of Tom Sawyer*.

Because the two books were produced back to back, *Sketches* and *Tom Sawyer* share a similar decorative cover design on identical blue cloth. Most significantly, perhaps, several of the characters in this volume leaked into Williams' images of Tom, Huck, and Aunt Polly. His "Bad Little Boy" picking apples (51) is virtually indistinguishable from Tom (*Tom Sawyer*, 42), and "Huck Transformed" (*Tom Sawyer*, 268) owes his origin to the "Good Little Boy" in *Sketches* (60). Aunt Polly's appearance throughout *Tom Sawyer* is similarly prefigured in *Sketches* in "History Repeats Itself" (271).

Shortly after completion of *Sketches, New and Old*, Williams began illustrating *Tom Sawyer* with Twain's explicit approval, an indication of the author's satisfaction with his work. Even so, a letter from Twain to Bliss makes it clear that Twain's approval was somewhat tempered by reservations about the artist's dependability.

> You may let Williams have all of Tom Sawyer that you have received. He can of course make the pictures all the more understandingly after reading the whole story. He wants it, and I have not the least objection, because if he should lose any of it I have got another complete MS. copy.[12]

Given the intimate relation between the illustrations for the two books, Twain's response to Williams' designs for *Tom Sawyer* may suggest something of his estimate of the illustrations for *Sketches, New and Old*:

> Williams has made about 200 rattling pictures for it [*Tom Sawyer*] — some of them very dainty. Poor devil, what a genius he has, & how he does murder it with rum. He takes a book of mine, & without suggestion from anybody builds no end of pictures just from his reading of it.[13]

NOTES

1. SLC to Elisha Bliss, December 22, 1870, in *Mark Twain's Letters to His Publishers, 1867–1894*, Hamlin Hill, ed. (Berkeley University of California Press, 1967), p. 53.

2. SLC to Elisha Bliss, January 5, 1871, cited in *Early Tales and Sketches, Volume 1 (1851–1864)*, Edgar M. Branch and Robert H. Hirst, eds. (Berkeley: University of California Press, 1979), p. 574.

3. Nathan M. Wood, "True Williams, Pen Drew Literary Giant of Old," *Watertown [N.Y.] Daily Times*, August 30, 1938, p. 11. Until recently, very little biographical information on Williams has been available. Unearthed by Barbara Schmidt, instructional media coordinator at Tarleton State University in Stephenville, Texas, and a regular contributor to the Mark Twain Forum on the Internet, this article provides significant biographical information, including his dates and publishing history. We are indebted to Barbara Schmidt for generously sharing this reference and her pioneering research on Williams' later career, which she is working on for a forthcoming article. Biographical information on Williams is presented in greater detail in this series in "Reading the Illustrations in Tom Sawyer," in *The Adventures of Tom Sawyer*, The Oxford Mark Twain (New York: Oxford University Press, 1996).

4. Cited in *Early Tales and Sketches*, p. 641.

5. Twain's drawings are reprinted in Beverly R. David, *Mark Twain and His Illustrators, Volume 1 (1869–1875)* (Troy, N.Y.: Whitston Publishing Company, 1986), pp. 210–12.

6. Twain to Bliss, January 3, 1871, cited in Hamlin Hill, *Mark Twain and Elisha Bliss* (Columbia: University of Missouri Press, 1964), pp. 86–87.

7. William Lyon Phelps, "Mark Twain," *North American Review*, July 1907, pp. 540–48.

8. Cited in Hill, *Mark Twain and Elisha Bliss*, p. 97.

9. Albert Bigelow Paine, *Mark Twain: A Biography*, 3 vols. (New York: Harper and Brothers, 1912), 1:551.

10. Hill, *Mark Twain and Elisha Bliss*, p. 97.

11. But see n. 3 above. Nathan Wood's article and Barbara Schmidt's research fill out our picture of Williams' life and work, and serve as a partial corrective to sketchy previous accounts of his career.

12. SLC to Elisha Bliss, November 5, 1875, *Mark Twain's Letters to His Publishers*, p. 92.

13. *Mark Twain–Howells Letters*, Henry Nash Smith and William M. Gibson, eds. (Cambridge: Harvard University Press, 1960), 1:121.

A NOTE ON THE TEXT

Robert H. Hirst

This text of *Mark Twain's Sketches, New and Old* is a photographic facsimile of a copy of the first American edition dated 1875 on the title page. Although books printed from the first edition plates were manufactured until at least 1893, the earliest copies of the first edition came from the bindery on September 25, 1875. Two days later, Clemens told William Dean Howells that the book would be published "in a week or ten days." The copy reproduced here is an example of Jacob Blanck's "second state" (*BAL* 3364). A footnote mistakenly repeated in the first state has been corrected (119–20), and "Hospital Days," a sketch by Jane Stuart Woolsey which the publisher mistakenly included in the earliest impression, has been removed (299). "Hospital Days" was not removed from the table of contents, but removing the text itself made it unnecessary to insert the erratum slip which is found in some copies of the first state. Because this particular copy was inscribed "Nov. 1875," it was probably among the 12,979 printed and bound by the end of that month (*Early Tales and Sketches, Volume 1,* ed. Edgar M. Branch and Robert H. Hirst, The Works of Mark Twain, University of California Press, 1979, pp. 617–53). The original volume is in the collection of the Mark Twain House in Hartford, Connecticut (810/C625sk/1875/c. 12).

THE MARK TWAIN HOUSE

The Mark Twain House is a museum and research center dedicated to the study of Mark Twain, his works, and his times. The museum is located in the nineteen-room mansion in Hartford, Connecticut, built for and lived in by Samuel L. Clemens, his wife, and their three children, from 1874 to 1891. The Picturesque Gothic-style residence, with interior design by the firm of Louis Comfort Tiffany and Associated Artists, is one of the premier examples of domestic Victorian architecture in America. Clemens wrote *Adventures of Huckleberry Finn*, *The Adventures of Tom Sawyer*, *A Connecticut Yankee in King Arthur's Court*, *The Prince and the Pauper*, and *Life on the Mississippi* while living in Hartford.

The Mark Twain House is open year-round. In addition to tours of the house, the educational programs of the Mark Twain House include symposia, lectures, and teacher training seminars that focus on the contemporary relevance of Twain's legacy. Past programs have featured discussions of literary censorship with playwright Arthur Miller and writer William Styron; of the power of language with journalist Clarence Page, comedian Dick Gregory, and writer Gloria Naylor; and of the challenges of teaching *Adventures of Huckleberry Finn* amidst charges of racism.

CONTRIBUTORS

Sherwood Cummings is professor emeritus of English at California State University at Fullerton. A scholar of Mark Twain from the time of writing his doctoral dissertation at the University of Wisconsin (1951) to the present, he has published several articles and a book, *Mark Twain and Science: Adventures of a Mind* (1988). His current research project is called "The Five Jims in *Huckleberry Finn*."

Beverly R. David is professor emerita of humanities and theater at Western Michigan University in Kalamazoo. She is currently working on volume 2 of *Mark Twain and His Illustrators*, and on a Mark Twain mystery entitled *Murder at the Matterhorn*. She has written a number of sections on illustration for the *Mark Twain Encyclopedia* and her *Mark Twain and His Illustrators, Volume 1 (1869–1875)* was published in 1989. Dr. David resides in Allegan, Michigan, in the summer and Green Valley, Arizona, in the winter.

Shelley Fisher Fishkin, professor of American Studies and English at the University of Texas at Austin, is the author of the award-winning books *Was Huck Black? Mark Twain and African-American Voices* (1993) and *From Fact to Fiction: Journalism and Imaginative Writing in America* (1985). Her most recent book is *Lighting Out for the Territory: Reflections on Mark Twain and American Culture* (1996). She holds a Ph.D. in American Studies from Yale University, has lectured on Mark Twain in Belgium, England, France, Israel, Italy, Mexico, the Netherlands, and Turkey, as well as throughout the United States, and is president-elect of the Mark Twain Circle of America.

Robert H. Hirst is the General Editor of the Mark Twain Project at The Bancroft Library, University of California in Berkeley. Apart from that, he has no other known eccentricities.

Lee Smith is the author of *Oral History* (1983*), Fair and Tender Ladies* (1988), *The Devil's Dream* (1992), *Saving Grace* (1995), and many other books.

Among the honors she has received are O. Henry Awards in 1979 and 1981, the North Carolina Award for Fiction in 1984, the John Dos Passos Award in 1987, the Robert Penn Warren Prize for Fiction in 1991, and a Lila Wallace/Reader's Digest Grant in 1994. A professor of English at North Carolina State University, she lives in Chapel Hill.

Ray Sapirstein is a doctoral student in the American Civilization Program at the University of Texas at Austin. He curated the 1993 exhibition *Another Side of Huckleberry Finn: Mark Twain and Images of African Americans* at the Harry Ransom Humanities Research Center at the University of Texas at Austin. He is currently completing a dissertation on the photographic illustrations in several volumes of Paul Laurence Dunbar's poetry.

ACKNOWLEDGMENTS

There are a number of people without whom The Oxford Mark Twain would not have happened. I am indebted to Laura Brown, senior vice president and trade publisher, Oxford University Press, for suggesting that I edit an "Oxford Mark Twain," and for being so enthusiastic when I proposed that it take the present form. Her guidance and vision have informed the entire undertaking.

Crucial as well, from the earliest to the final stages, was the help of John Boyer, executive director of the Mark Twain House, who recognized the importance of the project and gave it his wholehearted support.

My father, Milton Fisher, believed in this project from the start and helped nurture it every step of the way, as did my stepmother, Carol Plaine Fisher. Their encouragement and support made it all possible. The memory of my mother, Renée B. Fisher, sustained me throughout.

I am enormously grateful to all the contributors to The Oxford Mark Twain for the effort they put into their essays, and for having been such fine, collegial collaborators. Each came through, just as I'd hoped, with fresh insights and lively prose. It was a privilege and a pleasure to work with them, and I value the friendships that we forged in the process.

In addition to writing his fine afterword, Louis J. Budd provided invaluable advice and support, even going so far as to read each of the essays for accuracy. All of us involved in this project are greatly in his debt. Both his knowledge of Mark Twain's work and his generosity as a colleague are legendary and unsurpassed.

Elizabeth Maguire's commitment to The Oxford Mark Twain during her time as senior editor at Oxford was exemplary. When the project proved to be more ambitious and complicated than any of us had expected, Liz helped make it not only manageable, but fun. Assistant editor Elda Rotor's wonderful help in coordinating all aspects of The Oxford Mark Twain, along with literature editor T. Susan Chang's enthusiastic involvement with the project in its final stages, helped bring it all to fruition.

I am extremely grateful to Joy Johannessen for her astute and sensitive copyediting, and for having been such a pleasure to work with. And I appreciate the conscientiousness and good humor with which Kathy Kuhtz Campbell heroically supervised all aspects of the set's production. Oxford president Edward Barry, vice president and editorial director Helen McInnis, marketing director Amy Roberts, publicity director Susan Rotermund, art director David Tran, trade editorial, design and production manager Adam Bohannon, trade advertising and promotion manager Woody Gilmartin, director of manufacturing Benjamin Lee, and the entire staff at Oxford were as supportive a team as any editor could desire.

The staff of the Mark Twain House provided superb assistance as well. I would like to thank Marianne Curling, curator, Debra Petke, education director, Beverly Zell, curator of photography, Britt Gustafson, assistant director of education, Beth Ann McPherson, assistant curator, and Pam Collins, administrative assistant, for all their generous help, and for allowing us to reproduce books and photographs from the Mark Twain House collection. One could not ask for more congenial or helpful partners in publishing.

G. Thomas Tanselle, vice president of the John Simon Guggenheim Memorial Foundation, and an expert on the history of the book, offered essential advice about how to create as responsible a facsimile edition as possible. I appreciate his very knowledgeable counsel.

I am deeply indebted to Robert H. Hirst, general editor of the Mark Twain Project at The Bancroft Library in Berkeley, for bringing his outstanding knowledge of Twain editions to bear on the selection of the books photographed for the facsimiles, for giving generous assistance all along the way, and for providing his meticulous notes on the text. The set is the richer for his advice. I would also like to express my gratitude to the Mark Twain Project, not only for making texts and photographs from their collection available to us, but also for nurturing Mark Twain studies with a steady infusion of matchless, important publications.

I would like to thank Jeffrey Kaimowitz, curator of the Watkinson Library at Trinity College, Hartford (where the Mark Twain House collection is kept), along with his colleagues Peter Knapp and Alesandra M. Schmidt, for having been instrumental in Robert Hirst's search for first editions that could be safely reproduced. Victor Fischer, Harriet Elinor Smith, and especially Kenneth M. Sanderson, associate editors with the Mark Twain Project, reviewed the note on the text in each volume with cheerful vigilance. Thanks are also due to Mark Twain Project associate editor Michael Frank and administrative assistant Brenda J. Bailey for their help at various stages.

I am grateful to Helen K. Copley for granting permission to publish photographs in the Mark Twain Collection of the James S. Copley Library in La Jolla, California, and to Carol Beales and Ron Vanderhye of the Copley Library for making my research trip to their institution so productive and enjoyable.

Several contributors — David Bradley, Louis J. Budd, Beverly R. David, Robert Hirst, Fred Kaplan, James S. Leonard, Toni Morrison, Lillian S. Robinson, Jeffrey Rubin-Dorsky, Ray Sapirstein, and David L. Smith — were particularly helpful in the early stages of the project, brainstorming about the cast of writers and scholars who could make it work. Others who participated in that process were John Boyer, James Cox, Robert Crunden, Joel Dinerstein, William Goetzmann, Calvin and Maria Johnson, Jim Magnuson, Arnold Rampersad, Siva Vaidhyanathan, Steve and Louise Weinberg, and Richard Yarborough.

Kevin Bochynski, famous among Twain scholars as an "angel" who is gifted at finding methods of making their research run more smoothly, was helpful in more ways than I can count. He did an outstanding job in his official capacity as production consultant to The Oxford Mark Twain, supervising the photography of the facsimiles. I am also grateful to him for having put me in touch via e-mail with Kent Rasmussen, author of the magisterial *Mark Twain A to Z*, who was tremendously helpful as the project proceeded, sharing insights on obscure illustrators and other points, and generously being "on call" for all sorts of unforeseen contingencies.

I am indebted to Siva Vaidhyanathan of the American Studies Program of the University of Texas at Austin for having been such a superb research assistant. It would be hard to imagine The Oxford Mark Twain without the benefit of his insights and energy. A fine scholar and writer in his own right, he was crucial to making this project happen.

Georgia Barnhill, the Andrew W. Mellon Curator of Graphic Arts at the American Antiquarian Society in Worcester, Massachusetts, Tom Staley, director of the Harry Ransom Humanities Research Center at the University of Texas at Austin, and Joan Grant, director of collection services at the Elmer Holmes Bobst Library of New York University, granted us access to their collections and assisted us in the reproduction of several volumes of The Oxford Mark Twain. I would also like to thank Kenneth Craven, Sally Leach, and Richard Oram of the Harry Ransom Humanities Research Center for their help in making HRC materials available, and Jay and John Crowley, of Jay's Publishers Services in Rockland, Massachusetts, for their efforts to photograph the books carefully and attentively.

I would like to express my gratitude for the grant I was awarded by the University Research Institute of the University of Texas at Austin to defray some of the costs of researching The Oxford Mark Twain. I am also grateful to American Studies director Robert Abzug and the University of Texas for the computer that facilitated my work on this project (and to UT systems analyst Steve Alemán, who tried his best to repair the damage when it crashed). Thanks also to American Studies administrative assistant Janice Bradley and graduate coordinator Melanie Livingston for their always generous and thoughtful help.

The Oxford Mark Twain would not have happened without the unstinting, wholehearted support of my husband, Jim Fishkin, who went way beyond the proverbial call of duty more times than I'm sure he cares to remember as he shared me unselfishly with that other man in my life, Mark Twain. I am also grateful to my family — to my sons Joey and Bobby, who cheered me on all along the way, as did Fannie Fishkin, David Fishkin, Gennie Gordon, Mildred Hope Witkin, and Leonard, Gillis, and Moss

Plaine — and to honorary family member Margaret Osborne, who did the same.

My greatest debt is to the man who set all this in motion. Only a figure as rich and complicated as Mark Twain could have sustained such energy and interest on the part of so many people for so long. Never boring, never dull, Mark Twain repays our attention again and again and again. It is a privilege to be able to honor his memory with The Oxford Mark Twain.

Shelley Fisher Fishkin
Austin, Texas
April 1996